THE CITY 8

While Derek rode, he kept his rifle at the ready. Helen did the same to his left but they did not encounter anything. No signs of life or other noises greeted them. There was nothing but the howl of wind over the frozen snow drifts.

What remained was the crunch of the horse's hooves as they pushed through the thin crust to the soft snow beneath and their own low conversation.

The wind whistled and the snow settled with a gentle sigh like paper being ruffled in a library. Trees snapped and crackled in the cold as they swayed in the wind. Birds that had not migrated south chirped and tweeted in the branches of the trees.

There was no one—not a single living person—to disturb the wilder symphony left in their wake.

Also by Kristan Cannon

The Kingdom of Walden Trilogy
After Oil
The Last Iron Horse (October 2015)
Ghostwalker (Forthcoming)

AFTER OIL

KRISTAN CANNON

After Oil is a work of fiction. Names, characters, places, and incidents either are the product of the author's imagination or are used fictitiously. Any resemblance to actual persons, living or dead, events or locales, is entirely coincidental.

Published in Canada by KCEditions.
Printed in the United States by Lightning Source and distributed by IngramSpark.

Anime North Pre-Release Edition May 2014 – Independently Published
First Edition July 2014 – KCEditions
Second Edition June 2015 - KCEditions

www.kceditions.com
www.kristancannon.com

Library and Archives Canada Cataloguing in Publication
Cannon, Kristan, 1980-, author
After oil / Kristan Cannon.
Issued in print and electronic formats.
ISBN 978-0-9937603-0-3 (bound)
--ISBN 978-0-9937603-2-7 (pbk.)
--ISBN 978-0-9937603-1-0 (html)
I. Title.
PS8605.A5753A64 2014
C813'.6
C2014-904999-4
C2014-905000-3

For Grampa;

For always pushing me to follow my dreams.

AFTER OIL

KRISTAN CANNON

There is no such thing as a sudden ending.

Even the most out of the blue catastrophe can come with enough clues and signs to warn people. The problem was no one wanted to change, so the gigantic flashing signs which warned, 'Either reverse your course now or fall over that edge and fall to your death!' were flatly ignored.

Until, of course, change was finally forced down their throats. By then it was too late to change the course. The skiff was way too far into the rapids and the waterfall now loomed in wait.

All one could do was hang on and hope to survive.

I know this from experience—up until that one, fateful, winter my life was as normal as they came for the time period. I had what I wanted and needed to live and perhaps a bit more...

... And then it all changed.

—From the diary of the First Regent of Walden

CHAPTER ONE

Green grass when you go to bed, thought Marissa as she walked by the front window of her home, shaking her head the sight of her neighbor holding his shattered shovel in his hands and starting helplessly at his driveway. *And then so much snow the next morning your shovel breaks…*

… And someone always assumes those cheap plastic rigs from the local discount store are enough, Marissa lifted a brow as she continued to sip her coffee. *Apparently he did.*

As she looked out into the yard, she marvelled at thick white blanket covering everything outside. Movement in her own driveway caught her eye and she realized it was her husband clearing it with nothing more than a shovel.

She opened the window and ducked her head out. "Derek, what the hell are you doing?"

He muttered under his breath and chose to not actually answer with something she could hear. Marissa shook her head and then ducked back inside the house, shaking the snow out of her shirt as she continued to watch him.

Derek sighed heavily and then returned to clearing the snow from their driveway. Marissa knew their plan to spend their holiday at Sheridan's was in peril unless he managed to first free his ageing Toyota SUV from the driveway.

Still, why he was not using his snow blower—something that would have made short work of their driveway—was a puzzle.

Finally, he managed to dig his truck free and he leaned on the shovel.

Derek and Marissa's driveway was at least now clear. But looking around, she could see that the street was covered in snow. It was not as if Derek had to dig through a snowbank to get to the grossly under plowed street.

That would have been at least amusing, if annoying.

To Derek, at least.

2

I'd hear about it all the way to Whitefish, she mused, as she turned away from the window and picked up her phone. *Which reminds me…*

Digging through a hardened snow bank left by a plow was almost a rite of passage anywhere in Northern Ontario and Sudbury had certainly never been any different.

Had Derek had to cut through it Marissa knew he would tell Sheridan and her grandmother Lorraine. Once they got out there and use it as an excuse for Lorraine to make him her specialty hot cocoas—a drink that had more than just mere cocoa in it for added 'warmth'.

But that was hardly her concern right now…

…The problem was that there was no snow bank at all for Derek to dig through to get to the street.

* * * * *

"You are actually going home sometime today, aren't you?" asked the Mayor as she walked out of the elevator and towards her car.

"Home, no, but to my daughter's and son in law's, yes," answered Daniel. "My daughter has a huge holiday week planned for those who want to show up. I think she'd have plenty for dinner or to drink if you went out."

"Thanks for the invite, I'd love to see Sheri again, but I have plans as well—so long as I can get there first," she answered as she rummaged around in her purse. "Blasted keys. Why do they always wind up in the bottom of my purse all the time?"

Daniel tilted his head. He leaned against the heavy cement support and watched as a few other uniformed officers left.

"Merry Christmas, Dan!" Shouted one of the local police officers. "Looks like more snow. Might want to get out of here while you still can. You too, Madam Mayor."

The Mayor waved her hand at him as he got into his personal car. Dan gave a half wave in reply as the other police officer drove by them.

When he was gone, Dan turned back to the Mayor as she continued to search her purse for her keys.

"Maybe if you had a smaller purse you'd find them faster," he suggested.

The Mayor looked up at Dan while lifting a brow. "Are you trying to tell me my purse is too big?"

"I'd never presume to—" he was cut off as one of the office assistants came running up.

"Oh no, I am officially on holidays," began the Mayor.

The assistant stopped, bending over to catch his breath before he stood up. "I'm sorry, Ms. Piacentini, but there's this Colonel from the Armed Forces insisting on talking to you. He said it was urgent and important."

"Always is," mused the Mayor. She sighed and gave up her search for her keys. "Knowing my luck I left my car keys up in my office anyway."

"All right, since I have to go back upstairs anyway you way as well arrange for him to meet me in my office. Have him wait in..."

"He's already waiting in your office," answered her assistant. "I'm really sorry, ma'am, but he barged in and..."

The Mayor sighed heavily as she brought a hand up to pinch her nose. "Dan, I know you're on your way out too, but I would really appreciate it if you were there with me for this."

"Why do you need me?" asked Daniel. "You're more than able to tear a strip off of people on your own."

"Yes, that's my point," she answered. "I think I'll need you to keep me from tearing too much of a strip off a pompous arse who thinks he can throw his weight around."

"It's not too late to run... I *do* have a car," Daniel pointed out as he followed her back to the underground entrance to City Hall and took the lift to the Fourth Floor. "What do you think he wants?"

"Don't tempt me," she said as she shrugged, screwing up her face at the same time. "I have no idea what he wants. I'll deal with it and I hope whatever it is can be handled quickly so I can grab my keys and go."

She paused and Daniel sighed. "Sheridan's house is in Whitefish."

"Don't tempt me—like I said, I don't get to see her often enough," answered Valeria and she grinned. "She still as horse crazy as I remember her being since grade eight?"

"More so now that she actually has horses," he chuckled as the lift opened and they stepped out onto the carpeted floor. "I'll stay here. I'm sure you can resist the urge to murder someone. If not, well, I guess I'll have to arrest you."

She stuck her tongue out at him as she walked through the maze of desks to her office, motioning to her assistant to open the door.

"May as well get this over with," Dan overheard her say from across the large open room as the door opened. "I'm sorry, didn't catch your name…"

What else she could have said or what the other man said in response was lost as the door closed. Daniel leaned against the rail and stared down at the brown hexagonal tiles of the mezzanine floor where a small group of uniformed soldiers milled below.

A group of armed soldiers—with their rifles in hand, he noted. The first inkling of worry slid into his veins.

This isn't a normal meeting, he thought. *What the hell is going on?*

* * * * *

The farm was in a small town clear on the other side of Sudbury. It was so far out the four lane highway along Highway 17 heading west out of the city ended. So small it was not even its own town and just barely within the city's limits.

Panache Lake was a quiet corner and that was the way Terrence Scapael and Sheridan Wither preferred it.

However, this morning Terrence had the clear feeling he wanted to live closer to the city where the roads were plowed more frequently than they were here. He awkwardly balanced his phone between his shoulder and ear as he drove the ATV with a plow attachment on it up and down his long driveway.

"That's what I said to Sheri this morning." He flipped the phone over to the other shoulder and lowered the blade of the plow again as he prepared to take another swipe at the snow down the drive. "If it keeps snowing this much, we'll be digging out clear through June." He paused to listen to the other person, again switching which shoulder the phone rested on. "All right, maybe not that long but the point still stands. One of these days I swear I'm moving to someplace without snow."

Sheridan walked outside and watched her husband as he cleared the driveway, shaking her head as she did so.

Terrence looked up and over at her, waving, and ignored her slight frown. "Are you and Marissa still coming over for New Year's?" he asked. "Great, I'll tell Sheri to expect you. Later."

He hung up the phone and slid it into a pocket as he drove the four wheeled bike up to the front steps. He saw his wife and stopped. "What?" he asked.

"You do know what you're doing is illegal now?" She stood there with her hands on her hips, staring at him. "And for damn good reason."

Terrence stared at her in confusion and asked, "What is?"

"Where do I start?" she wondered aloud. "First, lack of a helmet. Second, distracted driving. And while limiting the movement of your head by holding your cell and using the position of your neck to your shoulder which therefore ruins your ability to look around— something very important when it comes to driving."

"Relax, Sheri, it's only our driveway."

"More than eighty percent of accidents happen in the home or within the closest few kilometres," she retorted. "And I've seen enough of the worst which can happen to last for a lifetime. Please don't invite it to my front door."

With a sigh, Terrence had to admit to himself that if anyone would know it would definitely be her. Sheridan finally sighed at his sudden 'lost puppy' look. "When are they getting here?"

"Derek said he had to pick up a few things so he wouldn't be coming empty handed. But he did say he and Marissa should be here sometime tonight," answered Terrence as he swung his legs over the side of the bike while still sitting on it. "S'good thing too. I think one of the panels in the north field is on the blink again. Maybe he and your Uncle can see what's up and perhaps get our field back up to normal operations."

"Like you can't do that either."

Terrence chuckled. "Are you still planning on heading into Sudbury?" he asked.

"I expect so—I have to buy groceries if we're going to have a house full over the holidays."

"Could you grab some beer while you're there?" he enquired, even though he knew she was probably overloaded with preparations for the influx of guests over the holidays.

"Why don't you come with me and help me with all this?" she asked with a sigh.

"Still have to plow the back drive and then do the same over at Karen's," he replied. "Grab your uncle or your Dad."

"Uncle Russell is helping Karen in the barn before he leaves to head back to Toronto, and Dad isn't even here yet," she added. "Russell and I will likely head out at the same time and split off at Lively."

"Where's Nathan?"

"He's also in the barn."

"Jeremy?"

"Helping Karen."

"Is everyone in the barn?" asked Terrence in surprise.

"None of the regular hands showed up today," she answered. "Some of them didn't bother to answer me while the others said it was too far and they had to stick around their own barns. I'm not surprised because of the weather, I'm annoyed that some of them didn't deign to answer their phones, but I get it."

Terrence grunted in concern. "If I had my rathers, you wouldn't be going out there either."

"I'm only going as far as Lively," she answered dryly. "Not even all the way into Sudbury. I asked Marissa to grab some things on their way through from Garson."

* * * * *

Two cars pulled off to the side of the road just down from the overpass bridging Copper Cliff and Lively. Here the intersection had a set of lights so Sheridan could turn around with ease and go back into Lively. Russell got out of the rental, a newer SUV, and kicked at the loose snow on the ground.

"Are you sure you have to go back now?" asked Sheridan as she walked over to him.

"I should," answered Russell. "I'll stop by Uncle Kirk's and then head straight down through Parry Sound."

"The roads are atrocious," she pointed out.

"In town, maybe," answered Russell. "But not so bad on the highway. Once I get to the main highway, things will be far better."

"If you say so," Sheridan crinkled her nose. "I don't think it's any better anywhere."

Russell hugged his niece. "I'll drive slow," he pointed out as he turned back to the rental. "You drive safely… at least I'm driving something that's four-by-four. I don't know what to call *that*."

He pointed at Sheridan's car, which was an older Smart Car. She lifted a brow. "What of it?"

"Sheri, you're a surgeon and you drive that."

"Gas is too expensive—even for me," she pointed out. "It's what I could afford to drive from the house to Sudbury Regional, and around to the offices I need to bounce around to."

With a sigh, he hugged her again. "Well, you drive safe and I'll call when I make it to Parry Sound. Deal?"

"Fine," she conceded. "Just make sure you actually do. You know you'll drive Gramma spare if you don't. You know how she worries."

"I know," he answered as he got into the rental.

She watched him drive up the hill then settled herself in the driver's seat of her car. Before she could pull away, a line of military trucks drove past her down the hill, leaving one truck by the ramps and bridge.

Confused, she drove down the hill and to the grocery store.

CHAPTER TWO

"Stop! Dammit, I said stop!" yelled the soldier as her voice echoed off the cement walls and what few cars remained in the underground lot.

Daniel pushed the Mayor ahead of him, and then around the corner. She looked at him in askance and he held his index finger to his lips.

The sound of booted footsteps clattered and echoed making it difficult for Daniel to pick out exactly where they were. It didn't matter as the two soldiers chasing them went past the blind corner he had pushed her into. He felt her grasp his elbow and he looked over at her.

In a glance, he knew what she was asking.

Was it safe? Were those two chasing them now off their trail?

He honestly didn't know and he did not have an answer. Then again, he had never been in this kind of situation. Daniel was still having trouble reconciling his day and it felt like some kind of dream gone completely wrong.

He waited a few moments and nodded to her that it was clear now. She licked her lips and he followed her further into the rat's maze under city hall and through another tunnel that led to the police tower.

Unfortunately, the fenced area prevented them access but there were far more cars to hide between. He knew his own cruiser sat nearby and he knew that there would be some problem if he poked his head up; it would allow the two soldiers sweeping the underground garage to find them.

He slid down and crouched by the wheel well with a sigh while looking over at the mayor.

Thankfully those two soldiers kept giving away their own position. The underground lot was one large open space, with the obvious need of support pillars which were evenly spaced throughout. It was open enough for the soldiers to easily see each other and use hand signals for communication. If Daniel needed to tell the mayor anything outside of using hand signals, this worked both ways.

* * * * *

While he waited for Corporal Montgomery to come back from the military truck with his clearances, Garrett paced in front of his truck. It was taking too long and every hour meant more snow fell.

He was more than a bit worried that the advantage of the four by four truck would be nullified on the back road to High Falls. It was no more than a dirt road meant to bridge the gap between the mines and was dangerous enough on a good day.

However, the dam was the primary supply of power for the region and also fed half the eastern sea board's power grid. It was vital that it remain operational.

Unfortunately, he was one of the few qualified in the region to keep it up and running.

If he was kept waiting any longer, the issue of clearance for whatever the damned military was up to now would be a moot point.

The snow would simply make the passage up to High Falls impossible.

I just want to get up to the power station, get what I need done... make sure the poor buggers at said station have what they need... he thought. *And then back get down to Karen and Sheridan's for the holidays.*

Worthington and High Falls were just to the North of their farm and he hoped getting back down to them would be easy.

Garrett watched Montgomery come back.

"Well?" asked Garrett.

"Command has the clearance," answered Montgomery as he handed the packet over to him. "Might not want to go back through town, though, when you head back."

Garrett took a breath and asked, "Why not?"

"What the boy is trying to say is that for the time being there is a live action exercise and it's above his pay grade to say anything," came another voice, one that belonged to a woman with enough stripes on her shoulder and lapel that Montgomery immediately saluted upon sight of her.

"In Sudbury?" he asked. "I don't remember seeing anything like that."

"Yes, in Sudbury... and you drove through right before they close it off otherwise you wouldn't even be here," she answered. "Travel has been cut off to the south because of the snow. You'll have to travel all the way around and back through the main part of Sudbury. I can tell you the Colonel would have a bird if an unnecessary civilian wandered into the middle of the main part of his exercise. Where are you going?"

"High Falls," answered Garrett.

"I'd suggest going back through Hanmer, but the roads are probably not any better," piped up Montgomery.

"I have a four by four truck, and if need be I can get out the chains," answered Garrett patiently, although this patience was beginning to wear thin. "I'll get where I'm going for tonight, even if the drive isn't easy. I won't push it."

"And then what?"

"When the weather improves, I'll head down to my daughter's place," he answered. "I won't have to come all the way back here. She's not that far from High Falls."

Corporal Montgomery sighed as he watched Garrett's truck drive past him. It turned off the highway and up another paved road just as a bus pulled up to his own truck.

He lifted an eyebrow at this, walking up to the door of the bus as he thought, *Didn't they get stopped at one of the other roadblocks?*

"You do know the roads are closed, right?" Montgomery asked as he climbed up the stairs and approached the driver.

"Nope, must have been closed behind me," answered the driver, pointing his thumb towards the back of the bus. "Unless you have a better idea I have to push on to at least Espanola."

"Try not even close," answered Montgomery. "The roads are *closed*... unless you

17

have clearance from one of my commanders, I have to turn you around and send you back to Lively."

"Not happening," said the driver as he shook his head. "Either get off this bus and out of my way—I have a schedule to keep and my relief is waiting in Espanola—or pay for a fare and sit down."

"The snow plows and graders haven't even been through here," retorted Montgomery. "You won't even make it as far as Nairn."

"Watch me… better yet, don't," snorted the driver. "Get off my bus."

"Fine, have it your way," conceded Montgomery.

Moments later he watched the bus pull away as it continued west. "Crazy bastard," muttered Corporal Montgomery as he went back to his truck.

* * * * *

"Let me guess, you couldn't find her?" asked Colonel Harnet as the two soldiers came into the office once held by the Mayor.

"There are more nooks and crannies in this place than in an old castle," answered Zoe as she sat down heavily in one of the chairs. "And I suspect more secrets as well, for all its modernity."

Harnet snorted, "If you call this modern."

"Considering the comparison I just drew, sir, it certainly is more modern," she responded.

"Well, then I suppose we could turn to other matters," he pointed out. "I would like to head out towards Falconbridge and Skead—take control of the mines and the airport before one of the others gets the same notion."

He stood up and Zoe followed him to the filing cabinets and maps of city.

"Once we have these we can start circling the rest of the area, take the farms to the airport's west and control the whole city. We won't need outside trade," he said. "Which is a good thing, considering…"

Blinking, he gazed out of the south windows as a plume of black smoke rose from just beyond the rail bridge and over the mountain.

"Is that coming from the Armoury?" asked Zoe as she walked over to the window.

"Or very close to…" he said and his words trailed off as the lights flickered and died.

The emergency lights came on as the rest of the towers went dark, but City Hall was not alone in the dark. As they watched the city lights die, Zoe realized something. "The hydro control centre," she pointed out and they watched as the city darkened for the first time in over a hundred years.

Harnet nodded and he turned to Zoe. "Send a team to Garson immediately."

The door opened and another soldier ran in. "Sir, the city is coming apart at the seams. What do we do?"

"Forget the damn Mayor!" ordered Harnet. "Lock everything down. Use whatever you can to create walls around the towers of this block. Board and seal off any and all windows or other access points into here. Brick it all off. Use anything you can find, just make this compound secure!"

"Yes sir!" answered Zoe and the two other soldiers.

The three of them saluted Harnet and left to carry out his orders.

Harnet returned to the window while rubbing his chest. *I'm too young for a heart attack but this... this might do it*, he thought as he drew his attention back to the map. Locking the place down had a two-fold effect—the second was that it would prevent the Mayor and her staff from leaving—or calling in support. *I just hope I called martial law fast enough...*

* * * * *

Sheridan pulled into the driveway and parked her Smart Car in the garage. As the garage doors closed, she mused over the circumstances of her very unusual day. Terrence would tell her if the soldiers at the grocery store had been honest or pulling her chain. Her gut was in a turmoil about the encounter.

She opened the door into the house and called, "Hello the house! Can I get a hand over here?"

It was at this point her cousin, Karen, started clapping.

"Funny," said Sheridan as she pulled a face. "Now, seriously?"

"All right, all right," said Karen as she got up from the stool at the kitchen bar. "You look troubled."

"Had a strange day," answered Sheridan just as the lights went out.

"What in the name of hell?" muttered Karen. "Jeremy!"

"I'm coming!" cried her husband.

"Bring a flashlight!" yelled Karen back.

"Is everyone all right?" came Terrence's voice as he came up from the basement, with a flashlight in hand. "Sheri... thank the Gods... you're back."

"I only went to Lively," she answered, slightly annoyed. "Although, I have something to ask you."

"Hello the house!" greeted Derek and Marissa as they made their way into the house.

"Why is it so dark in here?" asked Derek.

"The power's out!" called Terrence.

"Naturally," came Derek's more than slightly sardonic answer as he moved closer, flashlight in hand. "Hello, Sheri, I see you got some shopping done..." He flashed the light at her car. "Good grief, woman, did you buy enough?"

Sheridan must have taken lessons from the game Tetris. Her car resembled the game in the way it was packed. The only area empty was the driver's seat but she had filled every conceivable space—including up to the dash level in the passenger seat.

"You want to eat over the holidays?" asked Sheridan sarcastically. Then she said in a serious tone, "I had the strangest experience in town."

"If was anything like mine, you and I have something we need to talk about," said Derek seriously. "Let me guess—the military was there?"

"Yes!" answered Sheridan as she looked up at him. "Why, was the military in Garson?"

"No idea. We came down through Coniston. They were there, though. Needed to pull in a favour from a friend of mine to get a 'travel permit' so I could even get this far. Would have been turned back if not for the fact that the road back to Garson was closed."

"What was their excuse?" asked Terrence darkly.

Terrence had military training and was a veteran from duties in the Middle East. He had been discharged medically from Iraq and Derek and Sheridan's exchange had his military sense screaming that something was happening. It was clear that Sheridan and Derek were aware of his suspicion. Their minds were on the fact that Sudbury was fully of innocent people who did not have access to Terrence's experience.

"Military training exercise—anti-terrorism using Falconbridge as the supposed target," answered Derek. "But apparently the main part of the city was the nameless Colonel's live fire zone."

Falconbridge was past Garson and it made very little sense for the military to cut off Sudbury proper if a smaller town on the outskirts was the supposed area for the exercise.

"That's strange, they told me the exercise was practice for natural disaster response up near Chelmsford as the target," said Sheridan. "They, too, were using live fire… and again, the downtown was limited to military business only."

This, again, was not actually anywhere near downtown Sudbury. Derek and Terrence glanced surreptitiously at each other.

"Fishy," mentioned Jeremy.

"Very," agreed Terrence. "It's not the flimsy excuse, it's the lack of central intelligence. The reasons should have matched exactly."

"What do you think it is?" asked Marissa.

"Don't know. And I don't know what to do about it either," answered Terrence as the group moved the groceries into the kitchen.

* * * * *

Russell Wither was not actually from Toronto. Like the rest of his family, he was born and raised in the North. A bit of snow would never scare him. While it did slow him down, it never stopped him from continuing past Lively once he said his goodbyes to Sheridan.

At least with this weather everyone else typically stays off the road, he thought. *Having no traffic to compete with is a definite highlight.*

Unfortunately, after the first hour of slogging through the snow, he decided to call it quits. He pulled over and waited.

After a few moments of waiting, he let out a sigh and pushed on until he could see a small lake. *Almost there… that new overpass should be close.*

The new overpass served as the turnoff into the Four Corners area of Sudbury where his aunt and uncle lived. He sighed with relief as he checked the time again.

It was in that one moment he took his eyes off the road that two things happened.

Beneath the deep snow was a coating of ice. The tires slipped and the small import SUV swerved in response. Russell looked up immediately as he felt the tires slide.

Russell tapped the brakes and then inhaled a quick breath. *Oh shit, that was stupid…*

The SUV's tires lost whatever tenuous grip they had on the ice coated asphalt and he his entire world slid even faster as the back wheels slid, but the front did not. Knowing that panic steering would only make the spin out worse, Russell allowed the SUV to follow its course, but corrected it gently, slowly.

A tell-tale rattle of his front tires on loose gravel told him what was coming next and there was nothing he could do at this point. With no sand and no salt on the pavement the tires simply had nothing to grip.

The impact caused a cloud of loose snow to explode into the air as the SUV spun backward into the ditch.

CHAPTER THREE

Despite wearing a seat belt, Russell found himself thrown against the window and dazed to the point of seeing stars. Russell took a moment while he willed the ringing in his ears to dissipate and then started to swear vehemently.

Stupid rookie mistake... he thought as he gingerly climbed out of the SUV and back up to the road, surveying the situation. He was quick to realise he would not be able to recover the vehicle on his own. He pulled out his cell phone and dialled.

Moments later, he stared down at the smartphone in his hand in confusion. "What do you mean, no network access?!" he asked the device. "I'm not that far into the boonies."

He stared harder at the SUV as if he could lift it out by mind power alone and put it on the road. Naturally, that didn't happen. With a frustrated sigh at himself, Russell realized he was stuck somewhere just outside of Sudbury proper with no shelter available.

Gingerly picking his way back to the truck, he pulled one of his bags—one with a few nifty items that would hopefully make life a bit easier. Especially if he had to beg shelter from a stranger. He climbed back up to the road to look around.

He looked around and learned that he could just barely make out a few houses on the lake itself. Knowing that the incline was not steep, he risked breaking his neck to climb down it. Then again, the snow drifts could have been hiding something worse under their surface. He just had no way of knowing, not without risking it.

Rather than die of hypothermia, he decided to risk the embarrassment of a tumble, he chose to live and wasted no time in pushing his way through the snow that was hip deep in some places.

Soon he was down on the back road that led to the houses on the shore of the small lake, thankful the slope was less steep than it had appeared.

The first house was completely deserted, and it showed no signs of having recent occupation. It was clear someone did live there but they had left days earlier.

Russell moved to the next home and noted that it, too, was a deserted house. Looking down the road to the last house, he could also see it was dark. There was an old-fashioned chimney, but no smoke rose from it. The first two were the same. With a sigh, Russell knew he had no choice.

He had to break into one of these houses. There was just no waiting for someone to come home. Not that they could reach their house with the weather this temperamental. There was no point hoping, if they did come home, that they would feel merciful enough to let him use their phone or stay until things cleared up even if they did.

He walked back to the first house, figuring that at least it would give him clear view of the highway if a plow or tow truck drove by.

The door was a solid metal door with small windows set into it. With a sigh, he checked around the wooden door trim to make sure the owner had not left a key hidden somewhere. Russell checked everywhere around the sparsely decorated entry. This search left him with nothing but a few splinters for his trouble.

With a sigh, he decided to move to the next house.

Breaking a window would cause a draft that would be difficult to plug up, and losing heat was no option.

The next few houses were locked tightly and their windows—being modern—were burglar proof. There were other houses on across the lake, but that meant a risky walk across the ice to get them. It was not a long walk across the lake but the houses were huge secured against intrusion.

He was familiar enough with the building code to know just how difficult it would be to get into them.

Russell walked past the third house and stared in disbelief over at the last house. There was a glimmer of hope as he saw an all too familiar black and white SUV in sight. It made him think that someone might actually be there. And that they might help him.

If he was incredibly lucky, it might be someone that might know something about his brother, Daniel.

Finally, a very wet, cold and exhausted Russell walked into the driveway.

A very conspicuously clean driveway as if someone had recently cleaned it out for his Ontario Provincial Police issue SUV to climb that hill safely. Or, in this case a puzzled woman in uniform. "Is there something I can do for you?" she asked.

"I didn't mean to alarm you," he began. "I'm just glad to see you. I came from up there," he added as he pointed towards the highway and her gaze followed him.

"You came from the bypass?" she asked incredulously. "Through the closed roads... no one is allowed in or out of Sudbury and you came from there? How'd you avoid the military?"

"What? What do you mean?" he asked.

"Where did you come from?" she asked.

"Whitefish... Panache Lake to be exact," he answered.

"In this weather and those roads?" she asked, her surprise clear. "I have to hear this... why?"

"Visiting family before I head back to Toronto..." And then he clued into what she actually meant. "Oh, you mean why *today*. Well, I have family out at Panache Lake, as well as near the Four Corners. I have an elderly uncle and aunt there ... figured I'd stay close to them at a hotel instead of out in Whitefish. I was driving back when my truck slid off the road and into the ditch. I don't suppose you could call me a tow? My cell isn't working."

"Nothing is," she answered and then moved out of the way. "Come inside and warm up."

He followed her in as the cold began biting into his joints saying gratefully, "Thanks, it's getting colder."

"So, you're from Toronto?" she asked blandly.

"Yeah, was driving back down tomorrow," he answered.

She shook her head and pointed out, "You picked a bad time to be between places."

He followed her in and realised they were not alone. For a long moment, he stood there in confusion. "What's going on here?" he asked.

"No idea," answered the eldest of them.

It was the officer who had greeted him who answered the question, her voice matter of fact and quiet, "As far as we know the power is out, communications are out... we're in a complete blackout."

"Jesus," murmured Russell.

"You can say that again," she answered. "So, we answered your question—what about answering mine?"

"I'm Russell... Russell Wither." He held out his hand and she shook it, with a small smile on her face. "As I said, I'm from Toronto and the rest of my family is still there. My plan was to stay one last night here and head back down in time for Christmas."

"I'd ask if you were in any way related to Daniel Wither, but I can see the resemblance," she said. "Adrienne Constantapoulos, and these are my parents."

"Nice to meet you and thank you for letting me warm up," he nodded to them.

"Well, are you going to make him stand there or are you going to let him get his wet clothing off?" asked the older woman, undoubtedly Adrienne's mother.

"I left my luggage in the truck... which is back up on the highway," he pointed out.

"You look about my size," said Mr. Constantapoulos. "I'll let you borrow something of mine until we can get up there or until the phones come back on."

* * * * *

Harnet paced from one end of the Mayor's office to the other and back again. A knock at the door caused him to stop pacing as Zoe came into the room. "Sir," she began. "I'm afraid I have some bad news."

"With everything that has happened so far, Zoe, I wouldn't be surprised if you just told me that the Mayor had managed to turn everything on its head," he answered as he motioned to the maps on the desk. "Look at this. Martial law is declared and we still have to deal with those who not only chose to ignore it, but those who only followed the law of the land because the police were there. I used to think my former neighbours were better than this."

Zoe stopped for a moment. Harnet knew she thought he was too young for his rank but the

General had left him in charge of the area and so Zoe followed his orders.

"I keep forgetting that you're from here," she admitted hesitantly.

"Spit it out, Lieutenant, you're never this nervous," he snapped.

"The team you sent to Garson just came back," she answered.

He whirled and faced her. "And?" he asked.

"Garson is gone, sir. There's nothing left."

Feeling dizzy, with ice seeping into his veins at her words, he returned to pacing. Everything about the situation was slowly unravelling. Even his contacts—ones he had cultured over the course of years were suddenly going silent.

Taking the city should have been easy.

Well, taking the city *had* been easy. *Keeping* it was now a whole other matter. According to his 'sources', Mayor Valeria Piacentini was a woman of agreement. She thrived on all parties agreeing to a common goal and then working toward it.

The problem was the reality… and now he had lost Garson too.

If only I had been quicker… but he pushed this out of his mind.

He could not afford to split his attention between that and the situation here, especially since without the Mayor he could not simply consolidate command with any semblance of legality and she had already used his minor mistake of losing sight of her for a single second to her advantage.

Sudbury's City Hall was not like its southern neighbours. The building could not hold that many deep dark corners for her and her few supporters to simply vanish.

But vanish she had.

Colonel Harnet turned as he cocked his head to one side. There was an ungodly ruckus breaking outside.

His best, and highest ranking officer came running into the office, gasping for air. "Sir, we found the mayor."

"About damn time," he grumbled. "Well? Where is she?"

"Here! With the police—and they're storming the second level."

Harnet's brow furrowed. "We have the tactical advantage. It's a foolish move on their part," he said.

"Sir, step away from the door now!" yelled someone, and his officer swirled in response.

Two things happened. First, the officer who had just reported to him went to pull his side arm. Seconds later he stiffened and then crumpled to the ground, still twitching. It was easy to see why.

The taser wires were still embedded into his chest and arm. Harnet held up his hands as the officer that had 'spirited' away the Mayor and another one came into the room. This first officer held a taser, while the other had his own side arm out.

"There's a second stairwell I don't know about, isn't there?" asked Harnet. "Used in these very circumstances?"

Neither man answered him and for a moment none of them moved.

"Do you surrender?" asked the first one and Harnet froze for a moment but the officer did not appear to recognize him like he did the officer.

This was only a matter of time, so Harnet shrugged, his hands still held up. "I'm not exactly going for my side arm, officer... ah... I never did learn your name."

He stepped across the gap; the second man still training his gun on Harnet. It never wavered while the first officer came up and lifted his hand to grasp Harnet's wrist.

Harnet was familiar with policing and had suspected that the local police would try to arrest him if they did not follow him. He knew they would fall back on arresting him for later processing and prosecution. Judges and juries would still be operating, he knew they would assume.

They didn't have his knowledge or if they did, they weren't accepting it as yet.

He waited for that moment when the angle was wrong for the officer holding the gun while his partner attempted the arrest

Harnet waited and the minute came. Knowing that the other man wouldn't let go, he let the first officer grasp his wrist and then pulled him toward him.

While it did not work as planned, the officer did in fact let go of him and stepped back, hand already on his own side arm—the momentary confusion allowed him to pull his gun. The second officer did not even have time to duck out of the way before he fell. When Harnet turned his attention to the first one, the taser had been replaced by his own colleague's military issue side arm.

"You're quick, I'll grant you that," admitted Harnet as they aimed at each other. "You may as well surrender. My people will invariably squash your little rebellion and will be up those stairs to back me up."

"You really think that?" he asked.

"I know that," Harnet spat the words out. "You're outmanned and under provisioned. We have the advantage."

"When Ottawa hears about this—advantage or no—they'll come for you if we do fail," he answered calmly.

Harnet laughed, "You really think there's still an Ottawa to back you? Wake up, officer. There's no Canada, no USA, no European Union. Nothing. It all fell. Think about the signs for the past couple of months."

He saw the uncertainty in the other's eyes, although the gun never dipped and never dropped. Harnet continued. "It's too bad—you could have been part of this. All the others had no idea what this city could offer and rejected it. Only I had the vision to make it happen. We build history on the men who make it happen. I'm that kind of man. You could have been part of that but now you're just a footnote."

Harnet waited a few more moments, wondering what had happened to his own people. The sound of fighting had slowly wound down.

Finally, they both heard running come to a stop outside the door. "About time..." started Harnet, but when he looked straight at those in the door, he was shocked.

The newcomers were not all soldiers and they were aiming their weapons at him.

Harnet ground his teeth when he saw his other 'most trusted' lieutenant among them.

"Not who you're expecting, is it?" asked the officer.

"You are goddamn traitors, all of you."

"It's over, Colonel," came the voice of the mayor from outside of the door. "Put down your weapon..."

Harnet knew when to surrender. They had the advantage and nothing could possibly be gained by trying anything stupid or melodramatic. He sighed heavily as he flipped the safety on his side arm and handed it over to the other man. "Still didn't catch your name."

"Daniel Wither," he finally answered.

Harnet held his expression neutral. The last time he had seen Daniel Wither he had been in high school and dating Daniel's daughter, Sheridan. They say service changed a man and twenty years had done much to change his appearance. Time had a way of blurring memories, too. The chances of finding Daniel Wither here and now had been so slim that even a gambler wouldn't have bet on the meeting.

Mayor Piacentini followed another officer in as they picked cautiously around the overturned furniture in her office. Harnet watched her carefully.

Daniel swore as the Colonel jumped across the short span between him and the Mayor, taking advantage of the situation. Valeria gasped in pain as the Colonel dug his back up weapon into her ribs. "The mayor and I are going to take a walk—and you can come with us, Mr. Wither, if you like."

"For the love of Christ, Colonel, it's over!" shouted the soldier that had helped him.

"I don't think so."

He backed through the door and through the officers and soldiers that had weapons trained on him. "Let my men go, Mr. Wither."

Daniel ground his teeth and Valeria shook her head. "I'm not that important."

"She's wrong about that," drawled Harnet. "If I kill her, the highest ranking authority—by law—in this situation falls to the next ranking official. Unfortunately I didn't see any of her council about. Christmas holidays and all that, no one's home. If you want any semblance or claim more 'right' than my own then she's very, very important."

"So kill her," said the soldier that betrayed him. "And, once word gets around the closest thing to government is dead we'll have anarchy. You'll have your excuse."

"Don't tempt me, Gavin," snarled Harnet. "My people. Now."

Daniel looked over at Lescelle, the duty officer for the Sudbury Police Service. "Dammit... do what he says," he ordered.

The police let those who supported Harnet back up and, again, two sides faced off. "Fall back to the mall," ordered Harnet. "Through the provincial building."

"Yes sir," came an answer as his soldiers fell back through the breezeway connecting the third tower.

Harnet pushed the mayor forward and into Daniel's arms and as he moved her behind him, the Colonel took advantage of the distraction and turned tail and fled. "Lescelle, seal off the towers from those access points," ordered the Mayor. "If he's right..."

Lescelle nodded and he, with a few others, followed the tunnel and disappeared out of sight.

* * * * *

Garrett arrived at High Falls shortly after the sun sank into the west horizon. The lonely dirt path behind him disappeared into inky darkness. With a blink, he stared back down the road and past it.

This is strange, he thought. *Normally at night—particularly in winter—the lights from Sudbury are bright enough to light up the horizon. Even when clouded over, the light bounces off the clouds and give it a hazy presence.*

There was nothing but the dark.

He shook his head at this oddity and locked his truck – not that it was necessary. The dam and station were miles away from civilization or any sort of major highway.

One of the workers came running up to him. "Garrett! Thank God you're here!"

"What the hell is going on now?" he asked. "Why does it look like we've got a major blackout in Sudbury?"

"That's just it. We're supplying the power just fine and the grid didn't show a blip of a problem. It's as if someone pulled the plug connecting us to the rest of the grid."

"What does head office say?"

"Can't get a hold of them."

Garrett stared at him and asked, puzzled, "What do you mean you can't get a hold of them? We have a satellite Internet connection directly to them. Let me see…"

He followed the younger man up to the office and into the control room. Gone were the days of dials and hard switches. The power station only needed a few computers to run. The on site server was directly connected via a high speed internet T1 satellite connection to Hydro One head office which could, theoretically, run the dam remotely. Nothing could replace human instinct, however.

Garrett sat down at one of the computers and punched in a few of the commands. He blinked.

The young man was right—it was as though no one was home at Head Office. The command went out but nothing, not even the servers at the other end, answered back. He was no computer expert but he was guessing that his colleague was correct—someone had pulled the plug.

"What do we do?" asked the younger man.

Garrett sighed and asked, "Did you try calling them?"

"We couldn't even call you to see how long you were going to be," he answered. "We even tried your home number and there wasn't anything, not even a dial tone. So…" he ended up shrugging.

Garrett shook his head and then looked up at him. "Until the roads are cleared and we can contact someone to get up here, we can't do anything but wait it out."

* * * * *

Dawn over the small lake was clear and—much to Russell's dismay—far too still. Adrienne brought him coffee and sat down beside him. The dining room, and table, in her parent's house had a large picture window overlooking the lake. The view was often spectacular, especially in the autumn, when the leaves changed to fiery reds and oranges and reflected off the lake.

"The emergency channels are all still down," she pointed out.

"That's not good," he answered knowingly.

Before his retirement, Russell had been a network administrator for the City of Toronto.

The emergency network was engineered to survive collapses. There was really only one way the entire network would vanish. It had been purposely turned off. The mere thought of *why* this would happen was utterly chilling to Russell. No reason was good enough to warrant that outside of the government doing it on purpose to limit communications in the case of civil war. Unless an act of war had destroyed it.

No, it was more likely that someone in Ottawa had ordered the action but who was the real mystery.

Either way it did not matter.

Far more important to think about was what they needed to do now in order to survive until someone—the same someone or another who turned it off—in Ottawa saw fit to turn everything back on. What little there was around the tiny suburb outside of Sudbury would not sustain them for much longer. Russell knew that they needed to move if they had any chance at all of surviving the next week let alone the rest of the winter.

"There are some people on the lake," said Adrienne's mother as she made her way to them.

Adrienne crinkled her brow. "People?"

"That's what your father says," answered her mother. "Maybe you should go look and find out what he means."

Russell groaned inwardly and followed Adrienne to the other side of the house. People meant others searching for supplies that the small group currently had to little of. Reaching his position, they looked in the direction her father pointed.

"Is it me or does something feel wrong about this?" asked Russell.

The people he saw were clearly coming from the city, why, he had no idea.

This tiny suburb was too far to reach casually. Adrienne checked her weapon and headed out to the deck as the first person stepped foot on land.

Russell waited just inside. He had no idea what he could do if she ended up needing back up but it did not sit well with him to leave her alone.

A few moments later, she backed back into the house and half turned to him. "They're from the city…" she began, her tone subdued.

"And?" asked her father.

"I think it's best if we all sat down around the table," she answered, nodding in their direction. "All of us, *including* them. We need to discuss just how long this is going to last."

* * * * *

Sheridan rubbed her arms to ward off the cold as she walked down the central set of stairs to the main floor below to light the fire. There was a main central fireplace that could heat the whole house. The stones that formed the foundation of the fireplace also formed the foundation of the house and ran straight through the house as a solid load bearing stone wall.

This in turn kept the house warm like central heat. It was still a bit cool for comfort. Enough to prevent pipes from freezing in the winter and—if worse came to worse—hypothermia if someone forgot to light a fire.

This system was old as some castles in England and France and worked even in the coldest of Canadian winters. It did work far better in warmer climates but with proper planning it worked just as well in theirs.

Terrence learnt the idea at university in San Francisco and Sydney, Australia. There 'green design'—while still up and coming in Canada—had been in vogue for years and almost perfected. Thankfully, since the power was out and the other methods of keeping the house warm were out of order until the power came back on, it was a practical addition.

Once she lit the fire, building it to a roaring blaze for sustainability, she went to the front of the house and looked outside.

"What the hell?" she muttered aloud.

The roads still had not been cleared and there was no sign of it happening soon. In fact, there was no sign of any movement at all.

CHAPTER FOUR

The quiet during the night was a lie and they all knew it. Only a tentative cease fire had been called between the two sides once Harnet had slunk off to call the old heart hospital on the hill overlooking Science North across the conservation area and wetlands his new base.

As Daniel Wither paced in the centre of the rotunda that once formed the City Council Chambers, the mayor watched him with patience. The rotunda was not a large or impressive room, but it sufficed for their use.

As their meeting was by no means official, the mayor sat in one of the seats where citizens had once watched the council proceedings.

"He won't give up," she finally pointed out. "His type never does."

There was no doubt as to which *he* she referred to.

"I have no doubt of that, Madam Mayor," he answered.

"No more of that—if there's no Canada… or anything else… then I'm hardly mayor. And even if I am, what am I mayor of? A crumbling building in the shadow of a city of ghosts," she answered grimly. "Despite every effort we make, we will fade into obscurity."

He stopped pacing then and turned to look at her. "So, you want me to give up?"

She snorted. "Hardly."

"Then what do you suggest we do?" he asked.

She rose from the chair and leaned on the divider between the two sets of seats. "We survive and we take note of history changing around us. Like others did when they found themselves in the same situation, I am sure."

Spoken like a real politician, he mused. They were all about making a mark on history. She still had a point, though. He continued. "Easier said than done, given our present situation, Valeria."

She sent him a slightly sharp glare in response. He shrugged his own response. Part of him wanted to be thoroughly involved in making sure the core survived, but a very large part him knew it was already lost.

She just did not realize this yet.

"Who have you left behind out there?" she asked.

"In what way?"

"I can clearly see a troubled mind when it's before me, and yours is plainly fraught with something," she answered. "Family?"

"Yeah," he answered. "My daughter, and mother, as well as others are all out there. I have no idea if they're all right or if they're as dead as the majority of this city now is."

She sighed and looked up at the flags that hung behind the Mayor's seat. "You're not the only one. When I left my house this morning it was just like any other day. I had no idea what would unfold today and to remember hugging my husband on the way out, it kills me to wonder if it was the last time I ever will see him alive. I imagine it is much the same for you."

"You have no idea," he answered as he turned back to face her. "I wasn't even supposed to be here today. The OPP doesn't come to city hall very often, Madam Mayor, but... for some strange reason... I was here meeting up with another old friend of my daughter's over coffee this morning before she headed out to visit her parents. Fitz went to get a few last minute presents, and I came to visit you. And now we're stuck here like everyone else."

* * * * *

Lorraine woke up just before dawn as usual and had already built up a fire to warm up her room. The whole house dipped in temperature due to the lack of central heating. She was glad Sheridan and Terrence had held their own council and ignored advice not to build an old-style house from the start. The whole place felt much more like home.

Once she had a fire going, she didn't really want to leave it unattended even if the fire screen would prevent any sparks or cinders from escaping and igniting other materials int he room, although there was a general lack of anything flammable around the fireplace. *I wouldn't mind more sleep, but...*, she thought, she knew her own worry over the fire would prevent her from actually falling asleep or staying that way for any meaningful length of time.

Unfortunately there was not enough light to read, knit or crochet with, either.

She opened the drapes wide and moved the chair to face the field to watch the sunrise. Then she grabbed at the phone. If her sister was up it might be nice for a chat... Lorraine crinkled her brow.

The phone in her room was not a cordless phone which meant power should not have been a problem but there was no dial tone. It was completely dead. She got up and double checked the fire screen to make absolutely sure that there was no chance of it moving or letting a single little spark out of the fireplace. Wandering her way into the chilly hallway and then to the grand-central stair, she overlooked the grand and open concept living space below.

She was surprised to see that her youngest granddaughter was up and awake. Sheridan was already poking life into the large central fireplace to warm up the house. Opting to not startle her, Lorraine walked down the stairs and into the living room.

Sheridan looked up and over at her grandmother. "The phones are dead," said Lorraine.

"Use one of the corded ones."

"I did—the one in my room, actually," answered Lorraine. "Is the stove in the barn electric?"

"Nope, one of those old iron beasts from Grampa's camp."

"Well then, I'd best get dressed and make some breakfast for everyone. It'll be like at camp!" pointed out Lorraine.

Sheridan tried to ignore just how pleased her grandmother sounded at the prospect. While Lorraine enjoyed modern conveniences, she was a closet pioneer woman type who enjoyed the simple things far more. She had rescued many objects from her grandparents' camp and old house after her grandfather had died so that Lorraine could occasionally indulge in her pioneer whims.

"Good morning," Derek said as he wandered into the kitchen and poured his own cup of coffee. "I see the power still hasn't been restored. Bit unusual."

"Morning, Derek… Not the only thing 'a bit unusual'," answered Sheridan. "Road never was touched last night or this morning."

"What—at all?"

That's surprising… Derek felt a thin thread of worry work its way down his spine. *Power or no power a snow plow should've gone by to at least clear the road.*

"The phones are dead, too," Lorraine pointed out in a serious tone. "I tried to call my sister and not even the dial tone."

Oh, now that's just fantastic, he thought sourly. *How much worse can it possibly get?*

Derek had another sinking feeling. But he knew that panicking Lorraine would make the situation worse not better because it would stress her out—not a good move. He would talk to Sheridan later about his suspicions.

Better yet, Terrence or Russell would also be good to share this information with as either one would have a more tactical idea of how to handle any unwelcome developments.

* * * * *

"You can't just up and leave," pointed out the one uniformed police officer as he paced the small garage. "We don't know a damn thing about what is happening out there."

"Come on, Dave," said one of the firefighters. "What do you really think happened out there?"

David Radzinsky shook his head. He was not going to even guess what had really transpired but the one thing he did know was leaving a place of relative safety was suicidal. "It's forty below and the snow has crammed the roads to the point of making them dangerous. Your cruiser isn't even going to get out the damn lot let alone the highway," he pointed out. "Stay here where we're safe and warm. You gain nothing going out there and dying of hypothermia."

"And staying here is any better?" asked the same firefighter. "Listen, I'm up for surviving and all that. But, frankly, I'd rather take my chances and get to my family and spend Christmas where I know I can get to a grocery store."

David took a breath and released it. "You heard the radio—"

"So what? Some alarmist report on the news about unrest in Ottawa? Since when is that new?" he snorted and threw up his arms in disparagement. "Come on, man, we're in

Canada. It's not the end of the world out there. The power's only out and the phones are out. Big whooping do. It happens all the time in the winter—especially here. No reason to throw a panic."

"Doesn't mean we should be stupid and risk our damn neck on a road that is deadly when there's ice on it!" pointed out David.

"Your call, man, but I'm out of here," said the firefighter. "My shift was up awhile back anyway."

"What about your relief?" asked David.

"He made it here right before the roads closed!" he shouted back. "Check upstairs if you don't believe me!"

David watched the other man leave.

His partner looked over at him. "Listen, our shift was up and we missed roll already..." she started. "I'm headed back with the others."

"Not you too," he breathed. "Come on, we know better than this."

"Dave, get some rest... you're turning paranoid!" she called back as she hopped into the car with the other officer.

Mere hours later it was only David and Emilie.

* * * * *

Karen made her way through the snow and over to the barn, noticing that there was light in the house but not from actual power. The glow appeared to be from the fireplaces and candles.

Great, just what I need, she mused. *Another day without power.*

She walked into the tack room and the sudden wall of warmth surprised her as the delicious food smell wafted past. She could hear someone humming and it immediately lifted her spirits.

"Gramma!" she greeted happily.

"Oh, Karen." The older woman jumped in surprise. "You startled me."

"Sorry, didn't expect to see you."

"No power still, so we have to cook our food somehow. Can't expect an army to work on empty stomachs," she answered. "I'm guessing the power might be out all day so I'm going to keep the stove on so we can at least have a kitchen."

"I think that's also why Sheridan wanted the big fireplace in the main room—doubles as a hearth in a pinch," pointed out Karen. "You know how she and Terry are big history nuts... emphasis on the 'nuts'."

Lorraine snorted with laughter. "Given how long the power has been out I'd say it was more than handy at this point, wouldn't you?" stated Lorraine.

"Good point."

"The phones are out too," said Lorraine. "Tried to call your Aunt but no dial tone. What were the roads like coming in?"

"No sign of a snow plow for the past day. No idea how Sheridan got in and out with her Smart car... that thing is just not built for a northern winter... the only track on the road might have been hers but it's gone now." Karen took off her heavy outer wear and accepted a cup of hot chocolate from her grandmother, wrapping her hands around it for warmth. "It's dark and quiet as far as I can see."

"I imagine there are some very scared people out there now."

"I'll see if I can find that old radio that Grampa had, the one that cranked up instead of using batteries," said Karen. "It should be around here."

She started to look for it as Terrence came in carrying an armful of wood for the stove.

"Good morning Karen, what are you looking for?" he asked.

"Remember that old radio Grampa had? The one with the crank not the batteries?" asked Karen as she continued to search through cupboards.

"Yeah, it's in my shop area." He answered as he piled the wood up beside the door. "Wouldn't bother though. None of the stations are working."

Karen looked up at him sharply. Although his tone was conversational, she knew he meant something more serious. Lorraine failed to notice the way they looked at each other but Karen understood. She mouthed, *Not even the emergency stations?*

He shook his head, his eyes betraying his concern. He looked worried and *that*, in itself, worried her.

She took a breath and said brightly, "Well, it's a good thing there's lots of people about for you to cook for, Gramma—I'm going to need them."

* * * * *

Food was already in critical supply and Garrett had no way of preventing the fight that invariably broke out. He waded between the two, narrowly avoiding a punch himself, and pushed them apart. Neither of the two really stood a chance against him. While Garrett was not tall, he was solidly built and more than strong enough to stop any fighting.

"We have bigger issues at hand, here," he growled at them.

"Garrett, I'm hungry and this bastard stole my ration!" claimed the first one.

"I did no such thing! You lost it… fair and square…"

Garrett glared at him and asked, his eyes narrowing, "What do you mean 'lost it fair and square'?"

It was almost amusing to watch the both of them suddenly turn silent, but he did not have the patience for their excuses, not in their current situation. "I'm waiting," he said.

"Who made you king of the mountain?" asked the first one defiantly.

With a heavy sigh, Garrett turned to face the questioner and the other inched away almost as if he knew what was coming. The punch took the other by surprise and knocked him on his rear end. "We do not steal food from others," he said as he cracked his knuckles. He then turned to the other one. "Nor do we gamble our share away."

He gestured with his head and the other gave the remainder of his ill won gains back to the first. The first man pushed himself to his feet, rubbing his jaw. "So, what do you suggest we do?" he asked, a bit sullenly.

"Anyone have a fishing kit or some way to hunt and trap?"

The two men looked at each other and looked down. The second one started to laugh. "Well, not that I know of… but…"

"But?" asked Garrett.

"I'm sure we could rig something," he suggested.

They looked at the other man. "I think I might have seen a fishing kit in one of the trailers."

"Go look," suggested Garrett.

The two took off and Garrett sighed. He had been afraid this would happen after they lost contact with the rest of civilization. Unfortunately, with no way to clear the road back to town they were stuck up at the dam.

Supplies were running low. But with the right tools, they would be able to at least fish and trap. The error most people made when coming into the wilderness was that they assumed all animals hibernated through the winter but the truth was only a few did and were the exception. Others either did what they could to eat or stay warm or migrated further south. For some, this was south.

This meant it was still possible to hunt a small amount of game.

The two men returned and Garrett looked over what they had brought him. He inspected the pieces visually and then began to sort them into two piles.

The first one watched him curiously for a while and was silent as the second one asked, "What are you doing?"

"It's a summer kit which means it's meant for using on a rod and reel meant for casting. The lures are fake which means the motion of the rod is what gives it the illusion of life... it's what attracts the fish." Garrett continued sewing a different lure with the pieces gathered. "But if I can make a lure that will naturally twist and turn in the current, it won't require the motion of the rod and will still attract something. Hopefully something that won't break the line."

"Is there anything big enough out there to break the line?" asked the younger one.

Garrett nodded his head, and the first one said, "Yeah, some big sturgeon and muskie in the lake. They'd snap your line in seconds. You wouldn't even have a chance to react before the lure was gone."

He thought for a moment and then snorted. "Ironically sturgeon is good eating, if cooked right."

"That means going out on the ice."

"Yep," answered Garrett as he looked at the both of them. "Stay away from the dam where the ice is thinnest. The ice is likely a good few feet thick or more. You can drive a truck out onto it without any problems at all. The trick will be boring a hole through it to fish."

They were quiet for a time and the younger one appeared to be mulling things over. "There's an auger in the same shed," he pointed out. It's not exactly for ice drilling but we could use it as such?"

Garrett snorted. "How do you think ice augers got their start?"

CHAPTER FIVE

Daniel stared down from his crouched perch on top of the roof of the Ontario portion of City Hall. The ten story building was taller than most of the buildings that still stood over the downtown core.

Except for the office tower in the mall—just one very small block away from their current position—that was now the home of the people that were rushing the barricades below.

"We're going to have to beef up those barricades," said an older officer, a remnant of the Sudbury Police.

Daniel nodded his agreement.

"Never thought we'd be in a war zone," pointed out another officer. "This was always something you watched on TV... something from someplace else."

"It's going to get worse," Daniel murmured. He cleared his throat and continued, "Listen, I hate to say this but anyone trying to get in here and using violence to do it is now our enemy. They aren't citizens, and they sure as hell aren't victims anymore. If we let them in, all of us will be their victims, along with those we're sheltering. This is now a war and they are the enemy."

For a long moment the other three officers and the mayor stared at him in horror.

"My God, are you suggesting we open fire on those people?" asked the mayor.

"What else would you suggest?" he asked, staring straight at her, his breath frosting in the chill air. "You said it yourself yesterday that the world we knew is *gone*. There isn't a Sudbury anymore to be mayor of. What we have here is all that's left and even if it isn't, it's all we can lay claim to or help. Everyone else is either trying to kill us for what we've got or they are already dead."

Her answer did not immediately come. And he could see the other officers were coming around to his way of thinking, even though it was uncomfortable for them.

"Now you tell us—what would you have us do?" asked an officer.

"What right do I have?" she asked.

"You have every right, ma'am," answered another officer. "You were the mayor."

"'Were' being the operative term—an honour removed from me by the military when they called martial law."

Daniel shook his head. "Be that as it may right here and right now *you* still have final say, unless you choose to let that slide and then you have to tell us."

"No, you're right," she admitted and narrowed her eyes as she turned to the highest ranking officer. "I agree with Sergeant Wither. See that it's done," she affirmed.

"Yes, ma'am," he saluted. He turned and spoke into his radio. "Sergeant Lescelle."

A crackle in answer came through the radio. "Sir?"

"Give them one warning, and then you have my permission to defend yourselves with deadly force," he answered.

"Understood, sir."

Daniel heard the telltale screech of the loudspeaker, and then the warning went out in both official languages.

A few moments later the unmistakable sound of gun fire rose from below to reach their ears. The mayor looked away, and a few of the other officers looked down at the roof surface.

The rioters made a desperate attempt to climb the wall like ants over a blade of grass, but those within the barricades repelled them.

Finally, the screams and shouts and the gunfire died away.

"Sir," came a very distraught sounding Lescelle.

"I read you," the commanding officer said into the radio.

"I'd say most of them are dead but a few managed to escape back towards the mall. Do you want us to pursue?"

The other officer looked at Daniel.

Daniel shook his head. "No, Sergeant, bolster our defences."

"Understood, Lescelle out."

The radio silenced and Daniel said, "This is only the beginning."

* * * * *

Terrence, Derek and Sheridan stood in the main room of the manor house. The three stood close to the fireplace for warmth as the cold was enough to cause frost to build up on the glass windows and up the doors.

"There is no sign of anyone from city works," said Terrence. "At least not this far down the road. The phones are dead and even the emergency stations are out. Now, to prevent jumping to conclusions or panic, it could still be a military training exercise but that excuse is losing its credibility."

"I'm with Terry on this, Sheri," Derek pointed out. "This has gone way beyond anything allowed to the military as part of their training—and this is also way beyond an actual military exercise. There are simply no communications of any kind and no power. It's as if the infrastructure just vanished out from under us."

"Which means what? The end of the world just happened?" asked Sheridan. "We're at war and the government just forgot to tell us?"

"Or they were on the way out and grasping at straws to keep control. Think, Sheri, what's the first thing lost when a government ceases to exist?" Terrence asked, an intense expression in his eyes.

"Their ability to maintain infrastructure in outlying areas... the ability to defend territory," she answered. "Terry, these are not the days of Rome and Byzantium. We have modern methods of communication—the Internet, phones, mobile phones and radios. And the ability to travel hundreds of miles in a matter of hours instead of days. A civilization can't just fall and no one knows it happened around them."

"It can—if the news reports aren't entirely accurate. If the information they're given isn't true and we get what they report, we wouldn't know a damn thing," said Terrence. "Think, Sheri. When I was in Iraq, I saw how easily information can be twisted and manipulated. You know it happens."

She looked away and into the fire. For a long, tense moment they were all quiet until Derek broke the silence. "What if—what if civilization, as we know it, is now gone? We shouldn't be arguing over what is and isn't possible. We should be planning what we are going to do about it right now and for the future. There is a long, rough winter out there that is breaking all sorts of records as the worst one. We're still only in December which means there is January, February and March to think about yet."

Sheridan looked back up and at him. "You're right, of course. Terry, what is the status of our supplies? I know we won't have enough but perhaps we can stretch them somehow?"

"Stretch, maybe, but not for that long. We'll have to venture out and get more supplies at some point. The larger issue is going to be defending what we have. If civilization has fallen, many people out there will be desperate to live and they are not going to be nice about asking for help. They'll just take what they want," pointed out Terrence. "There's a reason they call looting... looting."

"And with no help from emergency services to prevent it," added Derek. "We're on our own if it's actually happened."

"Wonderful," said Sheridan. "So, we need to supply ourselves and keep our supplies from looters. First things first—we need the defences then. I want anything glass, such as windows, boarded up."

"That won't really help," pointed out Terrence.

"Then what will?"

"Taking out the glass and bricking it up with solid timber reinforcement, as well as proper insulation, will do two things. One, it will prevent looters from getting access and, two, it will also conserve heat," he answered, blowing out a breath.

"What about Norse shutters?" asked Sheridan.

"Sorry, what?" asked Derek.

"You know when you see those movies about 'ye old medieval times'? The windows close by closing up wooden doors that swing inward on heavy hinges and bar from the inside like an old fortress gate... only in smaller scale?" asked Sheridan.

"It would be easy enough to build and add to the existing structure," mused Terrence, interest in his tone. "And insulate. Should be more solid than boarding them up."

"And we would be able to open them back up later if and when this all blows over," she pointed out. "If this is nothing but a scare, it'd be a curious and functional historically correct addition to an already historical English manor... in Canada."

Terrence snorted in amusement at his wife's comment but she had a point. The shutters would just add to the charm of the house if this whole thing was just a scare. He hoped it was just a scare—that it was just an exercise. If it was, then all of this was not just only annoying to him for the sake of inconvenience. There were probably so many scared people in the area who had no idea what was going on or what to do. On the other hand, if it was not just a scare then there would be thousands of dead people simply out of a lack of preparedness.

He was not going to let his family be one of them—and he also was not going to let someone else take it all from him just because the police were not there to stop them.

"So, if the world has suddenly come to an end, what are the side issues we need to consider for the near future other than issues with looters and a supply flow?" asked Sheridan. "We also need to keep in mind that without regular supplies we will have to supply our own medicines and deal with our own injuries."

"Thank God we have a doctor," said Derek. "Without you, Sheri, we'd be screwed."

"I'm just one link in this. I can't deal with this on my own," she pointed out. "I need those shutters on the windows now, gentlemen. And we also have to think about a way to cook our food, not to mention the food in the freezer."

"I wouldn't worry about what's in the freezer right now. It's cold enough in here, let alone out there, to keep," said Terrence. "But cooking it when we need to will cause a problem. We'll have to move that old wood stove from the barn to here and move the electric one out."

"No power," sighed Sheri.

"Unless—and this is just an idea because there's nothing we can do about it now—we move a solar panel or ten to the roof and set them up for net metering. That way if civilization hasn't fallen, you won't run into the 'Dammit, the power's out again' annoyance," suggested Derek. "And still be supplying the grid with your extra power."

"That's why we bought a few extra panels." Terrence chuckled as Derek's eyebrows rose. "I just haven't had the time to get them up there."

"What? Where the hell have you been hiding those?" asked Derek.

"In the shed."

Derek shook his head in disbelief. "Well, all right then. We'll install those for you, Sheri, when we aren't in danger of breaking our damn necks. Can we use that massive fireplace for cooking for now?"

"Easily," answered Sheridan.

"Then we'll move the furniture around to accommodate," finished Terrence. "Now…"

There was a sharp knock on the door, and then the sound of a timid voice. "Hello?"

Terrence's eyes widened in shock as he spun to face the front door, then he looked pointedly at Derek, whose lips drew themselves into a compressed line. Derek saw Terrence's concern.

People—an unknown factor—had suddenly just appeared not only on their very doorstep but had walked through their front door. They looked around the corner warily. Two people one with hair that had at one point been a fiery red but was now turning silver and a man that made Terrence look small.

"Don't mean to give you a start," said the man as he held up his empty hands. "Couldn't help but notice you have light and warmth where there really isn't any anywhere else on the road."

"And?" asked Terrence pointedly as he felt Sheridan's elbow jab him sharply in the ribs as she moved around him.

"You must be freezing!" she exclaimed. "Come by the fire and tell us what you've seen up the road."

The two knocked the snow off of themselves as best they could and followed Sheridan the rest of the way into the house.

"I'm Sheridan, that's Derek and Marissa…"

"…And the glowering darkness behind you is Terrence," finished Marissa.

"I'm Tyrell, and this is Helen," the man introduced as he looked over at Terrence and Derek. "I'm sorry if we just barged in on you, but Helen noticed that the bell didn't work and knocking wasn't having much effect."

"A little hard for a bell to work without power," agreed Derek, poking Terrence in the ribs.

"The major problem of security has just been painfully made obvious, though," he pointed out, shrugging as Sheridan looked up. "Not saying that you two are going to be an issue. Actually, it being you instead of someone else not so friendly is a good thing."

"If you need a hand, I'm up for it," said Tyrell.

Terrence nodded and offered his hand and Tyrell shook it. As Tyrell finished, he turned around from the fire to face Sheridan and the others. Sheridan looked over at Derek and Terrence.

"Well, you're welcome to stay, of course," said Sheridan. "If you can help with horses, it will be a good news for my cousin, Karen. She will be more than happy to welcome the help in the barns."

"Barns? As in more than one?" asked Tyrell.

"There are three horse barns," answered Terrence.

"Is there anything else we can do?" asked Helen. "I'm not much use in a barn."

"I'm sure there is," answered Sheridan, and then she sighed. "I didn't think it would get to this point." She turned and looked at them sharply. "You said you came from further up the road. Was there any signs of life or even a snow plow?"

"None, and the phones are dead too," answered Helen.

Derek waited until Terrence led Tyrell and Helen off to the barn to see what help they could offer in exchange for staying.

"At this point we'd best call it for what it is," began Derek. "With no way to confirm whether we still have government or order, we are on our own and we need to start thinking that way."

"As much as I hate to admit it... I think you're right," agreed Sheridan. "You and Terrence were right—we need defences. Tyrell and Helen may be friendly but the fact that they waltzed right up my driveway and through the front door of my home makes it painfully clear that we need some way to prevent looters or others from doing the same."

"I have an idea. Since you're blessed with natural barriers here they may just save us," began Derek as he laid out his plan.

Sheridan's farm occupied its own little valley with an escarpment that ran along the north property line. The road, with the river on the east side, cut a climbable path up the cliff. The Vermillion River ran along the east property line before looping around the south and following a line of low mountains further south and was wide and deep. In recent years it rarely froze completely over but this year was an exception.

The property had once been a golf course but Sheridan had snapped up the property for a reasonable price. The northern half had been another horse ranch owned by someone else. A few short years later Sheridan brought that property, too.

Sheridan's house was on the northern half where the old ranch house had been. The southern fields that formed the old golf course still lay mostly empty.

On the other side of the river was the Whitefish First Nation Indian reserve. "With no help from authority, we're going to have to *be* the authority. There are going to be a lot of scared people out there that aren't road trash. We have an opportunity to start something here instead of watching what's left of our civilization vanish like a puff in the wind. We can do something very real to drag ourselves out of the dark ages," he finished.

"Is this what it is?" Sheridan mused, lifting a brow and looking over at him. "The dark ages?"

"Well, I wouldn't know."

"No, I think you're on to something there," she pointed out. "Rome was very much like the modern world. Terrence and I have often seen the parallels. The US even modelled their society on it. The White House looks like a Roman villa with its columns, and most of the traditional homes along the east coast had those same Roman columns. But even Rome fell on itself and was reborn. I think, unfortunately, history just has repeated itself."

"If that's the case, what are we?"

"I don't know," she shrugged. "Celtic England before it we called it that, perhaps? After all, it was the remnants of Rome that intermarried and set aside their Roman trappings in Britannia and eventually it became Britain. The ancient reborn into something new built on top of the old."

"So Rome has fallen, so does Canada?" asked Derek darkly.

"Canada was a colony of Britain, and in many ways still is... Was... who knows until we can confirm that the government either doesn't exist or has lost grip on the rest of the country. Rome did the same—it simply lost grip on the outlying areas and collapsed on itself," she answered. "Rome fell, perhaps now its remnant has and we are in the modern equivalent of ancient Britain."

"If that's the case, where's my broadsword, dear?" came Terrence's voice as he walked in on the last part of the conversation. "What's this?"

He looked down at the paper where Derek had drawn a rough sketch of the area and his plans. "An idea I have—if 'Rome' has indeed fallen."

* * * * *

The road between the rest of the city and the university on the south shore of Lake Ramsey no longer existed. Or, at least, for all appearances it did not. No one could see it or travel on it. The snow had clogged it so much that the only way to guess where it was by the houses that faced it and the slow, flat, meandering path back to the city.

No buses came, no trucks, no cars even. The road was empty of vehicles and Robert Kaine found himself waking up to a dark room lit only by the dull red of emergency power. "What is going on here?" he grumbled as he sat up from the cot he kept in his office

He had no family, no one waited for him. His apartment was nothing more than a place to register an address and to occasionally entertain a guest or two.

He let out a sigh before sitting up and hobbling over to his desk. He slipped his glasses on after checking them for dust. Peering through them, he checked the data on his computer screens.

I thought I'd have more time, he mused, sitting down heavily. *I knew this would eventually happen… but now? Why now?*

The initial shock faded and Kaine pulled open a drawer. Taking the notepad and a pen out from the drawer, he drove his attention back to the screen. Already some of the others were blank as communications failed between the university and other points in the world.

"Who the hell is Harnet?" Kaine wondered aloud as he looked up while crinkling his brow. "I mean I know who he is, but I don't remember him being my age…"

Muttering to himself, he moved to the next screen. As he finished marking down the name of the commander in Lively, all the computer screens went black before he could make note of anything else. *Dammit it all!! I didn't have time to take all that down!* he railed.

One by one, the rest of the screens went blank. All that remained was one satellite feed and the radio scanner and he could go over their archives later. The ones that had gone dark for security reasons did not save their messages once the power was cut. Whatever information had been on them was now lost.

"Damnit all to hell," he swore. He sank back into his chair, rubbing his knee realising he was already out of time.

Well, this winter is just going to be fan-tab-u-lous... he mused as he drummed his fingers on his desk. *At least I'm stuck here and not at home. That's something.*

CHAPTER SIX

Derek's breath caught as the shock of the sub-zero air caught in his lungs, and fogged in the air when he finally managed to exhale as he walked outside. The bottoms of windows were crusted with ice and frost as the panes of glass failed to keep out the cold.

While Sheridan had not specifically asked him to head out and look for her neighbours, it certainly beat the alternative of sitting on his behind as he waited for news.

Terrence walked around the corner in his heavy winter clothing. He nodded to Derek as he walked by and joined them.

"All right—we'll be heading across the bridge and to the south first. There's a small enclave of cabins and houses not too far from here," said Derek.

"What's past that?" asked Jeremy.

Derek shook his head. "A campground and marina. It's normally closed this time of year. I mean, the owner could still be there, but it's easily ten k's down and at the very end of the road."

"No chance they would have wintered there?" asked another.

Terrence thought for a moment and then shook his head. "I doubt it. Even before all this the drive down that way was nasty. You needed a four by four to make it and half the time the plows never went that far. I think they shut it down at the first hint of snow—maybe after hunting season ends at the latest—and check on it time to time but after winter sets in it's pretty much abandoned. Anyone still down there is more than able to handle this by themselves."

"So, we're not risking it," finished Derek for him. "We go as far as the camps and homes that could be occupied and then we head back."

He led them out into the driveway. Despite the fact that no one was driving because the fuel was simply too difficult to get and too precious to squander, the driveway had been cleared of snow. Terrence's breath frosted in the air and he rubbed his hands together in a vain effort to keep them warm. "Damn, it's cold out here."

Jeremy was hopping up and down and shifting from side to side in same effort. "Oh my God, I think a certain part of my anatomy just shattered."

Derek snorted and shook his head. He walked over to his SUV and slid into the driver's seat. Terrence moved over the front passenger side and Jeremy sat behind Derek.

When he pulled out and headed down the south road, he came to two conclusions.

One, I was crazy to drive here in the first place.

And, moments later, *Two, I still have no idea how Sheridan's little Smart Car had managed to drive from Lively to Panache Lake Road and then down to the farm in at least a foot of snow, even if it had still been loose and fluffy.*

The first conclusion... well... if he had not made it here the point would be moot. With the power out and the general infrastructure collapsed he was actually quite happy with where he was. Garson would be a nightmare if there was no way to keep order and the area was surrounded by mines and one old dump... and it was a bit too close to the city for comfort.

There were only two strips of land where he could have considered hunting or foraging but he would have had to compete with the others in the area.

The area around Panache Lake was, in contrast, far better for foraging and hunting—even fishing—which meant for someone familiar with camping and hunting it was quite easy to survive. The competition for that survival was also far lower.

And I'm definitely not going to complain about the relative comfort of Sheridan's home.

He hoped others would be as lucky.

If they were not, then he had an ugly feeling that they were not going to find very many survivors. *Assuming we find any survivors at all...* he mused.

As the little SUV pulled into the first subdivision full of year round cabins and small houses, the first thing they all noticed was the smoke rising from the chimneys of most of the homes. And that was a good sign, although the other two houses were cold and seemed deserted.

When he stopped, a few people came out of their houses. One man walked right up to the driver's side window and Derek rolled down the window. "How are you doing out here?" Derek asked.

"Could be better... but definitely could also be worse," he answered. His eyes grew wide as he noticed that the person was Terrence. "Terrence! Seeing you just made my day."

"Rick, how much in supplies do you have?" asked Terrence.

"Not a lot," he answered grimly. "Why?"

"I've a bad feeling this might last awhile. Why don't you take what you need and what can be shared and come up to our place?" Terrence looked around. "We can send a sleigh."

"Give me the night and we'll pack it up. Come back out early tomorrow," answered Rick.

"You got it," answered Terrence. "Stay safe… wish I could stay and talk but we have other places to check out."

"No other houses that way but that camp and they locked it up before heading south for the winter. We're the end of the road here. The others who were further that way." Rick pointed down the side road that branched off. "Came up here to stay with us."

"You sure there's no one else?" asked Jeremy.

"All accounted for," answered Rick.

Derek nodded and then turned to Terrence. "Let's head back to your farm and we'll draw up a plan to come get them for tomorrow. I don't want to use too much of my gas. With the way things were in town, I have no idea when we'll be able to get more."

* * * * *

Helen and Tyrell, who had joined them from up the road, were only the first ones to arrive on the farm and soon Sheridan had a dilemma. Her home was rapidly filling up with neighbours who were using her living room as a town meeting hall and the fireplace to warm up. The noise was enough to cause her two cats to vanish into the nether regions of the massive house—cold or no cold—and the two dogs had to be taken to the barn.

Lorraine was, naturally, in her element as she handed bowl after bowl of Irish stew to each of the waiting hands.

Terrence, Derek and Sheridan watched from the overlooking balcony on the second floor as Derek tried futilely to get an accurate head count. With a shrug, he finally gave up.

"How many?" asked Terrence.

"Well, I can tell you it's anyone that didn't rely on electricity—unless they were already off grid—for heat that's here," Derek sighed and ran a hand over his face. "Unfortunately there are quite a few people who didn't make it. We've confirmed at least ten households that are dead. Froze to death in their sleep last night."

"This is only one night," pointed out Sheridan. "There are hundreds of homes past us and further down the road. Hundreds unaccounted for—they can't all be dead."

"Even if they aren't, we have no way of getting to them," said Terrence. "And what would we do if we did? What *can* we even do?"

"Anything we can," answered Sheridan. "Everything we can. They're our neighbours... there are seniors and families."

Terrence sighed. Once Sheridan had made up her mind to help people he knew there was no way of dissuading her. It was because she couldn't sit by and watch other people in her community suffer. She saw herself as part of that community and being a doctor only made that sense of responsibility all the stronger. "We could get a few teams of horses together and sleighs, but we've only two actual sleighs capable of carrying any amount of people."

"What about the carriages?" asked Sheridan.

"In three, four feet of snow?" Terrence lifted his brow. "Sheri, I know this is hard—"

"What if we sent teams with a few horses as pack animals and the people with snow shoes?" asked Derek. "The horses could be used for the infirm and very young. The adults could walk, or even ski..."

Terrence sighed. "That would be better than nothing."

Sheridan leaned on the railing. "In the meantime, we have more than enough scared people in our home that need an answer of what's coming next right now."

For his part, Terrence had no idea what he could suggest to help them out. He knew that Sheridan would insist on everyone being aided somehow, even if it meant stretching their already thin resources to the very limit. He had no idea what she had in mind, but she suddenly stood up straight.

Uh oh, he thought. Sheridan suddenly having a flash of inspiration was either going to be very good or good but it would be hellish to accomplish.

Moments later, she turned to the both of them and said, "I have an idea."

"Christ," breathed Terrence. "Here we go, Derek."

Derek groaned and leaned his head on the railing.

* * * * *

Picking through the destroyed remains of anything was always depressing at best. It always made Daniel doubt his choice of career. Unfortunately, in the circumstances he found himself now, it was far worse.

Behind him stood one of the remnant of the Sudbury Police Service and he was equally subdued. "I still can't believe this is happening."

Daniel shook his head, crouching down in the rubble just inside the barricade. "You still have the same feeling of it being some horrible nightmare but... you just can't wake up from it. You open your eyes and the nightmare is still around you," said the Mayor as she walked up behind them.

"You shouldn't be out here," said Daniel.

"And where would you keep me?" she asked plainly. "Locked in some ivory tower while the barbarians are at the gate?"

Daniel looked around and then turned to face her. "No... the tower is hardly ivory," he answered. He continued before she could comment again. "I'm sure you've noticed the distinctive signs of an active war zone. The barricades are hardly able to hold long enough to keep another wave of them from coming through—and we've already established the fact that you are the last elected leader this region has."

"That we know of," she pointed out.

"If, and I stress if someone else survived they aren't here, which makes you our last leader. When order is finally restored, it will fall to you to sign the necessary orders."

"But not make them?" She asked. As Daniel was about to answer, took a deep breath and held up a hand to forestall him. "I know my strengths, Lieutenant Wither, and I also know my weaknesses. In some things—military or policing—I am not the best to lead. My role is mainly civilian."

"That's what I mean," he answered. "You'll need to decide if what we need to do is too far or not, or if we are under martial law or not. We can suggest the next course of action based on our own experience. But, let's be honest—this situation has no precedent in Sudbury. We're in uncharted territory."

"We all are," agreed one of the Sudbury officers. "And Daniel's right. If we don't pull together, we're all dead and what's out there will never see the light of day."

The mayor paced for a moment as she thought and then she looked at the second tallest of the three towers that formed the square. That was the home of the Sudbury police force. "Is there no way to open a line of communication to others?"

The local officer shook his head. "The old radios were switched over to a closed digital system that uses cellular technology. We'd need an actual radio station or a HAM to broadcast... and then they'd have to have their radio on and just happen to be on the same frequency. Unfortunately, AM and FM are broadcast only."

"At least we'd be able to give people hope..." she pleaded.

Daniel sighed. "If it ever gets safe enough, we can think about sending out a team to find a radio. But I haven't the slightest clue on where to start. We're talking needle in a haystack. To broadcast... well... the CBC station and that French one isn't too far, but the former is straight through those crazy bastards territory and the latter I think was hit by a tank strike."

"What about a HAM?" she asked.

"No idea where we'd find one of those," answered the local officer. "Those are typically used by hobbyists and enthusiasts. They aren't used as a real method of communication anymore. Most have, as I said, switched to cellular or satellite."

The Mayor turned to him in surprise and something akin to hope and a dawning realisation came on her face, "The cell towers I can see being off... but satellite never would be. It's just a matter of getting a signal..."

"Another long shot, but worth trying," admitted Daniel.

The mayor grinned. "Why don't you start in my car, Mr. Wither? I have a satellite phone."

* * * * *

David stared outside the fire door from the top of the EMS building and into the blizzard. *How bad is it when I can't remember just how many days have passed since we lost contact with our central communications at City Hall?* He sighed heavily. *Food's running low and I seriously have no idea how long this is going to last or if we'll actually survive it.*

Emilie came up behind him. "We could hunt."

"We may have to," he admitted as he turned from the door and then pulled it shut behind him.

A flashlight was the only thing that lit up the dark stairwell as Emilie flicked back on. "We also may have to figure something out for heat. The emergency generator is running low. We may have enough for another night or two—three at the most."

"No fuel in any of the ambulances?"

She shook her head as she led him back down the stairs to the gloomy, but still lit enough to see where they were going and the main floor of the fire hall. "Already syphoned off what I could."

He sighed heavily. "Well, thankfully this place is old enough to have an old wood stove hanging around. We could get wood and light a fire to hold us over."

She looked at the radio in his hands and he sighed again. Emilie looked away and then turned back. "What do you think happened?"

David compressed his lips into a thin line. "You sure you want to know?" he asked grimly.

"No, but knowing is better than being not informed," she answered.

"All right," he answered as he set the radio down. "The last burst clearly sounded like City Hall was under attack. All of downtown sounded like it was up in arms—and then it cut out."

"It what?" she asked, shocked.

"I don't think there's a government anymore. Em, I think we're it," he sighed.

"How can that be?" she asked, her voice rising.

They were both cut off when a loud knock at the main door echoed through the fire hall. He picked up his gun, checked it and handed it to her. "Hopefully you won't need this."

He picked up one of the rifles and turned to head back to the roof. "You head to the door they're knocking on. I'll keep the radio channel open so you can hear me. Channel forty-three, on secured. Only we'll be able to hear each other."

She nodded and headed over to the door while he sighed and walked back up to the stairs and out onto the roof. He looked over the edge at the four figures below and followed the footprints to where they led.

"You can stop banging on the door now," he shouted. "We know you're here."

"Thank God, we'd given up hope," a man answered. "Can we come in before we freeze to death? It's just my wife and my two kids with me."

He could easily see that the man was not lying. The small woman and the even smaller children gave that away. As pragmatic as David was about his own survival, he was not about to let people freeze to death. He was not sure how he would feed all of them but freezing out there was even crueler a death than starving. At least with three adults able to hunt and forage they could cover better ground while one stayed behind with the children and to watch the Fire Hall.

"Emilie, let them in."

"No one else hiding in the snow?" she asked.

David blinked then looked carefully at the drifts for any signs of disturbances. "No, Ms. Paranoia, just two adults and their two kids. Open the door."

The door opened from below and the four shuffled in. David kept watch just in case something else moved.

Not sure what disturbs me most… the fact that I'm looking for a threat or the fact that there's nothing out there at all. Once he heard the door clang shut, he headed back down the stairs to where the family were.

"Thank you for letting us in," said the man as he extended his hand.

David shook his hand and nodded. "Couldn't let you freeze."

"I'm glad for that," he answered. "I'm getting the feeling that this is not…"

David shook his head. "No, it's not short term."

"Daddy, I'm hungry," came the little girl's voice and David winced inwardly. "You said that when we found someone that they'd have something to eat."

The man looked over at David awkwardly. "We haven't been able to find anything."

David shook his head. "Don't worry about it. We might have something left in the kitchen, but our pantry is pretty damn bare."

"I'll see what I can manage if you take me to the kitchen," said the man. "I'm a shorthand cook."

"Oh thank God!" interjected Emilie. "David thinks cooking is hot dogs with nothing but mustard on plain bread. I was getting tired of being the only one cooking... well... if I wanted it to be *edible*."

"What's wrong with that?" asked the man, as he rolled his eyes. "It's all the kids will eat sometimes. So... your name is David, then?"

David groaned, rubbing a hand over his face. "Well, perhaps before we get too ahead of ourselves names would help."

"Ironic that the cop would forget that detail," pointed out Emilie.

"Shut up, you," snorted David as he shook his finger at her. "It's been a long few days. Give me a break."

CHAPTER SEVEN

"If I could have your attention, please!" came Sheridan's voice from above their heads.

Lorraine looked up, wondering what her granddaughter had in mind while believing it was along the lines of helping these people out. She had no idea how but she knew that Sheridan would the right person to do it. As the murmur and of voices quietened, they turned to look up at where Sheridan stood flanked by Terrence and Derek.

"I promise you that everyone here will survive the winter," began Sheridan. Lorraine raised her eyebrows but remained silent as she wondered how Sheridan was going to pull that off. "But I need something from you."

"What?" asked someone from within the crowd.

Another asked, "And how the hell are we going to survive all winter?"

Loud voices travelled back and forth as doubts filled the air.

Sheridan held up her hands that had begun to rise once more fell back to scattered murmurs before the room silenced. She explained, "We are going to have to work together on this but it can be done. First things first. We need to find any and all possible survivors in an area that can be reached on foot in half a day... half a day there and half back." She let that sink in and watched as people seemed to slowly back away from the thought, gazing around at each other. "These are our neighbours and friends, and some are even family. We cannot leave anyone without what they need to survive through the winter if we have something to help them too—and I promise you—we can."

Lorraine felt a stirring of hope at that statement, even she, like many others, had doubts. "I know you want to know how," Sheridan continued.

"Got that right!" a man chimed in. A few voices murmured agreement.

"Let me get to that—" Sheridan took a breath. "Shared between all of us are enough resources and this is the key point. We need to share evenly so that we all survive. Of course, those with special needs will be accommodated."

"How will we know who needs what?" asked someone.

"Sheridan's a doctor!" answered Lorraine.

The answering silence was almost deafening. It was as though the din had been a wall she was leaning against and the wall had abruptly given way. And then the noise suddenly erupted again.

"Medical?"

"Or are you a vet?"

Terrence whistled through the din and everyone silenced again. Sheridan nodded and answered, "Medical, and I'm a surgeon. My name is Dr. Sheridan Wither. Many of you know about my practise in Lively and that I also spend time at Sudbury Regional in the ER. My cousin, Dr. Karen Withers, is the vet." She smiled a bit. "We both have a thing for horses… in case you couldn't tell."

The comment allowed some of the tension to dispel. Lorraine looked around and saw that some of the more worried faces were suddenly not as worried as they had been. Given the circumstances she knew that knowing there was a doctor, period, in the immediate area that it had done a lot to help her peace of mind as well.

"Now that we have that out of the way, let's get into the nitty gritty of how we're going to survive the hardest winter we've ever had in living memory," she began again. "First—as I said—we're going to need to share resources. Food, water, blankets, tools and building supplies... There is literally a wealth of resources right under our noses. Secondly, and this isn't going to be pleasant, we're going to have to scavenge from those who didn't make it and therefore won't need their supplies."

A murmuring of discontent began but there were more heads nodding from those who could see the necessity. "What if someone doesn't want help... and doesn't want to share?" a voice asked.

"Leave them be," Sheridan answered. "We won't steal their resources, but if they don't want the help, we won't force it down their throats."

Terrence pointed out softly, "I can see a few of our more reclusive neighbours doing that."

Sheridan hummed in response and then turned back to the crowd. "If they choose to ask for it later, we're open to that possibility. But being overly aggressive about it at this stage of the game will not gain us any allies and that is what we need the most right now."

"How are we going to get around, Doctor?" asked a man.

"This is where the team work comes in. We are going to have to clear some of the roads ourselves—what roads we absolutely need—but only enough for basic foot and horse traffic. We don't need to go far as where we happen to move around the most will get packed down pretty fast," she answered. "This leads to the next big issue and that is where you are all going to live for the next few months. If your home is close, you can return to it if you want. And that leads to the next issue... how your house will be heated for the next few months."

Derek leaned over. "Sheridan—the wall."

"One thing—anyone who lives towards the highway and to the north of us will have to be moved south of us. If civilization—and our government—has indeed fallen the escarpment forms a wall of defence that we will be capitalizing on. Living outside the wall means I can't protect you," she explained. "Which means some people are going to have to open their homes to strangers to share. I am one of those people."

"What wall?" asked a man. "Did I miss something here?"

"Yeah, what wall?" came another voice.

Derek whistled and they quieted down.

"I'm turning the floor over to Derek and Terrence, who are handling defences."

Sheridan stepped to the side and Terrence stepped into where she had been, and Derek flanked him.

"Basically, along the escarpment we want to build a wall. At first, it will be a timber wall to prevent foot traffic from easily slipping past our defences if we need to defend our resources."

Lorraine did not like where this was heading. If Terrence and Derek thought it was necessary then they were in dire straits and she could tell she was not the only nervous at the disclosure.

"Listen to me," came Sheridan's voice. "This is going to be the hardest thing we have ever done, or considered doing. And if it's not necessary, then fantastic—we lost nothing and kept our hands busy while waiting this out." She took a breath. "But if it is necessary, then the two ounces of prevention will beat the pound of cure we will need if it comes to it. I would sleep better at night, knowing we took the precaution rather than not, and I know you all would too."

It seemed to settle matters, but Derek's next words did not. "That means we need volunteers to help build this wall and I won't lie and say it's going to be easy—especially without power tools. That's why we need to share tools. Axes, saws... if it can knock down a tree and dig a trench to sink these poles into, we're going to need them. And eventually we're going to be making a stone wall to reinforce that timber wall." He took a breath. "It is going to be back breaking and hot work in summer. But we still need to create temporary measures in a timber wall made from leaning logs and lashing them together and that will be both back breaking and cold."

"Can we not create an ice wall instead?" asked the same man that had been the most vocal.

Sheridan tried her best to spot the man who asked the question and it was Derek who answered, "It's something to think about, certainly. And would make the eventual permanent wall easier to build around if we didn't have to take down the other wall."

"Excuse me, sir," said Sheridan. "You seem to be quite interested in this. Can I ask your name?"

"Dr. Rick Kuretsky, Director of the Goodman School of Mines at Laurentian University," he answered. "I'm surprised your husband didn't recognize me."

"I'm surprised I didn't either," admitted Derek.

Terrence was laughing quietly. "What would you suggest, Rick?"

"Well, everything you have so far is good, but building a timber wall in the winter is going to be brutal. The ground is rock solid frozen and finding good trees that will suit is better done near the end of the growth season," he suggested. "If we pack the snow, it will settle solid like cement just as well as any rock wall and we have months until the thaw, if I'm not mistaken, which means the wall will serve the entire winter and can be erected far easier and far faster than what you're suggesting."

"Can you oversee that?" asked Derek.

"So long as I have Terrence helping me, sure," he answered.

"Done," agreed Terrence. "With that being said, what do we have in the way of expertise in the room right now?"

"Before you start yelling up at us with what you can do," interrupted Sheridan, "those who have professional or near professional medical experience, whether human or veterinary, go to the kitchen. If you have some sort of engineering background or trade skills in construction, go to the dining room half of the living space. If you have culinary—professional or not—stay in the living room. If what you can do doesn't fall into that, move into the entry area under this balcony and we will figure it out individually."

Everyone reorganized themselves accordingly.

"Okay, let's get this party started," said Sheridan in a lower voice as she turned to her husband and Derek. "Terrence, you go talk shop with the engineers. Derek, can you sort out what is what under the stairs?"

"You got it," he said as he headed downstairs.

"We'll reconvene when we all have a sense of what is what," said Sheridan. "Keep it short. We still have others we still need to save."

She leaned on the rail as she watched everyone below as Marissa walked up to her side. "Do you really think it's all gone?" asked Marissa.

"I have no idea," answered Sheridan, shrugging her shoulders. "But even if it hasn't we have a responsibility to keep those we can alive until help arrives. If it has, then we have an even larger responsibility."

"Do we?" asked Marissa, lifting a brow. "It seems to me like someone is taking too much onto her own damn shoulders again..."

"... Wonder who that could be," agreed Lorraine as she joined them on the landing. "Why not concentrate on what's under our roof before worrying about the rest of the area, Sheri?"

"Because I can," answered Sheridan.

"*Can* does not always equate to *should*, Sheri," pointed out Marissa as she watched Terrence break off from his group and Derek climb the stairs. "Like *should* also doesn't mean you *can*. Just remember the difference."

Terrence jogged up the stairs to the landing and noticed Lorraine had joined the group. "Hello, Lorraine, I'm a bit surprised to find you up here."

"Sheridan wanted my input from the ground, so to speak," said Lorraine.

With a nod, he stepped up into their little circle as Karen joined them.

"So, what do we have?" asked Sheridan.

"In the trades we have me and Rick with engineering degrees of some sort. He's mining and I'm civil. In skilled trades we have four Masters—Tyrell is a Master Welder, Pavi is a Master Stonemason, with landscaping experience. We then have Jason and Jean who are both Master level mechanics. As for the journeymen... well... we have a bit of everything. We also have two apprentices. One is an apprentice wood framer and the other is a roofer. We easily have what we need to rebuild if it comes to it," said Terrence. "A little of everything may not be great on one thing, but at least we're not missing anything critical."

"That's a good thing," pointed out Derek. "In the 'everything' else we literally have that. Mostly forestry and resource management—tree seeders and growers and various labourers for those that are of an age to work. The rest are retirees. They still have a wealth of experience to draw on—artists, writers, historians, hobby gardeners. You name it, we've probably got it."

"So, if civilization is truly gone, we have those here who will be able to preserve and teach our next generation," said Sheridan, and Derek looked up sharply. "Also critical to a healthy community." She quickly moved on and looked over at Lorraine. "Gramma?"

"Well, of those in the kitchen you have everything you could need support wise. A lot of homemakers and at least one professional chef from the city, as well as a dietitian."

"And, in my corner we unfortunately only have me as the only licensed medical doctor... or doctor period. But, we do have one nurses but no personal support workers," sighed Sheridan. "Other than Karen... as the vet. I can hardly run a small clinic. I can't do anything intensive, but it's better than nothing."

Terrence looked over at her with a quirked eyebrow. "Not even a MASH unit?"

She punched his arm playfully and he rubbed it while sticking his tongue out in her direction. She turned serious and looked at the four of them. "Okay, we need to run a town and I guess since everyone is here and chose to come here anyway that the Manor is now Town Hall. Everyone we have here is now part of that town. We automatically assume that anything outside is hostile until proven otherwise," she decided.

"Who leads this dog and pony show?" asked Lorraine.

"We call for a vote," suggested Sheridan.

"Oh hell *no*," said Terrence. "I have no issue with helping people and sticking our necks out, but voted out of my own home? No way. Sorry. You're the Mayor, Town Reeve, or whatever you want to call yourself and I'll back you up on it."

Sheridan looked ready to object, but Terrence quickly added, "If they don't like it, they can fend for themselves."

"I'm with Terrence on this, Sheri," said Derek, sighing and shaking his head. "This is *your* house—bought and paid for by you and Terrence and with both of your money. You can share what you have so we all survive, and they will make things both easier and harder on us. We could have survived without them here—but they will make life easier later. If you want to smooth alliances now, that's all fine and good. But you need to stay in control."

"Why Sheridan?" asked Lorraine. "Why not Terrence? Or even Karen?"

"I don't own the property," said Karen. "It has to be Sheridan."

"Fine, but why not Terrence then?" asked Lorraine again.

"You really do *not* want him as the lead here," said Derek in a seriously. "You want him supporting, and defending, the leader. But put Terrence in the lead and this will turn sour very quickly." He glanced over at Terrence. "No offence meant, I just happen to know you that well."

"None taken, and I actually agree with you," admitted Terrence. "I also agree with Karen and Derek. It has to be Sheri. The property deed is in her name... it's not even in my name... so that is moot. This entire property is hers and she should choose who lives on her land. She's the Lady of the Manor. If they don't like it, they can leave."

"If I'm the 'Lady of the Manor' as you put it, then we will need to present a unified front. No countering or questioning me in the open. I have no issue with concerns brought to my attention, but there is a time and a place for it," she decided finally. "Are we together on this?"

"Absolutely," answered Terrence.

"About time," breathed Derek as he looked up at the sky.

Lorraine paused. "I still don't like this whole thing, but I'll stand by it. Terrence made his point abundantly clear and I'll stand by your decision to agree with it."

"None of us like it, Gramma," pointed out Karen. "But it's the only way to survive this and still come out ahead." She looked at Sheridan. "I'm behind you all the way."

Sheridan nodded and then turned to face the crowd below. Terrence whistled to get everyone's attention. Terrence nodded to Sheridan to come forward once all was silent.

Sheridan looked down at the expectant faces and realized, *Every single last person here is counting on me to bring them through this... Now I'm about to place myself as their Lady... perhaps even their Queen. Can I do this?*

She looked over at her husband and family. Terrence nodded as he knew what she was thinking and Sheridan took another breath to steel herself. *Should I do this?* She looked down again. What right did she have to demand the equivalent of fealty to her in exchange for survival?

Sure, it was her property—they were here on her sufferance.

But they were living, intelligent beings and she was about to proclaim herself their Lady to whom they owed their lives and if they didn't like it... *leave?* But then again, what choice did any of them have? If she did not lead them there was no way any of them could survive the winter.

She took a few moments, considered her choice. She said, "Ladies and gentlemen, after careful consideration I have decided that there is only one real way we can possibly survive the winter and then the future. If civilization has indeed fallen, then it falls to us to create it anew. In this room is more than enough talent and expertise to do that. Each person here has a purpose—a reason to be here.

She paused to let her words sink in. "If Canada is truly no more, then what are we left with? So many of you have already told me that on your way here, when you checked on your neighbours, you told me that over three quarters of them were already dead. Frozen to death in their sleep or while trying to huddle around a long dead candle.

Again she paused. "We know that if we are seeing that here and now, then it is likely everywhere. I hope not, but the reality is this means only one thing—our government has collapsed in on itself. There is one predominant historical precedent and that was Rome. I believe we are seeing the end of ancient Rome all over again in Canada. I hope it's only in Canada and that eventually international help may yet still come but I have my doubts. If it were coming it'd already be here and our radios filled with at least their reassurances—not that we have any power for them."

People were exchanging eye contact as she described out how bad things had become. Someone was finally saying out loud what everyone already knew within themselves.

"So does that mean we fall with it? No!" she cried out. "Does that mean we let it all crumble around us? Again, I say no! Not when each of us can rebuild it. We have the artisans, the tradespeople and the scholars among us to preserve it. We have the ability to rebuild it— even if in this little corner of our world. And perhaps, like another great Empire that eventually built itself out of the ashes of fallen Rome we may do the same." She paused for a second and shrugged. "Probably not in our lifetime but it is an aim we can aspire to."

There were some chuckles in the crowd while Sheridan took a short breath. From the despair of knowing the world had ended, Sheridan had provided them with a spark of hope in its place. The easy part of regaining that hope and giving it back to them was over.

Now came the hard part.

"But we can't do it without leadership and someone at the helm of this ship. Someone pointed out to me that we are using my land as the core of our new community and that you are looking to me for leadership," she added. "Which means I will be that leader, and anyone who does not wish to follow me is free to leave. I will not force you to stay or share, and you are welcome to return later. But make no mistake — this is still my land and you are all on my property. It is because of what I have built here that you now live through another night. It is because I have decided to allow this and defend you past the wall on that escarpment that this becomes possible."

All eyes were focussed on Sheridan as her words redefined their world. The silence was profound as small conversations suddenly stopped in shock.

"So... you're our Queen now?" Rick's voice was hesitant.

"I wouldn't go that far," she answered and she was more than a little horrified at the thought.

"Why not?" asked another in a thoughtful tone. "You have a point. This is your land and we're here on your mercy. You could have turned us away or turned us out, but you didn't.

You could have then demanded we accept this... and you didn't. I'd say that sounds like a right and proper Queen."

"First, I don't have enough territory to go that far," answered Sheridan honestly. "And this house is far from a castle or a fort. Call me Reeve, Mayor or some other term. Or call me the Landowner... or even call me what I worked the hardest to get and that would be 'Doctor Wither' and you'd be correct and I'd answer to it. I'm not pompous enough to go past that and all the way to Queen."

"Fair enough," admitted Rick.

"Anyone who doesn't agree with this decision is free to leave at first light tomorrow morning." Terrence stood up and leaned on the rail in view of everyone. "We won't force you to make any snap decisions. Think on it and sleep on it. If you're still here by noon tomorrow, we'll know you've decided to stay on under our terms." He looked around. "Now, I'll ask if anyone has decided to stay, even with those terms, then I need some volunteers. We said we wanted to go after survivors. We need to discuss who can go look for survivors and can start out at first light tomorrow."

Hands went up in the crowd and the number surprised them.

"All of you?" asked Terrence, the surprise clearly in his tone. "Who is actually leaving— doesn't like the terms?"

"Can I say something?" came Jason's voice.

"Go ahead," said Sheridan.

"I'm with that other person who said you should be Queen. I think I speak for most people here. If you want to keep us around, you're the boss and we'll gladly work under your terms as you've laid them out. You've treated us fair and been honest so far I can't see you suddenly changing now."

There were nods of assent throughout the crowd and Sheridan smiled as she looked down at everyone. "Good... can I come down from here now? I do my best thinking on the ground and in the team, not above it."

There was some laughter and then the cheering began. Sheridan stopped for a moment shocked at the sound of the support. But she was even more shocked as the sounds continued to build until everyone was yelling and screaming their support until the windows rattled.

* * * * *

Daniel knew that there would be another attack soon and he was glad that he had ordered everyone to increase the solidity of the barricades. The barricades now resembled to a wall made of cement and other bits and pieces of debris. Sharpened spikes and barbed wire topped the wall to prevent anyone from climbing over the barricades.

The wall would prevent the square being overrun by gangs of half-wild raiders.

"Should we open fire?" asked Lescelle.

Daniel shook his head. "Only if they look like they might actually breach the wall. If not save the ammo for when we need it."

The clamour from outside the wall was almost deafening and the chanting was sociopathic. But the chanting and taunting was all meant to do one thing—get those inside to do something incredibly stupid by going outside, thereby opening the gate for the now neo barbaric horde to swarm inside.

Lescelle let out a deep sigh and said, "I shudder to think of what happened to any of the better citizens of our city got left outside."

"I'm not very happy about this either," answered Daniel. "But we're not much good to them if we're dead."

"No argument there," said Lescelle. "We will have to venture out eventually to find supplies. What's left inside that cafeteria and the few vending machines is now running dry. We're out of food."

"Assemble a team, then," said Daniel. "Send them out at the break of dawn to see if they can find anything, but make sure to send them in the opposite direction of the mall. I think the gangs are coming from there."

CHAPTER EIGHT

As the night fell, the teams that had been sent out to find survivors began to filter back in. Sheridan watched as each team came in through the foyer. She frowned as she realized that there were very few new faces with those who came back in. From the teams' expressions, it was not because people had refused their help.

Derek took each team leader aside and listened to a very quick report, and his expression grew grimmer and grimmer with each one. Finally, he patted the last leader on the shoulder and joined Sheridan where she sat at the top of the stairs. "The news isn't good," she stated.

"No, it's not. I sent teams out in every direction and it's the same story. Some have lived, and can survive on their own and have done the same as us here. In the spring, they will venture out and talk to us—if we're all still alive. A few of the ones that were desperate came with them and have joined us. Only a few of the most hostile of hermits refused to talk or come out." He took a breath and continued. "But, that's the exceptions. For the most part at least three out of four houses with people actually in them—those people froze to death."

"Would you suggest we keep up the search?" she asked.

"For a few more days, sure," he answered. "There are places the teams haven't checked yet. But I have a feeling that it will go from one out of four surviving to one in eight, and then there won't be much point."

"Do you think the worst has happened?" she asked seriously.

"I think we both know the answer to that." He patted her shoulder and stood up, helping her up, then following her to the railing where she saw a demoralized group of people. "The real question is how are you going to counter this?"

Sheridan whistled over the low murmuring that signified a drop in the people's spirit. It signified that morale was quickly sinking and her whistle broke through the low level sound. "Listen to me!" she called out. "Look to your right."

Everyone did so.

"Now I want you to look to your left," she ordered.

There was a long pause, but they eventually did and the expressions were now of puzzlement.

"Every single person you see with you now will survive the winter. If they weren't here yesterday, that means that every single that is now here will also survive the winter—we did that. You did that." She pointed out to them and around the crowd. "So long as we are breathing we have that hope and that ability to get us through this winter."

There were some nods, but she could see that she had not broken through to them all yet. "We've lost—well... we've lost a lot of people. And there's no getting them back but we can survive and remember them. But we do no one any good if we lie down now and die." Sheridan looked around at them and continued. "So we have more mouths to feed. So what? We also have more hands to supply and work to keep all of us alive. We have more with us and we will all survive."

The worst of the morale was lifting, but she could see that she needed to get them rallied.

"We can do this!" she shouted, punctuating each word with a slap on the railing. "We can do this!"

Derek saw what she was doing and joined her, slapping the railing with each word and falling into time with her chant. "We can do this!"

One by one each person followed picked up the same chant, clapping their hands and slapping a table or a counter near them. With each word, the voice grew until it was loud enough to hear clear into the barn. Sheridan suddenly stopped and everyone continued to cheer until it just quieted on its own. Although it was quiet, morale had been kicked up into a roaring fire that reignited their hopes for survival.

"We will eat and we will feast tonight. And then we will rest in the warmth of our beds—and tomorrow morning we will get back up and we will do this all over again until we know that we have found every last survivor. We will continue the work on our defences and we will continue the work that will get us through this winter," she affirmed, pausing. "Because this will not defeat us. Together nothing can defeat us. Are you with me?" she asked.

"Yes," came a few voices.

"Are you with me?"

This time she was sure the cheers carried straight across the river.

* * * * *

A few days later, the teams came back without any new faces, only more supplies and dark news of more people frozen to death. Her rangers had either found them huddled around candles or some other source of heat. More foolishly, others had taken to burning bits of debris which resulted in deaths not from freezing, but from suffocation. Others they found outside, along the road—half buried in the snow—as they tried to find somewhere safer or warmer. It didn't matter which direction the searchers went anymore because now they had reached as far as they could possibly reach without positive results.

Sheridan rubbed a hand tiredly across her face while Suni brought her in some tea. "I take it that the news is bad?" asked Suni.

Suni was the daughter of one of the survivors. Her mother, Pavi, had insisted on the younger woman assisting Sheridan as her 'handmaiden'. *Something that makes me altogether uncomfortable...* thought Sheridan, even though she had accepted on her mother's insistence that she would need some sort of support.

"Unfortunately, yes," answered Sheridan, sipping the tea. "We have ranged out everywhere and now no one else is being found alive. The reports are... not good."

"But we still survive?"

Sheridan nodded and looked up at the young girl. "How old are you?"

"Twenty-one," she answered, surprised by the question.

Sheridan nodded and suddenly realised that no longer were they looking after adults—there were young children and seniors, as well as household pets now living in the barn.

"I think I may have been... neglectful... of a certain need of any civilization," realized Sheridan. "I haven't given thought to its soul. I've taken care of its spirit and body, but forgot that one thing to keep it all in balance."

"Yes, you have," answered Suni, with a short bark of laughter. "You didn't directly address it but you didn't exactly forbid it. You've left it to be private—and really, in my opinion, that's how it should be."

She lifted her brow and looked at Suni. "Really?" she asked honestly surprised by the young woman's answer. "How do you know this?"

"My mother and I still have our faith, and I am sure it is the same with everyone else. I know I have heard singing in one of the barns." Suni thought for a moment. "In fact it was in the one closest to the house."

"Speaking of you and your mother..." began Sheridan, and Suni lifted a brow. "Are you happy with this?"

"I'm perfectly happy being alive considering the alternative."

"I meant you being my 'handmaiden'," answered Sheridan, feeling her nose twitch at even saying the word aloud.

Suni snorted. "My Mom is old fashioned and comes from a family who was proud of their 'service' to the British when they had control of India."

"And you are not," stated Sheridan.

"No, but I recognize the fact that you're just as uncomfortable with this as I am," she answered, grinning slightly. "And, I'm sure the 'handmaiden' thing will be temporary until you find something else for me to do that we *both* can agree on."

Sheridan nodded and left it at that, and they both looked up when Terrence came in with Karen close behind.

"We're out of hot chocolate," she stated. "And your coffee and tea supplies are also running low."

"That's a relatively minor thing that we were all expecting," pointed out Terrence. "It will be uncomfortable for some, but Derek and Lorraine know how to find Labrador tea in the bush, so we have bush tea if all else fails." He paused, looking over at Sheridan. "We have a bigger problem."

"Medical supplies," Sheridan answered. "I know about that particular problem. Helen already talked to me about the supplies in our clinic. Given our burgeoning population, I think we'll have issues soon, especially considering the labour going into that snow wall on top of the escarpment."

Terrence nodded. For a long moment there was an uncomfortable silence in the room as the true impact of what was happening around them started to sink in. "We need to head to someplace and scavenge," he suggested. "There's an emergency services depot at the end of the road near where our road meets back up with the back highway between the four lanes and Whitefish."

"We're going to have to head there," decided Sheridan, turning to Karen. "I want you to send Derek, with a small group of his choosing, on horseback to that depot and get everything they can carry."

"With the weather, even on horseback, it's going to take them at least two-day round trip," answered Karen, concerned about where this was going. "And there's no guarantee that place hasn't already been looted."

"It's a chance we have to take," stated Terrence. "If we wait any longer it *will* get looted. We need to do this and do this now."

"Agreed," said Karen. "But I want to go with Derek. I know the roads from riding them every day. He won't."

"I don't like it," muttered Terrence, but his mutter was still loud enough for the rest of them to hear.

"And I don't like having to send Derek but she's got a point," pointed out Sheridan, who then turned to Suni. "Could you send someone to get Derek? He's likely up on the escarpment with Rick."

"Yes, madam," answered Suni as she darted out the bedroom doors and down the stairs.

"She's quite the handmaiden," said Karen.

"Assigned to me," answered Sheridan. "It's taking a bit to get used to but the personal assistance is welcome. I have more on my plate than I was expecting with all this. And for the record—" She turned to face Karen. "—I don't like you going as much as Terrence doesn't. But I understand that you need to. You just make sure you come back."

* * * * *

Derek watched as the volunteers and those from Terrence's group of tradespeople worked on the first part of the snow wall.

And the work had not been easy.

The first day had consisted of gathering enough snow to start packing the snow and ice into gate posts on either side of the road at the top of the escarpment. They decided, after much deliberation, to build the most critical part of the wall first. Snow packed into cement like hardness and shaped into bricks formed the gate. It meant that each cart full of snow — and one cart was roughly equal to the back of a half-ton light duty truck — only yielded a fifth of that in bricks. They easily laid bare of snow the main road all the way down to the farm as well as the bridge to the south of the farm by the full width of the road. All this to just build up the gates and the first part of the wall on either side.

And those gates were only six to seven feet tall and, by necessity, three feet wide at the base and tapering off to approximately two feet at the top. Only one car could fit through the gate in the middle of the road. Right now there was no way to close the gate but at least it pinched and controlled any traffic to only foot traffic and funnelled that foot traffic through a choke point. They did not shovel any snow from the road outside of the gate in order to make it more difficult for anything to gain real speed to ram the walls.

Derek knew it would never prevent any real attempt at sweeping down into the valley. Even if — after sitting overnight — the snow did naturally solidify itself into a hardened mass of ice by sheer weight alone. In a fortnight the wall would be as if made of concrete instead of snow, and just as heavy.

Work on the rest of the wall along the side of the escarpment was beginning and the wall began to disappear into the bush. The rest of the wall would be the same. The gate would continue to be fortified until a person could climb up to the top and keep watch without fear of falling down or the structure collapsing underneath. When they built the gate part of the wall up to that point, he would feel better about the solidity of their defences. The wall would then likely stand up to a solid hit by a heavier duty vehicle.

"The wall is going better than expected," observed Rick. "We've all but stolen the snow from the fields and every driveway and walk in the area. Mind you, that's not a bad thing on our side of the wall. I'm noticing that getting around is significantly easier."

"I think the wall might last a bit into the spring, even with the melt," pointed out Derek. "Major snow banks were always the last to melt and were heavy until the end."

Rick nodded his agreement.

They both looked over as a young man ran up to them. The fact he could run drew their attention to the lack of snow in the compound due to the building of the ice wall. "Derek?" he asked, nervously.

"I'm Derek," said Derek.

"Dr. Wither is looking for you," he said. "Suni said to come get you and tell you to come back to the main house as Madam Sheridan has something she will need you to do—but she needs to tell you herself."

"Okay," drawled Derek, and he turned to Rick. "I think you've got this handled. I'd best head back to the house and see what she needs."

"You got it," said Rick.

Derek followed the much younger man back to the house, kicking off the dirt and snow from his boots. Sheridan was sitting waiting for him at the bottom of the stairs and she stood up as he came in. "What do you need?" he asked as he met her.

"I need you and Karen and a team to go on horseback to the emergency services depot at the end of the road. You choose the team. Scavenge what you can in medical supplies, food, and anything else you can carry back here," she answered. "I'd normally not ask you to do this, but we're in that kind of situation."

"Okay, that means I need Marissa too," he said plainly. "Us three and a two horses as pack can be there and back in two days. One day there—given the snow—and a day to search. We head back on the third day."

"Good, leave at first light tomorrow."

"Is the situation that bad?" he asked, concerned.

"I won't lie—yes it is," she answered plainly.

"Ma'am, if I could be so bold," came Helen's voice from behind her and she turned. "I can ride too, and I think I could help. I'm a retired RN so I know what we're looking for."

Sheridan looked at Derek and he nodded. "Then that's settled. Prepare what you think you'll need to take with you and get some rest," she said. "You'll need it."

CHAPTER NINE

Tyrell looked around the table at everyone and then out the massive glass window to the field outside.

"Has there been any news at all from the rest of the world?" asked Terrence.

Rick shook his head. "Nothing on any of the emergency channels and one of the nurses had one of those satellite phones and the only thing he's getting is the stand by."

"That's not good," said another person. "That means the rest of the world is as in the dark as we are."

Terrence nodded. "Rick, you suggested the ice wall. What do you think we need to do to get this done?"

A short bark of laughter was his first response from the other engineer. "Lots of shovels. We're going to have to pile up the snow and even take the snow off the grounds to do this. I think if we cleared the roads where we plan to defend, that will be a good start and should give us a good supply," answered Rick. "Not to mention off the ground where we'll build the wall."

"For defences' sake, I wouldn't suggest taking it from out of the bush outside of the intended wall. Inside, yes, so we can patrol it and build it, but impassable snow outside will create difficulty to those who would approach it—slow them down a bit," suggested Tyrell. "Also, I wouldn't clear the road too much outside of it. Just a thin walkable track."

"So, we're in agreement on how we're building this?" asked Terrence. There were nods around the table. "Okay, split off into the agreed teams and tap the shoulders of those you will need and of anyone else who volunteers to act as labour. Let's get our defences up now."

Terrence got up and walked into the side room where Sheridan pored over a map with Derek across the table from her. She looked up as he walked in.

"Well?" she asked.

"The work is starting on the wall. Tyrell and Rick have it in hand," Terrence answered. "I have a different problem—while we're building it, and then even after it's done, we'll need some way to defend it." He took a breath before continuing, not entirely sure how she would take his next suggestion. "We need a militia."

"I trust you can figure that out?" she asked.

"I was just making sure you were all right with me doing so," he answered honestly. "So, what's going on in here?"

"Organized chaos," she answered as she sighed and sat back in her chair. "Rick and Tyrell appear to have our structures in hand, and Derek has a plan for scouting for other survivors so I'm placing him in charge of scouting trips. You will concentrate on protecting our home and land. Karen is in charge of the horses and other work animals, and Lorraine and Marissa are in charge of all things domestic. I have a head nurse to report to me regarding health issues. Meanwhile I am regulated to… well… regulating."

"It's your land, your house," said Terrence. "You're the Lady of the Manor."

"Indeed," she mused. "And now we have departments, or ministries, and those who report to them. It seems almost surreal that this would even happen here. I am not sure how I feel about this but I suppose, given the circumstances that it's better than the alternative."

"That being we're all dead or out in the cold and on the run?" he asked. "You can certainly say that again."

* * * * *

Adrienne's decision to leave her parent's house and move further away from Sudbury was difficult, but it was their only chance to survive. "But this is our home," maintained her mother when they had decided to leave. "Where will we go?"

"And if we're not the first to head down that lake, what then?" asked one of the others, who had found themselves there in the first place. "One entire side of your house is glass, ma'am. If someone wanted in here they'd be in here and where would that leave you?"

"They'd have to know we were here first!" she shot back.

"We knew you were here," answered the second one. "At night you can clearly see that something is lit up over here. The next step is getting here."

"The boy is right," said Adrienne's father. "If the city has gone to hell, then this is no place to be—it's not safe."

"She does have a point, though," said Russell. "Where the hell are we going to go?"

"We head across and up the road a bit," answered Adrienne. "There's a back way into

Long Lake and numerous houses between. I patrol up there regularly so we'll have plenty of places to stop and rest. Some of them have wood stoves and if someone is alive, they may be able to put us up for a night or two... maybe even longer if we can share resources."

Silence reigned as they considered the option. Russell turned to Adrienne's father and asked, "Any chance you have snow shoes or skis?"

The older man thought for a long moment but Adrienne cut in, "He doesn't need to. I'll take us in the cruiser."

"What cruiser?" asked one of the younger ones from across the lake. "Wait a second... are you a cop?"

"OPP," answered Adrienne. "I have a large OPP issue SUV sitting in the front driveway with more than enough space for all of us. All we have to do is pack what we need and I can get us up to that road."

The other three nodded their agreement and her mother sighed heavily, looking around her house. She walked over to one of the chairs—it was a beautiful Queen Anne style arm chair and she leaned on its back. Adrienne watched her mother.

"If I have to leave then at least give me the time to pack what I need to bring... and want to preserve. You can't ask me to throw everything away," said her mother.

"Mom…" Adrienne sighed. "You have until morning."

* * * * *

The meeting room was hardly crowded. There were only a few professors left on campus as the holidays loomed close and most had left to be with family elsewhere. Kaine and a few others were the only exceptions as they had stuck around to grade papers when the snow started in and now were stuck at the university.

Not that I don't normally stay here anyway, he mused looking over at the others who appeared to have just arrived and were breathless. The members who had just arrived seemed curiously rushed, not having combed hair or ironed their clothes. Kaine sat down at the table and looked around.

"The streets are crammed full of snow," said a professor. "Still."

"I realize that," pointed out Kaine. "Ah, Neil… you did make it in."

The others looked up as the university president walked into the room. Unlike most of the others, Neil was clean and looked smart, just as he did every day.

"Why do you look like nothing is wrong?" asked Kaine, confused.

Neil was not supposed to be here, and Kaine shifted slightly. *I have those connections to get us through this… he's only interested in putting his head in the bloody sand,* Kaine frowned as he thought this. *And that was uncalled for. We need all the resources we can get and he's exactly that.*

"I live just down the road from here. My daughter noticed that the streets looked untouched, so I figured I should come and check in."

Kaine paused slightly. He had never paid attention to where the others lived and instead had focussed on his work but that habit had just bit him on the arse. Had he paid the attention, his plans for this situation could have included Neil in his usual role but now? Kaine thought to himself, *Now I'll have to re-tune everything. Oh well, no point in crying over spilt milk now. I suppose I'll have to live with it.*

"Do you have any idea what's going on?" asked one of the professors.

Neil shook his head as he sat down at the head of the table, moving Kaine's cup to the side as he put his own down in its customary place. Kaine ground his teeth but then picked up his cup and moved to another open seat.

"I was about to point out that I have a rather substantial inkling of what probably happened," began Kaine.

Neil waved it off and Kaine lifted his eyebrows in surprise. "I'll call the city and find out what exactly happened. We'll be back to normal in no time," said Neil, and he finally looked over at Kaine. "What else could it be?"

"I seriously think you should listen to what I have to say," said Kaine. "And what I have to suggest—"

"Dammit, Robert, what else could it be?" asked Neil, and there were a few nervous titters around the table. "I know you have connections in Kingston and Ottawa, but that 'project' of yours is simply theoretical."

"Look, we've argued this point before, but this time it's not just a theory!" exclaimed Kaine, and then he sighed and rubbed the bridge of his nose. "I have rather substantial backing to this now."

Neil blew out a breath. Kaine's eyes narrowed. "Of what? Our world just ended?" asked Neil. "Come off it. I love reading your reports and the theses that come from your students but we've had this come up in previous years too. The snow just falls, and then it takes the city a few days to catch up. No big deal."

"And the power?" asked Kaine.

"It's gone out before," answered another professor. "Happens when the snow and ice gets a bit heavy on a line. Give hydro a few hours and the power will be back on. Our back-ups are more than sufficient to hold us over in the meantime."

Kaine looked around the room, but refrained from shaking his head. *You all have no idea and*

sitting with your heads in the sand will only cost us...
he sighed. "Very well, I will proceed with a bit
of caution," conceded Kaine. "I can wait..."

* * * * *

When Sheridan said first light, Derek knew
she actually meant them to be out the gate by
first light. It was with this in mind that he and
his team decided to hit their beds not too long
after dusk in order to wake up fresh and ready at
the time required.

Marissa and Derek packed in silence, only
pausing to pass each other supplies for one or the
others packs.

They were of a similar mind. Derek's pack
contained everything he could possibly need for
at least five days out in the bush in the middle of
winter. Marissa packed her backpack in a
similar fashion. This offset each other's skills,
although it assumed that they would not likely
be eventually separated. It was not the absolute
best idea. There was always a chance of
separating, however he and Marissa had been
working together for so many years that they
knew each other's mind.

His pack consisted of the same basics as hers
did—sleeping bag, winter cover for the sleeping
bag and their respective covers for carrying.
Emergency 'foil' blankets—two each and
enough dry clothing and spare dry socks to last

more than a few days. Dry clothes were the make or break of survival, especially in the winter when wet and cold could literally mean a very swift death.

Other things in his pack were enough dry food and other edibles just in case foraging or hunting failed while out there. He also made sure he had what he needed to hunt with ammunition that was easy to replace as well as regular rifle ammunition. He had both a hunting rifle and the compound bow Sheridan gave him.

Marissa was not much of a hunter. Where she did excel was at trapping so her pack leaned heavily on that nearly lost art instead, although she also carried a shotgun just in case.

They both carried a small supply of hunting and portable knives and other camp kitchen supplies for lighting fires and cooking food. Once they had finished packing they settled into bed for the night and fell asleep.

The next morning, before the sun was even up, they met with the others in their group.

Derek noted with relief that everyone had thought the same as he and Marissa. Everyone brought various weapons, and carried full packs. Karen and Helen had saddled the best suited horses for the duty and led the group into the horse barn to meet them.

These were no light riding horses, but massive and intimidating animals that dwarfed other horses Derek had ridden before. He did not think they were Clydesdales but they were a similar size to that particular type of horse. The feet were smaller, and did not have the telltale hair around them. All of them were pure black. They immediately brought the words Knight's Charger to mind.

"What breed of horse is that?" asked Marissa.

"Friesians," answered Karen. "Sheridan's favourite horse and the signature of this ranch. Well suited for riding, equestrian show jumping and eventing. Not the classic choice for fox hunting, which is what Sheridan loves to do, but a very good alternative given the breeds other strengths and size."

Before she allowed them on the back of any of the horses, she gave everyone, including Derek and Marissa who were accomplished riders, a quick rundown of each horse.

Derek saw that Helen was eyeing the saddles and tack warily. "Everything all right?" he asked.

"Never ridden English style in my life," she answered. "Always been Western."

"On this particular saddle you won't notice that much a difference," said Derek, but he noticed there was a snort of laughter from Karen and he paused before and continuing. "Despite what Karen maintains."

"If you like English style, you'll notice a difference between the two," said Karen.

"I've ridden mostly Western and the hunter style of English saddle just feels less clunky and less in the way," he answered and turned to Helen. "First thing you'll find missing is the horn for tying off and the stirrups are closer up and there's less to them. I find it easier to get my feet in them and the seat more comfortable."

"Are they more comfortable for the horse?" asked Helen.

"They are lighter, that's for sure," said Marissa. "And the horse is able to respond quicker, so I imagine the lack of horn and other components means the horse is better able to move."

"These are also made to conform to the horse's back contours without creating pressure points," explained Karen. "Not that a good Western saddle—made by a good company—won't also do that. The big difference is like comparing a steel frame camping backpack to a lighter one of the same but only without a frame. You can't get the same amount of stuff onto or into a smaller pack that lacks a frame that you can the framed one, but at the same time you get a trade off on how much you're carrying. The hunter saddles, by their name, suggest that these have more to them. Naturally, the point to them is as it suggests in their name."

"Given what we're about to do, would it not be to our advantage to use the Western?" asked Helen.

"Normally, yes. However, these horses are English trained. If we suddenly changed saddle and tack type, they would need a few days to get used to the feel of it. This isn't a good time to wear a brand spanking new boot without giving them the time to break them in first," she answered and motioned to Helen. "You first."

Helen let Karen boost her into the saddle. Once she was in the saddle and settled, she immediately felt the difference in her riding expectations and settled with a contented sigh.

Karen grinned. "Not all hunter saddles are created equal. These are top of the line saddles meant for long periods of time on horseback, but you can very quickly dismount and remount the horse."

Helen slid off in a graceful dismount, surprised and pleased by how quick and easy that was.

Moments later she stared up at the saddle, wondering just where she was to grip the saddle to remount. Karen patted where the horn normally would be but instead a small rise and roll of leather was all that presented itself.

Her first try was rather embarrassing—the saddle slid sideways and the horse nickered his displeasure.

Karen took that moment to show her the differences in adjusting the saddle. Helen tried again and this time, while not as graceful at the dismount, she was able to mount the horse on her own.

"As a hint, because he's huge, sometimes leading him to someplace where you can get some height advantage on him goes far. But knowing how to do it from the ground is helpful," said Karen.

"The big difference is that I have to put more of my upper weight over him first before I put my feet in the stirrups," said Helen. "I wasn't expecting that. I mean—you still have to with Western—but you can get away with more on the stirrup than English. You almost have to lay over him and position your butt first before put your feet in the stirrups."

"The good news is that riding after that is nearly identical. The tack and bridle, again, have less to them and you need a gentle touch—but everything else is the same. Watch and listen to his cues," said Karen. "They're trained for riding over terrain and jumping stone fences chasing after a fox. They will see and hear things before you do, but they're trained to let you know so you have the tools to respond."

"Like any horse," said Helen, with a smile. "It's not the rider…"

"…It's the horse," smiled Karen. "Good, you'll do fine."

Marissa and Derek mounted their own horses while Karen, once she herself was mounted, took the leads of one of the pack horses and Marissa the other. Jeremy waved a hand as they passed through the doors and closed the barn door after them. With one final look at her own husband, Karen led them up the hill and through the gate of ice. Someone had connected the two sides with a bridge made of planks that had then buried on the two sides in snow. Thankfully, the gate was now tall enough so someone could ride under it on horseback without having to duck. On either side, there was now a tower made of snow and ice.

Derek had concerns on the stability of the towers as snow had the tendency to topple and collapse without some sort of structure. But there was little he could do about it now other than ask Rick once they returned. He was sure Rick would not leave it unstable.

Unfortunately they still had not figured out how to make a real gate to put in the opening. All the gate did now was restrict flow to two horses at once with a little bit of space in between. Still, it was better than nothing.

Life inside the wall was vastly different than that outside and it was very swiftly apparent. Inside they had almost forgotten that civilization had ended once everyone had sprung into gear. The roads and driveways were perfectly cleared—sure, that was mostly due to the need of snow to build the wall. Now people were throwing their efforts into keeping it clean even if they removed snow to build something else.

Activity was also high inside the wall. There was light in the windows and warmth in the houses, even this early, and something seemed to say 'civilization still exists here'.

Once past that gate to the North all hints of life vanished.

Houses were dark, cold and snowed in. Windows frosted to the point that the glass was opaque with rime. The roads were completely hidden and the only hint of where they once were being the clearing between the trees. They stopped just outside the wall and looked at each other. Helen swallowed thickly. This could have been her and Tyrell if they had not decided to make for the farm, she realised.

They realised, then, that there were no survivors. The search parties had been through here and found only death and the occasional hermit that had always been off the grid to begin with.

"Well, we can't do anything by staring at it," said Derek thickly. "Let's get this done and get back."

They were in silent agreement as they rode out of the gate and back down the other side of the escarpment. It was not as far a ride down the other side. Sheridan's side of the valley was lower than this side, but the ridge still served as its own natural wall sheltering the valley.

The snow made it almost impassable as the horses laboured through the drifts. "It's going to take longer than I thought," said Derek with a heavy sigh as the morning sun came up and began to track through the sky. "What time is it? Nine, ten?"

"Quarter after nine," answered Karen. "And we're only a third of the way."

Thankfully, the ride so far had been uneventful. The horses were not bothered by the snow. As they rode into the flat farmland, it became apparent by the drifts that it would be both harder and easier to get through the road. The drifts were like sand dunes — they had high sides and low sides and the wind would blow the drifts into rippling waves.

On the low side, the ground was almost visible and easily ridden. It was the navigating through and over the high parts of the drifts and trying not to break the leg of the horse if the snow gave way beneath them that was challenging.

While Derek rode, he kept his rifle at the ready. Helen did the same to his left but they did not encounter anything. No signs of life or other noises greeted them. There was nothing but the howl of wind over the frozen snow drifts.

What remained was the crunch of the horse's hooves as they pushed through the thin crust to the soft snow beneath and their own low conversation.

The wind whistled and the snow settled with a gentle sigh like paper being ruffled in a library. Trees snapped and crackled in the cold as they swayed in the wind. Birds that had not migrated south chirped and tweeted in the branches of the trees.

There was no one—not a single living person—to disturb the wilder symphony left in their wake.

CHAPTER TEN

Their intent to make it to the Fire Hall by nightfall, naturally, did not come to fruition.

In truth, Derek was not really surprised by this. It had been ambitious to think that they would and the minute it was apparent that dusk was falling and making visibility poor, he called it for the night.

Karen dismounted and they looked around. "We can't stay out in the open, we'll freeze and so will the horses."

"I know, but we can't keep going either," pointed out Derek before nodding at the horses. "If we can't see, then neither can they and we'd run the risk of them falling into something and breaking a leg. Can't risk that."

Marissa blew out a breath and looked around. She then pointed to a deserted house that had a sizable garage attached to it. "What about there? It's large enough for both the horses and us. If it has a cement or dirt floor, we can make a fire pit and keep the doors open enough to allow the smoke to escape. Between the fire and the windbreak, we should be fine."

Derek and Marissa checked the deserted house to see if there was anything suspicious inside. They then checked the garage for non-human habitation. Not that bears would be awake at this time of the year but it was better to be safe than sorry. "Clear," said Derek, and Marissa nodded her agreement.

"We could check the house for supplies," suggested Helen.

"It was probably checked already," pointed out Karen.

Derek sighed and said, "Can't hurt to double check it."

He and Helen entered cautiously, finding signs of forced entry and walked through the rooms. The very first room off the garage was the kitchen and mudroom. The sight before them stopped them in their tracks.

Huddled around an electric oven was a family of four. In their desperation they had turned it into a wood stove.

Their bodies frozen in the exact same position in which they had died.

Their deaths likely came from hypothermia but since they had tried to burn something inside the electric oven was just as possible to have been carbon monoxide poisoning. It was heartbreaking especially since the one child, the eldest of the two, could not have been older than eight. Derek cleared his throat and looked at Helen again as they silently moved past them and to the fridge. It felt wrong to rifle through their cupboards with their silence watching them, but to leave something there that could otherwise feed the living would have been a waste.

"Who puts a can of paint under a kitchen counter?" wondered Helen aloud.

Derek shrugged his shoulders and while he checked the bedrooms, she checked the living room, den and bathrooms.

There was nothing useful for them to pick over. "Take a note of the house," he said when they returned to the garage. "We'll have to send burial teams when the weather isn't as bad to cremate the dead."

As the last of the light from the sun faded in the twilight, the sounds of the animals and birds along with the wind outside faded. Not even crickets dispelled the frozen silence.

Once the surroundings grew quiet, they stopped their conversation, almost as though something held them quiet. He could not put it into words if he tried but it was not fear. At least it was not for him.

The only thing that broke the silence was the crackling of the fire.

It was as if all that remained of the world — even though they knew that just over the ridge was Sheridan and the farm full of survivors — was the small space in that garage. It was humbling and, while terror wasn't applicable, there was a certain amount of trepidation of what the next days could possibly hold.

Logic said that they could not be the last of everything. Someone else — somewhere else — had to have also survived this but where they were and how they did may never come to light. They could be the next town over and no one would know until someone got curious enough to range out and find out if it were true.

It was humbling to see just how large the world really truly was. Life before…

Derek stopped himself at that very thought.

…*Life before… life before what?* What exactly had happened to end everything as decisively as it had?

Was it nuclear war and now they would have to deal with fallout and nuclear winter on top of the typical Canadian winter? Did a virus wipe out most of humanity?

He discounted these since there would have been some hint even among the survivors had that been the case. It had to have been something significant to bring civilization to its knees but he could not figure out what it could possibly have been.

Derek thought about the weeks leading up to all of this.

Gas prices had been going up sharply — this had been all over the news. But it meant little. Prices always did go up and fluctuate around. It was one of the main reasons that cars like the Smart car and Tesla had come out as an alternative to petroleum based fuel. It also was not the first time gas prices had spiked as the seventies had been infamous for a rather large spike in gas prices, as had the early 2000's.

He almost dismissed it.

But something set its hooks in the back of his mind and refused to let go.

Gas prices had not been the only hint of trouble. Granted, much of the furor over going solar and other alternatives was everyone who cared about it had been up in arms about carbon in the atmosphere and other greenhouse effects. But where before it had been mostly token efforts lately had turned into a major industry.

So major that some companies well known for oil and other fossil fuel exploration had turned to alternative sources of fuel and re-branded themselves as the purveyors of 'energy' versus oil or gas.

Derek sat bolt upright, nearly knocking himself out on a hanging tool on the workbench. "It's the end of oil…" he winced as he spoke, his voice loud in the silence.

The others jumped, startled. "What in the name of Christ, Derek?" asked Karen.

"What brought all of this—" he motioned around the room, but they knew he meant more than that. "—on in the first place."

"The end of oil?" asked Helen, vaguely disbelieving as she listened. "Why did you even… what gave you *that* idea?"

"Think about the news lately," he continued. "Gas prices soaring to unreal levels. Natural gas and the cost to heat a home at the ridiculous point… Some people even gave up on their gas furnaces and were using electric space heaters because even hydro was less expensive. If you had an oil furnace, forget it. I worked for a solar panel system installer—we had more calls for panels so that people could net meter… We had far more calls than we could sometimes handle. We had insurance sales people jumping over to our industry because it was the hot ticket to sell."

"So… we just ran out and the world toppled?" asked Karen. "That doesn't make any sense. The government would have warned us it was going to happen."

"Karen, you worked for Ontario Shared Services while in school… would they really?" asked Marissa.

Karen looked down at the ground. "It's not as if they'd go out of their way to not tell people. Well...at least the government workers and office administration wouldn't. If they had the information to give they'd give it."

"...But?" asked Helen.

"Well, I don't work for them anymore so I wouldn't have heard anything anyway. I can tell you that with bureaucracy even if they had the information there were always approvals needed and, well... It's not that they'd try to not get the information out, but whether it would be useful by the time anyone got it is the real question. And as I said, they'd have to know about it first. Can't supply a public service information bulletin without the information in the first place," she answered. "If all this were true and the government knew it wasn't 'the government' that would know per se. Just those in office with that decision making power to pass the information along."

"Would there be a report somewhere?" asked Derek.

He knew Karen's point having dealt with the government more than once. He knew, however, that the others didn't understand. Helen looked particularly confused as did Marissa.

"Okay, say your theory is right. If there was a report written that our resources in oil and natural gas were about to run out and we were all, globally, at that critical point... then, yes, there would be," answered Karen. "However not all government offices would know that even existed in the first place. Government and the bureaucracy just don't work like that."

"How do they work then?" asked Helen, still confused and her brows crinkled.

"Well, there would have to have been a study or a report on something that someone noticed. They'd write a report and send it to a supervisor in whatever office they were working in for whatever ministry that office was part of. That one report would have to cross a few hands to finally arrive at the Minister of whatever office in question; and it would be up to that minister to decide what to do with it. He or she could either sit on it and not pass it along at all... Or it could get sent to a committee of yet more ministers to decide on what to do about it," answered Karen. "Once they had finally decided, it would be then sent to yet another committee to decide on what policy needed instituting and they would then create a policy. Only at that point would word trickle back down the same channels through to the various ministries that need to know. If a public service announcement deigned it necessary, only then would a bulletin get released—after it had been sent for drafting, anyway."

"The problem is that we don't know what ministry would have known and if they even did," mused Derek.

"And what's the point of worrying about it now?" asked Marissa. "It's too late."

"She has a point," agreed Helen, as they turned to Derek. "Why bring it up?"

"Because if we know what caused civilization to topple we know what we're working with and approximately what it will take to survive in the future—as well as what others are going to be eyeing for supplies."

He did not say that Sheridan, as their new interim leader, would need to know why 'Rome' had fallen so that she would not base her new bastion of civilisation on shaky foundations. After all, to be informed was to be forewarned.

"There's nothing we can do about it now," said Karen. "We may as well focus on the mission at hand and tell Sheridan your theory when we get back."

"Theory?" asked Derek dryly.

"Well, it's not as if we can prove it—even it does make sense," she answered.

He nodded and silence descended on them again. Even though it was quiet enough not to need it, they agreed on setting a watch and Derek decided he should take that first watch. His mind refused to let go and he needed time to think and process his conclusion. Sitting a watch would be perfect to allow him to do that.

* * * * *

Sheridan looked out over the balcony to the chaos below her. Derek had been only gone for a day and already those who had looked to him for answers had gone from being able to deal with Rick and Terrence to wondering when he was going to come back.

And arguments were beginning to start on who would do what task.

She whistled over the din. "What is going on here?" she asked.

This did not help as the din only erupted again. She held up a hand and shouted, "Quiet!"

Thankfully that had the effect of bringing the din to a sudden and complete silence.

"Rick, you first. What the hell is going on down here?"

Rick took a breath and stepped forward. "We, ah, can't seem to come to an agreement on whose job it is to keep the roads clear, now that they actually are clear."

"Tell me this argument isn't about who's on first?" she asked.

No one was able to answer her.

She asked again. "So, what did you come up with?" the room simply erupted into shouting and arguing again. Finally, she whistled again and they quieted. "Okay, listen," she began. "I don't mind doing this

151

democratically, but clearly we need to know who has the most experience and ability to lead as a foreman for each individual task. Who can do that job in their stead if, for some reason, they can't."

"What do you suggest we do, Sheri?" asked Rick.

"If we need to, we are going to run our own government until we're shown inarguable proof that the proper government that we all voted in the last election is still in power. Until then we're it. Now, that means we need departments and we need to work for those departments. Obviously each department has to work with the other at some point. We're a bit too few to avoid others all the time, so... here is what we are going to do—" She took a breath and then continued. "Each department, or whatever you want to call them, is as we originally split into. We will all nominate who is to lead that department and vote within it for that leader. That way, at least nominally, each department agrees on a leader or a foreman that they agree is the most suited for the job."

There was some grumbling at this, but it appeared that they all split off into those areas and very quickly bent to the task at hand. Sheridan let her head sink to her hands as Terrence came up behind her, massaging the tension from her shoulders.

"A bit of a war zone down there, wasn't it?" he asked.

"A bit," she confirmed. "This is not going to be easy."

"Did you honestly think it would be?" he asked.

"No, I didn't, but I also didn't expect it to be nearly impossible either. I expected that people would want to work together... especially since it's work together or die. Literally... no need to be dramatic on that statement at all," she replied.

He grunted in agreement. "At least you whipped them into some sort of order."

"For however long it lasts until I need to do it again," she replied.

* * * * *

The next morning Derek and his team set back out just as dawn broke over the horizon. The horses were restless at this point and eager to get moving as if they knew another day of riding was ahead. This time everyone was on their horse far easier, even if from flat on the ground, and ready to go in minutes.

The second day was no quicker than the first even though they had figured out the trick to getting around the snow drifts.

Like in a desert, those drifts moved, shifted and were always changing. They were not as high as a dune in the Sahara as the sun had a tendency to melt the snow. They were high enough to create a hardened crust on top and loose snow would blow and settle, starting the cycle again.

Karen had brought special leggings for the horses to prevent the sharp edges of the ice from scratching and cutting into their legs. This meant the horses could plow through the snow with very little issue. The team paused while applying the leggings before they moved on, then taking it slow for the horses' sake.

Finally, at midday, they reached the Fire Hall and pulled up short.

There were definite signs of life around it with tracks in the snow and near the entrances. The only question was how happy those inside would be to see them and how wary they would be. They cautiously rode up to the parking lot, which appeared tamped down by someone's repeated pacing. Derek took a rock and knocked on the side door. The people inside probably were wary of strangers. At least if they did not surprise them, it could help smooth over any rocky beginnings caused by just showing up unannounced. Granted, with no communications, there was no way to warn them they were coming.

Their answer came from above them. "Where in the name of hell did you come from?" asked a voice from the roof.

"My cousin has a farm up Panache Lake Road," answered Karen.

"I'm guessing the one with horses," said the same voice, a man, and the tone sounded like he was being a bit facetious.

"Yes," answered Karen.

Derek looked at the door and noted that nothing appeared to be broken into. "I'm guessing by the fact that the doors are actually locked and there's no sign of break and enter that you're someone who actually works here."

"Yeah, I am," he answered. "Constable David Radzinsky, Greater Sudbury Police Service."

"Derek Moss, Dr. Karen Wither, Marissa Moss and Helen Mitchell," Derek introduced his team.

Radzinsky thought for a long moment and then looked from Karen to Derek and back again. "Wither... as in that huge horse ranch up the road?"

"Yes, sir," answered Karen.

After all long pause, a question came. "Why'd you come this far?" asked Radzinsky.

"Medical supplies," answered Karen honestly. "We didn't expect to find survivors. All we've found so far has been a lot of death between the farm and here. Saw one smoke column coming from a house. It didn't look burnt so we're guessing someone there is alive."

"And that's all you saw?" asked Radzinsky, a worried look on his face.

"You?" asked Derek.

"What few made it here I let in," he answered gravely. "Me, one of the paramedics and a few of the firefighters in the hall, plus a family from the highway, are all that's left. The other paramedic and the other firefighters tried to head back to Sudbury. I don't know… I doubt they made it."

For a long moment, they fell silent.

"There's very little food here, so if you're after that expect disappointment," said another voice, this time coming from the side of the building.

They turned to face the other woman still dressed in the winter clothing of a paramedic.

"Didn't come for food," answered Derek. "We came for what's in your ambulance and fire support vehicle."

"Medical supplies?" asked Radzinsky in disbelief. "Those are a bit advanced for the lay person."

"My cousin is a doctor—a surgeon to be downright technical," answered Karen. "She's the one who sent us."

"I thought you said you were a doctor?" asked Radzinsky, puzzled.

"I'm a vet," she answered.

"If they've got a doctor, Dave, our best hope for surviving this is going with them," said the woman.

"She just said she was a vet..."

"My cousin's the doctor; and she's the one still at the farm," pointed out Karen.

David thought for a moment and then nodded his agreement to Emilie. "All right, you've a point." He turned to Karen and Derek. "You've got two extra horses, and we've got kids here."

"You got something we can rig as a sleigh?" asked Karen.

David laughed. "We have something better than that." He nodded to the woman. "Emilie, open the garage door and let these people warm up their horses."

Once inside, Karen wasted no time in checking each horse over to make sure there were no injuries. The ice and snow outside had been progressively crunchier as the day progressed. And she had concerns that the leg wraps had shifted or had been torn. In the numbing cold the horses would not have felt anything untoward.

Derek did not say anything and let Karen do as she pleased. "You said you had something better?"

David nodded and led Derek to the back of the garage and pointed, saying, "I'm guessing it's for parades, although why it's out here I have no idea."

Derek stopped and stared at what he saw and then started to laugh. David looked at him strangely, but Derek just continued laughing. "Karen!" Derek called.

Karen took a few moments and then walked over, looking where Derek was pointing. "For the love of…" she breathed. "How long has that been here?"

David shrugged but Emilie answered, "Oh, that… it belongs up at the old Anderson Farm as part of their exhibit. I think the city brought it here for storage. Why here specifically I have no idea."

David looked over at Derek and saw him trying his best to stifle his laughter. "What is it and why does Derek find it funny?" asked David.

"It's an old firefighting wagon, but it's modified to slide on skis," answered Karen. "As to why it's here, it's because the original Fire Hall it belonged to was this very one—or at least the one that once stood close to this spot before this one was built a few years ago to replace the one they had to tear down."

"I'd feel better if we it brought back to the farm," pointed out Helen.

"If you bring us with you, you can have that," answered David.

Derek nodded. "Done." He turned to the constable and pulled him aside. "Any idea what the hell is going on out there?"

"You mean why we suddenly have no government?" he asked and snorted a short bark of laughter. "Yeah, yeah suspect I do."

"So what happened?"

"The government, our own government, has been lying to us for years," he answered. "We ran out of oil—period. Nothing was actually producing anything but pollution, if you ask me. It was all for show. And the proverbial mess hit the fan because people found out and demanded answers."

"Who did and how?" asked Derek, suddenly feeling as if he could not get enough air.

"I don't know the details. What I suspect is the Americans were buying from us and we were digging up what we could, but cutting with oil from somewhere else. Who was stealing from someone else," answered David. "It was at the point where it was like paying a credit card with a credit card, but only having so many credit cards."

"You run out of credit."

"Right. So we keep shuffling the balance around from card to card or sharing the load. Doesn't seem so bad. But the demand kept creeping higher and higher, and the available balance kept creeping lower and lower," explained David. "Eventually the bubble just burst. Apparently the Middle East attacked Russia, then Russia moved into another country that had the rumour of having oil—and they didn't. The US and Canada went after Russia, which in turn went after China... and suddenly everything went dark. The last we heard from any sort of 'person in charge' was that we were all under martial law. No one knows who gave the order. But I think someone discovered that no one actually had because Ottawa ended up bombed the hell out of."

"And the US?"

"No idea, but if there's no 'intervention' or even rumours on the airwaves, so you can guess what happened," answered David. "We went to war over oil—and everyone lost."

"Did it go nuclear?" asked Derek.

"Not that I know of," David responded thoughtfully. "Before it went silent there wasn't anything said about expecting nukes or firing them off, so, thankfully, I think we're clear on that."

"When you said Russia..." Derek trailed off. "So, Sheridan was right. Rome has fallen."

David looked at him in confusion and then he nodded as realisation hit him. "So it has," answered David. "Much as I hate to say it, we're screwed. How screwed and for long remains is the question we need to ask."

* * * * *

Rick sat at the table and was not all that surprised when the nominations pitted him against Tyrell, Derek and Terrence. He did not actually relish the thought of leading this and when it came to be his turn he said politely, "I decline the nomination. Pick someone else. I'd rather be the adviser. Less stress."

Tyrell lifted a brow. "Funny, but Terrence said the same thing when he refused to be part of this. He said he had something else he was working on."

"Like what?" asked someone.

"Dunno, but it was related to the wall, but not in an engineering fashion. Something about 'going medieval'."

Rick chortled and suddenly knew what Terrence had in mind. "That answers that, so it's down to Tyrell and Derek."

"I vote we defer this until Derek gets back for us to decide between the two of us," said Tyrell. "It's far fairer that way. I have no issue with leading this in his absence, though."

"Are we agreed on that course?" asked Rick and a show of hands revealed a unanimous agreement. "All right, Tyrell, you're Acting Head of Infrastructure until Derek gets back."

"Then I'd like to put something else on the table while we're at it. I want to run it past all of you before I run it past the other heads of the other departments," said Tyrell and with various nods, he continued. "I think we all know that much as we don't like it civilization as we know it is gone."

"Yeah, and?" came from Rick.

"Then Sheridan is right—we need to rebuild from the ashes. Rome has fallen, and so rises a new empire—as she puts it," said Tyrell. "I vote we nominate that we make this permanent, even though this is her land and all and that means we're swearing our allegiance by stayin' on her land. But I vote we make it official. She's the Queen of our land and we're her people on said land."

"Queen?" asked another, and by the tone he sounded a bit disbelieving. "Seriously?"

"Seriously. We're already calling ourselves the Heads of Departments. In reality you may as call it the Ministry of Infrastructure and the role of running it the Minister of Infrastructure. Another department the Ministry of Health, and so on," answered Tyrell as he turned to Rick. "Tell me this isn't a crazy idea."

"It really, really isn't," admitted Rick, and he turned to the others. "Think about it; our country is gone. It's now the old world like a few thousand years ago when the old Roman Empire fell. Granted, our new 'country' isn't as big as the old, but none of the new nations that sprang up when Rome fell were as big as Rome either. They grew… like this will."

"But Queen?"

"It's her land, and we're here by her invitation, what else would you call her?" asked Tyrell. "There is no vote on who runs this land. We like it, or we leave. That's our choice. And I, for one if it came down to it, would be willing to defend it and her because without this one thing to strive for we're dead already. Maybe not in body, but definitely up here." He tapped his head. "And here." He tapped his chest. "Because a man is nothing without something to live and fight for. She can give us that—and so far she hasn't led us astray."

For a long moment Rick worried no one would go for it, but Tyrell had his point.

Rick pointed out, "As he said, this is her land. Many of us wouldn't be alive if not for her direction to come and even find us and take us out of the cold. For many of us here that means quite literally that we owe her our lives. Instead of being tyrannical about it, she's chosen to share her land with her so long as we live by her rules. And there's the crux and vital thing... *her* rule, which basically makes her our Queen."

"All right you two, you've convinced us," The man pointed up to the balcony. "Now you have to convince her."

CHAPTER ELEVEN

They stripped the Fire Hall, the ambulance, and fire support vehicle of everything useful. The only problem was that they could not rip out anything built into the ambulance. And, much as Derek wanted to, there was no possible way to drive the vehicle back to the farm.

While it had the necessary fuel to do so, the road was simply impassable. The horses had no issue because they had feet and the ability to jump over obstacles. The truck would only get bogged down and stuck.

The unexpected boon was in the form of the historic fire wagon that was set up as a sleigh, perhaps for a parade. But the skis looked original to the rest of the wagon. Derek suspected that it was always meant to be a sleigh and not a wheeled cart. Especially since Northern Ontario was prone to blizzards that could drop snowfalls in excess of four feet in a day. When the typical daily accumulation gathered, pulling a wheeled cart behind a team of horses was not only impractical but also impossible.

Karen pointed this out to Derek. "You know this greatly depends on the fact that there is the right tack and harness for the horses to even attach to that sleigh and that it wasn't somehow 'fixed' for towing behind a truck."

Again, luck was on their side when she looked the sleigh over and saw that it was never changed over—the yoke and bars were still intact and in good shape. They just had to find the harnesses.

After searching the fire hall, they found them in a store room and Karen immediately checked each length of the leather for signs of wear and tear.

Finally, after a few hours and right before the sun went down, she proclaimed, "Everything looks good. It will take at least four of our horses to pull that rig and the yokes are intended for that big a team. We'll have to extend the harnesses to get them set right, but with four of the horses on the sleigh and the other two riding guard we should be fine."

They retired for the night after helping Karen prepare everything.

Again, Derek found himself alone with his thoughts.

The world, as they knew it, was gone. Anything that resembled government had toppled and scattered and it was not just Ontario, or Canada—it was worldwide. That one thing, even if a well substantiated rumour was enough to make him wonder if they could do it. Could they survive this?

They had to.

If they survived the winter their chances of surviving the following winter went up astronomically. This spring and summer meant that they would have enough time to prepare for the winter. It was like going back to the old pioneer ways in the hardest and cruelest way possible but if a Northerner was anything it was a survivor. The adjustment from what they knew to what would become the new normal would take some time, but he suspected that they likely could bounce back eventually.

After all, when old Rome had fallen there had been a setback, but not a total loss of available resources and people had bounced back. Civilization had bounced back - just with new governments and power bases.

It had happened again but they would survive it and bounce back.

He honestly had no idea how easy it would be for people to accept this but he was already beginning to accept it himself. The young would simply forget-- they were too young to have really have gotten used to the old world in the first place. Not like their parents and grandparents who would find this transition extremely difficult.

Derek caught himself.

Old world.

He had already begun to think of life before the end of oil as the old world and this new one after it as a new world with the potential of a new civilization—and new centre of power—springing up around Sheridan. Whether she realized this was another matter. She had the property and now she had the defences around it, as well as the people around her, to make it happen. Derek knew Sheridan. She was not attracted to power or prestige. Everything she did she did to prove to herself—and others—that it was all possible.

Terrence, on the other hand, would do it for the power he would have and hate every second of it. He was an interesting paradox. Derek never knew what to make of his friend. On one hand the man was friendly enough, if a bit brusque with people and not exactly the best person to put in a customer service oriented career. He swore like a sailor and then, in the strangest contrast, preferred the peaceful hobby of shore fishing with a bobber at the end of his line. Pursuits that included reading and games of strategy instead of anything directly active were some of his favourites.

Sheridan was also a bit on the shy side and preferred to read on her own or spend time with her horses, and the small group she gathered around her. She never had really liked crowds but, unlike Terrence, she could not leave a person without help... And it never mattered what kind of aid either.

He supposed that was how she ended up becoming a doctor in the first place.

They were not the first choice of leading a new nation but by sheer luck they had the resources, and when pushed, Sheridan definitely had the ability to lead. That, he knew, had everything do with being a surgeon. She might not like dealing with people but she could at least be diplomatic when the situation called for it.

When pushed she had the ability to make snap decisions without waffling. This would take them out of any potential dark age and give them more than a fighting chance to survive.

The thought that haunted him was how lucky they were.

From what he could see in this little corner of the world the winter itself decimated the population. Only ten, maybe twenty, percent had survived the winter and he knew that there would be more deaths coming.

Even on Sheridan's farm.

Derek kicked his feet around the ground, and something strange, that was not snow or ice caught his boot and bounced away. He crinkled his brow as he walked over to it, picking it up.

It was a rock, almost perfectly rounded — likely one of those used in the garden as a border.

He had no idea where it he could use it but decided he would take it with him. He slipped it into his pack, still wondering at his own sanity for taking a bloody rock with him when space was so valuable.

The morning was clear, crisp and cold. Karen had harnessed four of the horses to her own standards to ensure the four would work as a team.

"The next question is who will drive the sleigh?" asked Derek.

"This I can do," answered Helen, smiling as she climbed up to the driver's seat and buried herself under the layers of blankets.

The two children and David climbed up and joined her as did Marissa and Emilie, although David and Marissa faced the back as a rear guard. Karen and Derek mounted the other two horses and led the sleigh out into the sunny morning. Before, the only sound other than the crunch of snow and whinny of horses had been minimal conversation. Now, the jingling of the harness and the four beat staccato of a team of horses pulling the heavy sleigh through the snow greeted the morning.

Derek found himself smiling at the sound, even though it was an old-fashioned sound.

"It's like Christmas," chimed one of the children. "We could sing Jingle Bells!"

The adults smiled at the child's sense of adventure and all laughed softly while Derek found that his mood was far brighter and lighter than the previous day and night. "We could," he admitted. "Why don't you start?"

The two kids started singing and the adults joined in as they made their way toward Panache Lake. This time laughter and singing rang out in the still atmosphere with the children pointing out objects that caught their fancy as they passed them. The older of the two seemed interested in the driving of the sleigh and Helen indulged him when they had finished singing.

"What day is it?" asked Emilie, suddenly and surprisingly.

"Sunday," answered Helen, after she looked at her watch.

"Christmas Day," mused Derek, reflecting on the singing of Jingle Bells. "What did you want Santa to bring you?"

"I got it," answered the oldest of the two. "I wanted to ride in a fire engine, but I got something even cooler... a ride on a fire fighter's sleigh pulled by horses through the country on Christmas. It's like being in a Western."

"And you?" he asked the younger of the two, the little girl.

"I wanted a horse. I didn't actually think I'd get one..." she admitted.

Derek snorted in a short laugh. "Yeah, me neither."

The day was very quickly falling to dusk and he was rather surprised to note that he hadn't been aware of the speed with which time had flown past. They were going to need shelter for the night and the mother was not looking very good. He looked up and noticed a column of smoke from a house that was a good distance from the road. He knew that house. It was the shop and garage for a major electrical lines contracting company. The fact that someone seemed to be alive was promising. "We could see if someone there is up to some company," he suggested.

They turned the sleigh up the driveway and stopped by the fenced yard where numerous large trucks, the kind used for fixing electrical lines, sat abandoned. Some were missing, but no signs of forced entry hinted that those inside belonged—as if they simply never left.

* * * * *

"The team we sent out yesterday didn't check back in," said Lescelle as he walked into the council chambers.

Daniel looked up from the map of the city he was poring over and his eyebrows crinkled. "What do you mean they didn't check in? You mean they didn't return?"

"Same thing in this day and age," answered Lescelle.

He leaned back in the chair and crossed his arms. "All right, we send out another team. Pick up their trail. It stopped snowing two days ago so their tracks should still be easy to find."

"You want to send another team out there?" asked Lescelle, obviously not pleased with Daniel's suggestion.

Daniel stood up and stretched. "I do... but I'm going out with them. I'll lead the team and we'll track them down. Maybe they found something and haven't been able to figure out how to get it back here."

The look on Lescelle's face told him that he clearly did not indulge in Daniel's optimism. In truth, neither did Daniel. But he hoped that it was true. The alternative was that they had just sent out eight good men and women to their deaths, and tomorrow morning were likely about to send another eight.

And one of those eight would be him.

* * * * *

While Garrett had no idea who had said it first, he was a thorough believer in the old saying, "Idle hands are the devil's playground."

At least that was the gist of what he understood. Garrett was not a man given to spending too much time lost in the bowels of a library like his other two brothers might. That was not to say he did not have his own library but the contents of such were far more likely to contain practical things such as books on hunting, fishing or carpentry. Or his beloved collection of Encyclopedia Britannia.

Sure, they were grossly out of date but as his daughter and niece often said the historical data and some other items within were still accurate.

And they looked fantastic on his book shelf beside his other collection of antique cameras and hunting knives.

He had no doubt that the workable supply of fish at the work camp at High Falls had a direct link to the fact that he had read the Britannicas.

The influx of protein and food served to re-energize the small group up there and it also raised their spirits.

The situation had gone from fighting over their limited supplies to real suggestions on how to continue the trend of survival using what they had on hand. They had almost made a game of it.

Garrett only cared that it served to raise their morale. Life seemed a whole lot brighter with a belly full of fresh fish and edible berries. Although while he was glad of the full stomach now he was not sure he would be too happy with it later when it needed to continue its way out as it naturally would.

The other major surprise was the HAM radio one of the women had found in an old-fashioned control room.

"Hey Garrett, I had an idea," came one of the ones that he had caught fighting.

Garrett looked up from what he was working on. The radio's circuits were dusty and he suspected there was a short somewhere in it as well. It just refused to work at all and, in truth, it began to frustrate him.

The distraction was actually welcome.

"Well, out with it," he grumbled.

"A few of the others had this idea for setting up a trap line and using the backs of some of the mesh chairs as makeshift snowshoes."

"The first idea is a good one," agreed Garrett, with a sigh. "The second... Well, I know what movie you took that idea from and unfortunately it won't work. The mesh and the frames aren't strong enough to even hold up a small child."

"You sound like that's from experience," said the other man.

"It is. My daughter tried that with my grandson. They lasted all of two minutes and he was through them with the frames up around his knees," he answered, barking a laugh at the memory. "If he hadn't been so disappointed, it would have been funnier at the time. At least now it is."

"How old is he?"

"Seventeen," answered Garrett.

"Wait, the movie we're talking about would have come out while he was maybe thirteen…"

"Didn't say we got the idea *from* the movie," pointed out Garrett. "Just said that unlike the movie it doesn't work."

"So, what should we do?" he asked.

Garrett shrugged and leaned back. "Not sure, but I'm sure we could figure something out. We've managed this much already."

The other man looked over the scattered parts of the HAM radio. "I'd ask if you were having any luck but I can see that you've got your own work cut out for you."

"Actually, I've made progress," answered Garrett.

As frustrated as he was with the radio, he had made great leaps on getting it to work—so long as the right parts were available. "I figured out what's broken, so if we can rig a replacement I should be able to get it to work."

"What kind of parts?" asked the other.

Scratching at his chin, which had grown from stubble to a full-fledge beard, Garrett took a long moment to answer. "Transistors, resistors, various electronics. Some things look a bit like they got too warm. I managed to repair the short that caused the damage."

"I'll keep an eye out for anything you could use," answered the other as he turned to leave. "I'll bring some food up later."

"Fantastic, and thanks," answered Garrett as he bent back to his task and the other man simply waved as he left the room.

* * * * *

Two men and a few others huddled around a fire in a barrel. Behind them, the water ran through the dam and into the running channel to the next power turbine that frothed throwing up a fine mist that coated the trees and rocks in a glassy layer of ice.

While the caged and directed river was not frozen over, it was still so cold that falling in meant near instant death from hypothermia.

"I don't know, man, he hasn't led us astray yet," said one. "We were damn near starving to death and now we're not even rationed."

"The problem is that he's not the best for the job, if you know what I mean," said the first, the same one that had been talking to Garrett earlier that day. "We can do better with different leadership. I mean, look, accidents happen all the time. The old man took a walk and slipped on the rocks. Aw damn, now we have fresh blood leading."

"Are you insane?" asked another. "We're talking Garrett bloody Wither, here. If we fail, we'll be the ones taking a long walk off a short dock."

"We're not going to fail," he answered. "So long as we all do our part it'll be over long before anyone else catches wind." He turned to stare pointedly at the one that had been voicing the most concerns. "And we keep our mouths shut. If the old man catches wind of our little coup, it's over before it starts."

CHAPTER TWELVE

Derek and David watched as the surliest man they had met since the power went out came out from the shop door and up to the fence.

"If you're looking for food, you're barking up the wrong tree, mate," the surliest man said.

Derek looked the man up and down and the emphasis was on up. He was tall and bit taller than Terrence was and Terrence was a tall man himself. "We're not looking for food," answered Derek. "We're wondering if you needed anything, and even if not, if we could shelter here for the night before moving on."

The man seemed slightly taken aback by this. "Move on to where?"

Derek pointed back to the road and to the south. "There's a farm down the road, just on the other side of the ridge, offering refuge for those who want it. Has all the basic necessities of life to survive the winter."

The man thought for a long moment and continued, "All right... but only because I'd like to know more about this farm of yours."

He unlocked the chain link fence gate and moved it far enough out of the way for the sleigh to move inside it. Once they were inside, he closed and locked it up again.

"Issues?" asked David.

"Had some would-be looters try to jump the fence. And, no, they weren't interested in sharing," he answered. "They were more interested in destroying what I had and they did some damage too before I managed to run them off, not before one of them managed to put a hole in one of the tires to the pole driver. Given that the world has come to an end, I'm guessing we're going to have difficulty replacing that."

"Understandable," he agreed. "I'm Derek, that's Karen, Marissa and Helen."

"I'm David, and this is Emilie, Aaron and Nora, and their two kids Kaylie and Liam," said David.

"George," answered the contractor. He then drew his attention to the two kids, looked at them meaningfully and said, "Kids. You would have to have kids."

He spoke the last loudly and it carried into the wind. Derek felt a sudden sinking feeling in his gut as he realized, glancing at the now locked gate, that this had been a carefully laid and executed trap for people just like them. He and David looked at each other. They shared the same disbelieving gaze as neither of them had even suspected that George was anyone but who he claimed to be.

As he suspected, on the roof was now at least five armed people with their rifles trained on their sleigh. He was glad that he had not warned them of the defences Sheridan had on their farm—only that it was there and offering shelter.

"I'd think it best if you got down off that horse, Derek," said George evenly. "You've got kids and I don't want to have to hurt them, but that sleigh is worth a lot."

"It's worth more to Sheridan!" exclaimed one of the kids, Kaylie by the sound of it. "She's a doctor!"

"There's a doctor up the road?" came one of the voices from the roof. "Take all you want from anyone else, but she'd be useful."

"Shut up!" yelled George, and he turned back to Derek. "Derek, get down off that horse."

By this time, Marissa and Helen had their rifles up and trained on the roof. David had his police issue shotgun trained on George. Emilie already fired one shot off a warning into the air before training her gun on the person sneaking up behind her using the heavy equipment. Derek's rifle was aiming at George, and a quick glance showed that the children very quickly ducked behind and under the sleigh.

Only one person had not responded and that was the children's mother, Nora.

Derek suspected she was already dead. She had likely died on the road from the cold. His priority, however, was making sure the rest of them made it back alive, without the needs of testing Sheridan's clinic. "I think you'll find that we'll be leaving," said Derek. "I would have invited you back, but I can clearly see where you want this to go."

"You think we're letting you leave?" asked George, laughing. "Let me tell you how this is going to go, even if I open that gate for you... You'll have to sleep with one eye open and push your horses all the way back through the dark because me and my men will be on your tails the entire time. We take what you have now or we take it later."

"Third option," came Karen's voice. "If you're actually the original owner of this property then you should be familiar with Terrence Scapael. These are *his* horses... and Sheridan is his wife. We're here on their say so."

That gave George pause as crossing Terrence now that the law was not there to stop him from going a bit old fashioned on everyone was a real threat. Terrence seemed an all right fellow before the law ceased to exist. But there was always something just brewing under that surface that screamed like a wild animal just barely kept under control. All the same, George was fairly certain that even if he did rile Terrence he could fight him off.

While George was contemplating his options, Derek was also running through possible outcomes. If, by some miracle, he allowed them to leave, George was right. They would chase Derek and his people all the way back to the farm and those defences would be tested almost immediately. The only advantage they had was the horses and the wall that they were a good distance outside of. If they relinquished what they had they would have to still get back to the farm somehow and more of them would likely die on the trip there.

"And that third outcome is?" asked George.

"You can *try* to take what we have. If you somehow succeed on taking it and at least one of us makes it back to Sheridan's farm—and I can guarantee you someone will—Terrence will raise a mounted fighting force and come at you with everything he has," Karen answered. "Just remember—Sheridan and Terrence are history fanatics and historical reenactors. You should see some of the medieval gear they have... Weapons of war from a time before cars or guns, and they have those as well although for hunting... You sure you want that on your doorstep in less than a week?"

"We could leave!" answered someone from the roof.

"And he'd only track us down until he got everything back," yelled George back up at him, before turning back to their group. "Quite the little stand-off we have here. I take it that wasn't the third option."

"Nope, that was a statement of reality. The third option comes from you standing down, letting us leave with what we have tomorrow morning and we make like this never happened," said Karen. "Because if you know Terrence and I think you *do* know him... you let this go down and even Sheridan won't stay her hand to stop him."

"You're not going to let them?" yelled the same voice from up top.

"Shut up!" yelled George. "You think you can do better?"

"Yeah, I think I do!"

Moments later the rest of his reply came with the sharp echo of a gunshot. George looked surprised for a second at his own blood as it steamed and bounced off the frozen snow before he crumpled in a heap.

The rest happened quickly, and Derek jumped from the horse. He rolled behind one of the cherry picker trucks while his horse fell heavily, twitching and thrashing as the bullets tore through its flanks. *Damn*, he swore. The horses were too valuable to lose. Even one would be a terrible blow to their resources.

David was just as pinned down, but at least they could see each other to signal what to do next, except David was taking aim at Derek. For a moment, Derek could only stare in shock and betrayal and prepared himself to die. It was out of his hands.

The gun shot he expected to feel did not come, even if he heard it. A dull thud of a body hitting the snow beside him made him turn and look. He laughed in nervous relief when he realized that he wasn't David's target as David shot another man trying to shoot him. Derek gave David the thumbs up in thanks and recognition at his shooting ability and for saving his life and ducked out just enough to see past the massive wheels of the large truck he was hiding behind.

The children were hiding under the sleigh, and Karen was using the back of the seat for cover. Derek was behind the sleigh, as was Marissa. Helen was face down in the snow, dark red blood pooling out from under her, her hair splayed out around her.

Emilie was... he looked around and saw her making her way to the side of the building, apparently part commando in addition to being a paramedic. One of the men on the roof made the mistake of looking over the edge for her and she shot him. She just barely moved out the way as he fell off the building and landing where she had been only moments ago.

With that man's death, the gunshots from the building stopped abruptly and a voice, from behind another piece of equipment on David's side, said, "I give up!"

They whirled on the young man as he came out with his arms above and behind his head. He knelt in the snow and David checked him over. "He's unarmed."

"Was he always, though?" asked Derek.

David shook his head, unsure. Karen jumped down from the sleigh and ran over to Helen, rolling her over. With a look of sadness, she looked up at Derek and he could plainly see that Helen had died immediately. Either a crack shot had taken her out or someone had been lucky with their shooting. Either way, she wouldn't have felt it hit her. "She likely didn't even get a chance to duck for cover," said Karen. "She was right beside me!"

"Karen, check the horses." suggested Derek, pushing into a task to take her mind off it. "I know at least one is dead."

"Okay, who are you and how many others of you are there?" asked David as he pulled the young man to his feet and got a closer look at him. Surprised at what he saw his next question was natural. "And how old are you? Sixteen, seventeen?"

"Fifteen, sir," he answered. "My name is Patrice. The one she—" he pointed at Emilie. "— Shot was my Dad."

"That bother you, son?" asked Derek.

Patrice shook his head. "I mean, it should but it doesn't. When everything—stopped— went dark… *whatever*… he simply snapped. He wasn't my Dad anymore. Even George went different. It's like they had this notion that they could make this little empire out of the shop and make people do what they wanted them to do to support them. But what could I do? He was my Dad and George was his best friend."

Derek patted him on the shoulder. "You can help us now—if you want to," he suggested gently. "A good solid hand would be valuable. If you don't want to stay you can provision yourself and leave after spring melt to make your own way in the world."

He nodded and looked back up at David and Derek. "I'd think I'd like that, sir, if you'll have me."

Karen came up beside Derek as he leaned against the back of the sleigh, staring out of the fenced gate, and put a key into his hand. He looked up at her and at the key in his hand. "It's labelled as the gate key," she explained. "It was on the bastard's key chain. I figured you should get this."

He lifted a brow in surprise. "After your show of force back there? I'd think you deserve it."

"All I did was cause a fire fight."

"No, you split the fire fight into two groups fighting over us instead of one cohesive group pinning us down," he answered and tapped his head. "You played a head game with their leader. Caused them to question him, which in turn split them into two factions... not to mention cut the head off the snake before it could bite us. It could have gone down a whole lot worse than it did. You did well."

She thought about it and then smiled. "Yeah, I did, didn't I?"

He returned her nod, smiling. He then looked at the sky, her eyes following his.

"The stars are brighter now," she said. "Normally they aren't this clear."

"No light pollution anymore to stop us from being able to see them," he answered. "A true sign of just how desolate things are. Normally, even this far out of the city, the lights from the city—and down south—are enough to make them seem dimmer. No light pollution means no lights on anywhere. We're right back to the 'days of old'."

"You think that maybe this is only temporary?" she asked.

"I hope it is," he answered. "But I don't think it is."

She nodded a bit sadly. "There's a lot of people out there that we were close to that if this this thing really means that civilization is gone we're likely never going to see again. Family that was on the other side of Sudbury but for all intents and purposes could be on the other side of the country now."

He nodded his agreement and then sighed. "You didn't come out here to talk to me about stars, did you?"

She shook her head. "Casualty list," she answered.

He sighed heavily. "Lay it on me, Karen."

"The first is Nora, the mother of Kaylee and Liam," she began. "From what I figure she died on the road between here and the Fire Hall... and we didn't even notice. Aaron... Aaron is of course torn apart at the loss of his wife and the even heavier weight of having to raise two young children in this world... Let alone how hard it would have been before."

"I'm sure we'll help him," he said, taking a breath. "Next."

"Helen."

Derek looked down and punched the back of the sleigh with his hand. She was someone that had come out with him because he had asked her to. He was directly responsible for her death.

"On the other side of things, George and his cronies are all dead. There weren't that many of them." She looked around and then continued. "We lost one of the horses in the fire fight."

"Mine?"

"Yeah, and he was a good horse too. I'll let you explain that one to Sheridan, but, given the circumstances, I don't see her being that upset. Upset that we lost him, and others too, but I imagine she will understand we did what we could," answered Karen and then paused while looking around before leaning in close. "As a suggestion, and the others are in agreement, given what Terrence is like I'd suggest saying we found Patrice at the Fire Hall and that he wasn't part of this."

Derek winced, but nodded in agreement. "I think that would be for the best, yes."

* * * * *

Driving through snow was not as easy as it seemed. Snow did not give way once left to settle. Instead of moving aside in fluffy drifts, it instead took on the consistency of half set concrete.

Even Adrienne's massive police issued SUV—with snow chains on the tires and the push bars on the front—began to labour to climb up the small hill until finally the tires could only spin as it began to slide sideways. Russell took a deep breath recognizing the slide that had taken him clear off the road.

Adrienne backed back down the hill and got out of the SUV. She walked around it while kicking the snow out from the wheel wheels, resetting the chains, and then got back in. Putting in a lower gear she turned to Russell. "One more try and if it doesn't work we either head back to the house or walk."

Russell nodded his head once.

Adrienne let the truck gain some speed and momentum before tackling the hill again. When they reached the same point the truck shuddered as it hit the now bunched up snow bank but bounced up and over again like a boat over a wave.

And then it kept going.

A cheer rose in the truck once they finally crested the hill. "How many more hills like that between here and where we need to go?" asked Russell, as this road was not one he had ever taken before.

"A whole lot more, but, we shouldn't need to worry. Once we reach the first set of houses we should be all right. It's downhill from there so the momentum of the truck should help greatly so long as I can keep it from sliding sideways."

A half hour later they pulled into the driveway. Adrienne looked at the fuel gauge in worry and Russell followed her gaze. The needle was under a quarter of a tank. Under normal circumstances this would have been enough to run around with but the constant high impact usage meant that it was far too little to continue for much further.

They would need more fuel... and soon.

* * * * *

Daniel stood just inside what had once been the main entry of the parking garage underneath the city hall. Unlike the other side that led out onto the four-laned boulevard, this one led out to a two lane street and a park. The gate was still closed and when he looked out it appeared quiet.

Another seven—all police officers or other emergency services, except for one army reservist—stood behind him.

It had taken far too long to find another team not only willing to go out, but also possessing the right set of skills. This was not the usual patrol. It was a walk right into an urban battle field.

"All right," he said. "The first priority is supplies. No supplies will mean we don't eat and the rest of our people starve to death. Second, we find our people. Understood?"

There were nods all around.

He signalled to the gate keeper and the gate slowly slid open. Daniel winced at the clattering and creaking of the gate. The noise was enough to alert anyone listening that the gate to City Hall had finally been opened. The amount of time it took to open was a way in for anyone waiting for that opportune moment. He made a cutting motion with his hand and the gate keeper stopped the gate from opening any further.

Daniel led the others out and then signalled again to the gate keeper to close the gate. Again, the creaking and grinding sound of the gate closing was far too loud, causing Daniel to wince again, and once it closed everything turned quiet once more.

"Maybe we're lucky and the gangs are sleeping off a rough night," said one of the officers.

"One could hope," admitted Daniel. "All right, stay sharp. I wish I could say by the book but I don't think any of our books covered this. Just be damn careful out here."

They moved out to the street and Daniel led them toward the arena, which was just to the south of City Hall. Strangely, while it would have made for another prime shelter like the mall, no one was ever spotted going in or coming out of the building. Tracks were non-existent and Daniel led them that way first.

Up until a few years ago, the train station had always been semi-deserted. Now, in the summer at least, it had become the Farmer's Market. There were numerous restaurants and cafes along the street facing the tracks. All deserted. If they looped around the arena and down that run and then into the downtown core again, they could cover all the restaurants and boutique delis and stores.

Hopefully the nuts in the mall had not already come to the same conclusion.

Funny how before all this, the walk had always been short, even pleasant, when those same stores had been open. Once off work, he would often share a good coffee at the roastery that sat right across from the arena. His friend, Derek Moss, had addicted him to the place as they were both coffee hounds in their own way. Sheridan also loved the place. She, however, tended to frequent places closer to her end of town and even if she ventured further in she preferred the Italian place on Regent.

He sighed.

He had no idea if he would see her, or his friends, again. At least he knew that if anyone survived it was likely to be them so long as she had not been at the hospital when everything went out.

Derek... well...

The last reports of what happened in Garson and up that way were as grim as downtown.

He turned his focus back to the here and now. As easy as this walk would have been before, it was not simple anymore. The streets were clogged with snow and abandoned vehicles and other debris that they had to move around and double check.

Daniel was thankful of one thing only.

The cars were at least completely abandoned – no one had opted to remain with the cars and therefore it was unlikely that they would discover a body within any of those parked along the way. Considering his choice in career, he had seen more than his fair share and it never got any easier.

After fifteen minutes of careful plodding through the snow to the corner by the train station and the arena, they could clearly see that the area was completely deserted. There was absolutely no sign that the gangs had even made this far from the mall.

"Well, this is anti-climactic," stated one of the others, and Daniel turned to glare at him. "Not that I'm complaining. Just stating a fact."

"Well, let's check the restaurants. Maybe there's something still in them."

The first one they checked was the coffee shop. It was not as if he was expecting a whole lot in the way of food in there as it did not actually serve heavier meals. He suspected this was due to the very tiny space it occupied less than the fact that it was right beside two places that did serve food. But, and he would admit it was because he really missed his morning coffee, he knew that they had had regular—and huge—shipments of coffee beans that they roasted and ground right on the premises.

And it looked like they had had a big one right before Harnet declared martial law.

Daniel would have danced if his instincts were not on high alert for any sign of danger. Some of the beans never had a chance to be even roasted yet which that meant with a bit of tender loving care they could still be coaxed to grow into a full plant.

Strangely enough, they did have something that could nurture these plants like a year round multi-level farm. The tower that housed city hall was encased in glass on almost every side. The roof was already accessible and often used as a daycare's play area. Each floor within the city hall was open concept and while north facing the greenhouse effect within could serve as a place to grow their food.

Starting with the coffee.

Now they just had to get some actual food seeds and he knew just the place where to get those. Luckily, it was also downtown. In fact, it was right across the street from the square—if on the side that was regularly raided.

Still, it was a chance they would have to take.

CHAPTER THIRTEEN

It took almost twenty-four hours for the various departments and teams to come to an agreement. Sheridan was expecting those leaders to come up to her but she was a bit surprised that they went to Terrence in his study just off the main room. Terrence winked up at Sheridan and joined the twelve others in that room.

Everyone else had scattered—seemingly because the now had more defined goals for their various teams. At least that's what Sheridan sincerely hoped.

With a sigh, she went back to what she had been doing before chaos had broken out below which was going over what they had for medical supplies and how best to run her team. With a wary look to the clock, she realized Derek was now overdue. They expected back last night or this morning but there still was no sign of him. The watch on the gate had reported hearing shots in the distance to the north. This worried Sheridan and the others but they had little choice but to continue their work to make the farm safe, secure and well stocked.

Later that afternoon, the door opened and in strode a very tired looking Derek and Karen.

"Thank the Gods," exclaimed Sheridan. "I was worried. The watch said they heard shots to the north."

"Unfortunately that was us," answered Derek. "We ran into trouble... and... Helen is dead."

Sheridan sat down heavily. "Dear God in Heaven," breathed one of the other nurses.

"Was anyone else lost?" she asked.

"Nora—" At Sheridan's confused look, he answered. "Someone we met at the Fire Hall who agreed to join us. She left two young children and their father. Those three survived. We also found three others out there."

"Patrice, his father died," answered Karen. "We couldn't help him. Also David and Emilie. David is a constable for the Sudbury Police, and Emilie is a paramedic."

"So six more to add to the survivors. I'm glad you found someone... but why the shooting?" asked Sheridan as she caught how Derek and Karen looked at each other. "What happened out there?"

"We had an... altercation with a group of people, and I use the term loosely—who decided they were going to lure us in on our good intentions and wanted what we had," answered Karen. "We had no choice, Sheri, it was us or them."

"I wasn't going to blame you," said Sheridan. "I wasn't there, you were. You did what you had to do and this world is going to force a great number of those kinds of decisions on us. We don't have to like it, but we do have to accept it if we are to survive."

That was the problem with this, she realized. Those hard decisions that once were hypothetical and bandied back and forth between people as a philosophical 'what if' now had become very brutally real. Decisions needed to be quick and the hard ones did not have the time or luxury of debate over what was right and wrong for humanity as a whole. It had literally come down to decide what was right for the group and hope they could all live with it at the end of the day.

Sheridan did not think she was the kind of person who could make those decisions. Or, at least she used to think that she was not. Now, however, she had to make those sorts of decisions every single day.

It was like triage, only the stakes were much, much higher.

And it seemed like the longer time went on the more that everyone around her depended on her decisions to get them through and she just didn't know how long she could keep doing it.

A few moments later Terrence came in and motioned for her to follow him. He acknowledged Karen and Derek, and pulled them with him as well. "Sheri, we need to talk."

* * * * *

The first house they came to had a furnace that relied on oil and when the tank ran out, the furnace had quit. Russell leaned on the door of the SUV and Adrienne looked past him, shaking her head.

Instead of risking moving to another house, those within had attempted to burn something else to keep warm but instead had burned their house down. The entire back half was a write off, even though the front part looked untouched.

They didn't realise that the house was burnt down with its occupants inside until they pulled into the driveway and saw the damage.

"What do we do now?" asked Adrienne's mother.

"We keep going," answered Adrienne.

Everyone climbed back into the SUV and Adrienne backed out of the driveway to continue south down the back road. She had been right about one thing. The uphills were now getting rare and they were heading down far more than they headed up. However, there were numerous dips and valleys where the road would climb down one side and up another side.

This was eating into their already iffy situation with fuel.

Finally, at the top of one final hill, the engine spluttered and died just at the end of another driveway. Unlike the first house, they could see a thin curl of smoke from the house that overlooked a lake. The house seemed to cling to the top and side of the hill by the lake and the patio at the back must have had a truly fantastic view.

They walked up the curving driveway.

"The SUV would have never made it up this hill anyway," said Russell.

Adrienne nodded as they finally reached the front of the house. Two people came out of the house and when they spotted Adrienne, they sighed in relief.

"Talk about a sight for sore eyes…" said the man as he came down and shook everyone's hand pumping Adrienne's the most. "With what we heard on the radio about martial law and then nothing else we assumed the worst."

"I can confirm it," admitted Adrienne. "Can we come inside?"

"Of course you can!" exclaimed the woman. "Hugh, how could you not even think of basic hospitality, especially now with how cold it has become. They look half frozen."

They followed the couple inside and Russell looked around at the ample supply of paintings and other artwork that decorated the living room. Adrienne knocked off her boots and the others followed her example. They all allowed the couple to strip them of their wet clothing and to wrap them in blankets. The first thing put into each person's hand was a cup of hot tea.

"Oh, this is heavenly, thank you," said Adrienne's mother.

After a moment, while they warmed up, Adrienne finally said, "We have it on good authority that our government has fallen. What we knew is now gone."

"Are you serious?" asked the woman.

Russell nodded. "There's some strong circumstantial evidence, as well as firsthand reports." He motioned to the three young men who had ventured across the ice. "Apparently the city has fallen into disarray and looting."

"And if Sudbury is gone, so are the rest of our cities, and perhaps the rest of North America. We've been thrown right back into the 1800's," pointed out Adrienne's father. "We came here because it's safer and because we've got nothing in the way of supplies. I'd hate to ask this but we're looking for shelter."

The couple looked at each and then the man sighed. "Well, we don't have much. But if you aren't averse to some hard work, we have no problem putting you up. Frankly, though, we're all going to have to work hard to survive. You have a problem with that?"

"You won't hear any argument from me," answered Russell, and there was a chorus of agreement from behind him.

"Then you're welcome to stay," said the woman. "My name is Laurie, and you've already met Hugh."

* * * * *

If they thought he was stupid or wasn't able to recognize the signs of dissension, then they were more idiotic than he had originally believed them to be when he first drove in here.

Garrett was neither stupid nor naive.

He was hardly surprised when the four men came up behind him while he was out checking the fishing nets and he was already turning to face them when they arrived. He said, "I heard you coming, so don't even bother being quiet about it."

The one caught gambling his share away led them and Garrett looked from one man to the other, noting that each one was armed with something, even if it was a stray piece of metal bar.

"No way this will end peacefully, I take it, eh?" he asked. "The old man has to die so the younger ones survive."

"Nothing personal, old man."

"None taken." Garrett stood up straight, his arms crossed over his chest. "Just keep one thing in mind. If you think I'm going to be an easy mark you'd best think again. If I'm going down, more than one of you comes with me and then you'd be pretty hard pressed to explain not one disappearance, but perhaps three? Maybe five if I'm lucky."

A few of them shifted uncomfortably. They knew he was fighting for his survival.

Garrett was not going to let them win this without it. "Well, come on, don't have all day," he sighed as he cracked his knuckles.

The instigator lifted the piece of re-bar above his head and took a step. Garrett kept an eye on him, but fully expected the strike from his opposite side from one of the others. What they did not expect was that he could read their actions way ahead of them.

He plucked the bar from that one's hand and let his own momentum continue past him as he took a small step back. Lifting one leg in a neat trip, Garret sent the man sprawling into the snow-covered gravel. When the decoy finally made his move, Garret shifted to his right and crouched, and then threw him up and over his shoulder as he abruptly stood up.

The scream behind him and scrambling sounds of metal on icy rock… and the splash… told him and the remaining four that the instigator had just slid to a cold, watery death. The current would carry his body to an even nastier end through the second stage turbines.

Garret turned to face the other three, except of course for the man still on the gravel that was just picking himself up now, his face one of horror at the fate of his co-conspirator. That one short scuffle and its end had just stolen their desire for further violence.

"Well, that it?" asked Garrett, tapping the bar in one hand. "Who else wants to go for a swim?"

They backed off and Garrett scowled. "I'd tell you to get the hell out of here but I'm not a cruel man. You can stay until spring and then I don't want to see anything but the back of you. You're done here. You stay on the other part of this work site and away from the others. Consider yourselves all fired. Now get the hell out of my sight."

* * * * *

Kaine drummed his fingers on the table as he mulled over what could be done. The rest of the faculty still operated under the assumption that things would soon return to normal. He watched the students, still stuck here, as they milled around the common area.

This will only get worse, thought Kaine. *We have food for now but soon we will not. And until that happens my esteemed colleagues will do nothing.*

"This seat taken?" asked someone from behind him.

Kaine turned around and look up at him. His face reminded Kaine of the forgotten valleys around the university and his long hair had been pulled back into a braid that hung down his back. "No, have a seat," answered Kaine, motioning to the other chair.

As he sat, he introduced himself, "Most just call me Martin."

"Robert Kaine," answered Kaine. "Lately a professor here at the university."

"Lately?" asked Martin. "Where were you before?"

"Kingston," answered Kaine. "I used to work for the government, but I retired."

Martin tilted his head as he looked at Kaine. "But you're not old enough."

With a sigh, Kaine answered, "My leg and knees were injured quite severely during the course of my previous employment. It makes working in my previous vocation rather problematic."

"And you got nothing from it?" asked Martin. "Seems like a crappy thing for them to do."

"I never said that. I did—a rather substantial amount as well as full rehabilitation. I decided to use my degree in a more civilian..." Kaine sighed as he saw Martin nod his head and grin. "Dammit, yes—I was in the Army before."

"I know," answered Martin. "I thought I had recognized you, but I wasn't sure."

"And so were you," realized Kaine as Martin nodded in answer. "What branch?"

"Regular army, and—before you answer—I know where you worked, and who for, but I know better than to advertise it."

"Thank you," said Kaine, relieved.

It was not as if he wanted to hide it but the mere mention of what he used to do tended to make the majority of the students here nervous. Some of the faculty as well.

Neil tended to top that list.

Kaine sighed once more, and looked over at Martin. "What do you make of this situation?"

"I was caught in this situation before," answered Martin, his tone even. "Back in '92 during Desert Shield. The power's not coming back and we're not seeing the effect of it by virtue of our location and the weather. But it won't last."

"Then we're of the same mind."

"It would appear so," answered Martin. "Why do you ask?"

"Not here—but could you come to my office later? It would be better discussed there."

Martin stared at Kaine. "I retired as well... just so you know."

"I realize that, but it we're right then we're the only two here who know *that*, and what needs to be done. No one else does."

"All right, fine, where do I find this office of yours?"

CHAPTER FOURTEEN

"I was talking with the others and they've taken it into their heads to make you their Queen..." Derek saw the look of horror on her face. "Listen, it would be until we manage to find some sort of trace of what's left of Canada."

"This is a mistake," said Sheridan while looking at the thoughtful faces of Karen and Derek. "Don't tell me you're going along with this!"

"It does make sense," said Derek. "In a way. After all, you do own the property. What else would it make you?"

"Land owner, employer, nominal leader until we rebuilt our government…" she answered. "But a *Queen*? It's a bit pompous."

"No, it's accurate," stated Terrence. "Think about what a Queen is and you'll be much amused that you've already been one from day one, sweetheart."

Sheridan sighed heavily and looked at the three of them. She clearly was not comfortable with the entire idea.

Derek did not really blame her one bit on that. If he was in her position, he would not be either, but comfort level or no, if they were to survive this someone had to step up and lead them through the winter. And it was her land, well, technically, it was Terrence's as well but no one really wanted him to lead. It was not as if he couldn't but he would end up being as much a raider as those Derek had just fought off back at that garage.

And he was not an easy man to work for, either.

Sheridan was strong, decisive. She was able to make hard decisions but she also had a core of compassion that tempered Terrence's utter and complete ruthlessness. She could not have been a surgeon otherwise, let alone a doctor. He waited her out. She would come to that realisation herself without someone pushing her into it.

Finally, she nodded. "Queen. Slightly pompous as hell title to claim, but if it's what everyone wants... it's what everyone gets." She was about to say something else when a very out of breath Patrice came running up. "What is it?"

"Your gates-men, they've spotted people coming down the road... they appear to have followed the tracks of the sleigh in," he answered. "Um..."

Sheridan waited him out, wondering what it was that could have left him without words.

Derek groaned, knowing what the others did not and he asked, "More friends of your Dad, I take it?"

"I didn't think they even survived—they left and didn't come back since this all started."

"Wait a minute, I thought you said you found him at the Fire Hall with David and Emilie?" asked Terrence, crinkling his brow.

"Terry, we don't have time for this—" snapped Derek. "Patrice, your Dad's friend... did they work for him?"

Patrice shook his head. "Came from the road, as far as we could tell."

"The Fire Hall?" asked Terrence, his voice tense and tight with barely suppressed impatience.

"They tried to get into it, but I guess Dave and Em stopped them—it was too much bother to get into... I honestly have no idea," explained

Patrice. "Listen, these guys… they make my Dad look like a lightweight."

"His dad… what the Hell?" Terrence exclaimed and turned on Derek. "Is there something you want to fill me in on?"

Derek sighed, seeing no way to avoid it. "Would you have taken him in if you knew he was part of the same group that killed Helen and one of your horses?" asked Derek plainly and he could see Terrence's expression darken as he looked from him to Patrice and back again. "He's a *kid*, Terrence. He had to survive out there and at his age that was with his Dad. We both know that."

Terrence grumbled at this, but finally breathed out a heavy sigh and turned to Patrice. "Derek has a point, which is the only reason you're still standing here."

"How well do you know these other people?" asked Karen.

Patrice shrugged. "Like how?"

"What lengths are they willing to go to take what they feel they should have, kind of how," answered Terrence.

"Almost inhuman—it's like they embraced the fact that the law was gone. The first place they headed was the Fire Hall and they bragged about how they managed to break some windows and deface the building. Mind you, they didn't get in and they were disappointed. My Dad let them rampage around… it was better that way, he said. Animals like that didn't deserve to live inside. Better to let them roam like the wild animals they were," answered Patrice.

"So… no chance of negotiating or splitting them up like we did with your Dad's group," said Karen.

Patrice shook his head.

"Any idea where they came from?" asked Terrence, sounding far calmer than he had been only a minute before.

Derek knew that Patrice's sharing of information with them had managed to calm Terrence down somewhat.

Patrice shook his head. "All Dad said was that they were road trash, or even perhaps trailer trash. Beyond that, I can't say. I've never seen them around before."

"Your Dad was George, wasn't he?" asked Derek quietly.

"No, sir, he was the one on the roof… he only worked for George. He was picking up his Christmas bonus and I came out with him. But we got stuck when the roads got snowed in." Patrice looked down at the floor. "We left behind my mom—she didn't want to come out."

Terrence put a comforting hand on the young man's shoulder. "Okay, you've proved yourself. So far." Terrence sighed. "We'll see about at least finding out what happened to her in the spring when the roads get a bit clearer and passable."

"Thank you, sir!" Patrice beamed. "I swear to you I won't let you down!"

Derek followed Terrence outside. "How much time do you think we have?" asked Terrence.

He took a moment to think and after a while Derek answered, "With the snow and the fact they're on foot we have maybe an hour at most. Not even—that sleigh and the horses packed it all down pretty solid. They'd still have to contend with slipping and sliding, but they won't have to plow through the snow like we did."

Sheridan looked over at Terrence. "Go on, I'll help Derek into his armour."

Derek looked at her in confusion but followed her anyway.

Terrence left for another part of the house while Derek followed Sheridan down to the basement. As a gun enthusiast, he knew armour generally referred to Kevlar. *What did she have in mind?* He thought as he followed her into a room full of glinting metal armour. In the darkened room, the battery powered camp lamps made it look like he had walked into a medieval armoury. It seemed that much more dark and mysterious.

"Okay, you're a smaller, slighter man than Terrence. You like to take things on at range, am I right?" she asked.

"I do, but I have no idea why you'd need to know that," he answered.

"We are the last line of defence between the bridge, and beyond that, retirees and families. In the old way—or the old English way—that meant that knights and armsmen had to protect the farmers and others from barbarian raiders and invaders," she explained as she turned to him. "We find ourselves in that position again. So I ask again, are you the kind that prefers things at range or up close and personal?"

Derek met her gaze. "Madam, I am a hunter and wilderness scout. In the old English way, that would make me a Ranger. I prefer bows and guns, but if I have to, I can handle a knife. I prefer to travel light and fast and through terrain that a horse would find bothersome and that heavy armour would make impassable."

She nodded. "Leathers and chain, then," she said as she pulled the necessary pieces down. "You will wear the Kevlar under this. Modern armour is to stop bullets, but it cannot stop a sword or arrow. Chain will. Leather lacing in the chain will make it silent. Count yourself lucky. My father made the metalwork and my native friend did the leather work. The metal is not steel or iron, but titanium alloy. It will not rust. It is lightweight and far stronger. The laces within the links are moose leather and the armour is from the same moose."

Terrence came in at this moment and he nodded his approval at her choice. Derek stripped out of the modern and into the more medieval, with modern touches for warmth, under shirt over his clothes. Derek saw the layers as she laid them out and winced.

He already wore winter underclothes—a simple undershirt tee and long underwear, plus regular cotton socks under the woollies. Over this, he wore durable khaki coloured jeans and a matching collared shirt of a lighter denim. Over his denim shirt was a warm sweater hand knitted by Lorraine.

He dressed himself in the modern bullet proof Kevlar vest which appeared to be simply a black vest.

This was the last of the modern wear, however. Sheridan had him pull on leather trousers secured onto him with a series of ties and a plain, flat-braided leather belt. He pulled on the matching boots that had a modern work sole sewn into the bottom. The boots went past his knees and looked like something out of Robin Hood. They were warm, though, and their height would keep the snow out.

Sheridan tucked a boot knife into his right boot with the sheath sitting just above the ankle and below the knee. The knife was on the lower attachments and was roughly the length of his forearm.

He pulled on the woollen winter under padding for the armour, which draped on him like a sleeved hooded tunic.

Terrence helped and showed him how to undo the ties to take it on and off. It was like wearing a winter coat with a hood. The only modern part to it was that the winter jacket's outer shell was on the under padding and meant to prevent wind from going through the tunic which hung past his hips almost to his knees. The tunic had two slits from the bottom to just below his hips. "The slits for movement?" he asked.

"Yeah, not so great for riding but better than not having them," answered Sheridan as she brought over the chain mail.

This was also slid over his head, and had a hooded part, which secured the same way. It was long sleeved, and protected everything from the head down, except for his face and hands, to his knees. It covered his neck and underarms. He helped Terrence to cinch it in so that it didn't move or jingle as much until it fit him snugly. Over that was a dark brown leather tunic. "More wind break. Trust me, you won't be complaining about this outside," said Sheridan as she handed Terrence everything else.

Each of these pieces made of stiffened hard leather and there was a narrow strip beaded in intricate Native Canadian designs. Derek ran a finger along the beads and Sheridan said, "My great-aunt from across the river, on the reserve, said that my armour was 'too boring' and needed the beading."

"This is *your* armour?" he realized, and she nodded. "It doesn't look like it fits a woman."

She snorted. "Proper armour won't."

Sheridan lent him a set of archer's gloves as they had the same size of hands.

A very distinctive fur cloak which looked more like a leather trench coat made from the pelt of a bear and tanned with the fur on the inside and the dark, tanned leather on the outside was then draped on top of all this.

"Why does this not exactly fit in with the theme?" He asked, his voice tight as Sheridan was being brusquer with him than gentle.

"It doesn't," she answered, grinning. "But it's not exactly wrong either. I use that coat when I'm riding. The rest is pretty accurate, but that was made for riding. It still matches the rest once I put the last bits on."

Derek felt like he was dying of heat inside as tied a belt around his tunic just below his breast plate and pulled it tight enough to not slip but not so tight that it was cutting off his circulation. An Irish short sword and matching leather sheath was secured onto his belt.

"Okay, go on out to the barn and tell Karen to get her people to prep two horses SCA style for you and Terrence. And once she sees you she'll know how to give her to you." Sheridan gave him a playful push to the door. "Terrence will be there shortly."

Derek walked out of the house and was thankful for the numerous layers underneath his new armour and coat as he stepped outside into the cold. When he walked into the barn, Karen and Marissa turned to look at him.

Marissa gasped and said, "Oh my God, Derek. Where the hell did you get that?"

"That's Sheridan's personal set," said Karen. "She calls it her English Ranger set."

"It's real armour, though?" asked Marissa.

Karen nodded in answer as she led another horse out of a stall.

"Sheri said to set up two horses SCA style... whatever that means," relayed Derek.

Karen nodded again. "You and Terrence, or you and Sher?"

"Terrence," he answered.

He watched as Karen set out a completely different set of tack, and then put it on the horse. Although the saddle and tack was different, it still went on the same way and was properly fit to the horse. But, curiously, there was still a significant amount still on the floor. Much to his surprise, she put this over the horse. It was very quickly obvious that it was chain barding with the same leather strips inlaid into the chain mail to make it quiet. It covered the horse's head, neck and other vital areas. Over this, she put leather barding in areas deemed higher risk than most, including kick guards on the horse's legs. The final touch was a heavy cloth skirt like garment meant for a horse in dark green and brown. She laid furs just in front and behind the saddle, but left them somewhat loose to allow him to cover his legs for warmth and further protection. They could be easily moved out of the way and secured in a bundle near the saddle.

It all looked straight out of the Middle Ages.

She brought the horse over to him and he mounted, noting the difference in the feel of the saddle. The barn wasn't freezing cold like it was outside, but it was still quite cool and the added protection was welcome while he waited. Derek looked over at his wife and asked, "How do I look?"

"Very intimidating," she answered. "But you also look very warm."

"I almost was baked alive inside the house with all this on," he admitted.

Terrence came in moments later. Both Derek and Marissa looked at him in disbelief. Gone was the modern civil engineer and in his place was an armoured warrior. It was as if a page from history or a display from a museum had just walked in. If Derek passed for intimidating, then Terrence was simply frightening.

Terrence's armour consisted of chain covered by steel plate left bare and natural.

While it was not rusted, it certainly wasn't polished to a mirror shine. It also looked well used and fit him like a glove. His chain did not have leather interweave, but was a double weave of chain set so close that there were barely any gaps in the links. Derek's armour was nearly silent, but Terrence made noise—a metal on metal ringing and creaking of various bits of chain shifting with every move. His heavy stalking march only added to the intimidation he effused.

Strapped to his back, the two handed hilt peeking out from under his fur cloak was the sword that had once been on display above the fire place. On his legs and belt were two pistols and another—shorter—sword. The hilts of two daggers peaked out from behind his lower back where he could reach them by reaching back with his hands.

He was not wearing his helm, but he held it loosely in one hand and he already wore the leather under padding for it on his head. Karen had already prepared his horse and was bringing it out for him when he walked in. The massive Clydesdale was in barding made to match Terrence's armour.

"Where the hell were you hiding all of that?" asked Derek.

"In the basement, where Sheridan was hiding what you're wearing," he answered, grinning as he accepted Karen's help into the saddle. "It's not exactly historically perfect. There are a few modern additions, such as advanced hinging and weight management—not to mention the alloy of the metal—so that I can actually move around without a team of people to haul my ass into the saddle."

There was a crackle in the radio. "Front gate to Terrence," came the watch.

Karen tossed Terrence the FRS radio, and Terrence responded, "Terrence here."

Derek clenched the reins as Marissa put a hand on his leg. She looked up at him, and he took a breath in to steady his nerves.

Over the radio they all heard, "They're here."

Terrence looked up at Derek before mounting his own horse. "Are you ready for this?"

"No," admitted Derek, and he squeezed Marissa's hand before encouraging his own horse to move forward. "But I guess I'm going to have to be."

CHAPTER FIFTEEN

Their camp on the overpass was within view of City Hall and would have only taken perhaps a half hour to get to, even through the snow. But Daniel did not want to head back straight away. He wanted to check the numerous cafes and delis before they headed back by going down Larch Street.

Larch was the street running west to east down beside the northern border of the city block where the City Hall sat. The northernmost barricade ran along Larch, and the tallest tower — the provincial tower — was also the north tower. The block was not as big as it could be but it was big enough. It and one other street separated City Hall from the mall to the immediate north.

The spaces between the streets were very short. So much so if he were to stand on the top of the provincial building he could probably see who was standing on top of the mall's office tower with enough clarity to recognize them later.

Which made heading down Larch a very risky venture.

Unfortunately, if they wanted to search the restaurants and cafes they had to head up Durham, which linked the two streets, and head right down Larch.

This was the plan and the reason why they camped out in another small square next to a building where Elgin—the street that ran beside the rail tracks in a meandering fashion—and their next move would be to salvage what they could from those restaurants.

Elgin and Durham met in a tight triangle and split at this point. Elgin would lazily make itself north and Durham ran straight and true to the north up to Elm—which was where the mall sat.

It was at least laid out in a reasonable attempt at a logical grid. Brady ran under an overpass that the trains ran over, as did Elgin. Durham intersected, awkwardly, at this point.

It was across this bridge and in the shadow of the office of one of the local newspapers where Daniel and his team were currently camped.

He wanted to check the building for survivors. He had an odd feeling that the reason they had not found any food in the delis and cafes close by was because someone within this building had already raided them.

The fact that they had not attempted to make contact with anyone worried him a bit but he also realised that if law and order had broken down and he had been them, he would have done the same.

As the night fell, their fire was noticeable. The door opened and a head cautiously poked its way around the corner. Noting the armoured and uniformed officers in full winter gear, a man followed the head and let out an audible sigh of relief and said, "I had thought when I saw the last reports from the AP that everything was gone."

Daniel stood up and extended his hand. "Daniel Wither," he introduced. "We're out looking for supplies, survivors, anything of use that we can take back to City Hall. Of course, that'd be without stealing it from others."

"I thought I saw signs of survivors that way but I didn't know so I didn't risk going over there. I saw and heard just as much fighting going on," he answered as he took Daniel's hand and shook it. "Denis Plouffe. I'm a reporter here, sometimes assistant editor when they let me."

"What have you seen?" asked Daniel.

Denis shook his head. "You don't want to know…" He noted Daniel's expression and then sighed. "Or you've already seen it."

"Probably the latter, unfortunately," he answered dryly. "So, when we move on, are you coming with us?"

"Straight to the point, aren't you?" Denis responded with a bark of laughter, and then he turned serious. "I don't know if I want to follow you but I'll head towards City Hall. I won't be shot on sight, will I?"

"You shouldn't be," answered one of the others. "You definitely don't look like the gang members that have been tearing up the place."

"Fantastic," he said in a tone mixed with relief and dry humour. "I think."

* * * * *

Terrence and Derek rode out to the bottom of the hill on the road leading up to the gate. Someone slid a heavy set of planks into the gate in order to seal it. It was not the most solid solution, but it was certainly better than nothing. Guns and bows were handed out, but it looked as if they were in short supply of weapons to fight off the raiding marauders outside the gate.

"We're not ready for this," said Terrence darkly.

Derek blew out a breath. "What choice do we have?"

Those without guns armed themselves with whatever they could find, whether sharpened sticks fashioned into rough spears or, even, shovels to bash a person with.

There was no one on top of the gate, and when Terrence rode up, the watchman said, "They have guns and they certainly aren't afraid to use them."

Derek grabbed Terrence's arm and said, "Listen!"

Just over the howl of wind was a sound of a motor running in the distance... the sound of very heavy duty engine noise. Terrence looked over to the person on watch. "What is that?"

"A truck... SUV—I have no idea where they found it," he admitted, looking worried.

Terrence and Derek looked worriedly at the gate and then back at each other. "That gate isn't going to hold if they ram it," said Derek quietly.

"I know," answered Terrence, and he and Derek climbed up and just out of their view on the gate. "If you lay down your weapons, we might be tempted to negotiate."

He was not all that sure what exactly the large Ford SUV was. Unlike his wife's family, he was not that much of a gear head to be able to positively identify it. It was possibly the same chassis and engine used in the larger ambulances. It certainly held the right passenger compartment reminiscent of an ambulance only it was far heavier duty and higher off the ground. The driver who was then echoed by the others with him, let loose a long line of rude suggestions and expletives that would have left some people with blistering ears.

That is, anyone other than Terrence, who simply rolled his eyes and turned to Derek, "I've seen some interesting things on the Internet but that last even suggestion I think it a bit... awkward."

Derek took aim and with one arrow. He shot it and the front driver's side tire blew out. The sound of it blowing out exploded across the valley. With the full size SUV immobilized, it greatly evened their odds.

"Sir, I believe the proper term would be 'You first'!" shouted back Terrence. "One last chance!"

There was silence and then a wave of raiders came out. They grabbed ladders and slammed them against the snow walls.

"Archers! Fire!"

A hail of arrows rained their death on the hapless raiders, and another tire blew itself out.

For a long moment, everything was quiet till twenty more raiders ran out of the woods and to the wall.

"Fire at will!" shouted Terrence. "Knock down those ladders. Shoot anyone that comes over that wall!"

The general of the raiders came out, and he wore a mish-mash of chain and heavy modern combat armour that didn't fit well but covered him completely. He held a riot shield in one hand and a combat shotgun in the other.

"Son of a bitch…" breathed Derek as he took aim and fired.

His arrow bounced off and only scratched the paint. He swore colourfully and pointed out, "Terry, we have a problem…"

Terrence looked over, swore and drew his sword. Derek had only seen the blade once and that was on display. In Terrence's hands it looked far more menacing and maybe even longer and wider than it had above the fireplace mantle. The hilt was clearly meant for two hands but Terrence could wield it either one-handed or two-handed.

The leader climbed one of the ladders, using his shield to prevent being shot off the ladder and his weight made it difficult to push the ladder back. He pulled himself over the wall and stood on the ledge behind. With a roar, he bull-rushed Terrence, coming at him down the stairs to the ground. Terrence swung his sword with both hands but the leader's shield was in the way.

David took a shot, aiming at the part he hoped wasn't protected. Unfortunately, the shell from his shotgun did not penetrate the first layer. Derek also kept up the pressure by firing off arrow after rapidly fired arrow until the leader of the raiders looked like some sort of psychotic porcupine.

Terrence jumped back as the raider stabbed his machete towards his midsection. Thankfully, his armour was there to save him and the clang of metal against metal was heard across the field.

Now the battle was fully engaged as more and more raiders poured over the wall, although only twenty-five percent survived. The rest were shot down by the archers by the trees.

A downward swing towards Terrence's head was deflected by his sword, and the raider then used his shield as a pummelling device to shove him backwards.

"Get that gate open!" shouted the raider leader. "Rush them!"

They had to end this before they were over run.

Derek found himself suddenly out of arrows, but he then spotted something. With a whistle, his horse came for him. He speed-mounted as she galloped towards him. A short ride later, he had a spear in his hand. The horse turned on a dime at his order and he brought the improvised lance down like a knight at a joust.

Terrence, at the very last second, jumped back and out of the way.

The raider was not as lucky as the spear— propelled by the force of the charger—went through his body armour and chain like it was nothing.

Derek could not stop the horse immediately. Thankfully he didn't have to as he caught another spear thrown to him by one of their own men so he could catch it as he rode by and turned again.

At the sight of their leader being so brutally cut down in such a medieval manner, the other raiders turned tail and ran. Most were cut down by arrows but others slunk back into the wooded areas to lick their wounds.

Derek slowed his horse down to a trot, then a walk and finally to a stop as he pulled up beside Terrence.

"You there!" ordered Derek "Form up a hunting party! We'll have to clear the bastards out before we can say it's safe beyond the wall."

Terrence looked up at him with thinly veiled amusement. "Thought you couldn't ride a horse."

"I learnt quick," quipped back Derek as they both laughed easily together.

David looked up at Derek and then over at Terrence, "I dare say that any of those who survive to wherever they came from today will be a day they won't soon forget."

Terrence nodded his agreement.

* * * * *

"All right, I'm here," said Martin as Kaine allowed him through the door and into the office. "Now, what did you have in mind?"

Kaine motioned to the desk and the chairs. "I am certain that the other faculty will not do a thing until it's far too late. Now, I have taken precautions in case, but I will need your help—and your expertise—in making sure the others don't catch wind of what I have before it's time."

"Typical of your ilk," Martin muttered softly but not softly enough to escape Kaine's hearing. Louder he asked, "And why would you want to do that? Why not let them in on it now?"

"Because they are still all operating under the assumption that is simply business as normal, but you and I both know this isn't true. I tip my hand now and the preparations I have made for such an eventuality as this will be twittered away," answered Kaine.

"Do you ever speak normally?" asked Martin, rubbing his face.

"I am," retorted Kaine.

"Maybe for your typical set, but not for mine. I prefer more direct speaking... such as what do you want me to do and where?"

Kaine sighed. "Just down the road from here, and close to the Laurentian Conservation Area, is a lab... specifically one of my labs. I had certain... supplies... shunted there when I had the chance. Typos that weren't—that kind of thing, you understand?" asked Kaine.

"If it were before, I'd not like where this was heading. But since we're dealing with a new reality now, I have to wonder if you knew this was coming," said Martin. As Kaine nodded, Martin leaned back in his chair. "Son of a bitch, you did. How?"

"Mostly the obvious slow decline or knowing, from history, that eventually all things come to an end to be replaced by something else. It's been an endless line of old empires that crumbled under their own detritus to be replaced by new... and the cycle will never end. But, a certain cadre I was involved with decided to make plans..." Kaine sat down in his chair. "We decided that if the world was to end, then at least we would prepare for it—beyond what the individual survivalists and 'steaders do—in order to drag our own empire back up out of its own ashes. Recover from a worldwide disaster that much quicker. But, we miscalculated just how quickly it would all happen. Certain other preparations could not be made. I have been cut off from the others and am now on my own. That being said I now recognize the need for a leadership prepared to drag itself up 'by the bootstraps', as it were."

Martin stood up. "Is that everything?"

"Yes, just go to my lab and organize a way to keep the others out of it until I say otherwise. No one else—just me, are we clear?"

"Crystal," answered Martin, and then they both turned when a soft knock sounded. "You expecting someone else?"

"No, I wasn't," answered Kaine, puzzled. "You have work to do, and I may as well see what the hell this person wants..."

Kaine pulled his door open and regarded the young woman outside. He had seen her before somewhere, but could not place her.

"We'll talk more later," said Martin as he left, nodding to the young woman as he went.

"Yes, thank you," answered Kaine, and then he asked the young woman, "Can I help you?"

"My name is Zara," she answered. "Are you Professor Kaine?"

"I am," he answered as he moved out of the way to allow her inside. "Now, again, is there something I can help you with?"

"My father is the University's president," she began.

"You're Neil's daughter?" asked Kaine, surprised.

She nodded.

"What can I do for you?"

"My father, much as I love him, can be rather stuck in his ways. There's something not right about all this and he just won't see reason. I overheard the others saying you got into another fight with him about it," she answered. "I came to see what you know that he refuses to listen to."

Kaine paused for a moment as he tried to pick the pieces of his shattered brain back together. "I'm sorry, what?"

"What do you know about all this?"

"I'm afraid not much, but it's more what I suspect that your father refuses to even entertain," explained Kaine. "I don't think anyone knows anything for certain."

"Then what is it that you suspect. And if it ends up being true, what do you think we should do?"

Kaine hobbled over to the couch in his office and sat down heavily. "Forgive me, you've just taken me out in left field here. I didn't expect you to show up here and want my input," he answered finally, tilting his head. *I could use this... I'm not sure how yet, but she could be very useful to me.* He then turned his attention back to her. "All right, have a seat over there and I'll explain my theory—mind you, it's just a theory."

She dragged a chair over to face him and sat in it before responding, "A theory at this point is better than nothing."

CHAPTER SIXTEEN

Derek followed Terrence as he stomped into the main room where everyone gathered. Instead of climbing up the second floor, he chose to stand within the ranks while motioning for Derek to head upstairs to stand beside Sheridan. "This was our first real test on whether we could defend our own," Terrence started, his voice carrying from the middle of the crowd. "Despite the odds being against us we passed. They failed."

A cheer went up in the crowd but it quickly quieted when they realized that he was not smiling.

"The problem is just that. There are only two options in life now." He took a moment. "Pass or fail. And something failed on our side."

"The wall," said Derek.

"The wall," agreed Terrence, holding up a hand to get those who would protest at how very hard they had worked on the wall to let him finish. "I'm not saying you didn't give your best with what you had on hand. You did. We all did. The problem is that it's obvious we need that damn wall more than we thought and we need a bigger one, a stronger one. Unfortunately, that's going to have to wait until spring."

"So, what are you saying?" asked David.

"Out there we fought with what we had on hand. And if someone else comes to take what we've got, we're not going to have enough on hand to fight them off. That truck up there drove up to the gate which means there is a big, obvious set of tracks leading straight to our front door," said Terrence. "And that means even more attention directed at us and it's obviously not always friendly. We need weapons and a way to fight them off, and we need to train so that we don't accidentally kill ourselves or who we're trying to protect by accident." He paused and let that sink in. "We need our own militia."

He looked around and saw everyone looking around with uncertain glances.

"Is that truly necessary?" asked Tyrell.

Terrence turned to him and answered, "Yes."

"Who's going to lead this militia... and train them?" asked Rick.

"I can," answered Terrence. "And I will, but I need to know if anyone else has any combat experience or skills."

David held up a hand, as did Emilie. There were a few other hands, but not all that many.

"Well, it's a start," he admitted. "So we have a new team—and a new ministry—to add to our growing government."

"We do indeed," agreed Tyrell. "Do you think now is a good time to go over that?"

Terrence thought for a minute about what Tyrell meant before he remembered. He clapped the other man on the shoulder and said, "Absolutely."

Tyrell nodded, and then waited. Derek chortled quietly from where he stood and looked quickly over at Sheridan, wondering if she knew what was about to happen.

Thankfully Terrence quickly picked up on the fact that Tyrell was uncomfortable with doing the honour, and he looked over at Rick.

Rick stood up and joined Terrence over by the fireplace. "Ladies and gentlemen," he started. "We are alive and we all damn well know who we have to thank for that."

There were murmurs of agreement through the crowd.

Once Rick was sure that they had enough time to think this over, he continued. "It's readily apparent that things are not—ever—going back to the way they used to. It's time we accepted this and moved on with our lives," he stated plainly. "And it's because of this woman up here that we can even think of doing that. Like you, when this all started, I immediately knew that I had days to live… at most… but when I agreed to live under her rules and on her land I suddenly had a future again. A different one, sure, but it was better than wondering if it was starvation or freezing to death that was going to get me.

"She organized us into teams and has proven to us over and over again that she has the ability to lead us through this. And, because this is her land, she alone has that right because she invited us here and she saved our lives. We didn't have to come here. Some of us could have lasted the winter. Would have been hard, sure, but we came here because it wasn't as lonely and shared work is lighter work."

Tyrell jumped in, finally finding his voice. "When those raiders came it was her preparations from wherever she dug that armour out of that saved us. We live by her rules—and there's the operative word."

Derek watched Sheridan's expression as this sank in, her eyes widening in dawning realisation as she saw what they were about to suggest. Inwardly he sighed, knowing it was needed and the convincing he would need to do to get her to figure it out. Suddenly, he remembered something. A rock he had picked up at the Fire Hall, a rock he had forgotten about until now and at the time he had rolled it around in his fingers with no idea why he had kept it.

Now he knew its purpose.

"Some of you already know this, and have already agreed to it," said Rick. "But we have got to have your support in this."

"Sheridan is our Queen," stated Tyrell plainly. "The teams are her Ministries. The team leaders are her Ministers. We have a chance to start new. Start fresh. The old world is dead—gone—and now buried. Time we stopped living in the past and welcomed the future."

"Long live the Queen," said Rick.

"Long live the Queen," echoed a few others.

The chant rang throughout the main room of the house as Derek looked sideways over at Sheridan.

He definitely had some convincing to do.

As the cheers died down and the room quieted, he noticed Sheridan disappear, like everyone else disappeared and went back to their chores, into her room with Terrence close on her heels.

Derek touched Marissa's arm and his wife glanced at him. "I think I have to talk a bit of sense into someone…"

"Let me guess, Sheridan?" she asked, and when he nodded she inclined her head. "Go on. She'll listen to you."

* * * * *

Leaning back against the wall, Daniel sighed as he pulled off his sopping wet boots and tossed them to the side, quickly followed by his equally soaked socks and trousers.

The air was chilly and while he shivered, he felt a little bit warmer. Covering his exposed legs with a rough blanket fashioned out of an old curtain from an abandoned hotel, he stared up at the ceiling and sighed heavily.

I was supposed to be out at Sheri's by now — enjoying a warm brandy with 'Rett and whoever else she and Terry invited, he mused, frowning as he did. *They'd be damn worried now and not able to do a damn thing either. Hopefully Mom didn't come into town for shopping, or to visit her sister... If everything went as planned they'd be out at the Manor by now... at least it's safer out there. Not so close to the chaos we've got here.*

That was something, at least. He could live with knowing they were all safe. And, perhaps, once they managed to get out of here he could somehow get them out of there. He could imagine what Valeria and Sheridan would be like in the same room.

Just have to get them all out there, he thought. *I'll keep that close to keep me going.*

He closed his eyes and sighed again. The wall and hard bench was almost comfortable with the time he had spent outside and on the streets. With a growl, he stood up, dried himself off and then pulled on dry clothing and socks before finding a set of shoes that fit him best.

People would be looking for him by now and he wa far too involved with them all now to let himself go missing for too long. When he did not hurry he walked briskly through the halls to the council chambers. Here he paused as he watched the Mayor—no, it was simply Valeria now—pace in the open rotunda of the chambers.

I can only imagine what she's feeling now, he mused. *I can pick up where ever I need to—she has lost everything that defines her.*

With a breath, he pushed the door open and walked into the glassed in room, making his way down the steps of the theatre to the central rotunda. "Valeria," he said, and she looked up. "We didn't find much out there, although by now a few stragglers should have managed to make it back here."

"And they have," she confirmed. "How are you holding up?"

"Me? What about you?"

"I am a very resilient, and resourceful, person," she answered. "However, you no longer have a police service to hold you. I imagine you are nowhere close to anyone in your family. You're as alone as I am, but I at least have my City Hall, and my duty, to keep me company."

"I think I could quickly find something to keep me busy too," he pointed out.

"Then stop worrying about how I'm holding up if you're not worrying about how you are," she retorted. "We will rebuild with what we have. We must."

* * * * *

Terrence followed Sheridan up into their room and she turned to Suni. "Could you give Terrence and I some privacy, please?" she asked.

The younger woman nodded and left the room, closing the double doors as she did. Sheridan faced Terrence with a dour look and he sighed. He knew she was not pleased with how things were shaping up and he was not sure he did either. But they had to deal with the cards as they fell. She knew this.

"Would you rather me as their leader and as king?" he asked plainly and she snorted in rejection of that very thought. "I didn't think so."

"But Queen?" she asked. "It's pompous, over the top and utterly ridiculous. I'm no Queen. Only one woman has legal claim to that status and she isn't me."

"Sheridan, there is one thing we all need to face up to—that world is dead and gone. There is no government anymore. What we have as the closest thing to resembling law, order and even modern civilization is right under this roof. Its leader and rightful 'rule' belongs to one person," he retorted. "You. And even by the old world's definition that makes you a queen, so whether you like it or not—you're the damn Queen of Walden."

There was a knock on the door and Terrence answered it.

Derek walked into their bedroom, nervous to intrude on them and nodded. "Terrence, could I talk to Sheridan for a moment?" he asked.

Terrence looked at Derek strangely, but acquiesced. Derek waited until the door closed and then brought out the rock he had found at the Fire Hall.

Sheridan held it in both hands, looking confused at what he had given her. "What is this?"

"It's a rock," he answered, simply.

She quirked an eyebrow. "I can see that. Why are you giving it to me?"

"That rock... I found it at the Fire Hall while doing some thinking," he started as he walked over to the window. The view was far better being higher than the other rooms. "All of this and I find one, smooth, rock while having some really dark thoughts about the state of our lives."

She waited him out, knowing that he would have a point eventually. He always did. Derek was an accomplished salesman and sometimes what he sold was not just something money could buy. Sometimes what he 'sold' was never for sale. In those cases, he simply had a point—a lesson—that he felt he could impart.

He was also far better travelled than any of them and had the most life experience and his advice, and observations, were often correct and this was the main reason she typically listened to him.

Derek turned back to Sheridan and pointed at the rock. "Do you know what that rock is?"

"No," she answered. "But I get the feeling you're about to tell me."

He chuckled, and then grew serious. "That rock is from the landscaping at the Fire Hall—a part of the building—and part of the old world. That rock is what holds this new world to the old. Our reminder of what can go drastically wrong if we screw this up." He licked his lips and finished. "It's also a symbol of hope. There are probably more rocks there—more reminders and more people out there. We're just one rock that makes up a whole."

Sheridan waited him out as this was actually a bit more complex than she was used to. "You brought up Rome, Sheridan. Rome was also a many headed beast of an empire when it was at full power. And then so was Britain... and then the US as well. All these, like Rome, fell. Out of them, like it was out of Rome, others rose. England, France—others—from Rome and even some of the Middle East. Britain founded Canada, Australia... held the USA for a time until the US also broke away. Nations came and went, but we always, always survived and the strongest always led us out of the darkest of times into better ones." He closed his hands over the rock. "This rock represents what was Canada. It now represents what will be—I don't know—whatever you end up calling your kingdom."

"If I take a kingdom," she pointed out.

He shook his head. "You will. And I honestly can't think of anyone better. Terrence would be a tyrant. He knows that, you know that and, hell, even I know that. But he makes a great military commander—*your* military commander. I could be the leader of your scouts or rangers, whatever you feel we should call ourselves now. All the various teams formed are now beginning to think of themselves as Ministries. Whether you want to admit it a kingdom has already been born and you're its Queen." He stared right into her eyes, closing her hands over the rock. "Now lead it as a Queen should."

* * * * *

"I have no idea where he'd be, Zara," said Kaine as he struggled to keep up with Zara and her sister. "Nor why you'd believe him to be here."

The two sisters stopped just outside their father's office. Kaine and the sisters looked from one to another.

"He said he was going to take a look into something but he didn't say what," answered Zara's younger sister, Niala. "He never came back."

Kaine crinkled his brow. *Now what are they on about?* He then sighed heavily and looked up at the ceiling before pointing at the door. "Well, which one of you has a spare key to the office?"

"I do," said Zara as she pulled it out of her pocket and turned it in the lock.

The door opened and Kaine waited, but then gently pushed the two young women aside. If something untoward was in the room, he did not want the daughters to see it. He had no idea what he was expecting but when he stepped into the room and saw Neil lying on the floor, he swallowed. "Niala, go get one of the other board members for the campus."

"Why?" she asked. "Why should I have to go?"

"Niala, just go," ordered Zara. As soon as she was gone, Zara cried out, "She's gone. What did you find?"

"I think I should—"

"I think you should tell me now," she answered as she pushed the door open and walked in. She stopped mid step and stared at her father's body on the floor of his office, the back of her hand over her mouth. "Oh my God, Dad…"

Kaine grasped her arm and although part of it was in reassurance, part of it was to stop her from disturbing the body. *I wasn't expecting this,* he thought. *Not the way I thought—or wanted—this to go either. What a waste of perfectly good resources…*

CHAPTER SEVENTEEN

The light had not even begun to climb up above the tree line when Derek found himself in the massive main room of Sheridan and Terrence's house. Even before the old world had passed into the new and dangerous one, he never found himself having that much time to simply sit and think.

While he poked at the fire in the massive fireplace to stoke it to a full flame, he found he had that time now—time that was becoming as rare as gold.

Barely a week had passed since Christmas and it was now officially New Year's day.

It felt far longer.

So much had happened in such a short time and the enormity of the fall of civilization made it feel as if it had been ages since he had left Garson. *Will we still count the year as 2016, or start all over again because of the change?* he wondered as he shook his head at himself.

Marissa came down from the upstairs room they shared. For a long moment, they stared at each other from across the room. While they had been together for the trip to the Fire Hall since then they had not had the time to actually talk.

"The fire needed someone to poke at it. It was dying down. Can't afford to let it go out now that it's what keeps us alive," he said.

"You're not talking about that fire," she stated.

"No, I'm not," he answered and turned back to her. "Am I too distant?"

She shook her head. "I'll admit it'd be nice to have you around a bit more often but, considering the circumstances, I'll live."

"You shouldn't have to just 'live' with it, Reese," he sighed and walked over to the couch, flopping down into it beside her. "If we could go back, would you?"

"Go back where?" She looked at him in surprise. "Back to Garson?"

"Back to the way things were before."

For a long moment she was silent and then she sighed heavily before looking into the fire. "I honestly don't know. It's a more dangerous life

249

now but at the same time it's all simpler." She grinned. "At least there are no more bills to pay."

He laughed then, a full and hearty laugh of real amusement. "That's true. Sheridan hasn't thought of what happens when a country requires currency. I don't think she's dealt with it all that far yet. Survival has come first."

"As it should," answered Marissa. "What will we do now?"

Derek honestly didn't know. Neither he nor Sheridan had given thought to long term plans whether currency or any other type of plans. So far they took everything as it came at them with no real chance to plan—only react. It was not the best way to respond to any situation. "I don't know what the future holds anymore. I've been living each day as it came. No time to do anything different, really."

"But we are going to?" she asked, surprised.

"I'd imagine so… at some point." He took a breath and sighed once more. "We just have to survive the winter first."

Once the sun had a chance to warm things up a bit more, people began to slowly trickle back into the main room of Sheridan's house. She stood on the balcony above the living room while leaning on the rail in a relaxed manner. Where she placed herself could be taken as a reflection of her attitude of superiority but the reality of it was that it was simply easier for her to engage with everyone if she could see their faces.

It was also easier for them to hear her without having to contend with her voice being lost in the crowd.

"Now that we've all had a chance to sleep and think this over," she began. "We have a lot more work to do. Even as your Queen I won't micro manage the hell out of you." There were a few chuckles at this. "We all have jobs to do and let's get to the core of the matter."

Court is in session, mused Derek.

"This is a new chance to direct our lives in a new direction. We didn't have this chance before," she continued. "I may lead you, I may legally own this land you all now live on. The territory may grow to include what is further south of us and perhaps in other directions."

For a moment, she thought about her next words. Sheridan was still plainly uncomfortable with the idea of being a queen. For all their sakes, Derek hoped she would soon come to terms with it. "But the fact that I lead you and oversee what each of our ministers do doesn't mean you don't have a say in your lives. I am no tyrant, no dictator."

A small grin lit up her face. "Honestly, that would take more time out of my life than I have currently to serve as your Chief Surgeon too." She grew serious again. "You all have your jobs and you know them well. I am just here to make sure that we all stay in the same direction without randomly scattering to the nine winds. I am here to make sure that priorities are set and then kept. With that being said, we now have the really hard work to do—we need to plan what our next step is and I know we don't all share the same idea of what needs to come first. I understand that you all held meetings within your respective teams and chose a Minister to lead you and speak for you. Court is open in the Kingdom of Panache Lake."

She brought down a solid stone against the thick wooden beam of the rail and the sound of the make-shift mallet rang out through the hall.

* * * * *

Kaine's ears ached from the shouting in the meeting room, but there was little he could do about it right now. With Neil's death, and still no way to contact emergency services, the calm now cracked within the University's leadership. *I told them this would happen*, thought Kaine as he watched the argument between the others. *And none of them listened…*

"Was it murder?" demanded one of the professors, a man Kaine never could remember the name of.

There were too many for him to remember so he gave the man a nick-name. It was not charitable, but until Kaine knew his name he decided this first one would be Long Nose.

The second, a woman he called Waxy Hair, and she laughed, but he could hear how hollow her mirth was. "Hardly. Might have been a heart attack but there were no signs of any foul play."

"We should wait until the police get here…" pointed out Long Nose.

Kaine sighed, "They're not coming."

Waxy Hair turned to him and asked in a demanding tone, "And how in hell can you possibly know that, Dr. Kaine?"

"I have my sources and I know no one is coming," Kaine answered, jabbing a finger onto the table for emphasis. "We are on our own here and we will have to be the ones to pull ourselves out of this mess."

"Even if that's the case, who's going to lead? Niel is dead, Kaine," pointed out Long Nose.

Kaine pinched his nose and sat down. "I know that - and I'm as distressed by it as much as the rest of you are. But we can't let this stop us in our tracks. If we do the, the whole university will be lost. We'll be dead too from either starvation or hypothermia."

"What do you suggest, then?" asked Waxy Hair.

"We tighten our belts, and we use what generous resources we have here to prepare for the eventuality that we will have to do it again next winter," answered Kaine before shrugging. "And if I'm wrong, no harm done. We just simply tested our emergency preparedness— something we should do anyway. It will be a morale building experience. And if I'm right, and I truly believe I am, then we have just ensured our own survival."

"Who will lead? You?" asked Waxy Hair with a bit of a snort.

"And why not?" asked Kaine, lifting a brow. "I have the experience and I had the foresight to recognize the writing on the wall when the rest of you did not. I think I should lead and my first order of business will be one of making sure we don't starve or run out of resources."

"Wait a second here," pointed out Long Nose. "We're moving too fast…"

Kaine stood up and the man stopped speaking, his mouth closing with a click. "No, we're not acting fast enough. Had we done so, perhaps Neil would still be in charge, perhaps not. I appear to have the vision and plan you all lack. No, I will lead and you *will* follow that lead or we will all die here."

CHAPTER EIGHTEEN

One day it seemed like the cold and the snow simply vanished overnight. After decades of the same, Derek thought he would have expected it. But, after a while, each day had blurred everything into the same routine. Even the discussions had blurred into the same discussions and then into each other. Planning for the spring simply seemed like he was spinning his wheels, but not actually getting anywhere.

And then, as if someone had snapped their fingers, spring arrived in Northern Ontario.

The warmth that greeted him that morning when the sun rose was welcome. It meant the core of the house that kept the entire structure warm did not need the back up from the fire at night and it was safe to let it bank back to embers. Individual rooms no longer ran the same risk of fire due to not even needing to be lit in the first place.

This, of course, meant that there were other issues to address.

Terrence was already up and deep in a discussion with Rick and Tyrell when Derek came down the stairs.

"The problem is that now that massive wall of snow is going to turn into water. It's already losing structural integrity," pointed out Rick. "The best thing would be to get up there with shovels again and scatter the snow to make it melt off faster and more evenly. While a few teams are doing that, and digging a trench for the run-off to follow, we need to send other teams to scour the country side for rocks and logs to build the permanent wall."

"How fast are we going to need to do this?" asked Tyrell, clearly thinking of whom to send and how many are needed per team.

"As soon as possible," answered Terrence. "Once the snow starts to melt, it'll be like a sudden cascade of failures in its structure. We're soon going to have an open road and a weak northern perimeter."

"The ground is still frozen," pointed out Derek as he walked up to them, accepting a coffee, or a coffee substitute, from Lorraine. "That will make digging anything extremely difficult."

"We're going to need some real digging equipment," said Tyrell, with a short barking laugh. "Considering how many mines and industries are around to support the mining, it shouldn't be too hard. The hard part is finding the fuel and getting the equipment here."

"That George fellow had pole drivers and the equipment in his shop," pointed out Derek.

"That's a start," said Terrence, and he turned to Tyrell. "I get the feeling you already have an idea of what you need to do and who is the best suited for it."

"I do," he answered. "I'm guessing we should get on this right now."

Rick nodded and Tyrell left the house, leaving Terrence, Derek and Rick.

"I have things I need to attend to as well. I'm borrowing your old drafting room, Terrence," said Rick as he got up and handed his cup over to Lorraine.

Terrence waved him off and Derek and Terrence stared at each other for a long time.

"How are you holding up?" asked Terrence.

Derek looked over at his friend. Terrence was a man that had been born in the wrong time. This sort of life suited Terrence who enjoyed roughing it and living a life from another time and another place. Before all this had happened Terrence had always participated in activities that took him away from modern life to a life less modern. It took him forever to learn to use a computer and then he had to be practically pushed into owning a cell phone or even getting his own car. Life before had not appealed to Terrence whose set of morals had always suited a more decisive time.

To say Terrence had taken to his new set of circumstances like a cat to cream would have been an understatement. For a man given to being vocal of his likes and dislikes, Terrence suddenly had far less to dislike than before.

Granted, he was far busier now than ever before.

Ironically, the Civil Engineer was no longer an engineer of structures—unless he was advising Rick or Tyrell—but instead had fallen back on his military background while leading their militia as a general, drill sergeant and captain all rolled into one. He had not been able to do any real drills other than teaching the theory of defending their homes and basic training. Now that the spring warmth was melting the snow in the fields and the risk of hypothermia was passing, he would start forming and training a real militia.

On the other hand, Derek had found his experience from his former life as a sales consultant less than useful in this new world. No one had access to money, and so his career suddenly found itself shut out.

Thankfully, his skills as an outdoorsman had literally saved him—numerous times, in fact. If he had had his sales skill only to lean on he would have been the same as the others.

Here on the sufferance of Sheridan.

As kind as she was, it was not something he wanted. He had been raised to walk on his own two feet and earn what was given. Still, though, this was not his home. Not originally. It was *now* but the home he had left behind with all his mementos and family photos may as well be on the other side of the planet. He felt bereft... like he was floundering.

How was he holding up?

On the outside he supposed he looked like he was holding up just fine. The reality was that he was not sure just how well he was really—truly—holding together.

"As well as can be expected," he answered finally, not noticing as Terrence looked not at him but past him. "How's Sheridan holding up?"

"Far better than you," Sheridan answered.

Sheridan had silently walked into the room behind him and her sudden appearance made him jump as he turned to face her. "Oh?"

"Let me see if I can sum this up. You're basically homeless at this point, even if you have a roof over your head. Everything that you held dear, outside of Marissa, is unreachable. What defined you no longer can," she said. "And yet you feel that you're in a far better position than others simply because you were lucky enough to know us."

He was quiet for a moment and then he laughed quietly, but it was without any sense of humour. "Isn't that the case?"

"No," answered Sheridan. "Every single person here, even you, is as rare and valuable as gold. More so because you still breathe and still can make a difference. That's the most important thing right now. You don't know if everyone is dead. While you still breathe and live, they have a real chance of finding you. I guarantee you that out there somewhere is someone just as worried that you're dead as you fear their deaths. That we all still live and survive is a victory, not a failure."

She flicked her long hair over her shoulder and then squeezed his elbow. "Come on, I have just the task that will make you feel better."

Derek looked at her sideways while remembering the trip out to the Fire Hall before following Sheridan out to the barn.

He was not that surprised to note that Karen was there and overseeing the monumental daily tasks of caring for not one but three massive horse barns. The main barn was the closest, even if it was not the largest, and held Sheridan's prized personal stock of Friesians.

The Friesian was a large breed and was also known as the Belgian Black and, before the apparent end of civilization, had been the favoured horse for the Royal Canadian Mounted Police for their rides. As such they were an even tempered but spirited and intelligent animal. They were also all black with only minor variations in markings.

The prize mare of this barn was Sheridan's personal favourite eventing horse, called Northern Shadow, as she was a massive black horse with no markings at all. In the dark of the barn she appeared to be a massive black shadow. Karen was exercising her in the ring and Derek found his eye following her. This was not new to him—he had seen Shadow perform before— but there was something that caused his eyes to follow the horse's movements in awe every time he saw it.

Northern Shadow was always given the best training an eventing horse could get and only ever entrusted to the best of riders until she was finally retired. Of the two foals she had just one remained here—although he was a yearling now and ready to start training.

Derek was surprised to find himself in the same paddock as Shadow Broker, the very horse dammed by Northern Shadow. He looked from

Sheridan to the yearling and back again. "What are you saying?"

"He's yours," said Sheridan. "I can't think of anyone better to take him into the world. Given his young age, we can train him for a new purpose other than show jumping and eventing. His sire, Breaking Storm, was a Friesian down south from a farm near Belleville. His owner didn't believe in breeding the new sporting breeds making this big boy a bit more in line with the older standard of the breed."

The confusion on his face made her continue her explanation. "The newer standard favours lighter horses interbred to remake the breed into a lighter, more sport, horse. Breaking Storm's owner and I were of the same mind—if the Friesian was ever meant to be a light horse, it would have been so. Neither of us subscribed to making a 'lighter' version of the horse. He's not going to be as big as a Clydes, but he's definitely going to be a big boy."

"Why me?" asked Derek.

"As I said—we all have to get used to some new roles. He will never be an eventing or show horse. He's going to need training to match this new world and he is going to be yours," she said. "Both of you will head out into that world in a new role."

Derek looked at her, crinkling his brow. He suddenly had this suspicion that Sheridan had an idea of where his life should go now. She wasn't going to force it on him but was giving him the option to take it and do what he wanted with it. "What did you have in mind?" he asked.

"Derek, you have a certain way with people that Terrence doesn't," she answered, her eyes on him. "We both know that. He's not the most diplomatic of people."

Derek snorted, "Understatement of the century."

"Indeed, but you also have his ability in the field," she pointed out and waited for him to make the connection.

Which he did. The realisation dawned on him. "You want me to be—what? An ambassador?"

"If required, yes—if not, your skills out there and your experience would make you a perfect scout. I'd never send you too far. I know what that would do to Marissa unless she chose to join you out there. I know that there has to be others who survived and I know we can easily reach them by horse," she answered. "I also need to know just what it is we are facing and you have that agile mind to be my eyes and ears outside the wall."

Derek sucked in a breath and looked over at Shadow Broker. "I'll do it if Marissa agrees to it... and comes with me."

"Fair enough," agreed Sheridan.

* * * * *

Spring melt held wildly different meanings, depending on who was asked. For those at High Falls it meant full capacity, perhaps even, over-capacity. Garrett did not want to release the overflow as he knew that as soon as he did, the flooding down river could turn catastrophic.

His daughter and niece lived on a river similar to this one. High Falls formed the head water of the Spanish River but there was a similar dam on the Vermillion. He had worked at both.

Finally, with a sigh, Garrett turned from the window he was staring through to the controller at the computer. "All right, let the river go. If we hold off any longer, it will be washing over the dam."

"Yes sir," answered the controller. "Full or half?"

"Quarter at first, then work your way into full. Don't want to cause the opposite effect of the controlled pressure release," he answered, patting the younger man on the shoulder before heading out of the controlling station and over to where he had managed to rebuild the old HAM radio.

He had not yet had any success in getting anyone else on it, but he would not give up until he managed to find someone.

Anyone.

* * * * *

Once the snow began to melt, the scene outside the walls of the City Hall was fully revealed. Unfortunately, the smell also matched. People had died outside those walls and now that the winter had released its stranglehold, things were beginning to thaw.

Some things, like bodies, were better left frozen.

Daniel knew that the death toll in the central part of Sudbury had been high but nothing prepared any of them for what met them in the spring.

The stench of thousands of rotting bodies hung over the downtown core like a cloud. Valeria, visibly distressed at the sight of the dead bodies as she came out to the rooftop gardens and asked, "How many people died out there?"

"Too many," he answered. "We were lucky."

"No, it was your idea of turning the municipal offices into an indoor farm that saved us. Luck had nothing to do with it."

"Yes, but…"

A shudder ran through the building and he stopped talking. "What in the name of hell was that?" he wondered aloud.

Two people ran up to the roof and stopped short when they reached Daniel. "Dan, we have a rather large and severe problem," began the first one.

"Which is?" he asked.

"The creek that runs under the building has leaked out of the cement channel that holds it, sir," she explained. "It's managed to work its way under the foundation of the provincial building and weaken the supports. The garage underneath is sinking, in fact it's already flooded and it's pulling the rest of the square down with it."

"What?" asked Valeria in shock. "The city engineers assured us that the Junction Creek tunnel would last at least twenty years before we needed to do any further reconditioning. The city paid billions to a contractor to make sure of it."

"The winter was particularly harsh, maybe," answered Daniel, desperately wishing his son in law, a civil engineer, although not for the city, was there to advise them. "Could have caused a crack... a frost heave..."

"How fast are we sinking?" asked the mayor.

Fitz blew out a breath. Fitz's father and Daniel were friends and he knew her well enough to know when Fitz said something was bad typically it was. She was one of those people who could fix anything with duct tape and shims, although she preferred to fix things properly, so for her to tell them it was serious meant that things were probably far worse. "Well, once the sinkhole opened up we started sinking. But it took days for it to worm under enough to sink the provincial building and it's larger than either of the other two. It'd sink faster."

Daniel nodded. "Still, to be safe, seal off the basement levels and the garage. They were our weakest points anyway and if they are about to be buried, it might be for the best."

"You do realize the swampy bed beneath us could potentially swallow everything up to the second floor of each building, right?" asked Valeria. "This roof we're standing on could soon be on the same level as the square below."

Daniel sighed again. "If it looks like that's going to happen, we move out of here. Head over the bridge to Lake Ramsey and away from the gangs. Leave the core to the nuts determined to take it."

"You want us to abandon City Hall?" asked the other incredulously.

Daniel turned to face them again. "What would you have me do? If this place is about to lose whatever advantage it had it would be better if we moved."

"And go where?" asked the mayor.

Daniel mulled the situation over for a moment and said, "If we can get to the canoe club, we can head across the lake, maybe. Head to the hospital, perhaps even the university."

Valeria nodded. "All right, but only if this place turns out to be unsafe."

* * * * *

"How many more feet have we lost?" asked Daniel as he inched carefully over to the young woman.

At first he had thought Fitz was crazy for volunteering to venture in the almost entirely flooded garage under City Hall.

It was getting darker and deeper every passing day. It was impossible to get under the provincial building now. The hallway connecting the two had already ruptured and spilled rubble into the companionway while the tallest of the three towers sank deeper into the murk below.

While the other two towers had not really sunk yet, both were noticeably had dropped by at least six inches. The provincial tower, being heaviest and the first undermined, had sunk almost by a story. The parking lot was now completely submerged and collapsed and the first floor was now where the parking used to be.

Instead of risking the safety of any of the survivors, the mayor had ordered everyone out of the provincial building and into City Hall itself—or into the police tower.

"At this rate, the third floor is going to be where the main floor's lobby used to be and you'll need scuba gear to find the second," she answered frankly, shaking her head. "Honestly, if it goes, it could take the others out with it."

"What do you mean by 'goes'?" asked Daniel evenly.

"I mean completely collapse—it's barely hanging on by a thread as it is," answered another and Fitz glanced over at him, then back at Dan. "And if the building comes down the whole square will be like a house of cards... if you want my honest opinion, we should pack up and move before that happens."

"What about other buildings?"

"Well, the creek only runs under City Hall and then meanders under the arena if I'm not mistaken. Or it runs under Brady, I'm not entirely sure, but wherever it goes I'd avoid it or we'll be right back where we started." There was a long pause as they listened to the structure groan from somewhere in the dark pit. "And the sooner the better."

Daniel nodded his agreement and clapped the two on the shoulder. "All right... let's get the hell out of here before it comes down on our heads and tell our mayor the bad news."

They had just climbed up out of the hole when a bottle—thrown from over the barricade—came crashing into the square. Daniel narrowly avoided it, and thankfully it completely missed Fitz as well.

A whoop sounded from outside and the three ran for cover. Just as they managed to get inside, more of the Molotovs came over the barricade, lighting the entire square in flame.

The mayor leaned over the topmost edge—ironically where her office was—and yelled down, "They've got ladders, Dan, and they're coming over the wall!"

Daniel was horrified as he looked at where she was pointing.

Their one line of defense was just breached and the only thing stopping them now was a thick pane of glass. He swore vehemently and yelled, "Everyone to arms! We're going to need every arm we can get!"

"Are they at the back?" asked another person.

"I don't see them," answered Valeria after she ran to check. "It seems clear—I think they're only from that side."

The young woman looked at Daniel. "We could make a run for the bridge... just leave this sinking ship to them."

Daniel hesitated a moment and then turned around. "Ben, take your people and the mayor and get them over the bridge. We'll keep them busy here and then join you later. Head for the canoe club!"

Valeria leaned over the wall. "No, Daniel... you can't do this..."

He turned away and shouldered the police issue shotgun as others came up by him, a bit more prepared as they were dressed in full riot issue. Twenty against at least fifty. He had seen better odds and while this was no movie he hoped that they could hold them off so they could retreat, too.

There was no avoiding the confrontation now.

* * * * *

Marissa stared out the window as the sun set. Derek sat beside her on the bed as they both looked out the window and to the river beyond.

"I told her I'd only do it if I had your blessing, and if you came with me," said Derek.

"What if I said you had my blessing, but I would rather I didn't come with you?" she asked.

Derek held his breath in shock.

She punched his arm and said, "I didn't mean we'd not be married, you old fool, I meant that sometimes I'd rather help Karen in the barn and not always be out there. I'm not as much a camper as you. I know you'll always come back—you always did when you were on the road as a salesman. The only thing that makes this different is how you're getting around."

"It's more dangerous."

"And the chances of having a deadly car crash were less?" She asked plainly and he had to admit her point. "Or the chances of being taken as a trespasser and shot?"

"All right, you've made your point," he conceded. "No way I can convince you otherwise?"

"You don't want to go out there?"

"Didn't say that, Reese, I meant I'd rather have you out there with me," he answered.

Marissa thought for a moment and smiled. "Maybe when the weather warms up more…"

"…and the bugs come out…" he pointed out and laughed as she shuddered at the thought.

"You, go, enjoy yourself. Do what you've always done, Derek," she said as she turned the bed back. "Bring back what you've always brought back."

"And what's that?" he asked.

"Yourself."

CHAPTER NINETEEN

The next morning Derek sat on the stone steps, with a pad underneath his seat, while drinking the 'tea' which now replaced coffee in the morning. He was not alone, however like Terrence, who had built a list of people that were to form their militia, Derek had decided to make a list for himself of people who were like him.

Finding these people had been easier than he thought.

A sales person was easy to spot—they were always sizing up a person to get inside their head and know what would serve as their hot button. A hot button was the flashy, right thing to say or do that could turn an objection around and into a sale.

In his opinion, these were the kind of people Sheridan needed to serve as ambassadors and scouts. Correctly reading people in this new world could mean the difference between life and death. But now, instead of training to read people and situations to make a sale, they all needed to learn a different set of survival skills for their main purpose of scouts.

He knew only one thig for sure.

The first thing he was going to when they got to whatever was left of Sudbury was find some real coffee.

"All right, I think you all know why we're here," he said. "We were all, at one point, sales people and sales consultants—however you want to slice it we were all in sales. We were hunters of a different species, and now we're going to be hunters in a very real sense."

"As in literally," piped up one of the younger ones.

The group chortled at the joke.

Derek nodded sombrely, "He's got a real point. This time we're not hunting for the next big deal—the next big sale. We've got something far more immediate—life and death—in our hands and we're the only ones that can get it done. Our skills and our talents are needed here—nothing else. What I'm going to teach you to do beside that is all you need to survive outside that wall. And then, we are going outside that wall and up into the mountains. We are going to test what we've learnt from each other by taking that theory and putting it to the test. Someplace where getting down for the amenities in this house is a pain in the butt. But we're also not so far that if we do run into trouble the cavalry can't get to us."

"Are you kidding me?" asked another one. "You're making us scouts?"

"You have anything better to do?" asked Derek. "What were we before but scouts of a sort? Our quarry was intelligent and what they had equally valuable. You had to use your smarts and your instincts to get, hopefully honestly, their money to buy what you had to sell and you had to prove what you had was of use to them. Sales was as much a game of smarts as wilderness scouting—and we were on the road as much as we will be now. We had to make do with seedy hotels for budget reasons, and an ability to read a map. Just use those same skills for this and you'll do better than fine. The new product knowledge now, though, is survival outdoors and how to ride. How to use a bow and a gun—but likely a bow because arrows are easier to replace."

There were a few sighs of long suffering patience.

Yet he did not actually hear anyone say that they would not work with him. "I'm not forcing anyone into anything, am I?" he asked. "If you would rather be doing something else, I'll understand. But once you accept this new task in front of you, I need you all to be on the same page and putting everything you have into it. When I say it's life or death, I'm not exaggerating."

No one left as he looked at each one of them. While they had sighed a bit, he could see that they were all up for this challenge. He grinned. "Good then, I think you'll like this as much as I do anyway."

* * * * *

"Goddammit," muttered Garrett in frustration as the radio fizzled out again.

At this rate, it was not very likely that he would ever get it running. He was not accustomed to failure and the radio was just not cooperating with any of his efforts to get it working. His assistant, when he got there, noticed him glaring at the wisp of smoke that rose from the radio again.

"Not having any luck?" he asked.

"Nope," Garrett answered as he leaned forward to poke at the radio. "I get the feeling this thing is beyond help. And no one has managed to find a CB radio in any of the trucks?"

"No CB's, no FRS', not a thing," he answered, shaking his head. "It's strange because it's clear they did have them at one point... and I think recently... you don't think..."

Garrett did think the missing radios were related to the near coup in winter. Someone still felt that Garrett was hogging power and leadership.

The strange part was, if asked Garrett would frankly rather not be leading the camp at all. While he was a good foreman he had still never liked being in charge of a camp itself. That kind of thing was better suited to someone with not only the temperament for it but also the inclination and skills for it.

Someone like his late wife—or, even, his mother.

The latter had once run entire camps while his father had overseen the work the camp was there to do. Between the two of them this camp would have been running in order—communications be damned. Their era had been exactly like this.

Garrett could admit he was out of his element. While he had indeed inherited his father's skills and ability he had been trained in an environment that relied on technology. Being without it crippled him.

"Yeah, I really do think," answered Garrett. "Keep an eye out. I'd like to live through this. Frankly, if someone feels they could do better, we could make a vote out of it if it's really that much of a big deal."

"You'd allow that?" asked the other, surprised.

He shrugged his indifference. "I'll lead if people want me to. Not the other way around. If someone else would rather take over, so be it. But don't expect me to be quiet if I happen to not agree…"

"You… quiet?"

He glared up at the man, but there was no heat to it.

* * * * *

Abigail stared out down the river and back at the camp where she had managed to survive and live over the course of the winter when forced to land her plane on the river.

After the snow had melted, she found herself in more of a soggy mess than a camp. With a sigh, she went back to the task of pushing the plane back out onto the water.

With no fuel she could not fly it, but it still could float and therefore be used to follow the current down river. At least then she could find the road and follow it to some sort of civilization, or at least find someone with riverfront property.

She knew there had to be. It was plain as day on the maps that such things existed it was just how far down river she would have to go before she found one... and if anyone would still be alive when she got there.

She supposed she would just have to see where the river took her.

I wish I wasn't so far away from my own house, though, she thought, chewing her bottom lip. *I wonder how many others were as stuck as I am...*

... And that's a depressing thought.

Abigail sighed again as she continued to pole and paddle the awkward bulk of the float plane down the river.

CHAPTER TWENTY

It took Derek a week to teach them everything he knew about the outdoors and camping. Some were able to fill in the gaps of the knowledge they picked up while others were not. In an interplay of knowledge and experience, the group of nine sales people turned into wilderness scouts were now comfortable with each other while sharing their knowledge among themselves.

On the last day, he sat them down outside on Sheridan's front step—something that had turned into a daily routine with them—and gazed at them all.

"I want you to learn one thing from me and it's this; we're a team. Yes, someone always needs to be team lead, but we can't be too shy to share something. If you know something that you know someone doesn't you need to speak up and tell them. If you learn something that will make all of our lives easier, you share it. That's our job description now. We watch, we listen and we learn. That's our mission and our code... if you will." He grinned as he picked up his pack and pointed to the North West. "Now let's test it."

They all stood up when Marissa came out in a hurry and half dressed for the weather. She was clearly distressed as she pointed down the south road and vaguely to the east.

"What's the matter, Reese?" he asked in concern.

Marissa was not often panicked to the extent of being wordless. "The river's burst the bank... it's up into the south east field and is threatening the outermost barn."

* * * * *

On the hill below three towers burned. The flames were bright enough to cast the entire downtown core in shadows and allow the former defender the ability to see where he was going as he finally fled the confrontation.

Daniel led his pursuers straight to the east and up the hill at the end of Cedar instead of to the south in order to lead them away from the mayor and her people. He had no idea if they would be able to ever meet back up—this part of Sudbury did not exactly connect up with the University but he would certainly attempt it if he could.

He was alone now—the others that had fled with him had all died to the last or were scattered.

I don't even know if Fitz made it out, he realized as he leaned heavily on a tree, panting from the exertion of climbing the hill.

The last he saw of Fitz she had been pushed up Brady and towards Lorne, which was in the complete opposite direction as the Mayor… or even Daniel himself. That would either lead west out to Copper Cliff, and perhaps out to Sheridan, or north to Chelmsford and Azilda.

The rest, when he ordered the retreat, they had been picked off one by one as they had wound through the streets.

After he had managed to climb the stairs to the street above, all signs of pursuit simply stopped as if they had lost interest.

The truth was he was likely as dead as the others and just did not know it yet. He was alone, unarmed except for his shotgun—which was out of ammunition—and his sidearm. He did not even have his body armour. Without food or any sort of shelter, he was pretty much screwed over.

Oh No point in dwelling on that now. He could only move forward. *When I get a second to catch my breath… I will. I'll make sure the word gets out.*

Daniel turned away from the burning downtown core and limped his way deeper into the other neighbourhood.

* * * * *

"The lake looks like it's cold," said Adrienne. She turned around as Russell walked into the house and made his way to the window where she pointed. "Why are you soaked?"

Russell rolled his eyes as he began to peel his clothing off. "Because the rocks are still a bit slippery and the water levels are still higher than normal… and I fell in."

She laughed, taking a sip of tea. "That will teach you to clamber around the lake side before the weather warms up. Why were you down there anyway?"

"Pump stopped working," he answered. "Unfortunately, I have no way of fixing it until the water is far warmer than this. I think the blockage is at the far end."

"So… we're carrying buckets up here now?"

He nodded. "Yeah, unfortunately." Russell looked over at her as she continued to sip from her cup, looking out over the lake. "How are you doing?"

She shrugged.

With a sigh, Russell dried himself off and then dressed again in dry clothing. He poked his finger through a hole and sighed again. "We're going to have to start figuring out a way to repair things, or even replace. Our clothes are threadbare and the plastic cooking utensils are getting old. We can only scavenge for so long before we run out." He grinned as he joined her by the window. "Don't suppose you have any carving or sewing skills?"

She crinkled her nose as she turned to him. "Nah, sorry, my hobbies were always sports and some reading. Once I graduated, work became my hobby." Adrienne looked down at the ground. "Dad could have carved some nice forks… and Mum could have fixed our clothes if they were still alive and healthy."

Her parents had died over the winter from the strain of having to live a nearly pioneer life. In truth, he though her mother died from the heartbreak of leaving everything behind — and her father had not lasted much longer.

A knock sounded on the door and the artist they had befriended came in. "Well, we're heading to Long Lake to see if we can do any trading. Did you want to come along?"

Russell looked over at Adrienne with a crooked eyebrow. Upon putting her cup down, she grinned. "Yeah, sure, why not," she said. "Better than looking at the same four walls."

* * * * *

Kaine shivered as he stepped from the outside into the common area. The winter had clogged it full of snow. But as it melted, he could at least step onto the paver's stones. The door opened behind him and he turned to see Zara freezing in the doorway.

"I don't bite," said Kaine.

"I wouldn't... I didn't..." she sighed and then she started over. "I never said that you would. I just didn't want to intrude."

"You're not. I only came outside because I'm getting a little sick and tired of being inside," he said. "How are you holding up? I know it's been a few months since you lost your father, but still..."

She shrugged. "I'm doing the best I can. All I have now is my sister and she keeps herself busy in her lab."

"And not you?"

"Well, I could. I do have my own work to do but I haven't found much in the way of inspiration lately. Who's going to review it when it's done? Who will even care?" she asked as she leaned against the door frame.

Kaine led her back inside, letting the door close behind him to cut off the cool breeze from outside. It was refreshing for a while but then his knees began to protest the chill from the still frozen ground. He glanced over at the younger woman-and thought for a moment. *She has a point... who will conduct our peer reviews now? Doesn't seem the same.* After trying to make sense out of the situation, he said, "I think I understand why our morale has been low lately, and while losing your father was a significant blow, I suspect he is just the tip of the iceberg... so to speak. I think we've lost our way and our purpose. It needs to be found again."

"How will we do that?"

"By being our own damn peers. We're a university full of professors and students... who else should be our peers but those who share the same interests?" he answered, smiling. "It may not be the best solution, but if it helps raise the spirits of everyone here, it may be the best course of action. Give us purpose again, and then we can also be that beacon in the dark."

Zara nodded and slowly smiled and the spark Kaine remembered began to light up her eyes again. "Now I know why you're leading the university."

He shrugged. "I don't know—I just couldn't stand by with my head in the sand. I had to do something that would at least help us... but I won't be able to do this alone either. Zara, I believe I need your help."

She perked up, her eyebrows rising. "You have it already."

* * * * *

Abigail could have jumped for joy when she bumped into the dock at the boatyard. It was a very large area covered in boats. *Should mean that now I'll be able to find something a bit more meant for negotiating the river versus the ungainly float plane. The real miracle was being able to maintain any control at all while drifting.*

She tied off the plane and then walked up the long dock, spotting the small fishing boat on shore straight away. The model was a type of bass boat, which meant it was low to the water with a flat surface. Poling, or even rowing, down the river in this would be not only far easier but also far more controlled.

Then even bigger—and jackpot! There was indeed fuel still left in the motor, and a quick check revealed that someone had wisely even treated it with something to prevent it turning rancid.

"Okay, where's that other shoe," she mused, amazed by her incredible luck.

After using the launch rails to get it into the water and to the dock, she unloaded the plane and loaded the boat.

An ominous creaking sounded from the dock. Abigail prayed as she ran down the dock and to the shore that it held.

It was then she heard something else—something far more threatening. "Oh no, oh no," she repeated as she ran to the boat.

She untied the boat as fast as she could and moved it up onto shore, using the launch rails and the hand powered come-along winch.

A few minutes later, the rushing sound of a river about to burst its banks turned into a heavier, lower sounding rumble. The water on the shore line began to ripple as if something was throwing a wake, but the problem was the water was slowly rising.

Abigail held her breath as water crept slowly up the bank. A groan reached her ear as the dock began to shift sideways and downriver. The plane slid to the side.

If I don't sacrifice the plane, I'll lose everything… Running as fast as she could, she used her hatchet to cut through the ropes, and barely ducked out of way of the wing strut. Once released from its securing ropes, the Cessna was quickly swept away.

The dock bobbed in the water, but did not move another inch despite the rushing water. *Willing to bet this is a yearly occurrence*, Abigail thought as she watched the chunks of ice and snow as they were swept downriver.

CHAPTER TWENTY-ONE

They all had forgotten the spring flood risk that came from living beside a major river. Now it was threatening their very lives and the lives of the horses, which were now their only way to drive the machines of life. Each and every horse was now worth their weight in gold.

The ride through the muddy grass and rock was treacherous and Derek found himself eyeing the footwork of his horse as he rode to the barn. He was a bit slower than Sheridan and Karen, but that was mostly due to the fact that it was their farm and their horses... and unlike him they had been riding for most of their lives.

That did not matter now. All that mattered was that barn and the horses.

Once they came around the last copse of trees, he could plainly see how high the river was. The water was breaching the first and closest wall. Within seconds, they had jumped down from their horses—Derek's knees protesting at the sudden move—and inside the barn.

The sound within was almost deafening. Frightened horses nickered and whinnied, desperate to get out the stalls they knew were now unsafe. The rising floodwater was like a slow rumble as it carved swathes from the ground below the barn, slowly seeping into the barn as it did so.

There was water up around his ankles as he led the horses outside.

Finally, Sheridan yelled, "Just open the stalls and let them run. It's better to let them run free than drown and if we stay any longer we're going to drown too!"

That was an order he was happy to oblige as Derek, Sheridan and Karen ran from stall to stall, opening the doors and guiding the horses out into freedom.

All of sudden, a new sound arose and greeted him—the glorious sound of hooves on dirt as they beat a staccato out into the daylight from the dark of the barn.

After the horses were freed, he rubbed his arms and fell heavily into the water, now knee and almost thigh deep. It was freezing cold and it was then that he realized he had fallen victim to the oldest and deadliest spring threat—hypothermia. "Sheridan!" he called weakly, but his voice was not enough over the sound of the rushing water.

"Is anyone here?" called an unfamiliar voice as a woman came around the bend. "Because if there is we have to—Jesus!"

Whatever this new woman had been about to say was lost to her shock. Derek groaned in appreciation as the woman, despite being smaller than him, hoisted him into a fireman's carry to the dry outdoors. However, that relief was short lived when he felt the still cold wind despite it being the middle of April.

"Someone help me!" called the woman as she laid Derek down on the ground, stripping off his wet clothing.

Derek numbly let the woman strip him something he would not have normally allowed and then, much to his eternal relief blankets still smelling heavily of horse but were still at least dry and warm were draped over and around him. He finally stopped shivering and came around enough to fully notice his own predicament. "Thank you," he breathed out finally. "When I went down I thought that was it."

"It damn near was," said Terrence. "If she hadn't come around just then... dammit... wait, who are you?"

"I should have kept a better eye on things," said Sheridan as they turned to face the newcomer.

"It could have been any of you," she answered. "And I'm Abigail."

With a final creaking rumble, the barn finally let go and slid down into the river to float away like some strange re-enactment of Noah's ark. Without the stone and cement foundation, the structure was flimsy. It quickly broke up into the river and washed away downstream as they all watched.

"Did we get them all in time?" asked Derek.

"Yes," answered Karen. "All fifty."

"That's something at least," he slurred, as he felt himself drifting, suddenly feeling uncomfortable.

* * * * *

A Chinese inspired dragon boat, that was once used in yearly races, finally touched the other shore. The former mayor stepped out of the boat and made her way into the shadow of the buildings that formed Laurentian University. The area surrounding the small cove in the south shore of Ramsey was at the bottom of a set of hills where on top the main part of the university sat.

Not only did it appear to have survived the winter, it showed definite signs of still being in full operation.

Lescelle stepped up beside her, his expression one of surprise. "How is this possible?" he asked.

She shook her head. "I don't know," she answered. "But if they're friendly, I would certainly welcome their inventiveness and ability from keeping this running."

"You won't get any argument from me," he answered.

She stood silent and still where a set of lights formed a crossroad before continuing to a second hospital—one for psychiatric patients—and the university. Given the order in the area, she knew that if the patients in that hospital had been the more violent type then the university would not look as pristine as it did.

Quite frankly she no longer judged things by how they appeared.

The rest of the city had been normal—full of regular people until the law and the ability to uphold it had vanished. Afterwards they had fallen head first into complete and total anarchy. Not just that—it would have been tolerable if a bit chaotic—but also into violent, angry gangs and mobs out for blood for no other reason than to take what the other had.

More worrying was that these scattered gangs had organized and equipped themselves enough to take on and force the police out of their own base. She knew just who had led them too.

Colonel Harnet.

But first they needed to just survive to the next day.

With one final decision made, she walked over to the point and plucked the bull horn out of the boat. "Madam Mayor…" Lescelle ran over to her to stop her but was not fast enough. "No, wait…!"

Even without it at full blast, the opening screech of turning it on was plenty loud. Lescelle got there and plucked it from her hands in turn and asked, "What the hell are you doing?"

"A large risk with a greater gain." She pointed up at the university. "Tell me if that looks like something like our gang would be so inclined to maintain a university—a institution of learning—to almost better it was before everything fell."

He looked where she was pointing and he sighed visibly. Up the sloping curve of the approach they could see a group of people.

The mayor started walking and kept her hands where they could easily be seen so that she would not be perceived as a threat. "Captain, this is where I come in."

Lescelle followed her as she met three others halfway.

"Good morning," she greeted.

"Madam Mayor," said the first one. "I am actually quite relieved to note that you survived the winter. Gives me hope that eventually we can rebuild—if part of our elected leadership still lives."

"It's thanks to these who held to their duty when others fell to chaos... and to others who, while lost, did the same," she answered gravely. "I don't come from a place of strength. In fact, quite the opposite. We were chased out and I think those who covered our escape didn't make it... which means what resources we have are what you see. We came here for sanctuary— unsure if we were even going to find it but to go back is certain death."

The man thought for a moment and looked over at his peers. He held out his hand and she shook it. "Well, you have it. My name is Doctor Kaine, and these are my colleagues Professor Chankrisna Pan and Doctor Nielsine Roy."

"Pleased to meet you..." the mayor answered. "My name is Valeria Piacentini."

* * * * *

The melt had tapered off, but the lake behind the High Falls dam was still higher than normal and the overflow gates still wide open.

Normally, at this time of year, the power generation would still be supplying full power to the grid.

It still was.

There just was nothing at the other end receiving what they generated. Garrett sat in front of the computer screen while stymied by what it was telling him.

No one sat at the other end—the computer and server still threw the same error. Signal left, went down the switch at the mine and then failed to continue from there.

For now, he had the whole system in standby because if he did send authorized power down the line he could do more damage to the grid. Downed power lines suddenly made live again would wreak havoc and be extremely dangerous on top of everything.

He hated to sit still but until someone gave him the all clear he was not going to risk putting people in danger. Mind you—normally—a technician should have thrown the breaker to the off position so that the circuit was not even live if there was any trouble.

But—and this is what concerned him most— if no one was dispatched or knew where to go those circuits were closed, and therefore on.

This was only one of the concerns facing him. The other was the coup on his leadership he was almost certain would happen. Paranoia was not in his nature and he liked to think the best of people.

The fact that it had not yet happened concerned him greatly. If they had changed their minds, then he had wasted entirely too much time worrying about it and that frustrated him. He had other things he could have done rather than constantly look over his shoulder for something that never came.

On the other hand—if they were waiting for him to drop his guard he wished they would just get it over with. He hated trying to outguess their twists in logic in order to be ahead of the game. That was a political game and he hated politics.

With a harrumph he decided that if they were that hell bent on being stupid then that was their problem, not his. He had already wasted enough time on it.

* * * * *

The newcomer stood up and Terrence eyed her cautiously before turning to his wife. "Sheri, she's soaked like the rest of us are. We need to get Derek and all of us back inside."

"Abigail," the newcomer spoke.

Terrence looked back at her and nodded. "Abigail."

There was an awkward silence between the two until Sheridan broke it and said, "Not to break up the romance there, but we have to get Derek back to the house and into something resembling a clinic, now."

"Will be he all right?" asked Marissa, hardly noticing her own shivering.

"So long as we act now…" Sheridan looked up and over to one of the horses. "Someone take the saddle off that horse and bring me the blankets and anything else we can use."

Abigail and Terrence moved to the horses and began unbuckling the saddles.

"Okay, Marissa, help me strip him," said Sheridan.

Marissa looked up in surprise. "Here?"

"Yes here," answered Sheridan. "The wet clothes are actually chilling him further. We need to get him out of them and into the dry blankets."

She took a closer look at Marissa. "How much warmer are you compared to him?"

Marissa shook her head and head out her hands. Sheridan took them and nodded. "Okay, you strip too. Your body heat will help warm him."

Marissa began to strip, not even caring or noticing Terrence was still there. Finally, she was down to her underwear and Sheridan wrapped her and Derek loosely.

"He's freezing," pointed out Marissa.

"Anything else?" asked Sheridan as she checked his eyes.

"I don't think he's breathing too well," she answered, her ear on his chest. "In fact, I'm sure of it."

Sheridan moved quickly to check for herself, first putting her ear to one side of his chest and then to the other. "Terrence, how fast is that sleigh?"

"They said they'd be a few minutes. Nathan needed to be able to get a team and then harness them and he's not as fast as Karen," he answered, kneeling down beside them. "Why?"

"I think he's developing something a bit quick is all," she answered, purposely choosing to not alarm them.

In reality she was very worried. The rattle she could hear and the fact that she could feel his body heat recovering—and rising—was not a good sign. While it could be something as minor as a cold she suspected that it probably was not going to be.

The sleigh finally came over the last hill with Nathan driving. "He learnt well," pointed out Terrence, turning to Karen.

"His mother's son," answered Karen, a small smile on her face.

Nathan clothes threw everyone a dry set of clothes. Those who had not already stripped did so without quibbling over who was there. Sheridan noticed the raised eyebrows from— Abigail, if she remembered correctly—but the woman still stripped down and dressed in the dry clothing brought to her.

Sheridan let out a bark of laughter when she noticed that all Nathan could find was their SCA garb which meant now everyone was dressed as though they had come out of the Middle Ages.

"Was this all you could find?" asked Karen sharply as she pulled the loose under dress and then a unisex T-tunic over her head, cinching it with the belt from her jeans. "Really?"

Nathan sighed. "It was the only thing I could find with any great amount of speed that was not only close at hand could adjust to fit no matter who I was trying to dress... and it still be warm."

"He doth have a point..." Abigail grinned archly as the stares in her direction met with an indifferent shrug. "What?"

"Oh, she fits in here," said Terrence as he looked over at Sheridan.

Sheridan sighed heavily as she directed the two boys to lift Derek up and into the back of the sleigh. They used the straw and a now ample supply of woollen blankets and cloaks to wrap him warmly. Nathan passed her the medical kit from one of the ambulances from the Fire Hall they had raided earlier in the year. "Okay, Nathan, get us back to the house now," said Sheridan. "But be steady about it. We can't afford to jostle him around too much."

Marissa climbed into the sleigh as Nathan led the horses in a loose egg shaped loop so that he could reverse back. Terrence nodded and waved as they headed back to the house. "Are you all right, Reese?" he asked quietly.

"As well as can be expected," she answered, and she glanced over at Sheridan.

She's hovering, realized Marissa. *I've only seen doctors hover when things aren't good, and then they just don't want to tell you that.* "Sheri, truthfully... what did you hear?"

"A rattle," answered Sheridan, shaking her head. "It could be nothing but I'll know more once we get him back to the house."

CHAPTER TWENTY-TWO

Waking was slow and sluggish. And if his head was anything to go by, it was also painful with a side of horrible. Derek's head throbbed and he moaned helplessly. Coughing, he rolled over and tried futilely to ignore the fact that his face was crusted over while his nose was too congested to let him breathe. He did not even want to think about what was running down the back of his throat, but that naturally meant that he did.

He rolled over and thanked the person who was helping him from falling out of his bed and into the bin as he dry heaved and coughed up more of the crap that coated the inside of his lungs.

That same person helped pick up his semi limp form and rolled him onto the pile of pillows, wiping his forehead in the process.

Finally, he gingerly cracked open his eyes to gaze at the face of a very worried Marissa.

"I'd ask how you're feeling, but I can guess," she said softly.

Derek wanted to answer her, but he could only cough and moan.

"Here," Sheridan said, who he had not noticed being present, helping him up as she slid an oxygen mask over his face. "Breathe that— it'll help."

At that moment he did not seriously think anything would, but strangely enough, it did. The taste of it told him it was not entirely just oxygen, but there was a faint tinge of something almost minty and it tasted off. Not bad, but just off. He just could not place what it was.

Whatever it was, it made breathing easier and his head clearer.

"How long?" he croaked through the mask.

"You've been in and out of it for a few days," answered Sheridan. "Acute hypothermia, which made a cold that much worse. You ended up with pneumonia, Derek. I'm treating you for that now and you'll be fine but you'll have to take it easy."

It was then that he realized that he was not even in his own bed — or his own room — but was instead in Sheridan's clinic.

He laid back down again, enjoying the respite that the oxygen laced with whatever she had concocted was giving him from the respiratory hell that pneumonia had caused. He drifted comfortably, not even caring that he fell asleep on any of them. He was dimly aware of a pat on his shoulder meant to be comforting before sliding completely back out again.

His days melded into each other and into a cycle of sleeping, enduring the burning embarrassment of being personally cared for by Emilie, who had taken over the role as Sheridan's head nurse, and periodic checks by Sheridan. He knew he could only expect yet more sleep punctuated by periods of misery brought on by coughing fits that made him feel as if he lungs had been coughed up and lay on the floor beside him.

His recovery took forever — at least that was how it felt to him. Eventually, he was able to hold a conversation without running out of breath or having to cough up his left lung.

Despite this, he was determined to return to something resembling what had become his normal routine.

Sheridan stared at him in disbelief. "You want to hold your morning meeting in here?"

she asked incredulously. "You should be resting."

"I am resting," he maintained. "Look, it'll just be long enough to check on reports and see how they're doing. I won't get up and do anything and we'll keep it short."

"I will allow it, but," she began, holding up a hand as he balked. "You have to hold to my conditions."

"And those are?" he asked, with a sigh.

"One, you don't get to lead these meetings every day... maybe once or twice a week until I'm satisfied with your recovery," she listed. "Two, you limit your meetings to half an hour, or shorter. Three, if I or Em see that you're tiring, you hand over the lead of the meeting to your second and you rest."

Derek did not like those conditions one bit, but he had to admit they were reasonable and fit his current condition. "It'll do," he grumbled, laying back.

He woke again in the afternoon and swore vehemently. Marissa chuckled. "And you were sleeping so peacefully too."

"I had a meeting to run," he answered. "And now I slept through it. They'll be in the field training by now."

"They're doing fine without you—as you trained them to do," she answered. "At least you're doing better. You're actually sleeping instead of that... whatever it was you were in before when your fever was so high. We almost lost you."

He sobered then and realized that he had almost died. If not for Dr. Wither, he would have been dead. Granted, if not for the same doctor he would not have been in this predicament, either. All things considered, he had still been very lucky. "I don't ever want to be in that position again, Reese," he said quietly. "When that water was up to my thighs and I fell into it… and it kept rising and the barn was making this groaning noise… I couldn't even call out loud enough for Sheri or Karen to hear me. It was blind luck that…"

He paused as he realized his memory was unclear on just who it was to pull him out. "Was it Terrence who came looking for me when he did?"

Marissa was quiet. "No, but the person who managed to find you didn't say what made her turn left instead of the right that the girls saw you head in last. She just did and then she happened to turn her head before you went under the water or she would never have even seen you go under. We'd have never found you."

Derek sighed and laid back. "You know me, Reese, I don't subscribe to God, or in Sheri and Terrence's case, Gods…but something was watching me that day."

"Or it was just plain luck," said Terrence as he sat down by Derek's bedside. "How are you feeling?"

"Better than the first time I woke up," he answered truthfully. "Not great, though. Apparently still a long way from back to normal if my random sleeping pattern and raspy breathing is anything to go by."

"Sheri says you have a few weeks, if not months, of recovery to go yet," said Emilie as she came over to check his IV and other tubes. "Okay, everyone out. I have to check him over and there are certain tasks that are best left unseen."

Terrence ushered everyone out. His apologetic shrug was the last thing Derek saw before the other was out of sight.

"When is this going to end?" he asked as he ran a hand down his face.

Emilie glanced at him and the look in her eyes spoke volumes. "You're lucky to be alive, you know."

"I know," he answered as he leaned his head to the side pillow.

To her credit, she was so quick he didn't have time to notice what she was doing. "You would make a good nurse," he pointed out. "I guess that's why you're a paramedic."

She chuckled as she stood up and washed her hands in the sink nearby. "Truthfully I started out as a nursing student, but there aren't enough paramedics either... so I did that instead."

She looked over at Derek, thinking in the prolonged silence from him that he had fallen back to sleep, but he was staring out the window. Emilie had a fair idea what was bothering him.

No one liked to be dependent on another and he was fiercely independent which only made it far worse. Most with his degree of independence were often the crankiest when they fell ill—true terrors within the nursing wards.

Derek was not, although he certainly had his own moments to test their patience, however, they were fewer than others. He swung to the other end of the spectrum which probably meant he was more bothered by the fact he was now a liability—to his own mind, anyway—instead of being out there and doing something useful.

"Can I give you my two cents?" she asked, before she grinned. "Although, given they stopped making pennies before all this went to shit anyway I know just how much my opinion will be worth anyway."

"Never say that," he answered, looking away from the window and back to her.

"You may want to hear what it is first."

She took a breath and continued, "Crap happens to everyone—I wouldn't have had a career picking up the pieces otherwise. And you are bouncing back really quickly. Sometimes getting this sick is a sign that it's time to take a break. Send the kids after any books you want to read and fall asleep with a book on your chest. You can run full tilt later."

"This isn't very relaxing," came his answer.

"Not now it isn't, but you're almost ready to go back to your own bed or at least be down here and not have tubes running everywhere," she pointed out. "In fact—I think—if we can get you standing up today, Sheridan said you could at least have that back."

Derek looked up, his eyes wide and a bit of hope returning to them. "Really?"

"Yes."

He grinned slowly before running a hand down the bottom of his face. "Can I get a shave with that too… perhaps an old fashioned one where I don't have to do it?"

"Oh, now you get demanding," she chided lightly, rolling her eyes before smiling. "Yeah, I think we can arrange that."

* * * * *

Before everything, this room had been a private living room. What some had called her "white room" as everything in here had been white and shades of pale cream. While the windows were not wraparound, it was a place of retreat and serenity after a long day.

It actually faced the front and was only accessible by going through a different room in the central hall between the kitchen and the garage.

Sheridan's personal desk and library were within this space. It was only natural that—due to its proximity to the garage—it would suddenly become her private clinic and sick wards.

It was here that, once everyone had retired for the night, she padded into the room—nodding to Emilie as she did so—to check on her patient.

Derek slept soundly and a quick check revealed that his chest was finally sounding far better than when Abigail had first pulled him out of the flooded barn.

Sheridan allowed herself a moment close her eyes and thank whatever deity for letting her skills save him despite not having everything she would have liked on hand.

She had no idea how she could have lived with herself—as a doctor and the man's friend—if he had died to save her horses

Sheridan was aware of his misgivings about his continued usefulness but the truth of the matter was she had no idea how to do half the things he did. Derek was far more important to all of their continued existence. She hoped he would forgive her for suddenly resembling a helicopter in her desire to make sure he stayed healthy this time.

There was no doubt in her mind that he would find some other way for her to have to use her medical knowledge and probably it would be on him again. However, it did not make her any less determined to make sure he stayed in one piece.

Both Derek and her husband were frustrating in that exact same way. She pulled the blanket up over his shoulders with a satisfied pat and got up to head for her own bed.

Sheridan never did see one eye open and follow her before he closed it again.

* * * * *

With less of a walk and more of a limp, Daniel found himself at the edge of Lake Ramsey. Here, the houses were nothing, but burned out shells and picked over. Nothing remained on this side of Sudbury.

He was not all that surprised — it was not far from the downtown core and easily accessed by the gangs. Once they had picked over the area for supplies, they simply destroyed it. Graffiti littered the walls and streets as testament to his observation.

The dead area made him safe simply because it had already been rejected by anyone still alive. At least the shoreline was reasonably untouched but, with his wounds and the cold water, the lake still had a few spots where ice floated. He had no way of leaving the area.

It was depressing that he would find his end here—with no way to tell his family or friends where to find his bones. Finding him would be like winning the lottery before—rare and not at all likely.

He sat down on one of the blackened rocks.

Unlike what was behind him the view in front of him was gorgeous. The leaves were starting to unfurl which gave the trees the appearance of having tiny green beads at the tips of every branch. The water was a dark slate which also betrayed its current frigid nature. The blackened rocks that surrounded everything—a throwback to when the old mining companies stripped entire region of everything and then the numerous smelters smoked it all out—grounded the picture against the white bark of the birches on the islands that dotted the lake.

It was quiet. Nothing broke the serenity of his surroundings except the occasional bird chirp of what birds had flown back north from where they had spent the winter.

His only regret in dying here was that his daughter would never know what happened to her father. He moved his hand away from his side and noted that the bleeding was as steady as it had been when he was first wounded.

The crackle of his radio coming to life surprised him and it startled the birds into flying away.

"Is anyone reading this frequency?" came a voice through it. "Can anyone hear me?"

It should not have been possible—the portable two-way radio, always affectionately called a walkie-talkie, was secure and meant for police use. Its frequencies required a special scanner to even here, let alone broadcast. Yet someone had—and not just anyone. He lifted his hand to his shoulder where his handset rested. "Lieutenant Wither here," he answered. "Adrienne, good to hear you're still kicking."

"Dan? You're still alive?" came another, far more familiar voice and Daniel started to laugh

Russell had survived. Relief flooded him. Out of everyone he could not confirm as still alive, at least he had one.

"Yeah, but unless I find shelter or something really soon I won't be." He took a breath. "I'm wounded, and I'm at the side of the lake. I'd give you my exact position, but I'm not sure who else might be listening in. Listen—City Hall's gone… the Police Service tower is probably in the hands of gangs. For however long, it stays standing, anyway."

There was a long silence and Adrienne came back. "Then it's best if we keep quiet too. Listen—we know a bit of what went down. I was at my parents' when it happened and by some stretch of luck your brother ended up off the road right by us. You and I know where that is. We headed a bit south of that to a settlement on yet another lake. If you somehow can make it..."

Daniel frowned and looked down at the water. "I don't know if I can but I'll damn well try. Listen if I don't Russ did Sheridan head into the city?"

"No, bro, she didn't. She went home. I'm sure she's in good hands," answered Russell.

Daniel nodded, even though no one was there to see it, "Yeah, I'm sure she is... and will be."

"As soon as you're there Dan?" asked Russell.

Except for the radio, the birds and the lapping of the water on the rocky shores all was quiet.

CHAPTER TWENTY-THREE

Sheridan walked back into the clinic and began her rounds as Derek watched. He did not often get the chance to watch people. A necessary skill as a salesman was being able to read people and to do that required a bit of practice by watching other people.

She was the surest of herself in this environment. He understood why. As a doctor and surgeon her home was a hospital but, unlike a nurse or personal support worker, her job was not to tend to the sick, injured or dying but to fix the problem. Diagnose, identify the issue and then formulate the plan of action to solve it—if it could be solved—or alleviate it as much as possible. Ease it if the worst was expected. The tasks for others were set down by her and followed as if they were law.

And they were... At least here they were but even in a hospital, her orders had to be followed.

Despite this she also had a core of compassion and kindness towards others. She honestly cared about their suffering and well-being, both the physical and the emotional, and always took that into account with her orders.

As a salesman, that had been the easiest part of his pitch when he had first met her. Her father had sent him to her and, at that point, he had no idea she was a doctor and so—since he had been building the company office to begin with—had also gone to meet her with the intent on not only selling her the solar system for her roof but also to see if he could add her to his team.

Selling the panels had been easy... she had already made up her mind that she wanted them before meeting him. However, when he discovered she was a medical doctor, he gave up trying to hire her. She already made more money as a surgeon than he did as a sales manager.

Sheridan had then invited him out to their farm and shown him what she and her husband had in mind which was an entire field of...

"Holy...!" he exclaimed, truncating what he had almost finished with when he saw the younger child sitting on Sheridan's desk while she examined him.

316

Sheridan looked up from the child's throat and over at Derek in puzzlement. "What is it?"

"We've been looking for power and a way to bring back a bit of civilization and it's sitting right under our damn noses!" he answered animatedly. "The solar field!"

"What about what now?" asked Emilie.

The realization was dawning on Sheridan as her face lit up. "By the Gods above, Derek..." she breathed. "I forgot they were even there."

"So did I!" he exclaimed. "We've been too busy surviving to even think about it. The only reason I did was because I've finally had time to stop and think but we could have real power."

"Do we have any way of harnessing it?" asked Emilie.

Sheridan grinned as she lifted the child off her desk. She nodded to child's father and he walked out with his child while shaking his head in amusement. As soon they were out of sight, Sheridan said, grinning. "You bet we do."

"Garrett," answered Derek. "We have Garrett Wither."

* * * * *

It was the sound of someone sitting down in the chair beside his bed that woke Derek from his light doze. Opening his eyes, Derek was relieved to see that Terrence, Rick and Tyrell-were ready to hear what he had in mind.

He took a moment to compose his thoughts while wiping the sleep from his eyes.

"Sorry to wake you," said Terrence. "Sheridan said you wanted to see us as soon as possible. I took that literally."

"She's right," he answered, his voice still raspy from sleep and his illness.

Thankfully, he had been moved to the far more private part of Sheridan's clinic. Instead of being close to her desk and under her direct eye, he now was able to sleep with a room divider between him and the rest of the clinic. Looking around, he noticed his wife was, again, missing. Considering she was now often involved around the farm and the growing town that was popping up around Sheridan's house, he was not all that surprised.

He looked back up at Terrence, then pointed to the pad of paper and a pencil that was just out of his reach and Tyrell handed it over to him. "I forgot about something," he admitted sheepishly. "And I think we all did—given the circumstances and what else has been at the centre of our attention." Terrence was quiet and waited for his friend to finish his thought. "The solar field."

Terrence leaned back in his chair as the realization dawned on him and the other two threw puzzled looks at each other over the head of the seated Terrence.

"The what field?" asked Tyrell.

"We have a field of solar panels in an area of the farm where nothing would grow normally and where the horses can't get good pasture anyway," answered Terrence. "The soil is rocky and destroyed from when it was a golf course way back in the day. Sheridan allowed the area to be used as a cooperative power generation venture—"

"And the company I worked for before all this happened supplied, and installed, the panels for it," finished Derek. "The worst part is that if they haven't been damaged they are still generating power... it's just not going anywhere."

"Wasted potential," said Rick. "Holy mother of God, you mean we could have real electricity?"

"If there's a way to re-route it and use it properly, then yes; our little community could have real power and some semblance of modern civilization," answered Terrence. "We'd need a power line engineer on top of an electrical engineer and I only know of one."

"Karen's Dad," answered Derek grimly. "Someone I didn't see make it here."

"He's a tough son of a bitch," said Terrence. "I have no doubt that he did survive... it's just where we'd find him and if we even manage to find him in the first place."

Everyone looked up at Rick. "Don't look at me... I can help build structure and tell you where you're going wrong if you needed a mine, but as for power lines and power generation? Sorry, man, you're barking up the wrong tree on this one."

"Do you know anyone?" asked Terrence.

"Again, one of the few I know in the area was—as Derek said—Garrett Wither and he was your neighbour, Derek. He'd be clear to the other side of Sudbury and a world away now," he answered and he turned to Tyrell. "What about you?"

Tyrell shook his head. "Not engineers. In a pinch I could suggest a few good electricians... and one fella I knew was part of that mess that killed Helen in the winter," he answered.

Derek leaned back in the pillows. "That's still a good place to start. There'd be tools and equipment we could use."

As he was about to say something else, his lungs decided that this very moment was a good time to act up and throw him into a coughing fit.

Terrence shooed the other two out and grabbed a bucket. It was a good precaution, even if he was not about to throw up he still had so much crap coming out of his lungs. Terrence put it back and a slight crinkle to his nose was the only thing that betrayed him.

Marissa followed Emilie into the room, holding a steaming cup of tea—something he was getting really tired of very quickly even if it did help—out to him. As sick as he was, he still took the cup from her, breathing in the vaguely minty vapour as it eased the spasms in his lungs.

"Better?" asked Terrence.

Derek nodded his thanks. "When did Sheridan say he would be over this?"

"Not for another week," answered Emilie.

* * * * *

Thankfully, the week passed quickly. Derek found that each morning became progressively easier to handle as his breathing became less of a fight.

Once he was helped up the stairs to his shared room with Marissa, he slept far easier. His health steadily improved until finally he was able to get himself dressed and back down the stairs into the living area.

Derek's movement alerted Lorraine. As she noticed his presence, she looked up and smiled broadly. "It's so good to finally see you up and around!" she exclaimed. "How are you feeling?"

"Better, thank you," he answered.

Lorraine handed him a cup of tea.

First my cigarettes ran out in January — thankfully Sheridan and Marissa were patient — now, apparently, it's the coffee. What next?

With an even heavier sigh he accepted the tea. "Thanks Lorraine," he said.

It just did not have the same pickup as coffee did, but he supposed it was better than nothing at all. The warmth of the hot tea really did do wonders for his lungs and throat. He leaned on the bar counter side of the kitchen island while he perched on one of the stools.

It could be worse, he thought. *Far, far worse… but still—it's like every day we run out of something else. It's a game of 'what next?'* What they had now needed to be either found and scavenged or built from scratch. *Not just of 'what's next to run out' but what's next for me? For Reese, and the others?*

Old roles and jobs in their former lives held little to no meaning.

Life was quickly being utterly and completely rewritten, and it had not even been four months since civilization fell.

That still bothered him intensely.

He was a man who liked to know where he stood and why he stood there. Not knowing for certain why civilization fell ate at him in a way that he could not fully explain—it just did. *Derek, you really don't need to know why. It just bugs you that your life changed and you need something to quantify it—but that's just it.*

Where do I fit in in all this? Money doesn't exist anymore. Everyone just asks for what they need—no one needs a bit of convincing.

It was the other reason that being so ill had greatly upset him to begin with.

I could go into Sudbury itself—there has to be some place that has some clue as to why we're all sitting here wondering what to do next. Why did our own government leave us to fend for ourselves... and what can we do to move on...

...Not to mention I'm pretty sure I could find something in the city we could use, and maybe that will make all the difference. He honestly did not think it would but he was feeling a familiar itch on the bottom of his feet to do something.

Marissa came down shortly after he did and sat down beside him, watching him drink his tea while leaning his head on his crossed arms. She laid a hand on his neck and he looked up and sideways at her. "You look like you're tired again."

"I think I am," he admitted. "Getting up, dressed and down the stairs on my own took everything I had."

"Why don't you sit on the couch in front of the fire for a bit and see if you can get a second wind?" asked Marissa.

Derek got up, and was a bit alarmed at the slight wobble to his knees. Getting down here had taken more of out of him than he thought it would and now he suspected his recovery was going to be rather protracted. He made his way over to the couch and slid into the cushions Sheridan had bought a few years ago. It was one that had an extension that turned one end of it into a settee so he could stretch out his legs and lie down without taking up the entire couch. The fire crackled pleasantly as he put his feet up.

Lying on the settee he stared up at the beams that cris-crossed the cathedral ceilings and around at the internal breezeway on the second floor which connected the two halves of the manor house.

With a sigh, he let the snap and pop of the fire lull him down into an early morning nap as Marissa threw a furry throw blanket over him. Things would be picking up later and the sleep would help him regain his strength for keeping up with the meetings he would soon find himself running.

CHAPTER TWENTY-FOUR

With a sigh, Derek rolled over and found he was no longer alone in the living room. When he had settled down for some light reading he had been alone. No meetings were planned that day so the living room was now just a common area. It was no longer a private living area but more of a comfortable community meeting place where town meetings were now held.

Other times people just spent what little free time they could here while Lorraine would hum and go about her business making sure they had light nibbles and never ending tea.

Sheridan's living room had become the central cafe of their swiftly developing town and

Lorraine ran the kitchen. Derek could see that this did not bother the older woman one bit. But Lorraine—being raised on a farm before working as a professional cook for mining and other work camps before 'retiring' to raise three sons and numerous foster children—was at home running all this. If she needed something by way of supplies—and those supplies were available— she had them.

It was a very homey and welcoming 'cafe' and reminded him far more of those old style Irish or English inns on the road—the ones always seen in movies or television. Given Lorraine was Scottish—with a great deal of English—by descent she was in her element. If someone came by for dinner it was whatever she had cooked that day. The days of the short order were now dead and gone. Lorraine spent the entire day in that kitchen making what would become the evening meal and also making sure it was enough to feed anyone that happened by.

What rooms on the main floor that once were private like the living room now were semi-public and their original purpose lost to whatever they needed now. To the right and closet to the front doors was Sheridan's examination office and clinic. This took up the entire south side of the house, including the entrance from the double sided garage.

To the left were various rooms where people could meet. One had become a sort of war room with a table top model overlay set up to look like the immediate area using modelling foam and wood. Maps of the area, what ones they had found or had drawn, were pinned up on the walls. Another one of those rooms was a library full of books that Sheridan and Terrence did not mind sharing. Immediately beside that was a room that really did not have a set use outside of a private meeting room or a quiet place to read and study.

However, today those he needed to talk with had decided to hold their meeting in the common area. Perhaps it was so that he did not have to move himself out of his warm cocoon. No matter what their reason, right now he did not care why they had decided to sit around the fire so long as he did not have to move.

"Good morning, Derek," said Rick. "You look a hell of a lot better than you did a few days ago."

"I feel it," he answered. "Better, but not right, yet."

"Sheridan did say it would be a few weeks to a few months, so you're doing well," said Terrence and then he motioned to the others. "I filled in what I could but we all agree that the only way to do this properly, without causing major damage to the panels or the lines, is by finding someone who knows what they're doing."

"I had the feeling that was the case," mused Derek, scratching his chin.

* * * * *

A few weeks later Derek followed Sheridan into her makeshift office and examination room. He hopped up onto the sturdy oak table and opened his shirt. He had a few layers on but thankfully she only ever needed to see the inner layer.

Sheridan stood for a moment, observing him as he sat on the table. "You haven't experienced any shortness of breath?" she asked. "No chills or other signs of illness?"

"Nope," he answered.

"All right," she acknowledged said as she rubbed the contact of her stethoscope to ease the coldness he might feel. "Breathe in as deep as you can and hold it."

"Okay, you can put your shirt back down," she advised at the end of the examination.

He settled his clothing back comfortably and buttoned up his shirt. "Well?" he asked.

"As far as I can see you've recovered, but the only way to really tell would be a chest x-ray," she answered.

"Which we can't do without the machine," he mused.

"Or some way to calibrate it," she confirmed.

"That reminds me—I was thinking about heading towards Sudbury on some reconnaissance. See if I could find anything useful or any news of what might have happened... maybe some neighbours to trade with."

"I don't know, Derek," she sighed. "You have a valid idea, but to head off on your own this soon after recovering from something that could have killed you? I know Marissa would have your head."

"She knows what I'm intending," he answered. "She knew before I got sick that it would eventually come to this."

"How about you give it another few weeks for the ground to dry up a bit and not be so mushy?" asked Sheridan. "It would also give your lungs more time to recover and your body to get back to what it was before you fell ill."

He nodded in agreement. "All right, all right, I'll give it another week or so—so long as I can start training my people again!"

"On the front steps, yes," conceded Sheridan. "Not in the bush... not for another few days."

* * * * *

"After months of waiting, you finally did something stupid, old man," came the voice behind Garrett.

Garrett closed his eyes and sighed as he turned and stood to face the three men who joined him over the spillway. One of the men was part of the original three but the other two were new. "I was wondering when you'd finally get around to it."

He turned to walk away and noticed that on the other side of the dam were another three on the other side, this time it was the other two plus another. This other surprised him—it was Dane, the young man from the offices that had always been so helpful.

So damn nosey, now that he thought about it. "Well, I'd be surprised but now that I think of it I'm not," said Garrett.

"Sorry, old man, but this new world belongs to the young and you did say you didn't really want leadership," Dane answered. "Kill him."

Bracing himself and lifting his hands in defense, Garrett was ready for the first one. He knew one would be impatient. Old man, indeed. He may have more years on him but he was far from old—and if they had tried that with his father the results would have been more than amusing.

Garrett was his father's son.

It did not take long for the first one to come in swinging the rebar and Garrett sidestepped him. Grabbing him by the scruff of his neck, Garrett yanked hard, pulling him off balance and into falling back.

He sidestepped again, grabbing the rebar from his hands as he pin wheeled and gave the man a further push off the dam and to the shorter drop off the deeper end.

The problem for the man now off the dam was that the sluice ways and spillways were in the full open. He was sucked through them in less than a second with no time to take a breath or to scream.

Garrett tapped his bar against the ledge while the others hesitated. "There's one... I did tell you that if you came after me you were goin' for a swim."

"He's one man against five of us... rush him!" yelled his former assistant, Dane.

Taking a short moment to point, Garrett shouted at Dane, "And you're fired!"

With a roar of rage, Garrett swung the metal bar with both hands, catching the first man in the side of the head. Blood sprayed in an arc and bits of grey splattered as he fell in at heap at Garrett's feet, making the others hop awkwardly to avoid him.

In a single handed back swing, Garrett caught another attacker in the face, breaking his nose and knocking him off the shallow part that gave High Falls its name. He screamed all the way down until he landed on the rocks below.

With his off-hand he grabbed a handful of the last one's left jacket front and tossed him off his feet and over his friend on the walkway where he landed on his rear. He scrambled back in a blind panic, realizing that he was slipping in his friend's blood and bits of brains.

The remaining two managed to bodily hold Garrett and lift him up and over the edge of the dam. Finally, able to regain his feet, Dane got up as he breathed heavily. "Throw him over."

For a moment all, Garrett felt was that sick feeling of weightlessness. Despite what he felt, reality would have told him that there was no long moment of hanging in the air motionless before he felt himself actually falling over the high side of High Falls, down the nearly one hundred feet to either the rocks, or the still icy water below.

* * * * *

It could have just as easily been the south shore of Lake Ramsey. While he did not have his brother's same gift with paints, or his other brother's gift with photography, Russell found words to be his art. He had no idea if Daniel had looked on the same scene as he now did.

He lived on a south shore and a brother died on a north shore.

They could have been the same lake and it still would not have mattered. With how quickly it happened even if they had been able to get across and been on the same lake all he could have done was see to his brother's burial. The only grace he had was being there—even if over a radio— so he was not alone.

I have no idea if I'll ever see Sheridan, or anyone else, again and I have no idea how long the radios will last… For all I know I'm the last of my brothers.

Adrienne came out and sat beside him on the rocks. Here the stones were shades of greys and pinks—sometimes even the quartz within made veins of white. The soot of the earlier smelter stacks had, for some reason, never quite stained the area around Long Lake as dramatically as it had closer to the core of the city.

Russell was a bit surprised when she leaned her head on his shoulder in silent support. Adrienne knew his pain—had already experienced the sharp sting of loss this winter— and instead of falling head first into it came to him in comfort.

His arm wrapped around her back and she leaned in closer as he drew in a shuddering breath.

"I'm sorry," she said.

Russell blinked before responding. "So am I. You knew him—worked with him. Were friends, by the sound of it."

"Well, working friends," she answered as she sat back up. "We didn't run in the same social circle outside of work. He was your brother."

"I feel as if I saw the glimpse of hope only to have it snatched away again," he said and then laughed. "He said I always had the touch of poetry. I don't feel much up to it now."

"Then don't," said Adrienne.

He pulled her back to leaning again him, resting his chin on top of her head. "Thank you," he whispered.

No reply was needed as they both sat in silence, sharing the emotion.

CHAPTER TWENTY-FIVE

It was a warmer morning than most, and this boded well for the weather. Granted, Derek had plainly seen the wall of snow and ice quickly disintegrate due to the melt. he ground was still soft, wet and mushy in the bush which made training his people that much more difficult.

Everyone was muddy, wet and cold and Derek knew they weren't happy about it. "All right, we're back," he said as he kicked the mud off the bottom of his boots.

"I wonder if Lorraine has a fresh pot of tea on," mused Abigail, who had since become one of his Seconds, or second-in-command.

His other Second, Gina, had already 'graduated' to leading her own teams and had not made it back yet as fare as he could tell.

"Clean up in the barn and I'll go check," answered Derek.

The forlorn group moved off towards the barn as Derek scraped off the dried and caked on mud from the leathers before moving into the inside foyer. He normally would use the mud room—which, given the weather right now, was now very aptly named—instead of the main front entrance. But they had always met on the wide stone steps leading into the house. He, however, did not move past that point, waiting until one of the girls that now worked within came by. "Hi, could you get Lorraine for me?" he asked.

"Yes sir!" she answered before running off. "Lorraine!"

"I could have done that," Derek mused as Lorraine came around the corner. "Lorraine! Tell me you have some tea on."

"I do," she answered. "Good heavens, Derek, what happened?"

"It's messy out there," he answered.

"Ah, Derek, just the person I'm looking for," said Sheridan as she walked down the stairs and she stopped once she caught a better look at him. "What in the name of hell happened to you?"

"Don't ask. I'll wait until we're altogether so I don't have to repeat it." he answered, shaking his head. "What did you need?"

"Has anyone checked the roads east?" she asked.

"I'm heading that way soon," he answered. "Right after I'm sure that the others can fend for themselves. Do you need me to look for something specific?"

"The usual," she answered.

With Sheridan it always came down to the same thing—medical supplies. Thankfully they had not needed to test what limited capability their little clinic had but Sheridan was determined to make sure they were well prepared. He was very inclined to favour her determination but he had another reason to head out in the next few days.

Certain other supplies were running low and he also wanted to see for himself what had become of the city to their east. He dreaded to think of what he could find given that no one had tried to contact them or come out this far since Christmas more than four months ago.

It had only been two weeks since he finally had a clean bill of health from Sheridan. He followed her into her office and hopped up onto the table to let her examine him.

Twenty minutes later Derek walked up the stairs, noting that his energy levels were by far better than they had been in the recent weeks.

He could still feel Sheridan's gaze on his back but he felt back to normal. The door to his and Marissa's room closed behind her and she leaned on the wall.

"I am better," he said before Marissa had a chance to even ask him.

"I know you're better," she snorted as she rolled her eyes. "I had thought we agreed that you would be more—theoretical rather than practical for the time being."

"Well, we did," he said. "I'm fine, Reese."

"You feel absolutely fine?" she asked again, warily. "No rasping, coughing or difficulty breathing? No sign of a sore chest?"

"Not one bit. I'm cold though, and I'd like out of these clothes," he answered.

"Oh, sorry, by all means!" she moved out of the way as he walked into the ensuite.

He wasted no time in peeling off the wet layers and carefully laying them to the side where they would not make more of mess than he had already made by walking up here in the first place. A hot bath immediately preceded by a hot shower would have been stellar, but without electricity there was no hot water or any way to pump it up from the supply.

Thankfully, many of the homes in the area were independent of the city water and sewer. Getting to the rest of normal living would hopefully be as simple as priming pumps and turning them all back on. Once they had power.

He also knew better than to expect it to be that easy.

Getting the power was the issue.

It was then that he noticed that the outside was almost dark and grey, but the house was brightly lit. He looked up at the light on the ceiling that he had flipped on without a second thought when he came out from the ensuite, his mouth dropped open in shock and he started to laugh. Wrapping a towel around himself, he ducked his head outside the door.

"Reese, how did they get the power back on?"

Marissa looked at him, smiling. "They may not have an electrical engineer to get the solar field up and running, but there are still panels on the roof that only need an electrician to flip a switch, I guess. Tyrell has a few of them working for him, so they turned the power back on. It's only for so long, though. Just enough to turn the inside of the fridges and freezers cold and heat up the water in the tanks. Terrence had everything insulated twice-over so that when the power goes back off we aren't left without."

"I can take a hot shower then?" he asked gleefully.

"A short one, but yes," she answered with a chuckle. "Hang on, I'm joining you. No sense wasting the water."

The short reprieve of real and working electricity ended not even two hours after all of

Derek's scouts had their chance to finally enjoy hot showers. The tanks were then given a chance to fill and heat up again.

Knowing that the various fridges and freezers were up and running again made the worry of how to store fresh food lighter. Life still had not completely returned to normal; he couldn't open or close the fridges freely without losing the cool within. The storage concerns had been mostly alleviated.

Derek and his various scouts sat around the large dining room table on the main floor of the house. Maps of the region were scattered around the table for them to look through.

Sudbury had not been a small city before everything came to a crashing halt. The people and neighbourhoods nestled anywhere houses could be built in between the craggy mountains, dips in the valleys, and in between the numerous fresh water lakes, swamps and rivers that made up the area. Also the natural challenge was it was firstly, and fore mostly, a city completely based off of the mining industry which meant there were also numerous mines, smelters—and tailing ponds—around the city.

This made for some interesting navigation issues especially if they were trying to get from one end of the far end of the region to the other while on foot or on horseback.

"So, who's taking horses and who isn't?" asked Abigail.

Abigail was an interesting woman to say the least. She had not come from within their community but from outside it. Derek was partial to her and was more than willing to admit that it was because she had saved his life from drowning in the river. Since being sick, he had not had a real chance to really get to know her outside of the fact that her survival skills were on a par with his.

Her sales skills were abysmal, but that was not surprising given that she was not into sales at all—even before the end of civilisation. Abigail had been a bush pilot grounded by the ever-increasing price of fuel to get her planes and helicopters in the air. It was clear that she strongly preferred to be in the bush and only came to the city to resupply or pick up passengers to fly them further north or into other, more remote, locations.

"Depends on comfort and riding level," he answered. "I won't make anyone ride a horse if they can't ride. We'll just get them to keep closer to the farm. But anyone who wants to come with me should be a fairly proficient rider."

"You're not leaving me behind," said Marissa.

Abigail put up her hand. "Nor me."

He nodded and looked around. "Anyone else?"

The others shook their heads and opted out. "All right." He leaned back and crossed his arms.

"I won't push but I wouldn't mind knowing why."

"I suck at riding," admitted one of them sheepishly.

"Scared of horses," admitted another.

He looked around at the other two who had not answered and could see why. They were of that age where travelling a great distance and roughing it on top of everything was not the most comfortable prospect. Every now and then with the opportunity to be able to retreat back to someplace warm, dry and with a soft bed... that was more to their liking.

Sheridan was looking at him like he should perhaps think along the same lines.

But he just couldn't. Not yet.

He had to know what brought all of this down for his own curiosity and the only way he could ever find out was by heading straight to Sudbury and to one of the news studios. He knew this was dangerous as it meant going straight into what had once been the centre of the city to the CBC radio station. He looked over at his wife Marissa who had no idea what it was he was planning to do and for a moment he felt a bit guilty.

There was no question about just how dangerous what he wanted to do was. There were three locations that he wanted to gain access to that he had a sneaking suspicion would have the answers he needed and they were all downtown.

The first one was the CBC radio station. All national, regional and local news went through there first. If anyone had heard anything about anyone that would be the first place to check. The problem was that the CBC station, and office, was located almost in the dead centre of the city's downtown core. He would have to negotiate a sizable distance on foot if he had any chance of getting in, and back out, alive if those who survived had become less than hospitable.

There was a chance—albeit minute—that those who survived were friendly. All he had to do then was make polite contact but reality was that likely those who survived were not the friendly.

The other two places he figured the information he wanted could be was City Hall— also downtown and not that far from the CBC— and just maybe within the Ontario Shared Services office inside the downtown mall.

The problem was that they were all downtown.

While cutting through the centre of the city would shorten their trip, it was still far safer to go around the city rather than through it. It was also far more likely that there were friendlier settlements of survivors than in the core of the city.

One such route was drawn on the map in erasable marker on the plastic sheet overlaid it. The route followed the old highway between Panache Lake Road and Copper Cliff. It was one thing to say they were riding to Copper Cliff but a whole other to look at it on the map and realize that that one part was likely going to take a few weeks. They had over fifty kilometres to traverse and the terrain would not be easy—nor would they be able to do this quickly.

Half of the journey would be just to get to Lively. With a sigh he realized that this expedition would probably be turned back at Lively and Copper Cliff.

But they still had to try. He would not simply throw his hands up into the air and give up on it. They just had to agree on how they were going to do this.

"I say this first trip takes us to see what we're up against," suggested Abigail, voicing his concern. "Once we have a real idea of what's out there we can properly gear up and really attack whatever it is you feel we need to find on the other side of town."

Marissa nodded her agreement.

With a sigh, Derek nodded his agreement. Being stupid about things never got anything accomplished. Usually, quite the opposite, if it did not simply result in someone's death. "All right, so, now that's settled what about our route?"

"Most direct path to Lively is through Whitefish," answered Abigail. "And, take my word for it, there's nothing up that way. At least I didn't see anything on my way down the river. Even the reserve was quiet."

"We should tell Sheridan that," said Marissa, looking at Derek. "She's been worried sick about her Aunt and no one has been able to get over there to check on that half of her family and no one came from there to us…"

Marissa paused, chewing on her lower lip. Derek knew she was remembering the winter and their discoveries of the people within houses who had simply frozen to death. He had no doubt they would find more death within any other homes they happened across. It was by pure luck that they had even managed to survive the winter.

"—And what?" asked Abigail.

"Did you go into any of the homes you came across on your way down the river?" asked Derek.

"A few," she answered and then she turned somber herself. "Oh."

The other scouts wandered off, leaving the three with the longest and more organized trek to plan their expedition. Some did not wander too far, ending up at the counter for Lorraine's tea.

"I realize it doesn't need to be said, considering the present company," said Derek.

"But supplies... what are we taking and what are we leaving behind?"

"If we're taking horses we need to think about their needs as well," pointed out Marissa.

Derek nodded in response. "I had remembered that. Considering the length of the trip, I think we need to pack as if we're camping with horses. A good tent with a rain cover that can serve as our camouflage to hide our camp. Cooking and water purification..."

"Goes without saying," agreed Abigail.

He nodded and then sighed. "All right then. Let's start packing what we'll feel we'll need in the garage. Lay out where we have space and where it won't get disturbed and start packing it up."

* * * * *

The little community centre just across the road from the shore of Long Lake was full to the brim with people that day. Russell and Adrienne sat near the back and watched.

"I say we should still decide things democratically," pointed out an older man loudly. "Who cares if the outside world isn't. Doesn't concern us!"

"What if we're overruled?" shouted another.

"We're still our own damn town—capable of deciding what goes on here!"

The argument devolved into bickering and Adrienne sighed, standing up and wading between them in order to break it up. Russell lost sight of the finer details of how she did it but the two were quickly pulled off as she stood in between them.

"Are you two seriously arguing over that?" she asked. "Grow up. We know we're our own town, and being overruled is a puerile reason to worry about a democratic vote. Just shut up and do it… and if you're so determined to lead, put yourself forward as a candidate."

They grumbled as they moved off to the side.

A tall man came up and said, "Thank you, young woman."

"You're welcome."

Moments later Russell pushed through the crowd, whooping with joy as he did so. Adrienne and the tall man stared at him.

"Russ—I'm glad to see that you're alive," the tall man grinned.

"Uncle Kirk," breathed Russell. "I had given up hope of seeing family again."

Adrienne looked from one to the other and then asked, "You two know each other?"

"This is my Uncle, Kirk McTaggert… he's the one that lives near the Four Corners."

Adrienne made the connection immediately and smiled, shaking Kirk's hand. "As in the uncle you were trying to get to?" she confirmed, and he nodded.

"Any chance you know if anyone else made it?" asked Kirk.

Russell's smile slipped and Adrienne looked down and away. Kirk immediately sighed and closed his eyes. "Who?"

"Daniel," answered Adrienne. "We managed to raise him by radio a few days ago but he died—we think—while we were still talking to him. He... he said he had been at City Hall and he asked about Sheridan."

Russell looked around but he didn't see anyone with Kirk that he could recognise. "What about you?"

Kirk shook his head. "Your aunt didn't survive the winter, and your cousins... well, I know where one could be, but I have no idea if he managed."

"Which one?" asked Russell.

"Oh, Brant went over to the university. When the weather turned really bad he decided to stay there since the para-buses... or any buses... were not running," he answered and sighed. "As for my other two sons... I have no idea."

* * * * *

Evenings were turning into a relief instead of the harrowing worry of how they were to survive the night. Did they have enough heat to make it through? Would someone die of hypothermia… or worse yet suffocation in the effort to stay warm enough to live?

Finally, as the days grew longer and warmer the evenings did as well.

Despite the lack of light, dawn and twilight had become Karen's favourite times of day. They were when she could get the most work done while no one was in her way and the horses were neither too warm nor too cool.

The barn closest to the house was where Sheridan had ordered all the best horses—and the breed her farm was famous for—to be moved to. The outlying barns were reserved for horses and other livestock that they happened to find or had been originally boarded there.

It was not as if the owners were going to suddenly return one day.

This barn held the horses that Sheridan decreed would carry her calvary and knights, if such a time came to pass. Terrence was adamant they needed a trained fighting horse—a horse bred for war with a steady, intelligent mind and fit body to carry an armoured fighter on its back.

It was an unfortunate necessity to even entertain it.

With a sigh, she ended up at the end of the row and walked over to the stall, running her hand along the horse's neck as he leaned into her touch. If Sheridan needed these gentle creatures to be turned into war horses Karen did so under protest, and conversely with great pride.

If any horse was well suited for these demands, it was those she currently cared for.

This was just the tip of the iceberg... Karen had still not heard from anyone. Her father— now the first priority for everyone because of his usefulness—was at least on everyone's minds because of how much they needed him here.

"Hi," came a soft voice from behind her.

Karen turned and blinked in surprise as Jeremy walked in behind her and rubbed a hand on the neck of the horse she was grooming. "What brings you out here?" asked Karen.

"My wife does," answered Jeremy. "It's late and she should be in the house... perhaps even in bed."

"I have to take care of the horses."

"They're already taken care of fine enough," he pointed out, and when she rolled her eyes and turned back to the horse he sighed heavily. "Derek is going through Coniston, you know."

Karen turned her head so that she could see him through her peripheral vision. "He is?"

"Yeah, while they didn't expressly state they were looking for Michael and Shiloh, he did state that since they were in Coniston anyway..."

"So they haven't forgotten about my brother and his kids," she mused.

"Hardly," answered Jeremy. "Yes, your Dad being found and brought back is incredibly important to our survival but family is still family."

"Good," she breathed. "I'm glad."

"Now will come back into the house and return to the land of the living?" he groused.

"Once I'm done. I did kind of mean that I have to take care of this big fella here and then I'll come in," she answered.

"So long as you actually do come in."

"I am," she retorted, throwing a bit of water in his direction.

He dodged out of the way easily, and the horse nickered warningly, stamping his own foot in protest at the sudden activity around him. Karen rubbed his nose in reassurance, noting that he still looked mostly sleepy and disinterested. "Then what was the stomp about, eh?" she asked the horse.

He simply pushed her with his head into Jeremy and the two fell sideways into the wall before blowing out a breath with his nose. "I think I like his idea," pointed out Jeremy.

"Great, Sheridan has a matchmaking horse," groused Karen, and then she sighed as Jeremy helped her back up to her feet. "Go on, Jer, I'll be up as soon as I finish with him."

Jeremy snorted in amusement before he turned and left the barn. Karen looked at the horse in the eyes. "Okay, Mr. Big Ideas. I get the point. I'll finish what I was doing and let you go to bed… and I'm off to my own after."

The horse only continued to munch on his oats.

CHAPTER TWENTY-SIX

Derek paced one way and then the next as he looked over what they had managed to pull together over the past few days. "Did I hear correctly that you were planning a serious expedition into Sudbury?" asked Terrence as he walked in and noticed the supplies laid out on the garage floor. "Apparently it's no rumour."

Derek shook his head, but other than that did not answer his friend as he returned to his list, checking what was on the floor against it. Terrence watched Derek, sighed once, and left Derek to his inventory.

I've lost him, realized Terrence. *Once he's out there there's a good chance with the way the world is now that I won't see any of them again.*

Terrence stopped and looked out the window, past the paddocks and the horses to the solar field beyond. *We need that field up and running, though*, Terrence groaned and ground the heel of his hand into his forehead. *I don't know if anyone else could attempt this—he knows Garrett, he knows where to find him… and he's got his own reasons to go back there.*

No one else can *do this.*

When he opened his eyes he noticed his wife staring at him. "What is it?" she asked, her voice quiet.

"Derek is in the garage taking stock of what's now in there for that expedition of his," answered Terrence, another sigh escaping him. "Once word got out that he was even making serious plans for an expedition to Sudbury the Rangers, my militia, and even our civilians gathered anything they could scrounge up. I don't think he'll be able to use or take it all, but at least he should have first pick of what's available."

"He's planning on selecting only what he can use," she answered, tilting her head and laying a hand on her husband's elbow. "Everything else goes to the other Rangers. Tyrell is planning on taking some of that and whipping something up that will be specific to their core."

"Well, that's something at least," Terrence relented, but he shook off his wife's hand and pointed to the garage. "I can't help but have a bad feeling about this. I don't want him to go — but at the same time I know I can't keep him here without locking him in the basement."

Sheridan snorted. "And he'd hate you for it."

"I know," answered Terrence.

"Then why aren't you out there helping him?" she asked. "If you're so sure you won't see him again, why don't you spend what little time you believe you have left at least making his job easier?"

Terrence sighed again, but turned on his heel and returned to the garage where he found Derek still organizing what he was planning to take with him. Terrence paused, and held his breath for a moment.

"If you think you've snuck up on me, you're wrong," said Derek, although he sounded muffled as his attention was focussed on the contents of one of the bags. The older of the two men looked up, "What is it?"

"Did you need a hand?" asked Terrence.

Derek lifted an eyebrow and his eyes lost focus for a second. "I'm sorry?" he asked finally, confused.

"A hand... some help... you know—figuring out what you're taking and then packing it up?" asked Terrence again, slowly.

"I'm not seven," came Derek's sharp reply, and then he huffed. "Sorry, you know how much I hate this part of getting ready for anything."

"That I do," mused Terrence. "I'd offer you a coffee, but I have a feeling that's the other part of why you're taking a wander."

Derek snorted, and then laughed. "You'd be right."

"So... what's the first thing on your list to find?" asked Terrence, looking around.

"A good tent—large enough to comfortably sleep at least three, and if the weather turns rotten can be comfortable to spend time in unless we find other shelter," answered Derek. "Thinking of one of those rapid pop-up multi-room things, if I can find one, plus a large tarp to go over it and extend past it... that way we're dry, and our horses are too. Maybe even our cooking area."

"I have one of those—Sheri bought it for going to the SCA with. It's big enough to house the both of us, her Dad, another couple we always went with... and it has this common room in the middle that's big enough to walk around in. It pops up easy and then folds down small enough to fit into the back of her car... the Smart, not my truck."

Derek spun around on one foot to face Terrence. "Where the hell are you hiding that?" Derek then blinked as he thought about it and laughed. "Let me guess, the same room you pulled my armour from?"

Terrence nodded, and then said, "In fact, you might want to check in there for anything else you think you might need. While we like historical re-enactment, Sheridan didn't like sleeping in the wet, the cold… or on the ground. Most of it came from that big camping and fishing supply place down in Vaughan… the one you can see off the 400."

Derek grinned, knowing exactly what store Terrence meant. "Well, that will make life a bit better out there."

* * * * *

Twilight held more than simple darkness now. The roads became darker than pitch, and no one had reason to be out there other than the Rangers.

As the sun went down it became progressively harder for Derek and Marissa to pack. Finally, with a heavy sigh, Derek said, "We can either turn on a light, or light some candles… or we can call it for the night and just go to bed."

Marissa shrugged, sliding her pack off the bed and onto the bench that sat at the foot of the bed. *Well, that was a decisive answer*, he chuckled as he did the same. "Everything all right?"

"Derek?"

"Yes?"

"Shut up and come to bed."

He looked up at the ceiling, although he knew she could not see him, and said, "Just a second."

Making sure what he packed was not about to fall and force him to repack everything, he carefully moved his pack over to lean against a chair before sitting on the edge of the bed.

As he stared out the window and to the sky, he felt her tug at the buckles and fastenings of his armour. "I didn't realise there were so many modern clips and buckles to this," said Marissa. "What are you thinking?"

"That not six months ago all I had to do to even go to bed was fall into it," he answered. "Now I have not only clothing but the armour I wear out of habit… and the weaponry."

"Which, and I'm going to thank you for this, you had the wisdom not to bring to bed with you," she answered.

"It has its own maintenance and that is better done where the tools are," he answered, shrugging off the first layer of armour as he helped her with the second. "Do you think we packed enough?"

A snort was his answer. "You pack like you always did for one of your trips into the bush—with just as many spare sets of socks."

"Can't have too many dry socks," he grinned as he turned his head.

Despite the sun being down and the room lit only by the stars and the moon, he could see her clearly enough. Once the last of his armour fell to the floor, he pulled at her hands until she sat beside him on the edge of the bed and she leaned her head on his shoulder.

"Do you think we'll make it back there?" she asked.

"We have to," he answered, frowning. "We can't make that field work for us if we don't find someone that can make it work. We may find someone else—but I'd still like to find Garrett… and I'd still like to get some things from our house."

"Same here," she answered.

"I wouldn't worry too much about it," he said, with a small shrug. "We're more than prepared to make it there, and back. If we avoid the city we won't run into anything major—and maybe we'll even meet a few other communities like ours."

"And once we get back to Garson?"

"We get what we want and need and we get our asses back here," he answered, and his eyes widened slightly.

After all we've been through, all that time… the mortgage and the payments… and I just gave up on my own house in order to return here, he thought to himself. *Have I changed so much in less than six months?*

"What about our house?"

"I… just had the same thought," he answered, and then he shook his head. "But, with the choice in front of us, which would you rather? Family or the house?"

"Family, any day," she conceded.

"Then we're decided," he said.

She nodded as she leaned into him again, and he held her tightly. There was one thing he knew that she did not… and to be able to return home would mean the difference between leaving a message for their children—who had not been expected back home this year—on where to find them and that they were still alive.

That was supposed to be my surprise for New Year's, he thought. *But that went so far sideways that even if Felicia or Alexander made it up here that they won't know where to look… but if they stuck around the area then maybe—just maybe—we'll find them or be able to leave something to tell them where to come and find us.*

And then we really will have all our family in one place…

… I hope.

* * * * *

Derek kept looking over at Abigail, back to Marissa and back to Abigail again. Marissa watched him, smirking a bit as she did, as she shook her head at his confusion.

Abigail is… she is definitely different, mused Marissa as she watched her husband falter every time he caught sight of the young woman.

It was easy to see why Derek was so caught off guard. *He's still not quite resigned to the new way of life*, realized Marissa. *He keeps expecting everything to return to normal—and this one to end without warning the same as the other did.*

Abigail had already accepted her new life and it was plain as she was a walking arsenal of weapons. She still, even then, took two machetes and two hatchets and strapped them to her hips and back.

Abigail looked over at Derek and, with a lopsided grin, said, "I still think you're going a bit light."

"I agree with you," said Derek. "I just haven't got to the full weaponry yet."

"You didn't think we were letting you three go on your own, did you?" asked David as he walked in with Emilie, the both of them already packed and ready to go.

"I was a bit worried that we were," answered Marissa. "Glad to have you with us."

"I need to find out what happened. If you're going anywhere near the core of the city, then there's a good chance we'll run into a detachment that still has a few good cops in it," David said, with a shrug. "Someone will know if there's anything... anyone... left in charge of this mess."

"Like Reese said, glad to have you with us." Derek nodded up to Emilie. "Em, you sure?"

"Dr. Wither has enough with the other nurses she's managed to train," Emilie answered. "You'll need me more out there and I need to know what happened too."

"All right then," said Derek. "Lay out your things and let's get ready to go."

"When are we leaving?" asked Emilie.

"Tomorrow morning," he answered.

* * * * *

The next morning was like deja-vu. Derek and Marissa walked around the front of the house, leading their horse as they did, the others also going with them not far behind. Terrence and Sheridan stood on the front steps and walked over to them. Sheridan checked a few of the straps of the saddles and their packs, and then stepped back.

Terrence reached out and Derek shook his hand. "You keep safe," said Terrence. "And come back."

"Don't worry, I will," answered Derek, turning to Sheridan who looked like she was just about ready to cry. "Don't look at me like I'm never coming back."

"It's not that—" Sheridan took a deep breath. "—All right, it *is* that. You've been gearing up to leave since this whole thing started. Just remember one thing, Derek. You do have someplace to come back to. You still have that yearling to train... Marissa, please make sure you all stay safe. I know how he is when he gets stuck on something."

"I will," said Marissa, staring at her husband. "Don't think for a second that the real reason I'm going is precisely to do that."

Sheridan nodded and then looked at everyone else. "All of you—don't forget the same thing. You may not have known us for as long as these two have, but you all still have a place to come back to... if you want that. This is your home, too."

"We'll be back," said David, smiling. "And thank you... for everything."

Derek looked from Sheridan to Terrence and then to Lorraine. "Keep your eyes on the north road—as David said... we will be back."

With one final wave, Derek led the other four up the road to the point where it crested.

CHAPTER TWENTY-SEVEN

Outside the community centre, Russell and Kirk leaned back on the wall and stared out the lake. With an inward cringe, Russell realised he had been doing this quite a bit. Normally, he would have something else to do in relation to his work or something in the city.

But, in being trapped here, he no longer had his usual pursuits.

"Adrienne seems to be a nice lady," pointed out Kirk.

Russell looked down. "She is, and she saved my life out there. We keep each other sane."

"I suppose since there's no chance in getting back down to Toronto it could be worse." Kirk had this funny way of saying things—it was direct but also forced a person to think. "Given the circumstances I believe God could understand," Kirk said.

Ah, he should have known.

Kirk and his wife, Sydney, were very Christian. Almost and if not full blown fundamental Christian with very simple and plain beliefs in how things should be. Things were, or simply were not, acceptable in their way of life and it was always guided by the bible.

Russell tried to see it their way and if could not then he at least tried not to cause fights and rifts within the family. His mother was a part of the same church and even went to the same Kingdom Hall as her sister Sydney and her brother in law, Kirk.

Well, before things had fallen.

He could guess why Kirk and Sydney had not been at home and had been over here instead. Their same belief also meant that as a part of their ministry it required going door to door.

Russell was a bit more liberal like the rest of this family except for Sheridan who was very liberal and vocal about it.

At least he could appreciate a few things. One, Kirk was always honest. Usually, rather brutally honest, which was a character trait he shared with Terrence, but he also cared deeply for those around him. He firmly believed, like those who believed similar, that it was his duty to see that his fellow neighbours were cared for and had their needs seen to.

Only Kirk took this a step further and also got a bit more involved in the local community than his wife would have even approved of. Most of his church insisted on remaining neutral in politics

Not Kirk.

He was not at all surprised that Kirk was actively helping keeping Long Lake running and also probably the one leading it.

"Well, I'll just leave it at that," Kirk grinned. "Wouldn't be me if I didn't."

Russell rolled his eyes but was careful to make sure his uncle did not see him do it. The older man would not be shy about cuffing across the back of the head for disrespecting him. Not enough to hurt but to startle. Kirk was never out to harm someone but he was just raised in a time where that had been acceptable. Even Lorraine was never shy about rapping knuckles with wooden spoons.

"So, you going to run for... whatever we're going to call the position of leadership... here?" asked Russell.

Kirk nodded his head. "I have nothing else to do right now outside of teaching others how to hunt and doing some fishing. With my knees, it'd be better if I stuck around town as the elder here. They could use it. Why? You thinking of being my competition?"

"Wasn't really thinking about it," admitted Russell.

"Why not?"

Russell turned to him in surprise. "You want me to?"

"Well, no, but if I can't be I couldn't think of anyone else I'd throw my support behind. Besides that Adrienne of yours… woman or no there's something about her."

A bark of laughter from Russell met Kirk's statement. "That might have to do with her being a regular OPP officer like…"

They both stopped at that. Daniel was still a raw wound on both of their minds and Kirk, after he had moment to think looked up again. "Did she know him too?"

"Well, sort of. She knew him in passing because of their work and they were the same shift, but not his partner or anything," he answered. "Still doesn't mean she's not in mourning the same as us."

Kirk nodded his agreement. "One day we'll meet again, you know that."

Actually, Russell was not about argue but, again, Kirk's beliefs were not necessarily his own. It was a nice sentiment and, in truth, he hardly wanted to argue that point, really. It was one of the few he really liked about their faith failing all else.

"But, right now the more important thing is the living," pointed out Kirk finally. "We've got a short summer."

Russell groaned. "If you want to be downright technical, winter and summer are about equal in length."

Kirk harrumphed and glared at his nephew for a long moment before he continued as if he had not been so rudely interrupted. "Be that as it may—it won't feel like it come winter especially if we let ourselves be caught with our pants down like we were this winter. We should organize and get supplies. Dig stores and the like."

"No argument here," agreed Russell.

* * * * *

"Tyrell, could I talk to you for a moment?"

Tyrell looked up and then over to where Sheridan leaned against the door jamb to his room and nodded. Sheridan walked in and sat down in the chair at his desk.

Tyrell was lying on his bed reading a bit before it became too dark and, in truth were told, he was a bit surprised at her visit.

After Helen's death he had been mostly left to his own devices and he had mostly turned to his own circle. "What did you need?" Tyrell asked.

"It's become abundantly clear the more people who come to us that we'll need to govern a bit more," she answered. "Up until now I have, more or less, led because I own the property. Out of default I'm the Lady of the Manor."

"Queen."

She waved the comment off and he grinned. Although it had been his suggestion, the fact that she found the title so uncomfortable made him like her even more. As someone who had such low regard for titles and power but yet rose to the occasion despite such distaste told him how well suited she was.

Even if she could not stand the thought of such a thing. "So what brings you to my door, my Lady," he asked.

She sighed and leaned back in the chair. "I think it's time—despite my misgivings—to formally start using the title you suggested I take. And, since I'm going that far, it's time I formed our government and court." Tyrell held his breath for a moment and was not entirely sure where she was going with this. Staring intently at him, she said, "I want you on that court."

"Me?" Tyrell asked incredulously.

She grinned slowly, "Well, if I'm to be Queen then you should be in my court."

"Doing what?"

"I was thinking your role would be as 'Lord Tyrell, Master of Arms' and you work directly with the military arm of my court."

He lay there as she let that sink in and then began to laugh. At least she had picked a good role for him. "And just how many are in this court of yours?" he asked.

"Ten, including you, with me as Queen making it eleven," she answered. "You will form part of my inner court and there will be others as we grow that will form the outer court."

He took a breath and thought for a moment. Well, she did have him on a few things. First he had suggested the whole 'Queen' deal and second she had him pegged in what he would excel in. He nodded. "All right, you've got yourself a Master of Arms. But I get to pick my people."

"I wouldn't have it any other way," she assured him as she stood up. "If they agree, the others on your half of court will have Terrence as Grand Marshall. You all will report to him. I don't think I need to explain why he's my Grand Marshall, do I?"

Tyrell shook his head. "And the others?"

"Karen as Master Knight for the mounted forces. Derek as Master Ranger, and I haven't yet decided on someone for our militia." She stretched. "Your 'civilian' counterparts are my grandmother—taking the counterpart of Terrence's role as Chatalaine. David as Grand

Justicar. Marissa as my Dean of Education, and Emilie as Assistant Minister of Health…"

"So who's the lead of health?" he asked and she lifted a brow. "Ah, right… you."

"Rick will be Minister of Infrastructure and Engineering," she finished.

"And you've told them this, I take it?" he asked curiously.

She nodded. "Except, obviously for Derek, Marissa and Emilie who are out with Derek on his expedition."

"So, what do you need me to do?" he asked.

She turned just as before she left. "Our first official court is tomorrow evening. We will be deciding what our future goals are. It will naturally be held downstairs where you decided my fate would be as your Queen."

CHAPTER TWENTY-EIGHT

In January and December, the snow drifts made it like a desert, thought Derek. *I expected the desolation* then... *I didn't expect it* now. After all, it had been in the middle of winter when the wilds of the Canadian north took on a decidedly desert like look.

"I didn't think it would be even more desolate in spring than in winter," said Derek as the trees gave way to sprawling, but empty fields.

He had thought that when spring arrived and the bare trees filled in with fresh green growth and the grasses in the open fields grew that it would feel less empty.

The reality was the total opposite.

"We haven't even gone that far," Emilie said, quietly. "We're not even as far as the Fire Hall yet... but there's not a single living soul past the gate."

"After what we went through, did you honestly expect there to be?" asked David as he shook his head, and gently convinced his horse to continue north along the broken pavement.

Nature had not taken long to reclaim the land now that humanity was not around to maintain its devices and buildings. What the winter had frozen and the snow had collapsed was now growing over in green growth and hidden in the grass. The road—no longer regular traveled by vehicles—had grass growing in the cracks of the pavement.

Strangely, while faced with this new life of trees, grass and wildflowers only served to make the feeling of desolation even worse.

In the winter it had been easy to think that the reason no one had come to check on anyone so far out of the city was due to how difficult it was to plow the road. If the road was not plowed then it was too difficult for a car or some other vehicle—even if pulled by a horse—to get this far.

Now that the snow had melted and the roads were clear—well as clear as they could be without anyone to maintain them. Someone should have been out this way to at least check on their neighbours. A patrol or two of the

Ontario Provincial Police from the highway or a cruiser from the local police service.

But nothing and no one had come down the road since the raiders back in January.

Derek looked at the other four and David said, "I had hoped we were wrong."

"I think we all did," said Marissa darkly. "Well, that confirms it."

"It doesn't confirm a thing, except that no one has been able to get out this far," said Derek. "We won't know anything until we get to at least Lively."

He coaxed his horse from a walk into a faster trot and the others followed. The trot was an easy pace for these horses, he knew, and they could maintain it for quite a while. The pace would see them at the Fire Hall—a trek that had taken a few days in the winter—in only an hour at most. As they rode they kept looking to the sides and to the ground ahead of them, always mindful of anything one of the horses could snag.

Grass filled the cracks in the road and some of the culverts had collapsed along the side but the ride remained an easy one. By the time they reached the old highway, a two lane side road that had once been the main highway, the sun had barely even rose into the sky.

The Fire Hall was a welcome sight and Derek mused at how easy it had been at this time of year compared to the winter.

"Hard to believe we survived as long as we did in there," said Emilie.

Derek, and David, kept their eyes on it fully expecting trouble but none came.   It was completely deserted. With a sigh, Derek said, "Come on, let's see how far we can get."

They rode past the Fire Hall and up the old highway instead of the new highway. The old highway was more likely to run across smaller settlements full of people of similar mind to Sheridan. At least that was what they hoped.

We'll need to trade, realized Derek. *A lot. Trading with neighbours will be crucial even more than when trade meant getting things, and sending things, overseas.   No one community can have everything and trading between would mean more choices for all of us.*

"Are we really back to the old days before the time of cars?" asked Marissa, and when he both shrugged and shook his head slightly he saw her raise an eyebrow.

Uh oh, I know that look, he thought. *It comes slightly before her asking if I'm all right. Truthfully, I have no idea.*

"Kind of funny how it all cycled around and came back to bite us in the proverbial rear," he answered.

"No kidding," said Abigail. "I never—not once—thought that I'd see something like this."

"I'm remembering a conversation with Sheridan a few years ago when she still lived in town and planned to bike everywhere—and by bike I don't mean a motorcycle," said Derek quietly. "I made light of it. Told her that a professional needed a car."

"She didn't dispute that part of it, if I remember correctly," grinned Marissa. "I remember that particular argument because I heard all the way upstairs. She said, where she was living downtown, that a bike made more sense because of parking and you told her that she was soft in the head. I think it was a good thing both her Dad and I were there to keep it from going farther than that."

Derek winced and Abigail looked over at him, quirking an eyebrow. "Oh, do tell," said Emilie. "I didn't get the impression that she could argue."

"She can," snorted Derek. "When you finally hit a nerve."

"Like calling her soft in the head," pointed out Marissa. "You know exactly how quickly her laid back nature will turn into a hurricane if you say that to her, or around her."

Derek grimaced and then sighed, "Now's not the time to remind me of times when I can be the same way."

Derek had also once thought her the same for being into historical re-enactment and building her house the way she had. *But back then I also shrugged it off as that being what made her unique. Now, though, I'm really very, very glad that she built her house the way she wanted and also collected the resources and items she now owned while still involved in that re-enactment club...*

He turned to look up and to the east.

"It's pretty," said Marissa. "Like an old road in Ireland."

"It *is* pretty," agreed David, with a heavy sigh. "The problem is there still isn't any sign of anyone having been out here at all."

"We can't be the only survivors of this," Emilie said. "There has to be others... somewhere."

"The winter was extremely cold this year," said Derek. "I know we looked in the immediate area of the farm for people we could help and bring out of the cold, unfortunately..."

"I think we're looking at it being fairly obvious that around ninety percent of those in the area froze to death over the winter," suggested David. "If the same rate of attrition had spread elsewhere then the possibility of finding others is kind of slim."

"Maybe others did the same as Sheridan and Terrence?" asked Marissa. "Built a home that wasn't so dependent on the grid?"

"Entirely possible," conceded David, as he looked over at Derek. "I can tell you is that the city probably fared worse as 'off grid' living was practically non-existent. Looting and crime would have exploded without any way for the police to gain control or stop it."

Not that I'm going to admit this—because she'd never let me forget it—but Reese was right. Going into the city is a suicide mission but it is also the only place I could think of that will have the information I need, realized Derek. *But... all that will be moot if we don't reach Lively.*

He knew from experience that according to Google Maps Whitefish was only a short distance away. It was perhaps two to five minutes away by car but walking it—even on horseback—took just the early part of the morning.

The tiny town was deserted and there were absolutely no signs of anyone having survived the winter. David was swearing vehemently as they rode through. "If anyone had survived they would have seen us and come out by now," said David.

Derek shrugged. "Might be hiding—not sure if we're friendly or not," he answered but he looked around – the trap at George's still fresh in his mind. It was not a mistake he intended on repeating. "Check the houses. If... if no one's survived, there could be something we could use."

The first house was deserted, but it showed signs of being that way for years. As he looked around, he realized that there really were not that many houses to begin with. As soon as the first horse passed that house, the crack of a gunshot broke the silence.

"That's far enough!" yelled a voice. "I don't know what you want, but you won't find it here!"

"We're not going to hurt you!" yelled back Derek. "We didn't think anyone had survived here and we're just passing through."

For a few minutes there was no answer and he had the feeling the person—which he could not figure was male or female—was mulling over whether he was telling the truth or not. "Prove you're not."

"How in hell are we supposed to do that?" asked Emilie. "And how are we supposed to know you aren't?"

"Are you from the shop down the road?" another voiced drifted over and sounded like it was from behind one of the houses to his left.

"No," answered Derek. "From the farm down Panache Lake Road."

Again, there was a long silence and then a few people came out from around the far houses. Judging by how thin they were and how their clothes hung from their bodies, the winter had been far harsher here.

"You look really well fed for this winter," said the first voice and now that Derek could see him he saw that the young man was no older than Karen's son.

Swearing under his breath he realised that not two minutes away from the Fire Hall had been a small community missed by everyone. It had been completely cut off over the winter.

"We were lucky," said Derek. "How many did you lose this winter?"

The young man shook his head. "Too many. None of the older ones survived and the really little didn't either." With a bitter laugh he turned back to Derek. "Hell, most of my age group didn't either."

"I'm sorry," said Derek. "If we'd known, we would have come and helped you."

"How?" asked another.

With a nod from Marissa, Derek continued. "There's a farm to the south on Panache Lake Road. Get to it and tell them Derek sent you. If you decide to stay, Sheridan will make sure you survive."

"How will we tell this farm from any others?" asked the young man, relaxing a bit.

"Oh, you'll be able to tell," said David with a chuckle. "It looks almost like civilization didn't fall there... it's not perfect, but it's better than nothing."

The small group looked at each and from the look of it they were holding a quick non-verbal vote. Finally, their leader nodded. "All right— we'll take your advice. You said we were to ask for Sheridan?" he asked.

"The rest of who's there has taken to calling her their queen... unless we find signs of the government elsewhere she's as close to real government you'll see," said David. "What's left of Canada will live on there."

"And who are you?" asked one of the young women in the group.

"Constable David Radzinsky of the Greater City of Sudbury Police Service," he answered then shook his head. "That is, if there still even is a service."

The leader of the group looked from one of them to the other and said, "I don't know about the rest of you, but I'm going to check it out at least. You can stay here."

"You're going to leave us?" asked the other one, shocked.

"If you stay here how long, will you survive off of what you've managed to find?" asked Emilie. "From the look of you, all I'd guess not long. What have you got to lose? Take two hours and walk there. At least the resources in between are better than here."

A third one in their group said, "She's got a point."

The young woman sighed and threw her hands up in the air. "Fine," she conceded. "We'll go."

"Good," Derek said as he turned the horse back to the road and east again.

"Wait a second, you can't be seriously thinking of going further up that road!" said the first one. "That's where the raiders came from."

"What raiders?" asked David, suddenly interested.

"Back in the winter, there were these raiders that came down the road," answered the young woman. "They didn't come back after they were through here and I have no idea where they went, but they took everything and kept going."

"Lovely bit of news" mused Abigail as she looked over at Derek.

Derek sighed heavily. He had known this was not going to be easy but also dealing with regular raids from bands of looters was not something he had counted on.

"Do we continue?" asked Marissa.

"Yes," answered Derek after thinking about it for a moment. "We do."

* * * * *

One of the biggest lecture halls at Laurentian University could just only fill with two hundred people. The problem was, the minute word got around that the city's mayor had survived and somehow made it to the university everyone wanted to hear what she had to say.

This meant that not everyone would fit in the formal hall.

Kaine had the meeting moved to the Grand Salon which would fit anyone who wished to hear her speak. Instead of the formal lecture hall that the Fraser was, this hall was far less formal, especially considering it usually served as the university cafeteria. One part also overlooked the golf club which sat behind the campus.

The hall was full of students who had been trapped here as well as the faculty. As a result, they had continued as if life never changed even though the challenges of doing so had made all their lives difficult.

She knew they were hoping for good news.

Unfortunately, she did not have it.

Without power to the Great Hall, she would have to project her voice as it was not amplified. Shouting would only warp the sound and make her unable to be understood.

"Most of you know who I am," Valeria began. "So I won't waste precious time with introductions."

"When are we going home?" came a question from the back.

"We aren't," she answered honestly and the whispering rippled from one side of the room to the other.

Kaine whistled and everyone fell silent again.

"I wish I had good news, but the truth is that the world we knew is gone. Sudbury is gone. We are all that's left and what can and will so is lead the rest back to civilization." Valeria waited until her training told her the crowd was willing to listen. "Here, at this one place, we have all the tools we need. It's been done before in history —

I won't bore you with repeating the basics—and we can do it again. It was always those like us that did so."

"What happened to the city?" asked someone.

"Raiders burnt it to the ground. City Hall is in ruins and we've lost too many already. We didn't come here to take leadership away from those who got you all through the winter. We're here because we had to run out and we have nothing." She looked at everyone in turn before saying, "I ask only one thing—let us stay. Let us help you rebuild our society. Brick by bloody brick if we have to."

* * * * *

Marissa could see the beginning of one of Derek's broods. The minute Whitefish was out of sight and they were further down the road he had fallen silent and focused his attention on the road again. *He's going to fight me on it*, she knew. *But I'd really like to know what he's thinking and he's going to talk about it so we're on the same damn page...*

He glanced over and sighed as he saw her staring pointedly at him. "We'll talk once we make camp," Derek conceded.

"So long as we do," Marissa pointed out.

"It didn't take long for people to become raiders and looters in the short time since the rule of law vanished," said Emilie, looking over at David. "Not even six months, if that."

It's like something out of a movie or a TV show — fantasy, not reality, thought Derek. *But I guess if the world really were full of rainbows and peace that someone like David wouldn't have been required even before the rule of law ceased to exist.*

Now that there were no police services the wilder side—the feral and the animal—had finally won over. The rule of law only existed with Sheridan and those willing to support it and he could see just how delicate that rule was.

They needed someone—even if as a symbol—to give them the feeling that the rule of law and civilization still existed. And if 'still' was no longer the correct term then they needed someone new to fill that void.

We need our Queen.

It was a sobering thought and it sent the cold chill like ice water down his spine as he realized this. *But we really need Sheridan to literally step up and call herself our Queen or what shaky foundation we have will crumble down around us like everything else just did. She might not be comfortable with the idea but she needs to get comfortable... and quickly.*

That was the real reason he needed to find out if civilization had indeed truly fallen and why.

CHAPTER TWENTY-NINE

If they thought the journey to Whitefish—even though the journey was short—was lonely, the road between Whitefish and Naughton was far worse. The highway between the two towns normally always had traffic. But now it was somehow worse than Panache Lake Road.

"I was hoping this stretch of road would be a bit better than the one between the Fire Hall and Sheridan's farm," said David as he slid off the back of the horse. "But it's actually worse."

"I don't know," said Derek quietly. "It could just be because we were expecting more signs of life here, not like on the road to Sheridan's farm."

"Which was never that great a road to begin with," said Marissa.

"Exactly—it's always been a bit of a patchwork quilt more than a road," agreed Derek. "Granted, this road wasn't that much better, as I remember it, but it was still better and more travelled than Panache Lake Road."

Perhaps it was simply because that was how it felt to Derek since the road to Sheridan's farm was a side road and never had really been well kept. Not like the highway. Finding the highway in the same condition with grass in the cracks and the potholes was more of a shock because he had honestly hoped for different. Seeing this deflated his sense of hope faster than the side road had.

"What else is eating you?" asked David, looking at Derek, and the older of the two men sighed heavily.

"I guess I could write off seeing Panache Lake Road as it was never a main road anyway— not travelled like this one. The quiet was expected..." Derek trailed off for a moment as he looked at the small, collapsed bridge in front of them. "But seeing this road like this—it just really hits home, y'know? This is it... what we suspected really is true."

"With our terrain, and the tendency for wash outs, no city works may mean no roads," pointed out Emilie. "The whole city will be cut off from each other."

"It kind of is," answered Abigail as she let the sandy soil run through her fingers. "The whole region is full of low rocky hill chains that formed the mountainous bowl of the valley."

"One big divot on top of a mountain, filled with sand," finished Derek. "Some places look green—and they are—but it can turn like a sandy desert if one thing is thrown out of kilter…"

He looked at David as he realized the other man was confused. "How long have you lived here?" asked Marissa, realizing at the same time that David could not have been around long if he only knew what the city looked like now.

"Not very long, just moved up here around a year ago," he answered.

I just explained to him last month why the city's rocks are so black… he thought it was natural," grinned Emilie.

The reason for this was simple—just over a century before Sudbury had either chopped it all down to fuel the smelters… Or the smelters thick smoke had choked out the life turning the area into the infamous moon rock of blackened granite and desert, sandy pits. For nearly sixty years their main landmark had been the destroyed forests with nothing but burnt stumps and stark, black slag piles.

The only thing that had ever seemed to grow was the blue berries.

"Oh my God," laughed Abigail. "Hello, stranger."

It had taken years of dedicated hard work by the citizens to, first, change the way the smelting plants spewed their smoke and then, second, to replant and regrow the landscape. The fact that the trees were still so young—less than a quarter century old—was testament to the former destruction of the land and its eventual reclamation.

The land was almost returned to its former glory before the roasting pits and smelters but signs of the former desolation were still easy to spot.

The trees were still smaller, still stunted. There were still large tracts of sand pits although they were slowly being reclaimed by trees and other growth. Rivers were cleaner.

"I had noticed it seemed somewhat flat, or stunted, until Capreol and Onaping," agreed David. "And then, once you're over the edge it's like everything falls away off the other side—like we're on top of the mountain but the mountain lost its top."

"Well, that's why," said Marissa.

"Long story short—that's a pretty good way of thinking about it," agreed Derek. "What's in that 'bowl' is a mix of rock and swamp… the water pools where it can and doesn't escape really easy, but that's not why the rock is exposed or why the trees are short… or why some places are the opposite."

"Before the Superstack in Copper Cliff, the only way to smelt the metal was to cook the ore in roasting yards—they cut down all the trees and then literally roasted the landscape. All the black is the result from, first, the roasting yards and then the old smelters which then coated the landscape with smoke and choked out everything else," explained Emilie. "Not twenty, or ten years, ago there were no trees, no anything but black rock and sand."

"So, what happened?" asked David.

"First, they built the Superstack, which only served to take what was spilling out of the smelters and send it up into the upper atmosphere... and spread it around further," said Abigail, ignoring the other's stare, and she shrugged. "Finally, with better environmental laws and regulation, it's better. Not great, but better... and there was also a re-greening and tree planting effort everywhere around the city. What you see is over twenty years of hard work to make it like it is now."

"Versus a landscape that only seemed to be able to grow blueberries," pointed out Marissa. "Behind our house it was just sand for years... sand and blueberries, the occasional tree."

Derek continued to poke around the collapsed bridge and then sighed.

"The ground isn't stable here," said David. "We'll have to find another way around."

"Damn it," swore Derek. "Well, we knew that it was going to take longer than it would have before."

"Did you suspect it would be this bad?" asked Marissa.

Derek shook his head. "No, I didn't. I really should have, though."

"There was no way you could have known," said Abigail. "I really should have known—I came down the river this way on that raft."

"I still can't believe you did that." Emilie pointed out. "Going down the Vermillion is a risky move on a good day—but during flood season? Crazy."

Abigail shrugged, "Didn't have much choice."

"No point crying over spilt milk now," Marissa said. "We should find a way around... unless you want to go back?"

Derek shook his head, making a cutting gesture with his hand in negation. "No, we find a way around."

* * * * *

Preparing for winter could hold different meanings depending on who was asked. Under Kirk's leadership, it meant only one thing— making sure there was enough food and enough fuel for heat to last until April, no matter how much snow fell or how cold it turned.

Russell and Adrienne spent their days helping in their own way—keeping watch on the northern roads between Long Lake and the city.

There was an overlook on the highway where they could see almost anything in the immediate area. It was from here they kept a regular watch using binoculars to the north.

As the days turned steadily warmer and the ground less soft and wet, they both knew that it was only a matter of time before someone—likely those same gangs from the core—could figure out there was a community living and surviving on the shores of a lake with plenty of fish in it.

Adrienne leaned back against the guard rail as Russell scanned the horizon.

"It's still quiet," he mused. "I would love to believe that we're safe but I can't shake this feeling we aren't."

"Trust those feelings," answered Adrienne. "Most of the time they won't lead you wrong."

He lowered his binoculars, looking at her. "Speaking from experience?"

She nodded as she took her turn to scan the horizon while Russell sat down on the edge of the rail. He opened his thermos flask and peered inside. "We're out of whatever that tea was Tara made."

She snorted. "Interesting little woman she is."

"You can say that again.

Tara was a pagan and in Kirk's eyes that was nearly worse than being in a gang. He considered her of loose morals and she felt he was overbearing. While she would never breathe the word rebellion against him she often spoke out versus his tendency to be more than a bit conservative.

The strange part was—despite the entertainment which resulted—between the two of them the community struck a balance right down the middle. What they did agree on was they were each other's staunchest supporter.

Both believed that the community was everything—without running into the lack of a private issue. Kirk was a deeply private man and Tara hardly liked people poking around her property much, either. Kirk was willing to admit that it was more Tara's territory since she had always lived in Long Lake and he was the visitor. Especially as they were of a similar age which meant Tara had been in Long Lake for decades. They both respected each other's skills and abilities.

However, their two wildly different views of faith and how one followed it often led to the loudest of fights.

Adrienne stood up straight and motioned to Russell suddenly. Looking where she pointed, he brought his binoculars up and looked through them.

After seeing exactly what she was pointing at, he dropped them again, turning to pack up their things. He hated being right... but at least—with the vantage point—they could see and know about threats a few days in before they arrived.

"Do you think they're part of the same group that killed Daniel?" asked Adrienne.

"I'm pretty sure they are," answered Russell. "Maybe not exactly the same... but definitely like them."

The group they saw was destructive, even from a distance, it was obvious that if they could not use it they burned it down.

It would take Adrienne and Russell a day to get back to Long Lake, but at the meandering pace the roving gang was taking they would still have a few days at most to prepare.

They were not going to waste time, however. While they were on foot most of the time they knew all the direct routes and shortcuts and their pace would be quick and steady.

Russell was not about to leave his community unprepared.

* * * * *

Even in early spring the bush was thick. Derek was extremely glad he had taken the machete and the hatchet with him as they had to cut a new path around the wash out through the growth. It was a shame to have to cut their way through the new growth but necessity dictated that if they wanted to get through they had to do it.

It was not as large an issue as it could have been. The small creek they had encountered — as flooded as it probably had during the early spring—was now only a quick jump over the shallow ditch.

"If this is only one of the small creeks, I'd hate to see what happened right beside the Vermillion," Abigail pointed out.

Derek sighed in agreement as they rode through and to the other side and back down the other side of the creek to get back to the road.

The embankment on the other side was in better condition. They were able to remain on horseback as the horses climbed up the small gravel embankment and back up to the road again.

Two minutes later David, who was in the front, started to laugh.

When they came around the corner, Derek realized why he was laughing. They had all forgotten about the large and very well stocked boat sales yard not even an hour by horseback from the farm. Since Sheridan's farm was on the main part of the Vermillion—as was the boat dealer—they had a quick and easy way back.

And perhaps a quick and easy way to Lively, now that Derek thought about it. "You think we can find a few large enough pontoon boats to get us and the horses up river?" he asked Abigail.

She snorted, "Easily… why?" she asked and then she quickly figured out where he was going with it. "Oh… now that's a smart idea and it could take a few hours off our trip. The problem is if there's even enough fuel there to do it or we're going to be paddling them up the river."

"I have a feeling we'll be doing that anyway," said David. "If fuel wasn't supplied to emergency services, then it certainly wasn't brought out here. They close in the winter so there'd be no reason to have it hanging around to turn rancid."

"Would it be worth checking out?" asked Marissa.

For a long moment they looked at each other as they all thought about whether it was or not.

"It could be—but on the way back," answered Derek. "And then, even if the fuel has gone rancid, getting any boat is easier when we're going downstream versus upstream."

"The river goes north very shortly after here anyway," said Abigail. "However, it may be to our advantage. There's a lake just after the first bend from here. The current is slow and I can tell you for certain that the road has to go over the river and the river has washed that bridge out completely. The creek was easy to cross with the horses, but the river won't be. It's too wide and too deep. We'd have to swim it and it's still too cold for that."

"How big is this lake?" asked Emilie, crinkling her brow.

"You had to have seen it," said David, surprised. "It follows the road. Most mistake it as the river, but, as Abby pointed out, the river goes north in less than half a kilometre."

"Wouldn't the boats—even if we have to paddle them—be easier, as Marissa said?" asked Emilie when she realized that. "And if the bridge is out we'd have a way across."

Derek blew out a breath and admitted, "You have a point. Okay, let's check out if they even have a big enough boat or two."

CHAPTER THIRTY

The first hurdle into the boat yard was getting through the locked gate. Jumping over it was not an option as barbed wire looped around the top like a prison yard fence.

The five of them split up, but remained within sight of each other. Derek stayed at the gate with Abigail while Abigail tried to puzzle out how to get the gate open.

"I knew I should have packed the bolt cutters," she mused. "I could have at least been through the links of the fence."

Derek rummaged around in his pack until he took out one of his rugged multi-tools and a set of heavy duty wire cutters and pliers. As he handed them over to her, she crinkled her brow.

"I don't think they're heavy enough," he admitted.

"Got a metal saw in that bag?" she asked.

"Yeah… I do," he answered, pulling the case out.

She grinned as she took it from him. Opening it, she whistled and waved everyone back over. "Now we're in business. I can cut through the lock with this. It'll still take me ages to do it but at least I can get us into it."

"How long?" asked David.

"No idea," she answered as she started to saw through the lock.

But Emilie stopped her as she pointed to the weaker anchor points in the fence itself. "Oh, now that's genius. Give me an hour and I'll have a nice big gap."

While they waited and listened to the sounds of the saw, they took the opportunity to take a break and eat lunch.

With a pop, one anchor was gone and Abigail took a break, letting someone else in the group to take over. Each time the telltale pop of an anchor let go, the saw would get passed to another person until each anchor point in a section of the fence was cut off. The whole gate simply fell to the ground on the other side of the fence with a clatter.

David and Abigail then dragged the gate out of the way of the road and the horses. "Let's see what we have," said Derek.

Derek walked around the boat yard aimlessly for nearly an hour.

Before the snow fell, he had been out this way and had seriously considered buying one of the boats in the yard. *Hard to believe that in such a short time — it had only been fall the year before — that the same yard only reminds me of what we've lost*, he mused.

The strange part was that the boatyard was untouched. No one had been interested in anything in it with survival being the first thing on their minds and without a way to fuel one of the numerous power-boats what was here was a bit useless.

I'm just not seeing anything of use and it's starting to get dark... and we haven't even set up camp yet, Derek grimaced as he put his hands on his hips.

All the boats so far had been bass fishing boats — too small for what they needed — and larger power boats but no flat top pontoon style boats.

The boat yard was large enough to spend an entire day in and they might not find what they needed.

Dammit, I give up — wait, what's that? Derek turned around the corner of the building and looked down to the docks.

Something surprising at the dock alerted Derek—a boat they needed greatly. Derek ran down to the dock and stopped right before walking onto it. He whistled and then waited a few moments.

Not too long after the rest of his group came down to the docks with the horses in tow.

"You find something?" asked Marissa.

"Look at this," he said, grinning. "All we need to do is straighten the dock out."

Abigail sighed. "More work than you think, but doable." There was another pause. "So... this is what this place looks like from this angle."

"Something for tomorrow," said Derek. "Wait, were you here before?"

"Yeah, it's where I got the bass boat to come downriver. I had been using the Cessna but it was too ungainly," she answered. "It's actually my fault that it's all crooked like this."

He nodded and shrugged, "No use worrying about it now. Let's make camp up from the river a bit and we'll get a fresh start of it in the morning."

Abigail nodded her agreement and pointed out, "This is going to make getting through that fence seem like a cake walk, you know that, right?"

"Yeah, I know," he answered as he pulled the pack for the tent off the horse.

Setting camp was a complex, but quick job. Despite the fact that they were only planning to stay one night, he wanted to make sure camp was properly set just in case fixing the dock took a bit longer than expected.

The first thing to decide was where the tent would be set up. A flat area of the boat yard, but still out of sight from the road, was chosen. David and Abigail went back to the gate and set the boat back to how they found it.

By the time they returned, the tent had already been set up with the ground sheet below it. Both these things—in the hands of Derek and Marissa—took less than ten minutes to do and the tent was up, secured and ready to use.

Abigail looked around and said, "Are you planning on staying awhile?"

"This didn't even take half an hour to set up," said Derek. "It will take the same to break down and if it rains tomorrow you'll thank me. Even if it doesn't, you'll still thank me for the shade."

* * * * *

The straggly group slowly made its way up the hill to the gate and came to a stop.

Unlike the raiders from the winter, these barely looked like they had the energy to continue, let alone try to rush the gates.

Terrence frowned as he looked down and counted them.

There were no more than ten of them and the oldest looked to be only around his mid-teens.

"That's far enough," he ordered down at them.

"We were sent here by Derek Moss and Constable Radzinsky," said the oldest. "We're what's left of Whitefish."

Terrence sighed and caught a few of the sideways glances from those patrolling the wall.

There was only one way they could have learnt those names—and then know to make their way here—and that would have been on Derek and David's orders. Terrence shook his head ruefully, wondering how they could help them but he turned around to the gate keeper.

He said, "Open the gate... let them in. Send a runner down to Sheridan and tell her she's got incoming needing attention."

"Yes sir!" was the crisp answer.

Minutes later, one of the patrolling militia ran down the road towards the farm. The bar reinforcing the gate and holding it closed slid to the side and the gate slowly dragged open. They had yet to figure out the finer details of fixing this to open and close easier.

They filed in through the gap in a thin line and once through Terrence gestured for the gate to be closed and barred again.

The children—as they were all no more than their mid-teens—stared around in wonder. Terrence suddenly worried about what the state of life was outside if these children thought that this was better.

"All right," he said as he came down to them. "Follow me and my wife will set you right."

"Will there be food?" piped up one of the younger children.

Terrence stood wordless in surprise and then sighed. "I don't how much there will be but there should something waiting for you when you get there."

They had not even made it to the bottom of the hill when a wagon pulled by a team of horses and driven by Nathan met them on the road. He was hardly surprised to note that Sheridan had come herself.

She took one look at their faces and turned to Terrence. "Put the younger ones in the wagon... it should take them all and we'll take them straight to the house. It's clear they need medical attention."

"One of the younger ones asked about food," said Terrence.

"Gramma already has that covered," answered Sheridan and a small smile wisped onto her face before she turned serious again. "For now it's a light but nutritious broth. If they've been without for too long anything heavier won't be any better."

Terrence saw her look across the clearing to the river in the distance. "I'm sure they're fine."

Sheridan looked at him in surprise. "Who?"

"Your mother's half of your family," he answered. "The ones on that Reserve... and the others scattered around."

A small smile, one not quite reaching her eyes, graced her face. "You know, despite what Hollywood would lead you to believe, we don't have mystical powers over nature. With things the way they are, my family—and the community—would be as bad off as anyone else."

"True," he admitted. "But your Uncle is plenty experienced with hunting—like Derek."

"Also true," she admitted, and then she sighed. "I just hope that my Uncle Garrett isn't the only one Derek manages to find, if he gets where he's going."

* * * * *

Kirk was just sitting down on the dock to throw in his line to go fishing when Adrienne, closely followed by his nephew came running up to him.

"Uncle Kirk, we have a problem," he said as soon as he managed to gain enough of his breath back to talk.

"Oh?"

"Raider gang spotted by the place my parents used to live and they are most definitely headed this way," answered Adrienne.

The older man blew out a breath and sat down heavily, ignoring the way the bench creaked in protest. He looked up at both of them and then shook his head. "I'd ask if there was any peaceful way out of this, but I have a feeling they wouldn't be interested."

"I doubt it," agreed Russell.

"Well, then don't stand there. Go sound the alarm."

CHAPTER THIRTY-ONE

The next morning rain nearly swamped their efforts. Derek gazed forlornly out of the screen and down at the docks as Marissa put her hand on his shoulder.

"At least the added preparation last night is saving us from some serious discomfort now," pointed out Emilie, looking pointedly over at Abigail.

"All right, all right," Abigail conceded. "Don't get me wrong I'm glad you made sure we're not soaked, but I wish we hadn't needed this. This is going to put us behind schedule."

"I didn't think we were even on a schedule," said David.

"We aren't," answered Derek. "But it doesn't mean that the rain doesn't slow us down. I could have done without it."

"It's still spring," said Abigail. "I'd expect rain to slow us down for a while yet. At least it isn't in the height of bug season."

Derek grunted his agreement.

'Bug season' in the area was brutal. Clouds of mosquitoes, black flies and other biting insects were often thick enough to see from a distance.

Even more reason to find some supplies, or even life back on Sheridan's farm would soon be unlivable as the bugs would simply make it almost impossible to get anything done. Given how wet and rainy it was already told Derek that it could also possibly be one of the worst years for them, too.

Just to add to everything they were already facing.

Rubbing a hand on his face he remembered another detail he had almost forgotten. It was spring—and past the spring melt. Another animal would be coming out of hibernation if it had not already done so.

The black bear.

He turned to the others and he could see that David and Abigail also had remembered the same.

"Oh… crap…" breathed Abigail. "I'm amazed we haven't seen any bears yet."

"My thoughts exactly," said Derek, pointing at her. "We not only have food—which they'd be attracted to—we also have horses."

"Great…" groaned David. "We *are* on a bit of a schedule then. "We need to get on the move as soon as possible. The longer we stay in one place the more likely it is we'll attract one… or two."

"Or two?" asked Emilie.

"Bears are not loners," answered Derek. "They can be, but they're also a social animal and can get along with others of its own kind if resources are rich enough. And given what happened—and the various houses now abandoned—resources will be plenty this year for the bears."

The grislier fact was that those who had died over the winter would also likely end up as food for the same bears. He did not voice this and he did not have to. The only upside to this was the distraction this would cause the bears.

The major, and far more serious, implication was that the bears would now have a taste for human flesh. Once a bear became a man-eater, it was a very unfortunate fact that it would always be one. The next generation of bears would go from fearing humans and human habitation to possibly actively hunting humans. Of course, this would add to the ever growing list of what a wandering person needed to contend with.

Anywhere a bear considered home was now hostile. Unfortunately, that meant all of Canada and into the US.

Derek sighed heavily, wondering how they were going to survive the summer. If they thought the winter had been deadly with the sub-zero temperatures and no heat the summer was now just as deadly with an active predator in their area. Those who survived the winter now had to somehow survive with also being hunted for food.

The rain continued to fall in massive torrents for another day. But it tapered off over night. By the morning of the third day, the rain stopped and a misty fog rolled in making visibility a bit soupy.

Abigail woke up first and poked life into the fire for Marissa, as the two found some way to make breakfast and boil water for tea. "Is Derek still asleep?" asked Abigail.

"He was sort of awake when I moved the covers getting up, but I think his eyes closed again after I was out of bed," answered Marissa, grinning. "He's not exactly a morning person."

Emilie came out of the zipped up side room of the large multi-room tent, wiping her eyes as she did. "Do I smell breakfast?" she asked, nodding at David as he came around the back of the tent.

Marissa nodded, and Emilie and David sat down on milk crates they had found yesterday, watching the dew and rain drip off the tarp. "Thank God that rain finally stopped," said Abigail, shaking her head. "Not sure what we would have done if we were stuck here another day."

"Watched my husband go insane," answered Marissa as she looked at the tent as Derek flipped the flap aside as he walked out to join them. "Oh, look who decided to finally join us."

Derek only grunted as he sat down on the last of the milk crates, wiping his face. "He's *really* not a morning person, is he?" asked Abigail as she looked over at Marissa, who shook her head while smiling.

"Are you talking about me again?" asked Derek.

"I'd never," answered Marissa.

"You absolutely would," Derek retorted, sticking out his tongue as he took his own mug of tea. With a sigh of relief, he noted, "I see the rain finally stopped."

After everyone had eaten their breakfast, and dressed for the day, David and Derek then followed Abigail down to the docks. She pointed to where one of the anchor lines had snapped and lost its mooring from the flood.

Abigail then explained, "We'll have to retie it, but we have to shift the dock back to where it should be to do it. After that all we need to do is reattach the anchors below the water. It's a floating dock so…"

They wasted no time and pulled the dock back into line.

Noon crept up on them and now the dock was fully repaired.

Abigail checked over one of the barges with David's help. "Well?" asked Derek as he jogged up to the dock and then walked gingerly on it.

Marissa and Emilie came running up. Emilie grinned and said, "We found a boat… and it looks like there's enough fuel for the motor."

Derek and David looked at each other. "How did someone miss that?" asked Derek.

David shook his head. "I have no idea but I'm not turning down that gift."

They followed the two women up to the boat.

"I have no idea how we're going to propel it, but it can be used," answered Abigail.

"Well, let's get it to the water and see if it even floats," said Derek.

They rolled it carefully into the water. As Derek let out a breath, Abigail tugged on the ropes to guide the boat to the dock.

Emilie and Marissa walked onto the dock with long paddles meant for a raft.

"Just in case," said Marissa.

David looked at Derek with his hand on the pull cord of the boat motor. "Here's hoping what we found is not rancid." He pulled the cord and engine rumbled. "Get the other tanks. By some miracle we have a working barge."

"That will make things significantly easier," said Derek, grinning.

"Lost a few days to gain one?" asked Emilie.

"No, it's not that," said David. "All we need to do is get back here and the current and the paddles will do the rest to get us back to the farm. We have a way to transport a whole lot more supplies in fewer trips."

"It also cuts a few days on the return," said Derek. "We can bypass the road and just head right downriver to Sheridan's farm. Perhaps it could even become a regular route, if we find another town or more survivors to trade with."

"Well, then, let's get this show on the road," said Abigail she threw the first of what they had brought with them onto the barge.

Marissa led the horses down the hill and onto the dock and stopped as the dock shifted. Derek and the others froze and Derek held his breath. "Bring one at a time," suggested Emilie.

Derek took the reins of the first horse and led it to the barge. "I'm amazed they're letting you do this," said Abigail. "They're very brave horses."

"There's a reason the RCMP, and other police organizations, chose this particular breed of horse," said David. "They are bold, for a horse."

The dock did not shift again, and soon the barge was fully loaded. "Are we good to go?" asked David.

Derek nodded. "Everything is here, and the barge is still floating. I'd say we're ready."

* * * * *

"I can admit when I'm defeated by popular opinion," said Dr. Kaine as he followed Valeria out of the Grand Salon and into the hallways deeper within the University. "Even if you didn't come here with the intent of taking over you just effectively did."

"It honestly wasn't my intention," Valeria answered with a deep sigh as she turned to him. "I do believe we can rebuild."

"I know—that's why I'm not upset over this recent little turn of events," he chuckled warmly, waving his hand dismissively. "Truthfully, it does give me more time to spend with my research. So I suppose I should thank you."

After a moment, he finally stopped and she came to a stop beside him. "I think it's time I showed you something. If you're determined to rebuild then I need you to truly know what it is you're up against."

Valeria whirled in shock, "What do you know?"

He smiled and used a key to open a door. Within sat a bank of computers with data scrolling across each screen.

"Before I came to Sudbury I worked in Ottawa," He explained as he closed the door behind him.

Valeria fought the urge to shiver and rub her arms in the room. The chill did not come from any actual feeling of being cold, but more from a certain feeling of discomfort now that she was alone with him. "And?"

He tipped his chin towards the computers and she moved so he could move past her to sit in the chair. "See this?" he asked as he pointed to one last line of code on the screen. "That was the final message I received from my old unit. It's a code word… it basically means the worst has happened and what my unit spent years preparing for finally happened."

"And that was?" she asked.

He turned to face her. "Doomsday."

For a long moment they both stood there and then she threw her head back and laughed until tears ran down her face. "Oh… you had me going for a second there." She stopped when she realized she was the only one laughing. "Wait, are you serious?"

"Well, if you excuse my flair for the dramatic… but yes, I am."

"So, you what?"

He sighed and ran a hand down his face. "I make it sound all dramatic and mysterious but to be honest we simply ran virtual..." He made a humming noise as he searched for the right word. "...Well, we ran simulations where we would put in certain perimeters and run the program. It would give us time lines. What could cause the downfall of everything, and also what would give the best chance of not only survival but also rebuilding society from the ashes. You see, CSIS and the NSA knew that eventually—like all things—everything we knew as a society would eventually simply collapse out from under us and we'd find ourselves in another dark age. It was never a matter of if... but when, and why."

"And you ran these simulations, why?" she asked curiously.

"To best plan our survival, of course," he answered. "And, hopefully, our best chance of re-emergence. We called it Project Ragnarok."

"Nice," she mentioned.

"Thank you, I must admit I had some part in picking the name," he answered. "Anyway, we knew that eventually there could be a second Dark Ages and we formed a group... completely unofficial of course... determined to prevent it."

"Prevent the fall of civilization?" she asked incredulously.

"No, no, that we knew would happen. But a second Dark Age, well, we figured we could attempt to thwart that." He sighed. "Unfortunately, if what you say is true, we weren't altogether successful."

"I wouldn't say you were unsuccessful either," she admitted as she walked closer to the computer bank, now a bit more at ease since learning what his giant dark secret was. "The university in one piece compared to what's around it is testament to this."

He inclined his head and nodded. "True enough."

* * * * *

The motor was not meant for speed and the barge trundled along up the river and into the wide part that signalled the start of the lake.

If observed from a satellite it would have looked like a vein that had burst. The river formed the vein as it ran into the lake from the north western point of the lake, and then less than a few hundred meters to the immediate south, ran back out of the lake.

The lake itself then branched out on its out for another few kilometres to the east as it wound its own way through the rocky terrain.

Once it ceased having to fight the steady push of the current as they went upstream it seemed to run smoother.

The lake was not big enough for any real waves or swells to truly threaten the boat or any of its occupants despite its length—it was simply not wide enough—and was mistaken for a river.

"How long will it take to get to the eastern edge?" asked Emilie.

"This lake is really long. It's a good couple of kilometres. We'll be there in the late afternoon if we continue at this rate," answered Derek as he flicked the line of his fishing rod into the water. "And, hopefully, we can have something a bit different and a bit fresher by the time we get there."

Derek spent the afternoon fishing while the others took turns, piloting the boat. He was a bit disappointed that nothing seemed to be biting. A fish or two of a good size would have been a welcome change to their diet. He had no doubt that if Terrence had been along he could have caught something or at least told him where he was going wrong since he had not managed to catch a single fish.

"I think the shore is in sight," said David.

Derek broke his rod down and put it back into his travel case with a sigh. "Well, that was disappointing."

"Not even a hint, eh?" asked David.

"Not one twitch."

The lake narrowed and they could see houses on the northern shore. A thin line of smoke was spotted from somewhere in the town and they looked at each other in surprise. "That could be good news or it could be bad," said

David, shaking his head. "But any sign of fire now means someone was around to light it."

The boat gently bobbed towards the shore as David cut the engine as the barge gently bobbed against the beach. Abigail drove a deep spike into the sand to tie the boat off. She then ran a second line to a metal pole sticking out of the concrete slab that formed the solid dock.

Derek looked around and turned to them. "Don't take the horses off the boat yet."

A short time later their caution was well served when four armed men came out of the clumping of houses. "Strange thing seeing a barge with a motor come from up the river these days," said the first one. "Where are you from and where are you going?"

"Down river," answered Derek. "Looking to get to Sudbury."

The four looked at each other, raising their eyebrows.

The second one asked, "Are you nuts?"

"Why? What have you heard?" asked Derek.

"Sudbury is dead, friend," said the first one. "You don't want to go there."

"How do you know?" asked David.

"I don't, but I can tell you that it's likely," he answered. "Look around you. If we're living like this, what is the city going to be like?"

The five from down the river looked at each other and Derek chewed his lip. He suspected that these four men were right but he still wanted to go. If they did not, there was no way they would ever find Garrett or what happened to him.

Derek said, "We're still going."

"All right," the first man said, with a sigh. "I can't stop you from something so stupid, but I can at least make sure you have a safe haven for the night. I'm Michel, this is Tony and his son Leo. The other one is François."

"You all that survived here?" asked David.

"No, but we're the first line of defence. What has come down the road hasn't exactly been friendly if you catch my meaning," answered Michel.

"We heard that from a bunch of kids down the road," said Abigail. "Any idea where they're coming from?"

"Yeah, I do. There's another part of Naughton just around the bend on the road. We've fought them off a few times over the winter and they retreat back there," he answered. "If you've a way to avoid them, I'd use it. The road sure as hell isn't going to be safe."

They looked past them to the boat.

"Will this work?" asked David.

There was a gleam in the older man's eyes. "Yes, I believe it will. Where did you come from that had horses?"

"A farm," answered Derek. "We rode up from the farm and picked up the boat when we saw the bridge was out."

The four men looked at each other and nodded.

"Makes sense. You're a resourceful bunch, you are," he said. "Come on up, Patricia will make sure you're all fed."

"We have to take care of our horses first," said Derek. "We'll be up in a bit."

"All right then. François will show you the way up when you're done," he said and he turned around with the other three and went back up to the houses.

Derek turned to the horses and the others. "Anyone else have a bad feeling about this?" he asked softly.

"Yeah, this is too much like that garage back when I first met you," said David.

"I think they are the ones raiding that everyone says is from 'just up the road'," said Abigail.

Derek nodded his agreement. "I think the same. So, how quick can we get out of here without tipping them off?"

CHAPTER THIRTY-TWO

Packing up and leaving was not an option in this case. If they did, after accepting the hospitality, it would probably cause the very confrontation Derek hoped to avoid. He sincerely hoped what he would find up in the settlement would not lead to a fire fight but he wanted to be prepared just in case.

David looked past him and up the beach to where more men and women were beginning to mill about. "Reese... tell me the ropes are easily untied," he whispered.

"I didn't even properly tie them off... just wrapped them once," she answered.

"I'd come off that boat if I were you," said their host. "Now, I did offer my hospitality and I was going to be nice about this; but if you make a run for it, then that hospitality is no longer in effect."

Reese watched Derek, but he did not make the motion to let the rope go.

"We're too exposed," whispered Abigail.

"I know," said Derek grimly.

There was literally nowhere for them to hide, except for maybe behind the horses but losing the horses was simply not an option either.

With a heavy sigh, he looked over at David and shook his head. David shrugged as they hopped off the boat.

With a smile, Derek asked, "What gave you the idea we were refusing? We've spent one too many days in a tent—thanks to the rain—and the tents are a bit wet. We were just discussing the best way to impose staying a few days while they dry out."

Michel looked from Derek and back to François and back again but the younger man pointed out, "In all honesty, it did look like they were rummaging through their packs and tying things off."

With a grunt, Michel glared at François and then his mood lightened abruptly. "All right, I think I may have overreacted a bit here. Let's all back up and just get you warm and dry... and fed." He clapped Derek on the shoulder. "No harm done, eh?"

Derek rubbed his shoulder and nodded. "Fantastic... I know I'm looking forward to someplace dry."

The tense feeling was still there, but it felt like it was dissipating. Michel led the others back up the path and François came up to Derek. "Between me, you and the fencepost... I could see you were trying to leave.

Derek looked at him in surprise. "Why didn't you say anything?"

François shrugged, "Michel is... touchy... but he's still a good man. Saw us through the winter where others wouldn't have been able to."

"François, I realize this is a sensitive question—but..." David thought about how to word his question. "Is Michel leading the raids?"

The long pause confirmed what they knew and François was quick to answer, "But we haven't killed anyone... really! He just huffs and puffs but if anyone pushes back, he retreats."

"So... he wouldn't have ordered you to shoot at us if we left?" asked Derek.

François looked down at the ground. "Look, you know what it's like out there," he pleaded. "If you had left... we'd have no way of knowing there were others out there."

"Raiding it isn't the way to do this," shot back David. "Even if the rule of law is apparently gone, we're still civilized."

François was looking at them with something in his eyes. "I don't know where it is you're from that the rule of law still applies—but out here it doesn't,"

"We're from further out," ground out Derek. "Wait—if it's this bad here… how bad is the city? Do you know?"

"So you are trying to get to the city?" asked François, shaking his head. "Michel wasn't lying—and he managed to fight his way here, tooth and nail, in the winter to get back to his family. He was downtown when the lights went off… when it all happened."

Derek backed away and David eyed him warily. "When what happened?" asked Derek quietly.

"It was the end of oil—the government had been lying to us the whole time about these big reserves and that it would last for God knows when… and then the bubble just burst. This—" François waved his arms around as he made a motion to include their surroundings. "—All of this… it's because of that. People went mad and the government simply stopped issuing orders. We all know the rest."

Derek walked back to the boat and sat on the deck. Marissa came over to him and sat down beside him. "What happened up there?" she asked.

"Michel was in the city when it happened," he answered. "He knows."

"Knows what?" asked Abigail. "So what? We still have a different mission at hand, if I'm not mistaken. Find that engineer... get him back to Sheridan. That ringing any bells?"

Derek had no answer for her and David made his to the boat and joined them. He said, "Michel is going to be looking for us shortly."

François ran up to the boat and looked at the crew. Swearing vehemently, he turned around and waved over one of the others. *"Allez chercher Michel et lui dire que les nouvelles sur le centre-ville a laissé un autre sans volonté."* At first the young woman did not move and looked a bit alarmed. *"Eh bien? Depechez vous!"*

The young girl ran up to the town, and they could hear her calling for Michel. François turned to the people in the town and said, "Sorry about that. She's a good kid but a bit slow on the uptake."

A few minutes later Michel called, *"Je ne vois pas un incendie. Quelle est la grosse affaire, François?"*

"I told them about what happened to you... what you had to do to get back here. This one isn't taking it so well."

Michel crouched down on the dock in front of the boat. The gleam from earlier was gone and in its place was a look of compassion. It was hidden behind a great deal of hardening—small wonder if what François had said was true—but it was there, nevertheless. "We do what we have to do to survive," he said again. "Come on... there's a fire and some fresh venison up in the town. Whatever you may think can wait until morning."

They led the horses off the barge and, with help from the others, brought everything they had up into the town proper. Michel, again, clapped Derek's shoulder and yelled over to one of the women who were cooking, "*Obtenez cet homme quelque chose à boire. Pendant que vous y êtes, Cecilie, voir de faire en sorte qu'ils obtiennent une part équitable de la venaison ainsi.*"

"I don't understand a word of what you're saying," lied Derek.

"He told her to get you something to drink... and make sure everyone gets their fair share of the venison. Tonight you'll be one of us. We can figure out what was going to happen later," said François.

"*Que sera, sera,*" said David.

Derek looked over at him, recognizing the title of the old song but not its meaning. "What will be, will be," he answered. "It's Portuguese... not French... but it fits."

"Oh!" François suddenly said. "And her name is Cecilie."

"Thanks, I think we caught at least that much," remarked Abigail, with a short bark of laughter.

Derek sat down on the upright cut log that had been set around the massive fire pit in the middle of the town. While their resources were drastically different than Sheridan's, he was pleasantly surprised to note that the same planning had seen them through the winter. It was unfortunate that the raiders along the road had been found and now he was right in the middle of their camp.

The drink handed to him was warm and the bite to it suggested it contained something alcoholic that he just could not place. He coughed over the sudden strength of it and caught Marissa's sudden look of concern, but waved her off. "That took me a bit by surprise," he admitted hoarsely. "What is that?"

Michel grinned, "Something of my own making from my own still."

Moonshine. It had to be moonshine and Derek cringed inwardly and sincerely hoped he was not about to literally go blind from it. "Not bad," said Derek. "Bit more kick than I was expecting."

It was as harsh as hell but he supposed that was why they had warmed it up. He decided he would—although he would not drop his defences—enjoy the night and let the fire warm his outsides while Michel's moonshine warmed his insides. It had been a while since he had been able to have a drink at all as Sheridan kept that under firm lock and key—it was the only thing she had for antiseptic at this point. That sent a cold finger down his spine.

Failing all else, the least he could do was open up some trade. Maybe Michel and his town would not have to raid if trade ensured that everyone had what they needed. He did not get his hopes up but, unlike the road trash from the winter, Michel seemed at least reasonable.

Cecilie, the woman who Michel had called earlier, brought him and David a plate and they ate while watching the fire. It was at this point that David looked around and shook the drowsing Derek. "Where are Em, Abby and Reese?"

Derek came to full wakefulness when he noticed that the women of their group were conspicuously absent. He turned to their host. "Michel, where are my wife and the other two that were with us?"

"Your women?" asked Michel, and he waved that off dismissively. "Off with the other women, I'd imagine."

"The men and the women don't... mix... here?" asked David.

"No," he answered, and his tone told them plainly that he thought the idea was utterly unappealing to him. "Why would you want them to? Best to leave them to whatever it is they do and the men to their work."

Derek and David looked at each other nervously, hoping that this was not something that Michel had thought up in order to prevent them from leaving. He still did not know what Michel had in mind, but the other man was not the type that would be hospitable on one hand and then leave them the next. It was up to Derek and his people to break that.

With an inward sigh, he decided to try a different tactic. "Well, that much is true," he conceded and caught David's glare in the corner of his eye. "However, where we're from the women and the men are a bit more... well... co-ed, if you catch my meaning."

"You don't think I'd do something with them, do you?" he asked.

"Oh, hardly," answered Derek. "But one of them is also my wife of some... wow... uh... thirty years... ish."

Michel laughed heartily at that. "Married for longer than you thought, eh? Don't you worry. She's not anywhere she wouldn't normally be. We did give them the option to stick around, but Cecilie can be rather convincing."

"So, where are they and I really do mind being separated from them," said Derek, the steel in his voice returning. "Call me a bit paranoid but as your guest I would like to *not* be separated from the rest of my people."

Michel looked at him and he caught something in the gaze that was almost like the other man was asking Derek for something—in fact—it was almost begging him. "Are you sure?" asked Michel quietly, looking around.

With a heavy sigh, Derek glared at him with all the force one stare could muster and the older man finally nodded. "Very well, I'll send for them."

Moments later Marissa and the three women joined Derek and David at the fire.

Derek turned to Marissa and asked, "What the hell were you thinking?"

She looked past him to one of the women who had followed her and he looked over to her and back again. "Something didn't sit well with me," she answered. "I did have Abigail and Emilie with me."

He took a breath and released it. Grasping her hand he reiterated, "Just don't do that to me again. It was not a particularly nice surprise to look around and wonder where you suddenly disappeared to."

Michel and Cecelia returned and sat down at the fire. He noticed that the other women had not and some of the men were also conspicuously absent. That same feeling of something not being quite right settled over him and he smiled thinly at his host.

* * * * *

"So why come to Sudbury?" Valeria asked finally.

Kaine looked at her in surprise. "I'm actually from here. My family are devout members of a certain church. Close minded the lot of them. They think science is heathen and contrary to God's principles," he snorted. "If they only knew."

He turned and locked the door, sighing once as he leaned on his cane before he turned to follow her back to the Grand Salon in time for the evening meal.

Everyone at the university somehow helped make the facility run. Given the talent and intelligence, it was a surprise that electricity had not yet been turned on for general use. Only for select purposes deemed important to university welfare—or research—had it been authorised. Dr. Kaine's computer research was one of those.

He was still running those simulations, only now it was all on survival.

More specifically, the university's continued survival.

"You do realize I am Christian?" she asked gently.

"Oh, don't get me wrong," he chuckled. "So am I. Just not the same type as my family. I'm a bit more agnostic, than actual Christian but I have met my fair share of others here who give me hope that their faith isn't misplaced… just my family has a cock-eyed view of the Bible."

They laughed a bit more easily now that she knew him a bit better. It was small wonder the man was so cautious around strangers. "How many others know about all this?" she asked, motioning to the bank of screens.

"You, the Chancellor of the campus, a few of my students… that's about it," he answered and shrugged. "The fact that I was in the military and worked for CSIS is well known. I never bothered to hide it. Didn't advertise it, but I didn't hide it. Just… watered down the details."

"Well, thank you for trusting me with it."

"Don't mention it," he smiled as he watched her head up to get something to eat. "Don't worry… you will have your part to play too."

CHAPTER THIRTY-THREE

Derek woke in the morning from a very light sleep even though his wife and the others had been returned to them. It was clear to David and Derek both that the women did not keep to themselves out of a desire to do so, but that they were more or less the men's property.

Derek motioned to David to follow him out the back and along the side where they could see a small gathering of the locals. Cecelie, the head woman, was talking to Michel, but the two men looked at each other in puzzlement—it was by far not Michel who was leading the conversation.

If anything, it appeared to be the complete opposite.

"The men are segregated from the women... by the women?" puzzled David. "Not what I was expecting at all."

"Terrence would call this the Avocado Jungle of Death scenario number one," mused Derek. "Our raiders are the women."

There was a snort from his wife at his comment.

"Gentle sex my..." David did not finish his thought as he turned to face the force of Abigail's glare, and he winced before asking Derek, "Do you understand a word of what they're saying?"

"I can," Derek answered. "Unfortunately I can't pick out what she's saying from here."

"She is telling Michel that where ever you come from is rich in resources—you have horses, supplies..." answered François from behind them and it took the two men everything they had not to jump from being sneaked up on. "Michel is telling her that while that may be true, it is also obvious that you can defend those resources and that travelling that far to get to some place we are not even sure of its location is foolish."

"So, the real leader of this little community is her, I take it?" asked David.

"Yes," answered François. "Come, you should not be found out here. Cecelie is scary when she gets mad and her displeasure is not something you want to be on the other end of."

They followed François back into the house. "She is a tyrant—as I said, Michel is a good man but Cecelie controls everything here. Do not trust any of the women... not even any of the girls."

He went back out of the house and back to his apparent watch. Derek and David looked at each other and sat back down until a knock sounded on their door.

"Are you awake in there?" came Michel's voice.

"We were just getting dressed for the day now," answered Derek as he opened the door, letting the other man in. "So, we had something to discuss?"

"You need to leave," said Michel. "I'll untie your boat from the dock under the pretense of sinking it. There's a path along the lake that goes to an inlet from this lake over to the other one... Take your horses and go on that path. She's not watching for you there because she thinks you'll either run for it on the road or by the boat itself... and if me and François take the boat, she'll watch the road instead."

"What will she do when you come back?"

"I have no intention of coming back... once you're done with the boat François, and I will wait for you with it. Going by lake means she cannot follow us. There's already been a few of us lucky enough to get away from her and they said they were heading to Naughton proper to live in that community." Michel pointed to his chin. "Now, make this look good for me, will you?"

David looked at Derek and Derek motioned for David to take the honours.

"You sure about this?" asked David. "Is Cecelie your wife?"

"No!" answered Michel. "She came from the north… we didn't stand a chance. The only ones that really survived the winter are me and Francois. The others all came from elsewhere— as I said on the beach—the raiders came from someplace else. I just could not tell you that they happened to choose to stay here as well."

Derek shook his head, "I seriously misjudged this situation."

"Do not be sorry—just do something about it now," answered Michel.

David took his swing and it connected solidly against Michel's jawline, sending the older man sprawling on the ground. He was thoroughly dazed, but managed to point towards the back door. The two men did not waste any time grabbing their things and leaving the house. François was, very conspicuously, nowhere in sight.

"I'm hoping that means he's off being the distraction and not running to this Cecelie," growled Abigail.

Derek nodded his agreement as they made for the path that Michel had told him about. Thankfully, it was exactly as Michel had described and where he had said. A nickering sound met him in the bushes and relief flooded him at the sight of François and their horses. Derek threw his pack on the horse and made sure everything was secure, as did the others.

"Did anyone see us leave?" asked François.

"I don't think so," answered David.

They led the horses through the underbrush and up the side of the mountain which led deeper into the bush and the promontory between the two lakes that Naughton was placed beside. Just as the horses were out of sight, they heard an outcry.

"Michel! Où sont ces autres?" came Cecelie's voice.

The answer was lost, but undoubtedly the answer that Cecelie had received was not the one she wanted. They all jumped at the sound of the sharp retort of a gun.

"Rechercher la région. Ils ne peuvent pas sont allés loin," Cecelie barked.

"Cecelie, les chevaux ont disparu!"

"Voir à la route! Vous, c'est leur barge parti?"

"Non, Cecelie, le bateau ils sont venus sur est toujours là!" came another answer.

"Alors Michel a dit la vérité... les trouver! Aller à la route et obtenir ces chevaux de retour!"

Derek swallowed and looked at the others. He understood what had been said and without the boat there was no way to go around them as the promontory led straight back to the road and far too close to Cecelie's part of Naughton. "I think they killed Michel," he said. "If I understood the thread of that conversation right, anyway."

François choked and looked away but turned back to them. "Michel was a good man. The *pouffiasse*... if we have to go through there again..."

"Do you think she killed him?" asked David grimly.

François nodded, "I wouldn't put it past her. The woman is ruthless."

Derek thought for a moment and then turned to the others. "We are going to have to go through them again and if we leave this 'Cecelie' to her own devices it will only be a matter of time before she turns into a real pain in our neck... and even if we manage to escape her, we're going to have come back through here to get back home. I say we put the *pouffiasse* down right now and right here."

Abigail nodded her agreement, "I'm definitely with you on that."

He looked at David, who only nodded, and he saw Emilie also nod her agreement. From behind him, François said, "I'll do it for my town... and for Michel."

Marissa was the last one he looked at. He did not want to drag her into this—it was one thing to explore and avoid confrontation, but a whole other thing to go walking into it wilfully and knowing that there was going to be a major fight involving guns and that people would die. There would be no talking this down—they were going down there to fight this out and kill Cecelie and anyone who stood between her and them.

A moment later she nodded once in agreement, and Derek pointed towards a rocky outcrop, following David as they carefully stayed out of sight of the town. Below, they could clearly see Cecelie as she walked around.

David checked his rifle over and took careful aim at Cecelie. "You do realize that if we get to Sudbury and find that civilization hasn't fallen what we're doing here is murder in the first degree, right?" he asked.

"Do you think we will find any sign of civilization?" asked Derek, looking at him.

David shook his head, "No."

Derek looked down to where he had told Marissa to use as cover. All he could see was the very tip of the barrel of her rifle as she was hiding well in the underbrush. Looking around to each of the other points they had picked out and agreed would be the best spots for this, he double-checked to make sure that each and every one of them looked ready before he took a breath. He thought for a moment and suddenly had a realization. "David, when you're in a situation... back when there was still a police service, was there ever a situation where a set of hostages were in direct threat and a sniper — such as a police sniper — had to be called in."

"Not in Sudbury, but I remember once having a situation in Montreal. Bunch of kids in a school. The reason they were all being held is fuzzy, but it was a tense one."

"What happened?"

"The sniper had to take the shot... the negotiations had gone south and the brass was sure that he was going to kill those kids. Had already shot their teacher," he answered. "She was only twenty-nine and left her husband and two little ones without their mother."

"One shot to save the others," mused Derek as he looked at David, meeting the other man's eyes.

David nodded, "I see your point."

Derek watched as David seemed to slow his breathing, stilling himself as he focussed everything down the scope of the rifle. "I have a shot."

"Take it," confirmed Derek.

The sharp echo of the rifle across the low plain rang out. And moments later, Cecelie simply dropped to the ground, unmoving. The raiders within Naughton did not fall into disarray but the next one in the chain of command took over.

Gunshots peppered the hillside and the trees they hid in. Derek and David had very little choice but to take sudden cover to avoid being shot at random. A sound of fury came from below as someone, likely their new leader, yelled, *"Les salauds ont tué mon Cecelie! Tuez-les tous!"*

"He's not very happy," said Derek. "Called us bastards and wants us all dead."

"Yeah, I caught that," snorted David. "Well, even if there is still civilization and even if I have overstepped the bounds for an officer of the law, I am still oath bound to do my best to bring them before the courts."

"And if they don't want to go in front of the courts?" asked Derek.

"Normally people give up long before this," mused David and he winced as a piece of the granite that made up the Canadian Shield shattered above his head and fragments showered them. "But, it's like in the States… we are authorized to use deadly force. If we have to… and only if there is no other way to resolve things."

"I somehow think there's no other way to resolve this," said Derek as he whistled in two short blasts. Return fire erupted from the other four of his group. "See if you can take the new head of this snake… and each time a new one pops up, take him out too."

"You got it," said David as he ducked back out again.

Derek watched as David shot the one that was now yelling orders and someone managed to wing another in the arm. Abigail was also an accurate shot and he was relieved to note that anyone who had decided to get involved had managed to duck, cover and then get behind something else. The only people on the ground were any who had fired back at where Derek and the others were hidden.

The entire fire fight took only minutes and they slowly made their way back down the side of the hill and into the square below. Those actually from Naughton came out while François ran over to where Michel lay and he knelt down beside the older man.

It was at this moment that a young woman ran out and hugged François and he clung to her in return, kissing her forehead.

He turned to Derek then and said, "Thank you."

"I only wish we could have also saved Michel," answered Derek. "You were right—he was a good man in a bad situation."

"You couldn't have known either," said François, and he turned to the woman, hugging her again. "We promised you a way around Naughton… you have it. The rest of Naughton is dead and gone… we are all that is left and what you see here is what we have managed to scrounge up. Take the highway to the north of here to Lively. Godspeed to you… and when you return I will make sure your boat is ready for you."

Derek shook Francois' hand. "We will." He turned to the others who were already mounting, then mounted his horse and finished, "Take care of yourself, François."

"You as well," he answered.

CHAPTER THIRTY-FOUR

Derek did not want to even think about just how very lucky they had all been in escaping Naughton without injury. While the loss of Michel was unfortunate he was relieved that no one in their little group had been lost. Unlike Helen the first time a similar situation had come up. The thought of it still brought bile up to his throat, especially after what she had had to do in order to even find them in the first place.

He could not afford to lose himself in such thoughts now or they would end up losing someone else. This new life was in many ways far harsher than his old life had been. Derek would give almost anything to be able to simply sit in front of his television and enjoy something as simple as a big game or even a movie.

He had to accept that those days were now long gone. His beloved den was likely now dust filled and the electronics—and all his photos and memories—left to the merciless freeze and then likely to rot as everything melted and leaked.

Much like the rest of Naughton.

It was all as Michel and François described. The deserted town added to the ever growing list of ghost towns that dotted Sudbury's landscape even before the end of oil.

Derek caught himself.

He had finally referred to the end of their old civilization—and the event that triggered it—as the end of oil and this new world was what would be after it… A world after oil.

He swallowed thickly at the mere thought of it. The feeling that came over him was akin to dread, but at the same time was different than it. It was not relief—not dread—but something not unlike those two mismatched emotions only mashed together into some new, and raw, emotional parcel.

It was not unlike the town they now rode through.

The houses within this part of Naughton were torn into and some even demolished leaving nothing but foundations of empty concrete. Those not torn down for their raw materials stood in mute testimony to the harsh winter they had survived. The grass—where once there had been lawn—was now as tall as his hips and knees.

It all lay abandoned.

After passing the third lake since starting their trek they finally reached the outskirts of what had been Lively as the terrain began to level back out again. It was a very gentle descent down and into the valley. Derek began to feel the same feeling of being watched as he had back in Whitefish only now there were far more houses and far more hiding places for an ambush.

As one they reached the first set of lights— which he noted were dead and slightly bent out of shape as if something had collided with them—at a major four lane intersection. This particular intersection had always formed the main point of entry into Lively and in fact was also part of the road north to Chelmsford. At this point Sudbury with its distinctive smoke stack well over a kilometre tall stood in the distance.

"Well, that's still standing," pointed out David sarcastically. "Wonderful to know that failing all else the world's biggest smoke stack still stands even after the end of the world."

Derek snorted in a short chuckle as he had been thinking the same thing. He pointed north. "There's a major clinic and Fire Hall that way, if

I'm not mistaken. Sheridan said her practise was always out of there. Maybe…"

His hackles rose at the same moment that the people came out of every nook and cranny that someone could hide suddenly surfaced and surrounded them. He looked around and held up a hand to Abigail, who was already reaching for her shotgun. Derek could tell just by looking that these were the survivors of Lively and not raiders.

"If you've come looking for trouble, you've found it!" someone from up the hill yelled through a bull horn

Derek raised his hands and shook his head. "We haven't!"

"Then where did you come from and why?" asked another one pointing at Abigail's stance. "I don't want to have to. But if I have to defend these people, I won't hesitate to do it."

"And that's why we're not drawing any weapons," said Derek, again motioning for Abigail to stand down. "My name is Derek… we're here because Dr. Sheridan Wither from Panache Lake sent us."

The other one, who had an open radio channel, spoke quickly into it. "They say that a Dr. Sheridan Wither sent them."

"My god, is she still alive?" asked one of the other ones holding a gun and he pointed the barrel to the ground.

"And well," answered Derek. "The name's Derek Moss, and…"

"The solar panel sales guy?" asked another one. "Of all the people to survive the end of the world is someone who can supply power…"

Derek looked at the others as they slowly relaxed in his group's company. The one with the radio shook his head and said, "Well, if they trust you, I suppose I can too. Lieutenant Kevin O'Neill, Algonquin Regiment… and as far as we know we're what's left of it."

"As simple as that?" asked David.

"Let's just say that if you prove to not be who and what you say you are, it won't really matter in the long, or short run. Raiders have come… and then they've gone," he answered. "If there is one thing we do and do well, it's to keep the citizens alive while the present circumstances allow us to."

A young man of Middle Eastern descent pushed his way forward after running clear down the hill from the clinic and Fire Hall. "Excuse me!" he yelled up at them as the throng did not let him through. "My name is Dr. Assad. Did you say that Dr. Wither is still alive? I don't see her with you."

"She is but her husband and the others protecting her and her land thought it best she stay there and keep things running," answered Derek honestly. "What did you need?"

"It's best if we continue this at the clinic. Let them through!" called Dr. Assad.

Derek and the others followed Dr. Assad and Lt. O'Neill back up the hill to the clinic which had been fortified. As soon as they came up the long curve and around the corner, David whistled at the sight of two armoured personnel carriers with their cannons pointed back down the hill. Portable fortifications of military make and engineering further protected the approach.

"I'm guessing you've had issues with raiders," said David.

"We have…" answered Dr. Assad.

"Constable Radzinsky?" came a voice as they came into view. "Oh my God, Dave? We thought you were dead!"

David looked up and his eyes widened and then he grinned widely at the sight of two more members of the Sudbury Police—others he had thought dead. Derek grinned at the reunion and the mood seemed to brighten substantially.

David turned to Derek and said, "Luis, Shana, this is Derek, Marissa, Abigail and Emilie… if not for them I wouldn't be here right now. Guys, these two are my colleagues… Lieutenant Luis Sanche and Auxiliary Constable Shana MacKenzie."

Dr. Assad suggested, "Perhaps more reunions are best done in the clinic where I can explain things better?"

* * * * *

The waiting area of the clinic in Lively was large and open concept. For now, it had been commandeered as a meeting room for Derek and his friends.

In many ways it reminded Derek of Sheridan's living room. But, unlike Sheridan's house, the structure was modern and the clean lines of something meant specifically as a medical clinic.

Not everyone could fit within the waiting area. Those in it included Derek and his group as well as Lieutenant O'Neill, Doctor Assad and a few others yet to be introduced. Assad appeared to be the nominal leader of the group and Derek noted that it, again, who led the community, was also another doctor.

"When the power went out we didn't know what to think," admitted Assad as he turned back to face them his coffee in his hand. "The lieutenant here was quick to focus his attention on fortifying this part of Lively."

Derek could see Marissa's amused face as he breathed in the fumes of his own cup of coffee in deep appreciation. He was more than happy to let David take the lead on this while he had his first real cup of coffee in months. And he was determined to appreciate it while he could.

"It was a good thing, too, as the rest of the world seemed to come apart at the seams once all contact was lost," said O'Neill. "Once Ottawa and the brigade leadership stopped responding, we knew all hell had broken loose… that the unthinkable happened. At Christmas it all came to a head when each tin-star brass decided to make a bid at carving their own piece of the pie under the guise of military exercises."

"So… there was no actual martial law declared," mused Derek as he looked over at Marissa. "It's a miracle we even got through to Panache from Coniston in the first place."

"I'd say so," answered O'Neill in surprise. "That's one hell of a trek at that point—especially since travel had been severely restricted between districts before Christmas."

Derek shrugged, not about to share his resources quite yet. Not that they apparently mattered anymore. "So, what happened then?" asked David. "The government?"

"Toppled like the stack of cards they really were," answered O'Neill. "As soon as it became plain that their fragile little illusion of resources they controlled was shattered, control simply fell. One party tried to take power, and then it turned into a free for all in Ottawa… and others parts of the world. The great engine of politics and government fell under the weight of the disarray brought on by a revolution gone drastically wrong."

"Surely not also in the US?" asked Marissa, shocked.

"Where do you think it started?" snorted O'Neill. "Once what everyone thought was holding the economy together was revealed as a fraud, it was overnight chaos—both here and there."

"How?" asked Emilie.

"It started with Russia," answered Assad. "And China."

Derek snorted. "Seriously?"

"Seriously—they both wanted more oil because their reserves had run out... But they couldn't tell anyone else this because Russia was a major exporter of oil and China a major buyer," answered O'Neill. "Russia began to buy more oil, under the table so to speak, to supply China... and that major supplier was the Middle East."

"Which had reached its own state of peak oil long before this—we knew... It's why Dubai and other places had become tourist trade meccas instead of just oil. The great mother oil fields were running dry," said Assad. "Which meant we also had to run further afield to find more oil."

"Which leads to Texas oil and the Alberta oil sands," said Abigail. "But Alberta has loads of oil—it's the major export."

"So they claimed," O'Neill added. "The reality was they were cutting their oil with Texas crude and off shore platforms, as well as squeezing every last dirty drop from the sands."

"But, the Texas oil fields were also beginning to run dry—which meant we had to search further into the ocean into high stakes drilling," said Assad. "Eventually, what no one was telling the other was that one was buying from another. Who, in turn, was borrowing from another, who then turned and sold it right back to the originator in order to appease each other."

Derek and David looked at each other and Derek then remembered David's analogy of paying credit with credit until finally there was nothing left. He swallowed.

"So what happened?" asked Emilie. "You can't tell me that the only thing that toppled the whole works was a credit issue."

"It wasn't—it was also the fact that they were relying on piracy to hide the fact that they needed to supply each other's oil. They were resorting to stealing it," answered Assad. "Until finally one country invaded another one for its oil—or for the oil they thought the other had."

"Which brought on trade sanctions and... oh my God," said Derek. "The whole thing came to a head and the truth was revealed..."

"Instant global anarchy," answered O'Neill. "Political suicides, assassinations, coups... and then finally they pulled the plug on any and all communications. No effort to regain control was made. Near as I can guess I think someone finally pushed a button and we went to war... only we weren't exactly invited. Civilization—

as we know it—is gone. Our governments have fallen and there's no leadership, no controls and no law."

"Sheridan has instituted laws, and government," said David quietly but despite how quietly he said it everyone heard it and turned to him. "In the absence of anyone else we voted her in as our leader for the community of Panache Lake. She made sure we survived the winter and we've given her our support."

"So why are you here, then?" asked O'Neill pointedly. "You planning on annexing us?"

"Hardly," admitted Derek. "We didn't even know you were here. Don't get us wrong; we had hoped someone survived that would be willing to consider trading and not killing us on sight."

Assad snorted in amusement, "So, we're a happy accident?"

"If you want to call it that, sure," answered Derek.

"What kind of trade are you looking for?" he asked.

"Knowledge, supplies, future options for alliances and more trade," answered David. "As well as a jumping off point for further exploration east."

"Are you insane?" asked O'Neill. "The only thing in the city is more death. You don't want to know what happened to Sudbury."

The five of them looked at each other and Derek asked, a sinking feeling settling into his gut. "What happened?"

"If you really want to know, it's best I show you," answered Kevin.

"First things first," said Derek as he held up his empty coffee cup. "Where did you get the coffee?"

Kevin laughed and answered, "The coffee shop down the road from here must have just got a shipment in before everything went to hell."

He led Derek outside and waved off his people, which effectively gave Derek and his group free rein in Lively.

"I would like to check out what's to the north... If you haven't already picked the grocery stores clean that way," said Derek, inwardly celebrating the chance to finally have a supply of coffee again.

Kevin shrugged his indifference. "We have, but if you find anything we missed, it's yours."

"How about we..." Derek trailed off as one of the young men from Kevin's unit ran up and saluted.

"Sir, we spotted a band of raiders in Copper Cliff.

Copper Cliff was another small town—only right next to the city of Sudbury and so close to it that it was all but part of Sudbury proper. Lively was immediately to its west which put the town of Lively in the dangerous position of being right next door to the most dangerous of areas now that the law was gone.

The city, as Derek had suspected, had crumbled into itself. The only ones to survive the implosion of control had been the toughest and meanest within the city. The real rough necks and the other less than savoury types who had no issues with taking and fighting for what they wanted—or, even, killing for it.

Kevin turned to Derek. "The grand tour is going to have to wait. I would suggest that you and your friends head back up to the clinic and wait this out with the others."

Normally, Derek would have taken his advice, and he was still inclined to do so. But something made him pause and think about it. Perhaps it was the time spent as a ranger himself and having to serve a greater purpose of protecting his fair share of the land Sheridan granted him to protect—and his new home—caused him to decide something entirely different.

"If it's all the same to you, I'm not a man that lets others protect him while he runs and hides," answered Derek, and then he shrugged. "Then again, I'm not exactly a head on fighter."

"Oh?" asked Kevin. "I have to admit that wasn't the answer I was expecting."

"I did ride on horseback through the desolate and raider ridden road between here and Whitefish," he pointed out.

Kevin nodded in acknowledgement of that. "What's your style, soldier?"

"I'm not—" Derek protested and then sighed as there was no point in arguing. At this point, he was a soldier... of a sort. "Ranger—from a distance and from where they never see it coming."

Kevin grinned, "I think I have just the place for you to be."

CHAPTER THIRTY-FIVE

Derek and Kevin climbed the ladder part of the way to the top of the radio tower. Now that they were high enough he could clearly see over the trees and into the extremely industrialized area that bordered Lively and Copper Cliff.

The view from the tower was incredible, despite the fact that the wind, while not very strong, still made the skinny aluminium tower sway against the thin tension wires holding it in place. He would never have climbed this tower or anything like it before this, but he and Kevin needed to gather enough information in order to formulate a plan of action to repel the most recent influx of new raiders from Copper Cliff.

"Do they always come from Copper Cliff?" asked Derek as he took out his binoculars and looked through them to see even further into what was left of Sudbury.

His stomach sank.

What little he could see of the city was not very pretty at all and he was glad that they had met Kevin in Lively instead of having to find the information he wanted in Sudbury. There was no doubt now that when the rule of law vanished like morning mist after sunrise, the city had fallen completed into anarchy.

The destruction was widespread and easily seen. Buildings and complexes that had existed since the early fifties were conspicuously missing—or only half standing. One apartment building in the distance looked as if half of it had collapsed. Smoke still rose from house fires and other fires that had yet to go out. Some places looked like they had been destroyed on purpose by some sort of rocket weaponry.

It looks like a war zone in the downtown, perhaps even all the way out to New Sudbury, realized Derek as his heart sank. *I guess there's little chance of even finding a house still there, even if we make it all the way out to Garson…*

"You're looking at Sudbury, aren't you?" asked Kevin, yelling over the wind.

"Yeah," answered Derek. After he stopped using the binoculars, he looked up at Kevin. "I see what you mean. There's nothing left."

"Considering the radio silence and the lack of response even by satellite radio, there's no one listening in any of the HQ's," said Kevin. "We're on our own out here."

Derek looked through the binoculars and down the road that connected Lively and Copper Cliff. There was a large gathering of people just inside the industrial complex bordering the road.

It was far larger than he expected, perhaps a few hundred strong. "We've got a problem," he yelled up to Kevin, pointing to where he was looking.

Kevin looked where he pointed and swore vehemently. "Well, that's not good."

A few minutes later they climbed back down to the ground where the police from Lively and Kevin's unit waited   Derek looked at the scant seven police officers—including David—and knew that at least two were part of the auxiliary corps and not regular and the other OPP was also an auxiliary. Of those two were OPP and one detective from the Royal Canadian Mount Police. In fact, he also knew the Algonquin corps was part of the reservists and not regular. That meant that most of what they had—while well trained like regulars—were civilians and not actually regular, full-time forces.

Some of the others were security guards and he figured he had at least four of those in their larger unit. Normal people comprised the rest — people that just wanted to defend their homes and families against those who once were neighbours and had now forgotten that fact.

"We have our work cut out for us," mused Derek.

Kevin agreed, "We don't have enough weapons to go around that are military or even police issue. The rest of what we've found has come from the various hunter supply shops and also what some of the people here had in their homes."

"Basically hunting weapons," said Derek.

Canada was not like the United States. There was no amendment that allowed the right to bear arms in defence of home and personal property or one's family. The only recourse, if someone wanted to be involved in defence in such a capacity, was joining the Reserves for the Canadian Military or as an Auxiliary for the various branches of police services. Both methods required rigorous employment screening and background checks.

Weapons as such were only supposed to be for hunting game and then only in certain areas. Again, the laws and regulations required to register were long and complicated. Most people simply decided that when they were going to camp it was likely to involve fishing.

Although, a simple hunting rifle without a scope was deadly enough. But their prime purpose was to take down animals—not people wearing modern combat armour.

"So, to sum up things… we literally have no idea what we're up against or even what resources these raiders would have to fight us with," mused Derek aloud, and Kevin nodded.

Derek looked up the road and thought for a moment.

The largest problem is access. The road from Copper Cliff was another a four lane highway set over the main four lane highway with a clover leaf interchange. This makes it easy to just stroll into Lively and back out again. The even larger issue is…

Derek followed the path of the road suddenly realized where the raiders—including those plaguing Panache Lake and Whitefish— always came from and just how they were getting to the area. *Oh… well, shit… this is going to be a rather large problem unless we do something about it.*

That very clover leaf gave them easy access down the four lane highway and to Whitefish by bypassing everything in their path. There was literally no one to stop them and then they easily could retreat back with their gains.

The bridge was their jumping off point and Lively sat right on it.

He looked at Kevin, "I have an idea."

* * * * *

Hours later Derek packed up his horse and loaded the saddle bags with junk and clothing. There was a fairly good chance the horse was going to bolt, no matter how well trained, and if she bolted, he did not want any of their precious supplies going with her. Marissa watched him dress in the armour that Sheridan had given him, but he also added a layer of modern flak armour underneath.

"I don't want you to do this," she pleaded. "Tell me you're not going to do it."

"Someone has to and I'm sending some kid out there to do it," he reasoned and sighed. "And it has to look like a trader or someone else... someone that would have been in our group."

"Why you?" she asked.

"Abigail and David will be with me."

"Then why aren't we all going?" she asked sharply.

He sighed again even he had to admit he could see her point. Why was she not going with him when he had always maintained that they stick together—no matter what? He knew the main reason he did not want her with them was purely because he wanted her safe.

Well, as safe as anything in the new world would be.

There was a good chance he would not be coming back from his little surprise for the raiders.

"Reese…" he began and then turned to face her.

"I *won't* let you do this," she said.

"Remember when I asked you if you would have a problem with me being a ranger for Sheridan's farm—her growing nation—and that it would likely result in me leaving you behind? How dangerous it was?" he asked.

"What does that have to do with this?" she asked.

"Everything," he answered. "I could have ridden out from that farm while you stayed behind and come here and still did all this. I'm asking you to let me do what you said you would let me do now."

Marissa nodded, her lips compressed into a thin line. "Fine—but don't do anything stupid out there. You come back to me."

"Wouldn't dream of doing otherwise," he admitted, pulling her into a hug. "I promise you—I'll come back, safe and sound, to you and we can go home."

"I'll hold you to that," she answered.

CHAPTER THIRTY-SIX

Derek led the others onto the bridge and then over to the other side while Kevin's people were placing charges using lengths of Primacord wrapped around the supports. David twitched regularly, as if looking for trouble but not quite sure where it would come from.

It was very unsettling to know that right under his feet were explosives that could go off at any second.

"Make this look good," said Derek in a low voice. "We're looking for supplies, we know there should be trouble and likely will be but we have no idea where they are."

"Except we do," said Abigail. "On your one o'clock."

Derek flicked his gaze over to where Abigail pointed to him and saw the brief little motion. "I see them."

He took a breath, finger loosely on the trigger of his shotgun. "Kev?" asked Derek into the ear piece lent to him.

"A few more minutes," came the answer. "My people are falling back now."

"We may not have a few more minutes," answered Derek.

"Incoming!" yelled David as the first of the raiders jumped out from behind the burned out husk of a car.

The first retort of the shotgun in the raider's hand was like a signal to the others. Knowing there was no point in hiding, they sprang their ambush and swarmed onto the four horses. Derek managed to shoot one that had almost managed to grab the reins, and then the raider yelled, "Back to the bridge!"

They retreated while Derek and his group had the horses. This meant they were able to put a significant distance between them in a very short time.

The Algonquin reservists and the police held their fire until Derek and the others were clear.

"Fire at will!" yelled Kevin and semi-automatic weapons fire filled the air.

The first wave of the raiders—funnelled onto the bridge as they had been—were cut down by the focused fire of Kevin's soldiers within minutes. Unfortunately, there were more of them behind the first wave. Derek and the others dismounted quickly and he slapped the horse gently and she ran away from the flying bullets. Four horses galloped down the road to the waiting people. And they help the horses escape from the fire fight.

Derek approached Kevin and yelled, "Are your people ready?"

There was no answer. When he touched Kevin's shoulder, he crumpled. With a wash of horror, Derek realized that the commander of the reserves was dead.

The control for the explosives was on Kevin. Derek searched the immediate area and saw the remote down the side of the hill. He slid down and grabbed it, looking under the structure of the bridge.

Gun shots peppered the ground. He ducked and hid under the bridge.

There was only one way he could end this and he was unfortunately right below what had to be blown.

He looked at the device.

He had promised his wife he would go back alive. He could hear the sound of the battle above him and the heavier thuds of the grenades.

The raiders were starting to spill out beside the bridge and down the ravine to the other part of the highway. Concrete dust rained down on Derek as the onslaught continued.

Gunfire was going in two directions and there was no way he could go back the way he came. *I'm trapped here*, he realized. Heart in his mouth, he closed his eyes. *And I just broke my promise...*

The thuds of heavier weapons seemed further away, but he knew it was still just above his head as dust and cement bits rained down on him. Derek picked his way to the other side and away from the invading marauders and to where the cement did not fall as heavily.

It was beginning to get quiet and somebody shouted, "Ammo out!"

Derek jumped the rest of his way down to the cement to the shallow creek below, ignoring the sudden flash of pain through his knee and leg. The bridge above him erupted in flames.

Screams met his ears. Bits of metal and rock rained down as a large piece of concrete landed near his head.

The pain caught up with him and his vision darkened. The cold water in the creek seeped into his clothing.

...I'm so, so sorry, Reese... he thought as he gave up on his tenuous grip on consciousness.

* * * * *

Marissa watched in horror as the column of smoke rose suddenly to her immediate east from where Derek had last reported from. While the raiders had not made it past the bridge in great numbers every last armed person had to protect the road.

She had never been one to run away from anything and if Derek had brought her with him then she, too, was going to defend Lively.

Even if the role involved little else but picking off anyone who managed to make it past the army.

Those who did had also turned at the thrumming feel through the ground and then the sonic shock wave that rippled the air. It never sounded like thunder. Movies had always made explosions sound like rumbling thunder... but this did not sound like that.

The sound had been like a whine, a zipping whistle and then the smoke and debris just lifted into the air.

The smoke dissipated far quicker than Hollywood showed it. One moment there had been a column as high as she could see and then it had all fallen back down again. All that remained was a thin thread—like that of a campfire in the distance.

All this in mere seconds.

The few raiders who had made it through simply lost their will to fight and sat down on the road. It was as if they knew what that meant, and what it heralded.

The police officers who had hung back simply fell on old habits and swooped in to take them off the road, dragging them down to where the grocery store was.

Marissa stood in the middle of the road, and waited.

Others arrived, and then one soldier brought back a covered body. "It's Lt. O'Neill," said Kevin's second in command, shaking her head. "I'm sorry, ma'am... there's no sign of your husband out there."

"You had to see something... someone did," insisted Marissa, as Abigail came over to them.

"The last we heard from Derek he had returned to Kevin's position—and Kev had the detonator. When the bridge blew we assumed it had been Kevin who pushed the button... but..." Abigail shook her head. "No Derek and no detonator... and if he was under that bridge..."

Marissa sank down to her knees. "Dammit, no, he promised me he'd come back. He told me to trust him—he said he'd *come back*."

Abigail hugged the older woman from behind as Marissa wept.

CHAPTER THIRTY-SEVEN

Sometime after twilight turned to night, Derek opened his eyes. In the darkness, there was nothing but cold—so cold that he could barely get his body to react. He ran his hand down the side of his leg and his ribs and then started to laugh.

I'm alive, he thought as he pushed a chunk of cement only centimetres from his head away from him. *I didn't think I'd survive this…*

He crawled his way, out of the water of the creek, and under the cement and stone. He stared in disbelief at the scene in front of him— there was nothing left of the bridge, but twisted metal and broken rubble and there was also no one in sight.

"Ow…" he breathed as he sat down heavily on the rubble below the remains of the bridge. *Not looking forward to rest of the walk up there.*

Derek staggered stiffly, and then climbed his way up through jagged chunks of concrete and twisted rebar to the Lively side of the bridge. The Primacord explosive had neatly cut the bridge from the road in a line and blasted the rest into chunks of concrete. The road was blocked with no way for anyone to cross the four lanes while the cars and semis were squashed beneath.

Derek stumbled down the road toward Lively and met a group of people. They stared at him like he was a ghost then ran up to him once they recognized who he was. A woman approached him. With no desire to question her intention, he let her guide him back down the hill to where the clinic was.

He walked those final steps in a bit of a daze, not even noticing anything around him—or the gathering crowd.

Derek came out of this long enough when he collapsed to protesting knees. "Ow," he said again, and then Marissa pushed her way through the other people and to his side, and he clung to her. "Never thought I'd see you again."

"I'm going to assume that was a hello," she pointed out, as he let him wrap his arms around her ribs. "Because other than 'ow' I didn't understand what you just said... Derek?"

"He's out," said Dr. Assad, as he checked Derek over. "I also seriously doubt he's heard a word of what anyone has said. I think he's deaf from the blast."

"Will he always be deaf?" asked Abigail.

Assad shook his head as they pulled Derek's arms, still gripping Marissa even while unconscious, from around his wife and lifted him to a waiting stretcher. "Could be only temporary, could be permanent," answered Assad. "Won't know until I get him into the clinic. Need to clean him up and get a better look."

Marissa followed them back to the clinic and into the examination room. She sat down beside them and took Derek's hand in her own. He never even flickered an eyelash despite all the activity around him. *He's exhausted*, she realized. *At least I hope that's the only thing it is.*

"Mrs. Moss, I'm afraid you need to move," said Dr. Assad. "Unless you plan on helping out."

"Of course I'm staying right here," she answered, taking a bowl of water and a few clean cloths from the pile. "And if that means helping then I'll do it."

* * * * *

Derek woke up and found himself in a warm bed with an intravenous line running into his arm. From the look of the room it was not a house, but instead someplace distinctly medical. It was too clean, and institutional, for an office and the facilities looked too much like a hospital. *Not where I remember being last...* he thought. *Wait... where was I last?*

"Oh my God, Derek, are you all right?" asked Marissa.

"Not so loud," he murmured as her voice, as soft as it was right now, was enough to send little jackhammers into his temple.

The shockwave of the explosives had still been enough to...

...And then he remembered. *Oh, that's right. I blew up the Lively Bridge... and somehow survived it... which means I must be in the clinic.* "Oh God, my head."

"Your *head*?" she asked, her voice rising in disbelief, and he rolled slightly onto his side as he groaned. "You're lucky to even *have* a head. Everyone told me they last saw you at the command post with Kevin, and then suddenly you simply vanished down into the ravine... and they knew you had the control... They told me you were under the bridge when you pushed that button. Derek... I thought you were dead and you *promised* me!"

Derek sighed heavily, "Trust me when I say that my promise was never very far from my mind."

Marissa leaned over and leaned her head on his shoulder, half on his bed but without disturbing his bandaging. Eventually he found himself nodding off and she looked up at him, watching him as he tried to fight it. "You need to sleep. Dr. Assad said you have a serious concussion."

"I don't doubt it," he answered, yawning before drifting into the foggy between of sleep and not quite asleep.

Marissa pulled the blankets back up over his shoulders, and patted his arm. "I swear if you ever do this to me again, I'll tie you to the bed posts by your damn ties," she threatened, but smiled knowing he could not hear her anyway. She leaned close. "Your *most* expensive ones, too."

"Promise?" came his whispered reply.

Marissa pinched her nose and groaned.

* * * * *

The days continued to roll by until Derek woke up again. Marissa hovered over him as he dressed, handing him pieces of his own clothing until he glared at her and sighed in exasperation.

"Are you sure you feel up to moving around this much?" asked Marissa as she followed him out of the clinic.

"I'm fine," answered Derek, staring at Dr. Assad who walked in. "And that goes double for you, before you ask."

"You're welcome," answered Dr. Assad, grinning. "How's your head?"

"Clear, for once," answered Derek. "Which is why I'd like to get out of here."

Derek let his wife grasp his hand as they walked out of the clinic. And soon after, he was met with thunderous applause. He released Marissa's hand and held up his hands and motioned for them to stop making such a fuss.

"Are you kidding? After what you did *and* managed to survive?" asked David as he tapped him on the shoulder. "And you tell us to play it cautious."

Derek shrugged, "It was all... well... I didn't think about anything other than what it would mean if we failed at the mission we gave ourselves. The raiders would have overrun Lively and I heard the soldiers calling the fact that they were out of ammo. I had to do it when I did... I just barely managed to get myself out from under the bridge when I did."

"You are definitely a serious bad ass..." Abigail trailed off. "So, what do we do now? Are we still heading to Garson to find Garrett?"

Derek looked across what was left of the bridge.

"Where are you going?" asked David, surprised.

Derek turned back to them, locking his hands in Marissa's. "I don't know about you, but I'm heading home. We have all we need right here."

Marissa's grinned and looked up at the sky, mouthing her thanks. "Amazing how it took nearly being crushed by a bridge for him to come to that conclusion."

* * * * *

It had taken weeks but the waters of the river had finally returned to their normal level and the water no longer frothed in angry eddies as it rushed down and through its course.

The trees finally had their full coverage of leaves and the underbrush was at its thickest. It was hardly quiet—the whole forest was awake now. Birds and squirrels wrestled over seeds and territory and the wind rustled the leaves.

A lonely cabin sat down river from the dam but was well above the flood point of the river.

Within, Garrett Wither wrapped a strip of cloth around his arm. *That took weeks, but the cut looks mostly healed*, he sighed. *Not the most professional job on the face of the planet but it will have to do.*

He walked to the door and pulled it open, barely dodging water from the roof as he did.

In the distance he could just barely see the dam.

From this far, the large structure holding back millions of gallons of water did not looking nearly as imposing. No one really knew it was there—just a few did or even what it meant.

Garrett was one of those few.

Not that it mattered anymore.

It's obvious no one is coming. Dane has what he wants, and I'm all alone out here...

Once his arm healed and he scrounged up a few more supplies he would leave, and attempt to make it down to where he suspected his daughter and mother was. If not, he was sure there was a small community of people in between that could use his skills.

All he had to do was wait.

ABOUT THE AUTHOR

Kristan Cannon was born in Kirkland Lake, Ontario and educated in North Bay and Toronto. She is a staunch supporter of literacy, reading, and young writer's programs. She also holds a current membership with The Indie Writer's Network and is a member of the NaNoWriMo Ambassador's program.

When not researching or writing, Kristan exists for sailing her classic wooden sailboat with her cat, friends, and family... or for video games and books when snow and ice have the boat locked in its slip and she can't get away.

More about Kristan on her website:
www.kristancannon.com

Acknowledgements

My decision to go independent at first instead of the traditional route means the team of artists, proofreaders and support was a little different. Not only did I have to balance writing this book but I also had to step into the shoes of a publisher and editor.

Despite being finally accepted by KCEditions I could not do it without help and I owe a massive thank you to the following for providing it:

My publicist Allan, and my regular employer Carmelo for letting me 'share the office' after hours and his office printer for the reprint of the final manuscript. I can easily tell you without either of these two this book would not be sitting in your hands at all.

Wilma for stepping in as the main editor when the computer, and the USB, decided eating over 75% of the manuscript only weeks before Anime North was a fantastic idea and forcing me to rewrite the book from the gathered scraps of previous drafts.

The original role playing group that portrayed a few of the characters in here.

Everyone who cheered me on.

The artist, Jeanette, for designing the fantastic cover and Vanessa for the amazing day at Lawrence Market and the amazing portrait photos.

And, of course, Steve... for not being completely horrified at the thought the character I based off of him decided he wanted to be the main character.

Preview of

THE LAST IRON HORSE

The next book in
Kristan Cannon's
Kingdom of Walden Trilogy

Available Now!

Karen found her godmother pacing in the white room—a room in the northern corner of the Manor which sat closest to the escarpment. Marissa never paced and this was enough to make Karen pause. In one corner sat her grandmother's paint easel, although Lorraine no longer had time to paint with keeping the kitchen organized.

"Reese?" Karen asked.

Marissa jumped a bit to the side, her hand on her chest. "Jesus, Karen, don't do that."

"Sorry."

The older of the two waved Karen into the room as she walked over to one of the long couches. "Karen, how has Sheridan been holding up?" asked Marissa. Before Karen could answer Marissa continued, "For that matter, how are you holding up? Lorraine? The others?"

Karen blinked. "I suppose we're all doing the best we can... why?"

"I'm concerned some of us taken on a heavier work load than others—and it's not because someone else is shirking," Marissa sighed again as she crossed her arms and looked over at Karen. "The opposite, actually. It's because someone isn't delegating."

"Sheridan," surmised Karen, and was hardly surprised when Marissa nodded. "You can't tell me you weren't expecting her to do it, though. You do remember this is the woman who was supposed to hire a personal assistant over five years ago and never quite did. I'm amazed she took Suni on, but I suppose Pavi didn't give her much choice in the matter."

"I was thinking, like Suni has for things medical, of taking on things administrative," said Marissa. "I have no idea what anyone will call what I do—Terrence and Sheridan are the history nuts and since we seem to be taking a large step back in time into a... ah... not sure what to call this and it's been years since I graded anything or had to look something like this up..."

"I'm sure in the library upstairs they've probably got something on the subject," suggested Karen. "Since you want to take up 'things administrative' I think you've got the first call on what you get to call yourself."

Marissa lifted her brows and leaned back in the couch. "Valid point."

* * * * *

The space behind the fireplace was a small room in a sea of larger ones. It always had been an awkward space with only a few bookshelves and a small desk. The advantage was that despite its odd layout—or its use as an odd shaped hallway instead—it was still private.

It was perfect as a small office.

The shelves held extra storage space for filing and organization. The small desk was more than big enough for someone to keep track of expenses and other things.

A few hours later Jeremy poked his head into the room as he watched Marissa shift things around. "What are you doing?" he asked.

"Sheridan needs someone as her second," answered Marissa. "Not medical, but administrative. Someone who can run things if she cannot."

"You?" he asked.

"Why not?" she asked in return as she looked up at him. "Come on, give me a hand. Maybe we both can whip this into shape."

Jeremy looked almost like he was going to say something but then changed his mind as he came the rest of the way into the room. Marissa had borrowed or outright taken certain things from other rooms. But the items, unused and ignored, were hardly missed by their previous owners. With a sigh, he helped her tweak her new office into the space she was looking for. "There," she said. "That should just about do it."

"Why did we just spend a day making another office?" he asked, puzzled.

"I already told you," she answered. "Sheridan has two big hats to wear but she's only one person. So, each role has someone to back her up. In the clinic I think she has Suni, and

Emilie if she comes back. But in running the farm, so to speak, she has no one to keep track of anything. We may as well be it."

Marissa linked her arm with Jeremy's as his eyebrows rose. "We?"

"You doing anything else?"

"Well, no. Marissa, you're a genius."

"I try," she chuckled.

* * * * *

The small group of people in the clearing at the bottom of the hill grew as more came from the bush. *I really hope they're just more displaced citizens*, Russell thought as he watched them meet up in the middle. *Just wanting shelter like us.* His thought was dispelled when the first shots peppered the building from the side.

"They flanked us," pointed out Willow in chagrin. "Damn, I should have expected it."

"No one's perfect," answered Adrienne.

"Yeah, unfortunately missing that particular detail may cost us our lives," retorted Willow. "I never excused missing vital details before from others and I sure as hell should not be doing it myself."

Adrienne sighed but did not argue as Willow had a valid point. Unfortunately, before they had entire teams of personnel to work with and rely on. Now it all rested on far too few.

"Willow, do you recognize those two?" asked Adrienne, pointing to the intersection and just past the lights.

Willow checked it with a pair of binoculars. "Son of a…" she growled. She then leaned back against wall and knelt down. "Yeah—was hoping not to see them."

"People we know?" asked Emilie.

"Marcus, its Jeff and Sina," called out Willow.

Marcus's only response was a loud, and empathic, "Shit."

"My thoughts exactly," agreed Willow.

"Who are Jeff and Sina?" asked Russell.

Adrienne sighed, "Two people we used to work with. I'm guessing they took off on their own when everything went sideways?" she asked Willow. Willow gave her nod. Upon receiving Willow's nod, Adrienne continued, "While we never could prove anything and no one ever pressed anything, we all knew they were trouble. But, since not even IA could prove it or do anything, we were stuck with them. We were all hoping they would quit, or something…"

"… Or *something*?" clarified Abigail. "That a different way of saying you were hoping they would do something monumentally stupid and get themselves killed?"

"Well, not *that*," answered Willow. "Nothing like that—but we were hoping they would slip up and get themselves nailed by IA, and then terminated from their jobs. I wouldn't wish that on anyone but they were dragging us all down."

"But now they're here to take the

detachment and I'm guessing they aren't going to have the same amount of mercy for us," said David. "And I get what you're saying. Excusing the cliché and all… it takes one bad apple to ruin the reputation… two or three is hell on wheels to recover from."

"I think that was more than one cliché," came Russell's voice, as he rubbed a hand over his face. "So, what can we expect from these two?"

"They're smart—Sina's got a good head for tactics," answered Willow. "It was unfortunate her head for tactics came with one hell of a temper and far too much ambition for her own good. Not saying there's a problem with ambition, but Sina never tempered it with patience or empathy."

"Like she forgot she was human, at times," added Adrienne. "No matter how much you tried to draw her into a normal relationship she didn't want nor welcome it. I don't think she understood it."

"And Jeff?" asked Abigail.

"Always a real wing nut," answered Marcus, and he made a circling gesture with his finger by the side of his head. "Hid it but… not that well, if you catch my meaning."

"How the hell did these two even get through training and human resources?" asked David. "I'd hate to point it out, but someone wasn't paying attention to the psych report if what you're saying about Jeff…"

"…He wasn't always like that," answered Willow. "He was transferred here from down South. From what his old colleagues said—he just needed someplace quieter to hold out for a year before he retired. So, I always gave him the less intensive assignments—traffic patrol in quiet areas, desk work… that kind of thing. I was in the middle of filling out his paperwork for retirement when everything fell apart around us. And he just snapped—disappeared—and I thought maybe he'd died over the winter… but I guess he met up with Sina somewhere."

This Sina, however, sounded like someone who would take advantage of Jeff—and, if Willow and Marcus were correct, she had, thought Russell.

"I wonder…" mused Emilie. "Would it mean we could split them up and cause a bit of a rift in leadership?"

David grinned, remembering another—and similar—circumstance from the winter. Karen and Derek had managed to split leadership in another situation.

"If we could, it would, potentially, split their numbers. Granted, we'd end up in a three-way fight, but if it works that would definitely split their focus and ruin Sina's day," admitted Willow. "I'm all up for that if we can do it."

"Willow!" came a shouted voice. "I know you've seen us! We outnumber you… there's two of you and quite a few more of us. Why don't you just give it up?"

Willow sighed. "I could have done with a

little more time to come up with a better defence than this."

"We still have the advantage, Sina," called down Marcus. "Locked up detachment, supplies enough to outlast you, and enough to repel you if you insist on trying to get in. Go crawl back under the rock you came out from under!"

"This is starting to remind me of something else," mused David as he looked over at Emilie while Abigail looked confused. "Before we met you, Abby, there was a bunch of raiding scum tried to take the farm by storming the gate. Terrence was the one who told them where to go and how fast to get there... and Derek fired the warning shot."

"Nice to know you've encountered similar," said Russell wryly. "Any ideas on how to repel this?"

"This is a little different. Then we had the advantage of blocking them off, and the numbers, to fight them off if they somehow made it through the gate," mentioned Emilie. "Not the other way around... and we're kind of surrounded here."

"Okay, not exactly the same," conceded David, as he looked around. "But we do have the high ground and we also have cover and the supplies. More so than they do. We just need to outlast their siege... wait a second, we also have radios... any way we can call for back up?"

Willow shook her head. "We've tried and all

we've gotten for our efforts was bump kiss… and overhearing you and Dan…"

Silence fell like a pall and swept through their ranks. Russell looked down at the roof surface and pulled out the picture of Sheridan. "We don't lose this place. No one will come for us. We have to become what the others need because we are the only ones who can. If we fall here, then the others will fall after us. We stand here, and now, and… even if there is no one but those raiders out there to know what we did, we still just sent a clear message. We won't let what's left of our world—of civilization—go without a fight."

A few of the bricks lining the roof exploded and caught everyone's attention. They flattened themselves against the surface of the roof and underneath the edge of the ledge.

"I didn't think she would give us long to discuss things," mused Willow. "Would have given us too much time to plan how to counter her." David sighed heavily and motioned for Abigail to move to the back corner, and for Emilie to join her. Marcus and Willow moved to another while him and Russell did the same.

Reacting instead of having a plan was no way to go into a fight if they had to defend their lives but unfortunately this was all they had. David sighed heavily and motioned for Abigail to move to the back corner, and for Emilie to join her. Marcus and Willow moved to another, while he and Russell each took up the other two.

"We'll have to move around as they move around us, but we leave one of us on each corner as spotter," ordered Russell. "Emilie, you're our paramedic so don't take this wrong when I say to keep your head down and out of the fighting. Run us supplies and keep out of sight."

"You got it!" she called as she moved to the centre of the roof and near the door for the access.

"One of these days you need to fill me in what the hell you were on about that gate fight!" called Abigail. "Strikes me as something I'd like to know."

"We survive this and I'll tell you all about it," answered David.

* * * * *

The cabin on the edge of the river was just above where the river would flood. It was an old cabin built before High Falls had been a town, let alone the ghost town it would eventually become.

Garrett had plugged the holes in the roof with whatever he could scavenge from the old ghost town and what sometimes washed down the river. Derek knew with proper tools, however, he could easily take the ramshackle log cabin and turn it into something five star.

The five of them fit into the cabin as well.

"So, why are you down here and not up at High Falls?" asked Derek.

With a snort, Garrett answered, "My so-called assistant decided to stage a mutiny.

Unfortunately, he succeeded… almost. I'm sure he thinks the fall off the dam after throwing me from it killed me and he definitely managed to mutiny because I'm here and not there."

Shit, thought Derek, feeling like the world had dropped out from under him. *This is worse than right before Christmas when everything simply ended. We really could have used that dam.*

"So, what happens now?" asked Aidan. "We found who you wanted to find. We could head back and make a few people extremely happy."

Derek and Garrett looked at each other knowing it was not an option.

"No," answered Gina for them. "We need the dam, and we need the solar field up and running. Both things up and running will give us an advantage."

The problem was the small group who mutinied—not the others at the dam. And using anything larger than small arms runs the risk of damaging the dam or the equipment. Neither one is an option. We just can't order what we need to fix what breaks, Derek thought as he paced the small space. Garrett poked at the fire inside the cast iron stove. "So, the big issue appears to be gaining control of the dam," said Francis. "What would happen if we just happened to roll on up there and talk to these people?"

"What do you mean?" asked Aidan. "You heard the man—they took the dam, by force, by throwing him off it."

"No offence—" Francis looked at Garrett,

and then back to the others. "—We just don't take Garrett with us. We go up… the three of us. Garret and Derek head up the other side with that long shot camera in my truck. We three talk to those up there while Derek and Garrett take pictures of those we talk to. Then we all come back here and Garrett identifies the troublemakers. Once identified we go in under the cover of dark and eliminate the issue. No mess, no fuss. The next day we take Garrett back to his dam."

"Makes quite a bit of sense," mused Derek. "What do you think?"

"It's smart," admitted Garrett. "And it would result in the least amount of property damage. I think we need to fine tune it a bit, but it's definitely workable."

"So, this camera of yours…" started Derek.

"It's actually mine," clarified Aidan. "And it's not anything fancy. Just a decent point and shoot."

"It's a start," said Garrett. "Go get it, if you're open to us using it, and Derek and I will figure out how to use it before we go so we're not trying to learn how later when we need it to work."

Aidan pulled his camera from his pack and handed it over to Garrett. "It's not that hard to use. I have more complicated SLR's sitting at home," said Garrett, after taking it from its case.

"Guess who's using this thing, then," said Derek. "So, where's the best place to take the pictures, then? We can't just pick a place at random and then we need to make sure we actually are in the area when you are."

Francis blew out a breath. "That I'm not sure about," he admitted.

"Might be easier to just scope out the area and not worry on timing. Send the three up under the guise of setting up a trading route between the two camps," pointed out Garrett. "Just don't mention the last name of either Karen or Sheridan."

"Or do it and we'd know who is who just by how uncomfortable they are," pointed out Gina. "Who gives who an uncomfortable side glance?"

"Good idea," admitted Derek.

"I like it better than hoping to take pictures," pointed out Aidan. "It still means we have to leave Garrett behind, or at least take him with us but make sure he's not seen until it's time to reveal the bastards in the lie. Then at least we all stay together." He turned to look at Garrett. "You said it was only a few who mutinied—not others. Those others may back you up. If it was me I'd be pretty pissed off."

"So would I," agreed Gina. "I'm with Aidan on this."

"And if things go pear shaped?" asked Francis. "We're talking some serious fighting we've just caused… with no cover other than the truck."

"Garrett?" asked Derek. "It's your call here. Your dam."

The other man thought for a moment. "I'm not one for sneaking around and people know it. If we go a bit more direct the good news is there is a spot, with plenty of cover, but nothing of any real value to meet the others at before we get to the dam. If we do it this way, I'd roll up there and then stop and wait for them to come to you."

* * * * *

Jeremy pored over the various bits and pieces of paperwork while trying to make sense of it. He could not help but think if he had access to a computer he could build a program that would do all this for them instead of using paper.

Actually… it was not that bad an idea.

There was a laptop—even if an older model—kicking around somewhere. It ran a version of Windows a few years out of date but he was not about to complain too much. It would do.

He just had to find it first.

"If I was a junk computer owned by Terrence, where would the rat bastard stick me?" he wondered as he walked out of the room while ignoring Marissa's laughter from behind him.

He walked down the back hallway to the other end of the house and into Terrence's office.

Terrence looked up. "Jeremy… what can I do for you?"

"Do you have an old laptop or something I could use… something still working?" he specified at the last minute.

"Uh, how old is old?" asked Terrence.

"New or a year or so," he answered. "An actual laptop with keys, though, not a tablet that thinks it's a computer."

Terrence thought a moment before he stood up and walked over to a filing cabinet, pulling out an old IBM ThinkPad. "How long have you had this?" asked Jeremy as he held it in his hands.

"Not long," answered Terrence. "It at least runs Windows Seven."

"One of those rugged beasts, then," mused Jeremy.

"Precisely," he answered, waving him off.

"How's Sheridan doing?"

Terrence sighed and looked down. "Not great, but she's feeling a bit more like facing the world again."

"Tell her I'm thinking about her," said Jeremy.

"Thanks, I will," answered Terrence.

Jeremy walked to the office space he shared with Marissa. Marissa looked up as Jeremy went in to the office with the computer in his hand. "I'd ask but…" she began.

"It's all fine and good to use paper but, seriously… where are we going to get the paper once we run out?" asked Jeremy.

"Good question," agreed Marissa. "And if it crashes?"

"We make back-ups," he answered. "And we can overwrite back-ups and other things.

Instant organization."

"Amazing… we've been forced to go paperless entirely by the end of the world," she mused. "In one part we are in the stone ages because of communications and in another we've jumped forward a few decades."

The Last Iron Horse
The next book in "The Kingdom of Walden"
Series
To be released October 2015

ALSO FROM KCEDITIONS

The Archer
Tony Spencer
Welsh longbow maker and archer, Will Fletcher, sees an ancient bow that looks familiar and is drawn into remembering a good deed that he has long strived to forget.

The Zombie, the Cat, and Barack Obama
Christopher Meade
This comic/horror zombie story quickly morphs into an outrageously funny satire on conspiracy theories.

The Complete Selena Grey Collection
Forward by Kristan Cannon
Compiled by Tony Spencer & MJ Spickett
From dragon living the life a human in the basement of hapless secretary to a ship's AI just wishing to be human—these short stories chronicle the beginning of Kristan Cannon's writing career *before* she dropped the pen name. The best have been picked by the board of KCE for this special release.